SWEET STRUGGLE

"Sweet Mary, but I'd not have you do this to me," she whispered in near anguish.

"Your body tells me a different tale," he murmured against her, as both his hands moved to cup her breasts through her undershift, his thumbs teasing the peaks that strained against the thin cambric.

She caught at his hands to stop them with her own, but she could not still the waves of desire that threatened to overwhelm her. It was as though even the lightest touch of his fingertips had the power to awaken an ache deep within her. Her pulse pounded so loudly in her ears that she was unaware he eased her shift upward until she felt his hand on the bare skin of her thighs, and suddenly she didn't care anymore. Every nerve, every sense in her body, was tuned now to his touch. A low moan escaped, while fire spread and engulfed her. She twisted against him, wanting him to feed her need of him. . . .

Fire
and Steel

Anita Mills

AN ONYX BOOK

ONYX
Published by the Penguin Group
Penguin Books USA Inc., 375 Hudson Street,
New York, New York 10014, U.S.A.
Penguin Books Ltd, 27 Wrights Lane,
London W8 5TZ, England
Penguin Books Australia Ltd, Ringwood,
Victoria, Australia
Penguin Books Canada Ltd, 10 Alcorn Ave., Suite 300,
Toronto, Canada M4V 3B2
Penguin Books (N.Z.) Ltd, 182–190 Wairau Road,
Auckland 10, New Zealand

Penguin Books Ltd, Registered Offices:
Harmondsworth, Middlesex, England

Published by Onyx, an imprint of New American Library,
a division of Penguin Books USA Inc.

First Printing, August, 1988
12 11 10 9 8 7 6 5 4

 REGISTERED TRADEMARK—MARCA REGISTRADA

Printed in the United States of America

This book is dedicated to
my grandfather,
Orson F. Tracy.
He gave me my love of history.

A special acknowledgment to my sister, Deborah Gavin, and to MARA members Christie Kennard and Kitty Bentch—their careful reading and their criticisms were an invaluable aid to me in the writing of this book. Also, my thanks to all members of the Kansas City MARA chapter of RWA for their encouragement and support this past year.

1

Late Summer, 1106

The great keep of the Condes loomed ahead of them, silent and forbidding, its new twelve-foot-thick walls rising nearly sixty feet above the rounded motte. It stood an aloof guardian to the cluster of wattle-and-daub houses that lay just beneath the wide river-fed ditch. The lead rider reined in, halting the thirty men who rode with him, and looked upward in admiration. Behind him, his squire and his captain muttered oaths as they too stared at the tall fortress.

"Jesu, but 'tis hot," Guy of Rivaux complained aloud as he removed his heavy steel helmet and wiped his sweat-drenched black hair back from his face with the sleeve of his blazoned surcoat. Squinting to stare again, he sighed. "Aye—we'd best hope that the Lady Eleanor lets us in, for 'twould take a year and more to starve the Condes into submission."

"My lord, your helm . . ." William de Comminges, his captain, sat uneasily in his saddle and darted his eyes toward a nearby brake of trees.

"Nay." Guy shook his head and pointed downward to where deep mud-dried ruts bore testimony to the recent movement of the machines of war. " 'Tis as Curthose said—the men have gone save for those that guard the walls, and we are out of range from there."

"My lord, I like it not," Alan of Poix muttered as

he edged his horse closer to Guy's. "Not even Belesme could breach that outer shell."

Guy turned his attention to his squire. "Nay, but God willing, Alan, we'll not have to try. We bear Normandy's banner and Normandy's writ," he reminded grimly, "and she cannot know why we are come."

"My lord . . ." De Comminges hesitated to repeat his argument against what they would do, but he felt compelled to remind his young lord once again of the risk they took. "If anything happens to the girl, Lord Roger will not rest until we are dead."

Lord Roger. There was so much respect and admiration in the old man's voice that Guy wished anew he'd not come—wished that somehow fate would have cast him on the other side in this senseless war between the Conqueror's surviving sons. Aye, for when it was done, good men stood to lose their lands if not their lives, while those who broke their feudal oaths would likely profit.

There was no question where Roger de Brione's heart lay in the bitter quarrel. Although he favored the younger brother, Henry, now King of England, he held lands from Robert Curthose too, and therefore chose not to fight for either of them. He'd quoted Holy Scripture about rendering unto Caesar, and he'd sent his Norman troops to Curthose and his English troops to Henry, but he himself had gone to wait out the war on the Welsh border, protecting his English lands from the marauding Welshmen. Henry, who counted Lord Roger as much a friend as any, had understood, but Curthose had not.

Guy himself had no such choice to make—everything he had he held of Robert Curthose, and he'd had to place his hands between the duke's to swear fealty for his patrimony. And now he would have to fight for the feckless Curthose or be forsworn. He accepted that as the price of being Count of Rivaux, but it went against his heart to do what he had been sent to do now.

"If 'twere me, my lord," de Comminges mused aloud, "I'd just say she refused to yield the girl. Let Curthose come himself and take the little demoiselle hostage. 'Tis he who fears her father, anyway." He leaned over to spit into the dirt. "Nay, but I'd not bring my lord of the Condes' wrath down on my head. Curthose is the fool in this." Casting a sidelong glance at Guy, he could see the young man would not waver. It was to be expected, he admitted to himself, for Guy of Rivaux did not take his oaths lightly. William, who had trained the boy in the skills of war, could take pride in everything about his pupil. Aye, but when he was scarcely seventeen, Guy'd won his spurs of knighthood. He'd had to take the field of battle to save his bitter, unloving father from the Count of Mortain's fury when that lord had been exiled from England. It had been an act of rare courage for a boy but lately trained in war, as William remembered fondly, reliving again how Guy had plunged into the thick of the melee to lift his fallen sire into his own saddle. Had it been William's choice, he'd have let the old man die, for he'd never seen a worse parent in his life. But Guy, armed only as a squire, had taken his father's sword and literally slashed their way back to safety, rallying Rivaux's troops and driving de Mortain from the field. Jesu, but the boy'd known no fear that day. And, as young as he was, he'd fought like a seasoned warrior ever since, holding at bay those who sought to encroach on Rivaux lands after the old count died.

Guy was silent, his mind troubled by the task before him. Finally his eyes met William's, and he shook his head. "If I would not have come, he'd have sent Belesme."

The dread name hung between them. Young Alan involuntarily raised his hand to cross himself, while William conceded the truth of Guy's words. No man, however hardened to violence and war, could want a child to fall into Robert of Belesme's hands. God's blood, but there were no simple answers in these quarrels between the Conqueror's sons. William spat again. "Aye, but I doubt Lord Roger will see it that way, my lord. And what are we to do with a small girl when there's an army to be raised?"

It was a question that Guy had asked himself over and over without answer. He'd no wish to be nursemaid, not even to one of the greatest little heiresses in Normandy. At nineteen, he'd a far greater taste for fighting than for shepherding a child to Rouen. Aloud he answered simply, "We take her to Curthose, and then we call up my levies."

"But there's no time."

"We leave in the morning, press on to Lisieux by nightfall, and have her in Rouen in the duchess's care in three days."

"Three days?" Sweet Jesu, but we travel fast." Alan whistled softly, shaking his head. "Can the child keep the pace?"

"She'll have to." Guy squinted into the bright sky, noting that the sun had reached its zenith already. "We waste time we do not have." Clicking his reins, he nudged his horse forward. "Have the approach sounded."

As a boy in Rivaux's red livery pulled out of line to raise his horn to his lips, William reminded his master again, "You'd best wear your helm ere we get into archers' range."

"Raise Normandy's standard above mine!" Guy shouted down his line before turning to his captain. "Nay—'tis hot, and I would have Lady Eleanor know I come in peace."

"Some peace," William snorted. "We are come to take a child hostage so that her father will not fight against Curthose, when 'tis more like that 'twill guarantee he will."

But Guy had already spurred ahead, his mail glinting hotly in the bright summer sun, his bared head glistening wetly, as both banners unfurled above him and Normandy's leopard paced restlessly across the bright silk.

The girl lay prone on the narrow stone bench, her fingers plucking aimlessly at the hairy stalks of pennyroyal growing in the neatly defined bed, her thoughts lost in self-pity. She should have been born male, she reflected bitterly, for then she'd not be treated so. She would not have been left behind with naught but her mother, three sisters, and a few old men for company. She'd have gone with Brian then, gone to fight on his father's side in this quarrel that had ruined her life. At least then she could have been with him.

Abruptly she broke off a stem and flung it viciously to the ground. Sweet Mary, but it did no good to wish for what could not be. Brian was gone, mayhap never to return to the great keep where he'd been fostered, and she had only an unwanted betrothal in her future. Sitting up, she dug mutinously with the toe of her soft kid shoe, trying to uproot the broken pennyroyal stub from the dry dirt. She didn't want to wed Robert of Caen—could not believe her father had agreed to the match—not when it was Brian FitzHenry she'd wanted. And it did no good for others to tell her that the king's favorite son was the better choice, she thought sullenly, for should not one royal bastard be the same as the other? And why could they not see, King Henry and her father, that 'twas Brian that she loved? But nay, they would not listen to her wishes in the matter, not the father who'd married for love or the king who would settle her inheritance on Robert of Caen. For once, she'd wished she were not her father's heiress— that Aislinn had been born the eldest child. That gave her pause. Nay, but she would not want to lose her position as the Demoiselle of the Condes to become merely the Lady Catherine. And, much as she loved Linn, she still got a measure of satisfaction in being a year older.

"Still in mourning for Brian, Cat?"

Catherine de Brione looked up, her reddened eyes sullen, her chin jutting stubbornly. " 'Tis no concern of yours if I am," she muttered.

Unperturbed, the younger girl plopped down beside her and leaned to pick up the discarded sprig. Sniffing it, she settled back comfortably and rested her head against the stone wall behind them. Cat eyed her suspiciously for a moment before deciding that Aislinn meant no malice.

" 'Tis so hot, Cat," Linn complained. "I cannot think how Maman stands it when she is so far gone with child."

"She's used to it—we've all been born in the heat."

"You know, you should not vex her so with your temper, Cat—not when 'tis not her fault that Brian left."

"She could have stopped Papa from telling King Henry that I would wed this Robert that I know not." Plucking another sprig of pennyroyal, Cat broke the leaf and licked it, savoring the minty taste. "And 'tis not seemly that you should chide me, for I did not think you overjoyed to take Geoffrey of Mayenne either."

"Nay, but I have considered the matter," the twelve-year-old girl admitted slowly, "and I know that Papa would not give me a bad husband. Besides, I know that 'twill be years before I have to leave the Condes." Turning light brown, almost golden, eyes to Catherine, she smiled encouragingly. "Come, Cat—'tis not so terrible for you. Papa says that your Robert promises to be a great warrior."

"He is not my Robert!"

"But he will be one day."

"Did Maman send you to speak with me?" Cat demanded angrily. "For if she did, you waste your words, Linn."

"Nay, she did not, but she wearies of this. 'Tis most unfair of you to worry her when her time nears." Pausing to smooth the soft fabric of her gown over her knees, Aislinn looked away for a moment. "You know, Cat, you can be sharper-tongued than an alewife when you do not get what you want," she observed quietly. "There's none here that thinks Brian is for you."

"I love him—and he loves me!"

"Does he? Cat, he is but sixteen, and two women here have borne his bastards within the year. What if he is too like his father—would you take a husband who would fill your household with his by-blows?"

Catherine tossed her glossy dark mane of hair back and lifted it away from her damp neck. Arching her head backward to profile a face that everyone said rivaled her beautiful mother's, she answered confidently, "My lord will not stray from my bed unless I will it."

"Sweet Mary, but you have a good opinion of yourself, Cat. To hear you tell the tale, only plain ladies' husbands are faithless, but—" Aislinn stopped in midsentence, her face suddenly intent on listening to the sound of the horn. "Cat, there are riders!"

Their small quarrel forgotten, Catherine climbed to stand on the bench. "Help me that I may see," she ordered imperiously as she boosted herself up on the low garden wall. "Jesu, but 'tis not tall enough." Jumping down, she ran for the gate, calling back over her shoulder, "If I reach the tower first, I wear your bells in my hair tonight!"

For answer, the younger girl lifted her skirts from her ankles and ran in pursuit, her excitement over visitors crowding out any worry that their mother might be displeased. She was no match for Cat's longer legs, and the steps were too narrow to allow passing, so she had to content herself with elbowing for the better position in an unmanned arrow slit. Kneeling in the deep cut-out, both of them watched eagerly as the column came closer. The sun glinted off the helmets with blinding intensity, but they could make out the red-and-gold banner of Normandy flying above.

" 'Tis the duke!" Aislinn breathed in alarm.

"Nay. He'd not come with so few." Cat squinted against the bright reflection, straining to identify the men. Her eyes took in the second pennant, also red, but with a huge black bird blazoned across it as though swooping for a kill. "I cannot tell yet who it is, Linn," she admitted finally as her eyes dropped to the rider in the lead. "But they do not mean to fight, for the one in front is unhelmed."

The horn sounded again, and apparently old Ralph, the keep's seneschal, was satisfied enough to order the bridge lowered. The ropes strained to raise the iron-and-wood portcullis that protected the entrance in the outer wall, and the iron chains creaked against their pulleys as the long wooden bridge slowly swung into place over the deep river-fed trench.

The column halted, poised for crossing, as the girls watched curiously. The lead rider pushed báck wet hair with his arm, affording a look at his face. Beside her, Cat heard Aislinn gasp in admiration.

"If 'tis Mayenne, I'll go now. Did you *ever* see the like of him?"

"Nay," Catherine admitted. "And 'tis not Mayenne, I'll warrant, for unless my eyes fail me, I think that may be the hawk of Rivaux that flies above his head." Turning back to her sister, she reminded, "And I get to wear your bells at supper."

Catherine crossed the open courtyard eagerly, her face flushed from the heat as she outran her mother's page. Taking the narrow, winding tower steps to her mother's solar two at a time, she paused at the first small landing to smooth her blue samite overgown down against the shimmering red undertunic. She hoped fervently that her mother would not remark that she'd chosen to wear her best gown. But then, it had been a fortnight since her father had left and there'd been no reason to wear it since. Giving her thick hair a lift off her neck, she let it fall forward over her shoulders so that it hung like a heavy curtain over her breasts. Brian had always admired it worn thus, and mayhap the stranger would note it also.

Carefully cuffing back the wide-banded sleeves to reveal the fitted red silk underneath, she wondered why she'd been summoned. How Aislinn had envied her, Cat reflected with satisfaction, when 'twas discovered that the visitor was indeed Guy of Rivaux. And though she'd never seen him before, it was exhilarating to think that she would greet one whose exploits were already sung in halls from Rivaux to Maine. Nay, but there were some things that made being the eldest worthwhile, for the page had said, "He would speak with the Demoiselle only," when Aislinn had demanded to come. Her only regret was that she'd not

17

had time for Hawise to weave her sister's bells into tiny braids over the back of her hair. Biting her lips to redden them, she finished the climb to the solar.

She found her mother in earnest conversation with the guest, but both fell suddenly silent at the sight of her. And, judging by Eleanor of Nantes's stricken expression, Catherine knew something was very wrong. For a fleeting moment her heart sank like a rock within her breast.

"Catherine, come make your obeisance to my lord of Rivaux." Nodding to the young man standing beside her, Eleanor added proudly, "My lord, this is my eldest daughter, Catherine of the Condes."

Guy stared, bereft of speech, at the girl who dropped to her knees before him. Somehow, he'd expected the Demoiselle to be a small child, but Catherine of the Condes was already taller than her famed mother—and she was equally as lovely. Looking down, he found it an effort not to reach out to touch the shining crown of rich, deep brown hair and assure himself she was real. And when she lifted her eyes to meet his, he had to suck in his breath. Jesu, but in all of his nineteen years he'd never seen any to compare with the girl before him. Her face was perfectly oval, her features delicately chiseled, firm and straight, her cheeks lightly blushed, her teeth white and even, and her chin well-defined. But it was the eyes that drew him, eyes so dark that pupil and iris were nearly one in appearance, eyes that were fringed with thick black lashes that curved luxuriously against pale, almost translucent skin.

"Demoiselle," he managed finally.

For once, Cat had to stare back. His fingers were strong and warm as they closed over hers and raised her up to where she faced the embroidered black hawk on his red silk tunic. Her eyes traveled upward, openly taking in his tall, well-favored form. He was freshly bathed and barbered, smelling cleanly of Hawise's strong soap, and his still-wet hair was plastered smoothly, to lie dark as a raven's wing against his face. His cheekbones were high, his nose only slightly aquiline, his jaw squared. A small, almost imperceptible scar cut through one black eyebrow, giving him a slightly quizzical expression. Had he taken the blow half an inch lower, it would have damaged his strangely beautiful eyes. Even as she stared, they seemed to change color as gold flecks radiated outward across irises as green as emeralds.

"Cat, Lord Guy brings us unwelcome news from the duke."

Eleanor's words broke between them. The smile that had frozen on Guy of Rivaux's face faded, and he stepped back, dropping Catherine's hand. For a moment Catherine had forgotten the stab of fear she'd felt, but now it returned. Wordlessly she turned to her mother, her eyes questioning.

Eleanor, still seated on a low bench, clasped her hands tightly over her distended abdomen and looked away to hide her anguish. Catherine, fearing something had befallen her father, moved quickly to her side.

"Papa . . . ?"

"Nay." Eleanor sucked in her breath and fought for composure. "Roger is safe at Harlowe, Cat."

"Sweet Jesu—'tis Brian! Brian's been taken—he's—"

"Cat . . ." Eleanor's face went white and her hand pressed more tightly into her swollen side. Closing her eyes for a moment, she waited for the pain to subside.

"Maman, are you all right?" Cat demanded anxiously.

"Aye." Exhaling slowly, Eleanor nodded and sighed. "I would tell you myself, but I find I have not the stomach for it." Looking behind Catherine, her eyes met Guy's. "My lord . . ." she appealed helplessly.

"Demoiselle." He waited for Cat to turn back to him.

"I do not understand," Catherine began slowly. "If 'tis not Papa and 'tis not Brian, then what . . . ?"

Guy sighed heavily. "Demoiselle—Lady Catherine—I am come from your duke, your father's suzerain." Seeing that he had her full attention now, he

plunged ahead. ''Robert Curthose fears that your father will bear arms against him in King Henry's cause,
for 'tis well-known the love he bears England's king.''

''But he would not—my father would not break his
oath! My father—''

''Aye, and even Curthose's own council disputes his
fear, but he will not listen, Demoiselle,'' Guy continued patiently. ''He demands a hostage for surety against
Lord Roger's returning to lead Henry's armies.''

''A hostage!'' It was a howl of outrage. ''Nay, but
he would not dare! Of all the men in Normandy, my
father would be the last to break his sacred oath! He'd
die first!'' She caught the sympathy in his face and
stopped still. The color drained from her cheeks and
her eyes widened in dawning horror. ''Nay, he would
not . . .'' Her voice dropped hollowly. ''Sweet Mary,
but I'd not go.''

He nodded. ''I'd not take you if there were a choice,
Demoiselle, but I bear Curthose's writ. You'll go to
Rouen to serve the duchess as one of her ladies until
this thing between the brothers is settled.''

''Nay!'' she blazed suddenly. ''Tell Robert Curthose that we'll hold the Condes against him first! Tell
him—''

''Catherine.''

Cat spun around at the sound of her mother's voice,
certain that Eleanor would never let her be Curthose's
prisoner. But her mother's face betrayed the answer—
she had no choice either. Stretching her hands out in
supplication, Cat pleaded, ''Nay, Maman, but I would
not go—I would not.''

''Cat . . .'' Eleanor spoke gently, keeping her own
voice low for control. ''When I was a year younger
than you are, when I was but twelve, my father sent
me to a convent against my wish. I cried even as you
cry now, but there was no help for it—I went. Seven
years I spent at Fontainebleau, Cat—seven years—and
I survived. This matter between brothers cannot last
beyond this year, child, and you will come home

again.'' Eleanor shifted uncomfortably in the summer heat, and shook her head. "Curthose is our overlord—there is no help for it.''

"We can fight! Maman, we can fight!" Cat cried desperately. "We can hold the Condes until King Henry comes—we can!''

"Demoiselle.'' Guy's voice was gentle as he came up behind her. " 'Tis folly to think it. I doubt you have twenty men left within these walls, and I have thirty ready to do as I ask.'' Reaching to touch a strand of dark hair that fell loosely down her back, he sought the means to placate her. "You'll be one of the duchess's own ladies.''

"And as I am King Henry's own goddaughter, my lord, I doubt she will be pleased with me. 'Tis not likely she will forget that, is it?'' she demanded bitterly, shaking her head away from his hand.

"Curthose would not harm a child.''

"I am not a child!'' Cat retorted hotly.

Eleanor pressed harder against her side and tried to ease herself. "You will go, Cat,'' she managed finally, "and you will remember that you are a de Brione.''

"Art craven like your sire, Maman!'' the girl exploded. "Aye, but you've no more spine than Gilbert!'' Whirling to face Guy, she declared defiantly, "You'll not get me to Rouen, my lord, and you'll rue that you ever thought to take me! I'll—''

"Cat!'' Eleanor reproved sharply. "Would you risk that Curthose sends Belesme? Lord Guy says that he will.''

"Belesme!'' Cat spat out the hated name viciously. "Belesme! Is there none save my father who is not afraid of Belesme? Sweet Mary, but even he cannot take the Condes!''

Beads of perspiration formed on Eleanor's blanched brow while she held her breath. Rising, she exhaled slowly and reached to grip an iron torch ring embedded deep into the stone wall. "When would you leave, my lord?'' she addressed Guy. "I would not have her go to Curthose's court like a beggar's daughter." Tears welled to brighten eyes as dark as her daughter's. " 'Twill take her maids two days to pack the sumpter horses."

"Maman!"

Guy ignored Cat's shriek to answer, "I have not the time, Lady Eleanor. We'll have to leave at first light." There was a hint of apology in his voice as he added, "I have mine own feudal obligation to meet before King Henry moves, else I'd stay longer."

"You will keep her safe?"

"Aye."

"You so swear?"

He looked to where the beautiful young girl stood shaking with rage, and pitied her. He had not a doubt but that her angry words hid a very real fear for her safety. "By the Blessed Virgin and all the saints, I swear it. I'll yield her to none but Curthose," he promised.

Eleanor met his gaze squarely, taking measure of the man before her. He was little more than a boy, and despite the reputation that preceded him, he seemed overyoung to wear the spurs of knighthood that clinked against the floor. Though he was nearly as tall as Roger, he could not be out of his teens, and yet she would have to entrust him with her daughter, an heiress to lands great enough to inspire greed in every baron. For once, she wished she'd not argued against the early betrothal to Robert of Caen.

Her eyes wavered and dropped. It was a difficult thing to do—to send her firstborn for hostage, knowing full well that a misplaced word, a whispered lie, could bring the duke's wrath down on her daughter. Robert Curthose might blind the thirteen-year-old girl in a rage and repent of it later. "God defend you if she is harmed, for Roger will see you dead then," she managed finally.

"I'll see she is safe—even in Rouen." He reached beneath the neck of his splendid tunic to draw out a crucifix suspended from a thin leather thong. "I'll swear by the Cross she'll come to no harm if 'twill ease your mind, my lady."

"My lord, do not promise what you cannot keep."

"I give Curthose five hundred men, Lady Eleanor. There's none but Belesme that can bring him more," he answered quietly.

"Sweet Mary, but is everyone mad save me?" Cat cried in disbelief. "You would let him take me to an unjust lord, and he would fight for a weak fool! Papa will never forgive either of you for this!" Angrily she stalked for the door, the silk of her undergown swishing against her legs.

"Demoiselle!" he called after her.

"Nay!" she shouted defiantly from the stairs.

"Leave her be, my lord, and give her time. She is, I fear, much indulged, but . . ." Eleanor's body doubled over with a new stab of pain. "Meekness is not in Cat, my lord," she gasped. Her fingers gripped the torch ring until her knuckles were white and her head pressed against the cool stone. "Holy Mary—"

"Jesu! Lady, are you all right?" In two long strides Guy was at her side to support her. "Demoiselle! Demoiselle!" he shouted as he encircled Eleanor's waist with his arm. The color had drained from her face, leaving it damp and ashen. Another pain convulsed her, depriving her of breath. He lifted her easily as she drenched the back of her gown. "God's teeth, is there none to come?" Helplessly he looked around the solar and then he began yelling in earnest. "To Nantes! To Nantes! To your lady!"

Catherine was nearly to the bottom of the steep steps when she realized that he was not calling her back in anger. Below her, servants ran in answer to his frantic shouts. She turned and ran back up.

"Maman! Maman!" As she rounded the last step, she could see him laying her mother across the curtained bed. One look at the scene told the tale. "Sweet Mary—'tis the babe!"

The women Gerdis and Hawise pushed past her and elbowed Guy away from the bed. Hawise felt of Eleanor's taut abdomen and nodded. "Aye, 'tis the babe, and 'tis early." Bright birdlike eyes flicked over Guy as Hawise took in the richness of his dress. "Get him belowstairs, Demoiselle."

But Catherine stood rooted to the floor. Stricken with shame for her earlier words, she barely managed an audible whisper. "Maman, I beg your pardon—there's naught of Gilbert in you."

Eleanor closed her eyes and nodded. " 'Tis all right, Cat."

" 'Tis my accursed tongue."

"Nay. Do as Hawise tells you."

Guy grasped Catherine by the elbow and firmly led her from the chamber. "There's naught you can do here, Demoiselle."

At the first landing, Cat stopped to murmur a quick prayer under her breath. Looking up when she finished, she explained, "I would that God grants my parents a son this time."

Surprised, he raised the scarred eyebrow. "Strange words for an heiress, 'twould seem."

"Nay, but I pray thus every time she is delivered, for seven times in thirteen years she's been brought to bed in her quest for a son, and she has naught but four daughters and three dead babes for her labor. 'Tis her mother's curse, she says."

Guy, who well understood what it meant to be unloved by a parent, felt a tug of sympathy for the beautiful girl. Laying a comforting hand on her shoulder, he murmured, "Aye—'tis hard to be faulted for one's birth."

She looked up at his touch and her eyes widened at the sudden warmth in his. "Nay, but you mistake the matter, my lord," she muttered as she ducked away. "My parents blame me not for what I cannot be—'tis I who would be a man."

Catching her arm to steady her on the narrow landing, he shook his head. "Nay, but you are as God made you, Demoiselle, and 'tis rare He grants such beauty." Moving below her, he turned to help her down the steep steps. "Are you betrothed as yet, Demoiselle?"

For a moment she could only stare. Then, shaking his hand off her arm, she brushed past him on the steep step. "God's blood, but you would aim high for yourself, my lord," she muttered scornfully. "My father promises me to a king's son."

He caught up with her at the bottom. "You think I ask for myself? Nay, but you mistake the matter, Demoiselle," he told her coldly. "I'd not take an ill-tempered girl, no matter what her wealth and beauty. Aye," he added at her outraged expression, "I'd not have you."

"Nay? Then why did you ask?" she shot back.

"Because I have sworn to protect you, Demoiselle, and the task would be easier if you were already betrothed," he responded evenly. "Otherwise, there are those who would persuade Curthose to grant an heiress, and the duke is a changeable man."

"He would not dare give me where my father would not."

"Then you are betrothed?"

"I will be given to Robert of Caen when King Henry comes to the Condes." She looked down to where her toe traced the edge of a cobbled stone. "And I like him not."

"You are unpledged, then."

"I cannot see the difference!" she snapped. " 'Tis as much as done, is it not? My father and the king have decided for me, whether I will it or not. And . . . and I shall hate him!" she finished vehemently.

"Robert of Caen?" Again the scarred eyebrow rose. "Demoiselle, do you know him? Nay, but there's naught to dislike in the boy."

"Naught to dislike! Brian says he is vain and ill-tempered and . . ."

"Then this Brian cannot know him, Demoiselle. Robert—"

"Brian is his half-brother, and knows him well, my lord," she interrupted. "And Brian FitzHenry would not lie to me."

"Then he is but envious of Robert, for I've seen none of this."

Her dark eyes flashed and her face flushed angrily. "He is not! And if he is, 'tis because of me!"

"Jesu," he complained, "but I know how 'tis you are called Cat—you are all claws and spit rather than wit."

"There's naught wrong with my wit!" she spat back. " 'Tis that I do not want Robert of Caen when I'd rather have Brian!"

"Aye, there is—'tis foolish to dislike that which you do not know and even more so when you speak of Robert. He can bring you the king's favor, Demoiselle."

"I care not."

"Art a strange little maid, then."

"I am not!"

She spoke with such force that Guy was hard-pressed not to laugh. As it was, the corners of his mouth threatened to betray him. "Oh?" His eyes traveled over her as he appeared to consider her. "I should be surprised to find you anything but a maid at your age, Demoiselle, and you are nearly an English foot shorter than I am, so you must be a little maid." Noting the defiant jut of her small chin, he could suppress his smile no longer. "And given that little maids are supposed to be meek and pleasant, I'd have to think you are a strange one."

"You are laughing at me!" she said angrily.

"Nay." His expression sobered suddenly. "I am thinking it will be a long journey to Rouen."

❧ 3 ❧

Catherine approached her mother's bed slowly, composing what words of comfort she could. The labor had been swift and hard and fruitless, and now Eleanor lay silently weeping within the shadows of the silken bed hangings. Her red-rimmed eyes opened at the sound of Cat's footsteps on the floor, and she managed a tired smile through her tears.

"Maman." Cat sank to her knees beside the bed and leaned to clasp her mother's fingers between her own. Despite her best efforts at control, her quavering lower lip betrayed her. "Maman, I am so sorry," she whispered as she rested her head against Eleanor's breast.

"Nay—'tis not your fault, Cat."

"But my accursed tongue—I should not have spoken so. I . . . I . . . Oh, *Maman!*" she wailed miserably.

Eleanor's free hand crept to stroke her daughter's silken hair much as she had done when the girl was but a tiny child. " 'Twas not you," she repeated gently. "Aye—the pains were coming before Lord Guy arrived even, but I had wanted to speak with you—to tell you of Curthose's writ myself—before I could not." Pausing to sniff, she admitted, "I was afraid this time, Cat—I was afraid without Roger." She took a deep breath and sighed heavily. " 'Twas a boy babe."

"Aye." Catherine was at a loss for something to say. Hawise had told her how the child had come forth strangled by its own cord. They'd blown into its mouth and rubbed its tiny body to no avail until Eleanor had finally ordered them to stop. "May the Holy Mother cradle him in heaven," she whispered at last.

"I . . . I have asked that Masses be said," Eleanor added haltingly, "but I cannot bring myself to write of this to Roger." Her fingers ceased stroking Cat's hair. "I would that you did so for me."

Catherine longed to ease, to give solace, to say that there would yet be other sons, but like everyone else in the Condes, she was loath to raise hope again. Four times in her memory she'd seen her mother brought to disappointment in childbed, and it was almost too much to bear.

"He will not reproach me—he never has. He never complains of the lack, Cat."

"He loves you well."

Eleanor sighed heavily. " 'I took an heiress,' he tells me each time, 'and I will leave an heiress, content that I have had Eleanor of Nantes for wife.' " Her chest shook with suppressed sobs beneath Catherine's head. "Oh, Cat!" she wailed.

Cat's throat constricted painfully, making speech nearly impossible. She'd quarreled bitterly with both her mother and her father before he'd ridden out, and she'd been ill-tempered and sullen since he'd left. "Maman, I am so sorry," she choked out.

"Aye." Eleanor shifted to turn her head for a better look at her daughter.

Catherine raised up and rocked back on her heels. Tears flowed freely down her cheeks now, streaking them, as she met her mother's eyes guiltily. "I . . . I have given you much to bear, but I never wished—"

"Nay, but you are my joy—and Roger's also, lovey," Eleanor consoled. "I am grateful to God for all of you—Aislinn, Philippa, and Isabella—but for you most of all. 'Twas the promise of you that gave me strength those long months I was captive to Belesme.''

"But Papa—''

"Cat,'' Eleanor interrupted softly, "I know you think him wrong where Brian is concerned, but he does what he believes best.'' Lifting a weary hand to brush at Catherine's wet cheeks, she murmured, "He fears that Brian is too much like Henry and constancy will not be in him.''

" 'Tis unfair! Brian *loves* Papa! He—''

"Aye, and Roger loves him also, but we were not speaking of what is between them, lovey, but rather of what is between a man and his wife. *I* think myself more his mother than the Welshwoman who bore him, but I am not blind to his faults.''

"But I'd wed with him, Maman,'' Cat protested miserably. "Surely you who fled with my father can understand that, can you not?''

"Aye—I understand. But I was promised to Robert of Belesme, else we'd not have run to England. And Brian is not Roger. Roger would never have gotten a bastard of every willing serving girl in the house.''

Catherine fell silent. Even now it pained her to remember her shock and dismay when she'd learned that both Agnes and Tyra carried Brian's babes. And even his assurances to her and Aislinn that the women meant nothing to him had not lessened the hurt of Agnes' gloating in her presence.

"Would you be like Henry's Saxon queen?'' Eleanor persisted gently. "Would you be content surrounded by your husband's bastards? I may never give Roger a son, but I know in my heart that no other woman will bear him one either. Whether he is gone from here a week, a month, or a year, Cat, he will lie with no other. Can you in truth say that would be the same with Brian if you were wed?''

Catherine bit her lower lip and shook her head slowly. "But there is no other Roger de Brione, Maman,'' she answered low. "Every man—''

"Nay, but 'tis not so. My cousin Walter looks at none but Helene, and Aubery would not stray from my sister Adelicia's bed—and I could count many who are not faithless, Cat."

"And you cannot know if this Robert of Caen will prove different from his father either!" Catherine retorted.

"Mayhap, but there's naught said of him yet in that quarter, while Brian—"

"Nay, I'll not listen! I'll . . ." The words died on Catherine's lips as she met her mother's eyes. She'd come to ease her mother's grief, not to quarrel with her again. And, after all, was not her mother's concern for her as great as her sorrow over the babe? she chided herself silently.

" 'Tis difficult being heiress of Nantes, Cat, as I can attest, and you will find yourself heiress to far more than that. You must have a husband who is strong enough to hold vast lands in both England and Normandy for you and your heirs one day."

"Brian—"

"Brian is good-tempered and pleasant to the ladies, but he is no soldier. Roger says the other boy shows more promise on the field, Cat, and that is what you will need when we are gone."

"You speak as though you will never have a son. You cannot know that—you cannot!"

"God denies me this—mayhap because I would not serve him at Fontainebleau—but he denies me." Eleanor closed her eyes and sank back against her pillows for a moment. Exhausted from both her labor and the pain of parting from her firstborn, she nevertheless summoned the strength to touch on that which worried her the most now. "But I would speak no more of the babe, Cat," she said finally. " 'Tis for you that I fear. I cannot keep Lord Guy from taking you to Curthose's court." She opened her eyes to see the girl's face set mutinously. "Nay, but we must not argue—'twill be done whether we will it or not. And you will be going

where your father's power cannot always protect you,
for a man who has risen as Roger has done gains many
enemies. Remember always that you are among
them.''

"Nay, but Curthose is Papa's overlord, Maman,
and—''

Eleanor silenced her with a tired wave of her hand.
"Cat, that you go for hostage tells that your father's
enemies already have the duke's ear.''

"But—''

"We must speak while we have the time.'' Raising
herself higher on the pillows, Eleanor fixed her daughter with the seriousness of her expression. "You must
behave as a gently bred lady, Catherine, and conduct
yourself always as befits the Demoiselle of the Condes.
But I would not have you draw attention to yourself—
there must be no cause for Curthose's complaint. Do
you understand?''

"Nay, but—''

"I'll brook no argument in this. You will be obedient to Lord Guy in all things also. He may well be
your only friend on Curthose's council, Cat.''

"A boy scarcely older than Brian!'' Catherine
scoffed indignantly.

"He is nineteen, but 'tis of no import how old he
is. He's won his spurs on the battlefield and he's managed to keep his lands intact against the power of great
barons in these troubled times. You cannot say that of
men thrice his age, and well you know it. We must
trust him to hold you safe.''

"But—''

Eleanor appeared to ignore the interruption as she
continued in the same vein, "He has given his oath on
the Cross that he'll not see you harmed, so I pray you
will not vex him. I would that I'd not spoken against
betrothing you to Robert of Caen before this began.''

"Lord Guy asked if I were betrothed.''

"Then he recognizes the task before him.'' Eleanor

sighed heavily. "Were you already pledged, none would dare to claim you."

"Well, I am glad I am not. I've no wish for Robert—not now, not ever," Catherine maintained stoutly.

"Alas, but I pray we do not regret 'twas not done." Resigned, her mother shook her head and sighed anew. "Come, Cat, cry peace with me and get you down to sup before Lord Guy thinks we do not mean to feed him. And promise me now that you do not mean to quarrel with him."

"I . . . I . . ." Catherine bit her lip until it reddened before she could bring herself to nod acquiescence. It would do no good to reveal now the plan that was forming in her head. Instead, she prayed silently that God would forgive her the deception.

"Give me your pledge, Cat, that you will strive to make Roger proud to call you his heiress."

The girl breathed in relief, certain that her father would not expect her to go meekly for hostage. "I will be my father's daughter in all things, Maman," she answered finally.

"I pray you are."

After Catherine left, Eleanor turned her face into a pillow and wept again, both for the son she'd lost and the daughter she feared to lose. And then she prayed that Guy of Rivaux would be able to keep his own promise to her.

The hall was more than half empty, with the blue-shirted men of the Condes mingling freely with those in Rivaux red at the lower tables. On the dais, the young count leaned forward, his elbows resting on the cloth that covered the trestle table, his dark head bent attentively to Aislinn. Catherine watched for a moment as her sister's hands moved descriptively in the telling of some story that brought a broad smile to his face. Somehow she felt it disloyal of Aislinn to be so obviously taken with Guy of Rivaux when, despite his handsomeness, he was the one come to take Cat away from the Condes.

As she drew nearer, he looked up, his strange eyes still warm with amusement, and the smile faded suddenly. Rising to greet her, he leaned over to ask in a low voice, "How fares your lady mother?"

"As well as may be, my lord, given that she lost the babe."

"Aye—I heard and I am sorry for it."

She bit back bitter words of accusation, reminding herself that he could not be faulted for her mother's early labor. Instead, she slid onto the bench as Aislinn reluctantly moved to make a place for her. As the elder, it was Cat's right to share Guy of Rivaux's trencher whether she wished it or not. With scarce a sideways glance as he dropped down beside her, she reached to dip her fingers into the bowl of scented water.

"Did you speak with Maman, Cat?" her sister asked eagerly. "Alice said Hawise came for you."

"Aye." Catherine took a towel proffered by a serving boy and dried her hands carefully before turning around. "And it is as you would think, Linn. She grieves for the son she has lost."

Aislinn nodded. "Hawise said 'twas strangled with its own cord."

"Sweet Mary!" Catherine muttered irritably. "If you had the tale already, why do you ask? Nay, but I'd not speak of it before strangers, anyway," she added with a significant glance toward the young count, who was seemingly absorbed in carving a haunch of roasted deer.

Unperturbed, Aislinn slid her trencher past Cat to allow Guy to place a chunk of the venison on it. "My thanks, my lord. I pray you will forgive my sister her lack of manners," she murmured.

"Linn . . ." Cat's voice dropped low in warning.

"The Demoiselle has much to plague her," Guy responded easily as he began cutting the meat he'd placed on their trencher into small pieces. Pushing half of it to Catherine's end, he made a place for the ale-boiled fish that a serving wench placed on the trestle table in front of him. "Do you take fish or some of the capon?" he addressed her.

"I am not hungry."

Thus answered, he divided the fish between them and reached for the bowl of stewed peas and onions. "I would not have you weak and famished on the road to Rouen tomorrow, Demoiselle. 'Tis my plan to reach the abbey outside Lisieux at nightfall."

"Lisieux!" Catherine's face betrayed her dismay. "Nay—'tis too far! My lord, I am no soldier to be marched from daybreak to sunset!"

"You do not ride well, Demoiselle?"

"Cat rides better than most men, my lord," Aislinn offered proudly.

Casting her sister a look that bordered on pure dislike, Catherine turned back to Guy. "I do not travel well in the heat," she lied as she furtively pinched Aislinn in warning.

"We'll take extra skins of water."

"My lord . . ." Catherine hesitated, unwilling to ask anything of him, and yet so very loath to leave her mother.

"Nay," he answered.

"Nay?" Her face flushed with indignation. "You presume too much, Guy of Rivaux, if you think to know my thoughts!"

"You wished to ask if I would stay another day." He fixed her with those strange gold-green eyes of his and shook his head. "Alas, but I cannot."

"But *why?* Surely one day cannot mean so much to you, my lord, and my mother—"

"Nay," he cut in patiently. "As I told the Lady Eleanor in your presence, Demoiselle, I have mine own feudal obligations to be met. Already Henry makes his move, and I will have to have my levies raised ere he marches through Normandy unchallenged." He pushed the laden trencher closer to her.

"Believe me when I say again that I wish I did not have to take you with me."

"Then do not."

"I bear Curthose's writ."

"Jesu! 'I bear Curthose's writ,' " she mimicked angrily. "God's blood, but you are a fool to bear arms for him, my lord! You will lose your lands and mayhap your life for a weak-willed duke who changes his mind as often as other men change clothes." Her dark eyes mirrored the scorn in her voice. "Do you not know that my father will hunt you down and hang your head from these gates if I am harmed?"

"I gave my word that you will be safe, Demoiselle."

"A vow you cannot keep! How many will listen to a boy, my lord?" she gibed spitefully. "Aye—you are but a boy playing at men's games in this foolish war!"

"Cat!" Aislinn gasped beside her.

"Well, I would not go—and I will not." In a calmer tone she added to Guy again, "You will not get me to Rouen, my lord. You forget that I am my father's daughter as well as my mother's."

His own patience strained by her outburst of temper, he picked up her small dinner knife and carefully speared a small piece of venison with it. "Aye—you'll go, Catherine of the Condes—you'll go if I have to tie you in your saddle and lead you all the way there. Now, eat your food and give me peace to eat mine." Reaching for her hand, he pressed the knife handle into her palm and closed her fingers over it. "We have many miles to travel on the morrow, so you'd best fill your stomach well." For a moment his eyes seemed more green than gold, and then his expression softened and they lightened. "Come, Demoiselle, let us not fault each other for what must be done."

"If Brian were here, he'd meet you for the insult you offer," she gritted between clenched teeth.

He skewered another piece of meat with his own knife and bit it off. Then, after carefully wiping the rim of their silver goblet, he washed the venison down with a sip of sweetened wine. For a moment he stared absently across the nearly empty hall as though he meant to ignore her.

"Aye, and he'd claim your horse and your armor for spoils, my lord," she taunted further.

"Your FitzHenry?" He turned back to her with raised eyebrow. "Mayhap, but I would doubt it."

"Art a conceited fool also, are you not? You speak as though you were Count of Belesme rather than Rivaux."

"Nay, but I try to give better than I get in all things, Lady Catherine."

"Brave words for a boy, I think."

The scarred eyebrow rose a fraction higher. "You mistake the matter, Demoiselle. While FitzHenry learned the art of war within the safety of these walls, I had to fight for every hide of land my father left me. Your father has been at peace these two years past, whilst I have defended my patrimony against those who would take it."

"Aye." Aislinn leaned around Catherine to address him. "And your successes are not unnoted. Our father says you acquit yourself well, my lord."

"I survive," he acknowledged simply.

"Until King Henry takes the field," Catherine muttered. "Then you will be in chains—if you live."

"Cat!"

"Well, 'tis the truth. Eat your supper, Linn, and cease making sheep's eyes at the fool. 'Tis bad enough having to share my trencher with him without your feeding his conceit."

Catherine's tart tongue prompted him to look heavenward and shake his head. "Poor Robert," he murmured in mock sympathy.

Both girls looked up at Guy. "Robert?" Cat demanded.

"Aye. He'll weary his sword arm beating manners into you, I fear."

"Nay, you mistake the matter, my lord. I'll not wed with him—I swear it. 'Tis Brian FitzHenry I'll take, and no other."

He took another sip from the wine cup and shrugged. " 'Tis of no concern to me whom you wed—I have but the task of getting you to Rouen."

4

Catherine rode in sullen silence, her thoughts bent on escape from Guy of Rivaux. Beside her, he too was quiet as he contemplated the tasks ahead of him. He was already late in assembling his levies, although he'd sent out his call to arms to Rivaux's vassals a fortnight before. His brow furrowed at the mental count of those who'd answered and those who had not. It was not easy to command men who had been betrayed by Robert Curthose's vacillating ways too many times before. Twice since he'd been count, he'd followed his duke against Henry of England, only to stand helplessly watching as Curthose had bargained away Norman lands rather than fight. And now there were those of his own vassals who held back, waiting to see what the two quarreling brothers would do this time, hoping to save their own patrimonies. Jesu, but they regarded their feudal oaths lightly. His frown deepened at the thought of Herluin de Braose, who had not yet responded to his call. If a man like de Braose chose to be forsworn, what hope was there?

"My lord, I would stop."

Without waiting for permission, Catherine reined in her white mare and slid to the ground. With a muttered oath Guy shook his head. She looked up to where he sat astride the black stallion, a horse huge enough to be used for a battle charger had it been gelded. From

38

where she stood, Guy of Rivaux appeared as magnificent and imposing as her father. She had to shield her eyes from the bright reflection of the hot summer sun off his helmet and mail. She could sense rather than see that he was angry with her.

"Nay, Demoiselle, but we do not stop again."

"I thirst."

In defiance, she turned and walked back along the mounted column to where Hawise rode with the pack animals and Guy's body servant. "Get me a drink from the skins," she ordered. Behind her, she heard him dismount as his spurs clinked against the hard-packed dry mud of the road.

The maidservant hesitated, unwilling to incur the young lord's wrath yet again, and remained uneasily on the horse provided her. With an almost furtive nod toward the advancing Guy, she hissed to her mistress, "You strain his patience, Demoiselle, and are like to gain nothing by it."

"I care not." Lifting her thick mane of hair off her damp neck, Catherine kept her back to him. "Sweet Mary, but 'tis hot," she complained, "and I'd go no further until I am cooled. He cannot expect to treat me as a soldier, after all. Get me the water, Hawise."

"Demoiselle."

She felt his hands on her shoulders and would have ducked away but for the firmness of his grip. Standing stock-still, she spoke evenly. "Unhand me, my lord."

"Nay." He held her steadily until he'd mastered his temper, and then he slowly turned her around to face him. "Do you take me for a fool, Demoiselle?" Still holding her by one hand, he gestured toward the bright, merciless sky. "Thrice you have caused me to stop, and 'tis scarce noon yet. I have not the time to spare for this, and well you know it, so I can only think you wish to delay me."

The gold flecks spiked across the green of his eyes from above his nasal as he fixed her with their intensity. The suppressed anger she read there made her

forget his youth. A sharp retort died on her lips with
the realization that defiance would defeat her purpose.
If she were to carry out her plan, she would have to
make him think her weak rather than stubborn.

"My lord, I an unused to traveling in the heat."
Lifting her hair again to show him her wet neck, she
explained in softer, more placating tones, "I should
have braided my hair—'twould have been cooler. Perhaps Hawise—"

"Nay."

"Then at least let me drink."

Despite the harsh side he showed his enemies, Guy
retained a kindness and gentleness toward those whom
God had created weaker. Staring down at her upturned
face, he reminded himself that she was, after all, but
a child still, and she was being thrust into the difficult
position of hostage through no fault of her own. With
a sigh, he relented. Turning to his perplexed body servant, he ordered curtly, "Get one of the skins and give
Lady Catherine some water."

The boy Arnulf slid down and hastened to remove
one of the waterskins tied to a packhorse. Rinsing out
a battered cup, he filled it and carried it to Catherine.
But for Catherine, a quick drink was little suited to
her purposes, and she sought the means for further
delay. Taking the cup, she held it out to Guy.

"As hot as I am, my lord, you must feel the sun's
heat ten times worse."

He eyed her warily as he took it. From his limited
experience of her, he'd not thought her capable of no-
ticing anyone's discomfort but her own. In the four or
five hours since they'd left the Condes, she'd kept herself aloof except when she'd demanded to stop, first
for water and then to relieve herself and now for water
again. Raising the cup to his lips, he drank deeply,
conceding to himself that he was thirsty, after all.

"I could not stand to wear a helmet on a day like
this," she murmured as he handed the empty cup back
to Arnulf. "Surely it cannot make too great a differ-

ence if you were to cool yourself for a short while.''
Even as she said it, she reached upward to touch the
hot metal that encased his head. ''My father complains
that 'tis like a pit oven inside when 'tis hot. Sometimes
when he and Brian would ride in, I would help him
take it off, and then I'd wet his head with water from
the well.''

''Demoiselle—''

''Sit you down, my lord, and let Hawise and myself
cool you down before we go further. You'll not reach
Lisieux if you are fainted from the heat.''

She spoke reasonably and he was tempted. Already
her hands tugged at the lacings of the mail coif that
protected his neck. Before he could protest, her fingers had deftly undone them with the skill of a squire.
His hands caught hers and pushed them away gently.
''Nay, Demoiselle, but I can do that. 'Tis unseemly
for you to care for me.'' With an effort, he wrenched
the helmet off his head, exposing his dripping black
hair and deep creases from the imprint of the nasal
against his cheeks. Dropping the helmet at his feet, he
brushed back his wet hair with his hands. Nodding to
Arnulf, he ordered, ''Tell the men to dismount. We
rest for a few minutes whilst the Demoiselle drinks.
And you can take water down the line so each can
quench his thirst also.''

The boy handed Catherine the cup and began un-
tying another skin while she slowly sipped the tepid
water. She watched as Guy found a tree to lean against.
Following him, she reached impulsively to touch his
arm. Telling herself that he was not so very different
from Brian after all, she gestured to the ground.

''Sit you down where 'tis cooler, my lord.''

Dropping to the hard earth, he watched as she unwound the cloth girdle she wore and poured the rest
of her water on a corner of it. After wiping her face
and neck with it, she leaned over to mop his brow
where an unruly dark lock of hair fell forward. He
closed his eyes to savor the relief he felt. ''Hawise,

bring the water,'' he heard her tell the plump woman, but he was unprepared for the sudden stream that hit his head, poured over his face, and splashed onto his blazoned surcoat. Sputtering, he opened his eyes to see Catherine standing over him with a nearly empty skin in her hands. "God's teeth, but you would drown me!" he complained as he tried to rise.

"Nay.'' She pushed him gently back down against the gnarled tree roots and began wiping away the excess. "I was used to doing this for Brian after he practiced with the quintains in the heat.''

She was leaning over him, her body but a few inches from his head. Her wide sleeves fell away from her slender white arms, revealing that she'd forgone the undergown in the heat. Staring directly into the swell of breasts that curved roundly beneath the fabric of the simple gown she wore, he was suddenly aware that the Demoiselle was already more woman than child. For the briefest moment he wondered if naked she would look like the castle whores he'd seen, and then he forced himself to dismiss the thought. She was, after all, but thirteen, and she was also, above all, Catherine of the Condes, daughter to Roger de Brione. Abruptly he brushed her hand away and pulled himself up against the tree trunk.

"My thanks, Demoiselle, but we can tarry no longer.''

"Wait . . .'' Cat stalled for still more time. "My hair—can Hawise not braid it quickly ere we go? 'Twill feel better, my lord, and I will not get so hot.''

His eyes narrowed for a moment and he scanned her face for some sign of guile. She stared steadily upward, meeting his gaze squarely and openly. And once again he was struck by the incredible beauty the girl possessed. Looking away, he muttered, "See that she hurries, then. Arnulf is nearly done, and I would be on the way as soon as may be.'' Bending over, he reached to pick up his discarded helmet.

Cat smiled slyly to herself as he made his way back

to the front of the column. Thus far this day, she judged she'd already cost him better than an hour, an hour that would make Lisieux difficult to reach by nightfall. A few more such delays and they'd have to stop before they got there, making the ride back to the Condes easier.

"One braid or two, Demoiselle?" Hawise asked from behind her.

"Two."

"One would be quicker."

"Two," Cat repeated firmly.

"I would not tempt his temper," the woman warned as her fingers separated the dark hair into thick strands. "He does not look overly patient to me."

"Leave me be—I know what I am about."

Hawise's hands ceased moving and her mouth drew into a thin line of disapproval. "Have a care, little mistress, lest your wiles lead you where you would not. My lord of Rivaux is no Brian ready to do your bidding rather than quarrel with you. Nay, but this one will not be so easily fooled, I think."

"Brian is no fool, old woman," Cat snapped irritably.

"Mayhap not a fool," Hawise conceded as she began anew to braid, "but too eager to please where he should not."

"You speak in riddles. Hold your tongue and do my hair—'tis why you are come with me, after all."

Reaching the front of the column of men, Guy handed his helmet to his squire, ordering curtly, "Tie it to my pommel—'tis too hot to wear."

Above him, William de Comminges still sat his horse impatiently. "God's teeth, but she delays us," he complained.

"Aye."

The grizzled old warrior threw up his hands in disgust as Guy looked back down the line to where Hawise still worked on her mistress's hair. " 'Tis nursemaids Curthose would make of us, my lord, for the little maid cannot keep a soldier's pace.''

"My lord"—Alan of Poix followed Guy's line of vision with a frown—"perhaps if we were to carry a skin up here, she would not have to stop again.''

"Nay," William snorted above them, "for then she will have to pass water, and we'll waste time seeking privacy for her." He eyed his young lord balefully. " 'Twould have been more to our purpose to have told Curthose to come after her himself.''

"I told you—he would have sent Belesme.''

"Nay." William shook his head. "Not even Curthose would be such a fool. Now, as 'tis, we must needs coddle a small maid.''

"She is not so small as one would think," Guy mused under his breath, his eyes still on Catherine.

"Aye—I have seen them wed younger than she is," Alan murmured beside him.

Guy's expression deepened to a frown. If a fourteen-year-old squire could see what he himself saw, protecting the Demoiselle of the Condes was going to be an impossible task. Tearing his eyes away from her, he muttered, "I would that she *were* wed, for then we'd not have her.'' With unusual roughness he grasped the reins of the big black and pulled hard to lead the horse to where one of the ostlers emptied the last water from a skin into a basin for the animals.

"Jesu, but he is short-tempered today," Alan complained to William.

"Aye, and with good reason. She costs us time we do not have.''

The boy stared for a long moment as Hawise finished binding Catherine's hair and stepped back. "By the Blessed Virgin, but I've not seen her like before," he admitted in open admiration.

William looked down suddenly, his black eyes sharp, and growled, "Lord Roger would hang you for the thoughts your face would betray, Alan. Nay, but she will bring promise of the Condes—and Nantes and

Harlowe also—to her marriage bed. Unless Lady Eleanor should bear a son, there stands the richest heiress we are like to see."

"Holy Mary."

"Aye."

Unable to delay any further, Catherine handed Hawise her wet girdle and walked back past the curious stares of Guy of Rivaux's men to stand beside her mare. She waited until the young count himself led his horse back to the line before drawing his attention. Pointing up to her saddle, she ordered him imperiously, "Mount me."

Guy's eyebrow shot up and the corners of his mouth betrayed the thought that flitted through his mind as the men behind him suppressed snickers. His flecked eyes flicked over her, taking in the dull red that crept unbidden to her face with the realization of what she'd said, and his grin deepened. "Alas, Demoiselle, but there's not time, and I'd not incur your father's certain wrath." Bending over, he cupped his hands.

"Insolent fool," she muttered to cover her embarrassment. Stepping up into his palms, she grasped the pommel and waited for him to throw her into her saddle.

She was lighter than he'd supposed, but then, he'd scarce touched any female other than castle whores, and they were usually thick-waisted and heavy from bearing their bastards. He lifted her easily and she swung her leg over the padded leather before settling into the seat. Wiping the dust from his hands on his red silk surcoat, he stepped back.

"God's blood, but you have the manners of a serf," she gibed above him.

"And you have none at all, Demoiselle," he responded dryly. Looking up to where William sat, he nodded. "Give the sign to mount—we've miles to travel in haste." Striding to his own horse, he took the reins, and without a backward glance at Catherine, he swung up and eased his mail-and-leather-encased body into the saddle.

"Wait."

"Jesu!" Gone was that brief feeling of charity he'd harbored for her earlier, replaced by a sense of frustration. "What now, Demoiselle?" he gritted out without even turning around.

"I . . . I . . ." Her face colored as every man except Guy stared at her, but her chin jutted determinedly. "I would be private, my lord."

"Nay."

"You would not wish me to soil my gown."

"Demoiselle . . ." Guy growled.

William cast his young master a look of resignation, muttering, "I told you she had too much water."

"Nay."

"Nay?" Her voice rose indignantly. "Nay? My lord, even prisoners of war are allowed to relieve themselves when they must."

The muscles of Guy's jaws twitched as he sought to control his temper. Finally, with a patent sigh of capitulation, he nodded.

The flecked eyes he turned to her were clearly skeptical, prompting her to add defensively, "I will hurry."

"I doubt that. Alan, get the woman to go with her." The scarred eyebrow lifted higher as he appeared to study her face. "And, Demoiselle, I take leave to examine the ground afterward for the puddle. If there is none, you'll not stop again this day—not even to eat."

"You have no courtesy, my lord."

"What did you expect from one with the manners of a serf?" he shot back. "And you could have done this ere you had me mount you." The emphasis he placed on the last several words brought another round of guffaws from the men. Her color deepened, and he was instantly sorry for the remark. She was, after all, little more than a spoiled child, he reminded himself, and he supposed she could not be expected to understand his need for speed, no matter how many times he explained it to her.

Ignoring Alan's outstretched arms, Catherine slid easily from the mare and started toward a brake of trees several hundred feet from the road. Behind her, she could hear the mutterings of Rivaux's men, and a slow smile of satisfaction curved her mouth. Let them think her weak and stupid—'twould serve her purpose well. If she could but make them lose another hour or two, she'd warrant that they'd not press on to Lisieux but would choose some inn or abbey closer.

To Guy, it seemed like she took far too long, and he was about to go after her when she finally emerged from the woods. This time, she walked quickly despite the heat until she reached them. Then, without further complaint, she stepped into Alan's cupped hands and let him throw her up into her saddle.

"I am ready, my lord."

Wordlessly Guy raised his hand and gave the forward gesture, and the column finally moved, with men and pack animals swinging into tight formation behind him. Alan hastily remounted and caught up, falling in beside his lord.

"I thought you wished to inspect the ground, my lord," Catherine chided Rivaux.

"I had not the time," he responded tersely.

Guy spurred the big black into a bone-jarring trot as the horses' hooves pounded rhythmically against the hard-packed road. Beside him, Catherine matched his pace and planned her next delay.

5

"My lord, there are riders ahead."

William de Comminges' urgency cut into Guy's consciousness, drawing him from his glum preoccupation with their slow progress. He looked up absently, followed his captain's gaze, and came alert with a jolt. As a line of green-shirted men drew up along the horizon, he sucked in his breath and the tiny hairs at the nape of his neck stood on end. His hand instinctively crept to the hilt of his sword, grasping it, ready to withdraw it from the sheath that lay flat against the side of his leg. Exhaling sharply, he swore a long and unsatisfactory oath that bordered on blasphemy.

Catherine, startled by his vehement outburst, leaned forward in her saddle to look. Even as she watched the approaching knights, their green-and-white banner dancing above them, Alan of Poix edged closer and reached for her reins.

"Take her back with her woman," Guy ordered curtly, frowning deeply. "And throw a blanket over her ere he sees her plainly."

"Who?" Cat demanded foolishly, her own heart pounding.

"Belesme."

"Sweet Mary."

"Aye."

All of her life, she'd heard of Count Robert of Belesme, knew of the bitter enmity between him and her father over her mother. Her flesh crawled at the thought of the tales she'd heard of his cruelty and depravity, and for a moment her heart threatened to stop. Alan leaned across his horse, blocking her from view as he led her toward the back of the line.

Guy shielded his eyes against the sun and waited uneasily. "I count but twenty of them."

" 'Tis not like him to ride with so few, my lord." William turned away and spat on the ground.

Belesme's men had halted also, and Guy could see one of them counting the red surcoats of Rivaux before conferring with his leader, the tall knight Guy knew for Count Robert himself. Even in the intense summer heat, Belesme wore his helmet and full mail for protection against his enemies. Not that Guy could blame him for it—Robert of Belesme considered no man his friend with good reason.

Suddenly the count turned and spoke with his captain. Then, as Guy watched warily, he removed his helmet, smoothed back black hair, and rode forward alone with the helmet dangling from his pommel. Reining in a scant ten feet from where Guy sat, he flashed a smile of greeting that did not begin to warm those cold green eyes of his.

"I had expected you before now."

"I was delayed."

"Aye. I heard Curthose sent you to the Condes." Belesme looked past Guy, his eyes flickering over the Rivaux column quickly, taking in every detail with the detachment of a seasoned soldier, apprising himself of the numbers and equipment of Guy's men. "You have the Demoiselle," he noted dispassionately as he stared toward where Catherine veiled herself with her cloth girdle.

"Aye." Guy's mouth was dry, his nerves taut.

"I would see her."

Before Guy could refuse, Belesme had spurred his horse past him, moving down the line to where Hawise attempted to shield her mistress. "Nay, I would but look at the girl, old woman." Edging his horse between them, he reached to draw away the wrinkled cloth. For a long moment he stared at her silently.

Catherine's fear faded, replaced by curiosity at the longing mirrored in that face. It was as though she glimpsed a vulnerability at odds with all she'd ever heard of him. Staring back, she could not help thinking he must've been extremely handsome once, sometime before a well-aimed blow had broken and caved in one cheekbone, disfiguring him. His green eyes did not set evenly now, and yet they were still arresting with their intensity.

"You favor her."

There was no need asking whom he meant, for men still sung the tale of his disappointment of Eleanor of Nantes. She nodded. "Aye," she answered proudly.

"Your lady mother—is she well?"

Somehow, Catherine did not think that either of her parents would wish her to discuss her mother with him, but she felt an odd pang of sympathy for this man despite what she'd heard of him. She exhaled slowly under that penetrating gaze and shook her head. "Nay—she lost yet another babe this week, my lord."

His face hardened and the green eyes went cold so quickly she was taken aback by the change in him. His curiosity was gone, replaced now by an expression of such bitterness and hatred that she wanted to flee from him. Willing herself to sit calmly, she denied the chill that crept up her spine. Then, like quicksilver, his twisted face changed yet again, softening, and his eyes traveled over her before returning to her face.

"Aye," he half-whispered more to himself than to her, "but you are very like her in more than looks, Demoiselle. She never cowered before me either."

"The Demoiselle is under my protection, my lord."

Belesme straightened in his saddle and turned to Guy. Appraising the younger man shrewdly, his green eyes assessing Guy's resolve, he shook his head. "Nay, but Curthose sends a boy for a man's task."

There was an open insult in both his manner and his words, but Guy would not be baited. Leaning forward to pat his horse's neck, he merely nodded amiably. "Mayhap, but he gave me his writ, Robert, and I mean to discharge it as I am able."

"You have not assembled your levies, and already Henry has landed," Belesme reminded him. "Nay, but I would leave you to do so now, and I will see the Demoiselle to Rouen for Curthose."

"I cannot allow it."

Robert of Belesme's eyes narrowed dangerously, piercing like shards of deep green glass, but Guy refused to waver. "You deny me?" Robert asked harshly.

Neither foolhardy nor unafraid, Guy knew he risked much in defying a man whose cruelty was legend in his lifetime, but he also knew he'd sworn an oath to Catherine de Brione's safety. His mouth was almost too dry for speech, but he managed to answer simply, "Aye."

"Art a fool then, for I can take her with me whether you will it or no, Guy of Rivaux," Belesme challenged.

"My Lord, I have thirty men sworn to fight where I choose. You are alone and unhelmed among them, and you have scarce twenty to come to your aid. I'd not fight you in this, Robert—not when we both are sworn to serve the same overlord in a far greater cause—but I will if I must." Resting his hand on the rounded pommel of his sword hilt, Guy faced the older count steadily and waited.

Thinking herself about to be the center of a blood-bath, Catherine stared in disbelief, first at Belesme and then at Rivaux. "By the blessed saints," she exploded finally, "but I think you are both mad! And I would not go with either of you!"

Belesme's usually inscrutable face betrayed him as

anger gave way to surprise. "Nay, I will not fight you for now, boy—not when Normandy himself will deliver her to me ere this quarrel ends." A slow smile played over a sensuous mouth and warmed the green eyes with an almost eerie light. "I give you one thing, Guy of Rivaux—art your father's son." Turning to Catherine, he sobered. "Until Rouen, Demoiselle."

"Sweet Mary," Cat breathed in relief as he rode off. "So that is Belesme."

"Aye."

"He must have been very handsome once."

Guy stared in surprise at her. "So I have heard, but not since I can remember. 'Tis said 'twas your father's blow that did that to his face, but I was not there. I was with the monks then," he added bitterly.

"You were destined for the Church?" she asked in disbelief.

"Aye, I was to atone for my mother's death. But I would speak no more of that, Demoiselle. Let it be said that my brothers died early, saving me from the life, and that is all there is to tell." His gold-flecked eyes followed Belesme as the count rode back to his own men, and he shook his head in puzzlement. "Though I cannot think Count Robert would have admired my father, for they were enemies—unless 'twas that they both were cruel and bitter men."

"Art a fool, Count Guy," Catherine murmured with unusual softness, "but I thank you for the service you gave me just now."

"Aye," Guy sighed. "I pray it does not cost me my head. Robert neither forgives nor forgets those who thwart him in even the smallest matters."

❧ 6 ❧

The abbey was still save for the deep rhythmic snores emanating from the pallet where Hawise slept. Catherine lay clothed and awake on the narrow cot, listening intently in the darkness, her ears straining for some sound beyond the tiny cell, her mind willing her body to remain alert. She judged that the last footstep had passed along the stone-flagged corridor an hour or more before, but she dared not move yet.

They'd not made it to Lisieux—they were far from it yet, she noted with smug satisfaction. A slow smile curved her mouth in the darkness as she remembered Guy of Rivaux's impatience with her. He would have liked to beat her, she knew, but his chivalry and courtesy to those weaker than himself forbade it. Instead, he grudgingly slowed their pace to accommodate a demoiselle unused to traveling in the heat. She could almost laugh at his exasperation with her as she remembered his irritation, his anger, and finally his resignation as she had demanded again and again to stop. Thus, when they'd reached the small abbey at Froilyn shortly before dark, he'd reined in and announced curtly that they'd ask for beds there. The older man, the one called William, had snorted and argued for pressing on through the night, but Rivaux had shaken his head, saying, ''Nay, but she can go no further this day.''

Her only regret was that he'd thought her too sick to eat and had sent her to the narrow cell with bread and cheese whilst he and his men had partaken of a more substantial meal with the abbot. She'd feigned illness too well, she decided with a sigh, and now she lay listening to Hawise's snores and her own stomach's growls. Briefly she wondered if she dared pass by the kitchen for food ere she left, and then reluctantly discarded the idea for being too risky. Well, on the morrow she'd be eating at the Condes, and that thought would have to sustain her.

Finally, too afraid that she would succumb to sleep herself, she rose stealthily from the cot and edged to the small, high window to listen for sentries. Hearing nothing, she was emboldened to pick up her soft leather shoes and tiptoe past the slumbering Hawise to the door. Leaning her head against the grated opening, she waited several minutes to assure herself that the long, narrow corridor was empty before daring to ease the iron handle upward. The door opened with a squeaky groan as it swung on ancient hinges. Waiting again for the sound of movement within any of the sparse tiny chambers lining the passage, she finally slipped out and crept toward the open courtyard.

Moonlight bathed the cobbled stones, showing them like hundreds of eggs lying in rows, shadowing them at the edges by the surrounding walls. Faint voices came from the depths of the shadows across the wide expanse of yard. Catherine held her breath and listened, determining that Rivaux's sentries shared stories and a skin of wine, before she edged along the wall on the opposite side.

The horses, tethered on a grassy strip behind the wall, moved nervously at her approach. Still barefoot and holding her shoes, she isolated her mare to lead it away. Rivaux's ostlers had removed her saddle and piled it with the others in a row to form a barrier along one side. For a moment she contemplated trying to find it and then decided it too much of a risk. Sud-

denly Rivaux's big black reared its head to shatter the
stillness with a piercing whinny that made her heart
rise in her throat. A knot formed in the pit of her
stomach as she held her breath and waited for the sentries to respond. The big animal's ears were laid back
and his nostrils flared. Timidly she reached to lay a
quieting hand on its long nose and whispered soothing
words. She could hear the men across the courtyard
pause and listen for what seemed a very long time.
Finally they resumed a desultory conversation about
full moons and skittish animals.

Picking up a riding whip, Catherine stopped to slip
on her shoes before grasping the mare's mane and
swinging up on its bare back. The big black whinnied
again and moved restlessly within the small area,
prompting others to shift about. With her knee, Cat
nudged her horse away while lying close to its back.

"Leaving, Demoiselle?"

A half-dressed Guy of Rivaux stepped out of the
shadows and grasped her reins. A tight smile of suppressed fury, coupled with eyes that glittered in the
moonlight, gave him a frightening aspect. Catherine
gasped at his sudden appearance. Raising her whip,
she brought it down with full force. He closed his eyes
by reflex and took the blow across his cheek, wincing
as the thin leather ribbon cut into his flesh.

"Unhand my horse!" she hissed furiously while
kicking the mare.

The animal tried to rear, but Guy maintained a firm
grip on its reins. It half-stumbled and would have
thrown Catherine had she not held tightly to its mane.
Tears of impotent rage stung her eyes and threatened
to spill onto her cheeks as she choked helplessly above
him.

With the back of his free hand, Guy wiped away
the blood that welled in the cut on his face before he
reached for her. Then, releasing the mare's head, he
grasped Catherine roughly by an arm and dragged
her down. She fell heavily against him and struggled

for escape. Kicking and elbowing, she fought while he held her. Warm, wet drops of his blood dripped on her gown as both his arms imprisoned her flailing limbs. Finally he brought a knee around her, forcing her to lose her balance and fall in a heap at his feet. She lay for a moment to catch her breath and then scrambled up.

"God's blood, but you are a fiery little maid," he muttered, his eyes on her heaving chest.

"You've ruined my gown!" she spat out.

His anger fading, he stared hard into her upturned face, thinking irrationally that he'd never seen any female, demoiselle or great lady, to compare with Catherine of the Condes. Her eyes, black in the moonlight, flashed defiance still. For the briefest moment he wondered if her mouth would taste like any other, and then blotted the dangerous thought from his mind. Instead, he reached for her wrist and pulled her into the open area.

"And you have marked me, so we are even, Demoiselle," he answered curtly. "Where did you think to go?"

Twisting her hand to loosen his grip, she found his fingers cut into her wrist like unbreakable bands. "You bruise me, my lord."

"Answer me—where did you think to go?"

"Mayhap I thought to meet someone!" she snapped insolently. "God's bones! Does it matter? I am found out, anyway."

"The only person you'll meet out there is Belesme." He watched those black eyes widen and nodded. "Aye, he travels less than a league behind, and has since we met him."

"But why? He would not fight you surely . . ." Her voice trailed off uncertainly as she recalled tales of Count Robert's treachery.

"Who knows what is in his mind, Demoiselle? He is, I think, more than a little mad, and mayhap thinks to gather more men before he tries to take you from me."

"Sweet Mary!"

"Aye. I had hoped to be to Lisieux by now—and would have been—and we would have been closer to mine own allies." The hazel eyes were heavily flecked now, making them lighter as he stared soberly, his brow furrowed with some distant thought unrelated to her. The slash against his cheekbone still oozed dark blood. Abruptly he looked down and considered her anew. "You still have not said where you intended to go, Demoiselle."

"The Condes."

His scarred eyebrow lifted quizzically. "The Condes? 'Tis leagues, child, and despite the moon, I doubt you could find your way."

"I am not a child," she muttered sullenly.

"You are thirteen, Catherine, and scarce prepared for such a journey. You could have ridden into Belesme's camp ere you even knew it, and I'd not have been able to aid you. Come on." He tugged at her wrist and started back for the cloisters. "I would rise early on the morrow."

"Nay." She pulled back, digging in the heels of her soft slippers against the cobblestones. "My lord, I would not go to Rouen—I would not," she repeated desperately. "What if Curthose should receive word—however false—that my father was in King Henry's train? He might blind me—or worse."

He stopped. "Nay. Too many of us fight for him because we must, Demoiselle, but we'd not stomach his harming Roger de Brione's daughter. 'Twould be folly—Lord Roger would be sure to come then, and even Holy Church would stand against Normandy if you were harmed."

"Yet you let him take me hostage—aye, you *come* to do his bidding," she accused.

"Because you will not be harmed."

"How can you know that?"

"Demoiselle, I *swore* you would not."

"You are but one boy. What if you cannot keep that which you promise? Will you grieve for me when I am blind or dead?"

The muscles in his jaw tensed until they ached. "Demoiselle," he answered finally, "I am but one man—or boy, if you will—but I will keep my oath or die. Now"—he grasped her roughly again and pushed her ahead of him—"I would sleep tonight that I may ride tomorrow."

It was useless to argue further and she knew it. She went without hurling the dozen or so barbs that sprang to mind, walking silently before him, knowing she was going to Rouen for a certainty. She'd been a fool to think it could be otherwise, she conceded to herself, but she'd had to try, else she'd not been Roger de Brione's daughter.

He shoved her unceremoniously through the cell door and woke Hawise. "Get up, woman, and watch your mistress until I return," he ordered brusquely. "And do not think to let her leave again. Next time, I'll beat her."

"Until you return . . . ?" Catherine stared.

"Aye."

Hawise blinked in the semidarkness and sat up. Catherine stood rooted where the moon made a wedge of pale light against the stone floor, her face as still as one of the carved stone statues in the chapel at the Condes. Then, before the plump woman's eyes, the girl's shoulders sagged and shook. "Oh, Hawise!" she wailed. "I go to Curthose! I shall die there!"

"Nay, nay, little mistress," Hawise soothed in alarm. "Come—'twill not be so. You'll be cosseted and petted as you were at home—you'll see. Nay, but none can look on you and not love you."

With an effort, Catherine collected herself and sniffed. It did no good to frighten one who could not aid her anyway. Dropping to sit on the cot, she nodded her head in dejection. "I thought to run away."

"Cat!"

"Aye, but he caught me."

"I told you he was no fool."

Catherine sighed. " 'Twas his horse that gave me away, Hawise, else I'd have done it. But he says Count Robert follows us, so I suppose it was for the best. Sweet Mary, but Curthose cannot be as bad as Belesme," she reasoned finally.

Hawise crossed herself at the mention of the hated name. A superstitious soul, she like many others felt certain that Robert of Belesme was the devil's tool on earth, for how else could he have done what he had all these years without retribution? Aye, Satan's spawn he was, and it was not healthy even to think of him.

There was a faint scraping sound in the corridor and then Guy of Rivaux reappeared dragging a straw-filled mattress by a corner. Pulling it just inside the door, he arranged it so that it blocked the opening. His back to them, he explained, "You'll not leave again tonight without waking me, Demoiselle, for I do not sleep deep."

"My lord, 'tis unseemly," Hawise protested.

"You can sleep between us, woman, and I will leave the door open for all to see she is unmolested." Even as he spoke, he drew his tunic over his head and discarded it in a heap beside the pallet. Catherine strained curiously to see how he looked naked, but his pallet was in deep shadows. As if sensing her thoughts, he added, "And I sleep in my chausses, Demoiselle." Easing his tired body down against the rough cloth that covered the straw, he rolled onto his side and cradled his head on his forearm. "Since you are recovered from your heat-sickness, Catherine of the Condes, I expect we will gain the leagues we lost today. We'll stop but once in the morning and once in the afternoon this time."

She lay still on the cot, pretending not to hear him. That he'd discovered her before she could flee galled her still, but even that could have been borne if he were not so conceited about it. She waited until she could hear him breathing steadily and knew he was slipping into sleep, and then she brought him awake by announcing evenly, ''I am glad I cut your face, Guy of Rivaux—I hope it marks you for the rest of your life.''

7

The city of Rouen bustled with the preparations for
war. Everywhere Catherine looked there were men-at-
arms on brightly caparisoned horses and common soldiers jostling for passage in the narrow streets. The
whole place was crowded, teeming with the sounds
and smells of armorers' and farriers' bellows blowing
smoke that mingled with the odor of bake ovens and
spits. Great cauldrons sent pungent clouds of steam up
as leather was boiled to toughen it for those unable to
afford mail. Peasants drove herds of sheep and swine
to slaughter within city walls, and the animals' cries
contributed to the din.

Catherine wrinkled her nose at the commingling of
garbage, animal offal, and urine that fouled the streets,
keeping the ragged, bearded cleaners busy in a hopeless effort. A filthy beggar, his right arm ending in a
blackened stump, clutched at the hem of her gown
with his left and cried through broken teeth, "Alms
for a poor soldier, gentle lady—alms for a poor soldier!"

William de Comminges would have forced the fellow out of the way with his horse, but Guy reached
into the purse that hung from his belt and threw a coin.
As the beggar dropped to grope on the ground, William growled, "You give too much, my lord."

"Nay, he lost a hand to his trade."

"Humph!" the older man scoffed. "I'd say he lost it for poaching or debasing coins, more like. Sometimes art soft as a woman, Guy of Rivaux."

"I care not how he lost it, then—he cannot work."

"God's blood, my lord, but you cannot feed every poor soul between here and Rivaux," William expostulated before his face broke into a reluctant smile. "Not that you would not try. The monks had you overlong—'tis a wonder I could teach you that a hand's for aught but writing."

Well aware of William's pride in his ability to read and write and cipher, Guy grinned openly. "Aye, but at least I know when the clerks would cheat me, and you cannot say that is not an advantage."

Beside him, Catherine covered her mouth and nose with her hand and rode in stony silence. She was in Rouen—she was effectively Robert Curthose's prisoner now. Before her loomed the ducal palace, ill-named thus for it was more fortress than anything, and this day it looked to be a prison.

"Art silent, Demoiselle," Guy chided her. "I cannot believe the Cat no longer means to hiss and spit."

"I was thinking the place stinks more than I remembered," she answered untruthfully.

He looked sideways at her, taking in her proud profile and thinking she looked more like a queen than a hostage. If Eleanor of Nantes had given her daughter anything of herself, it was that incredible beauty. Watching her, he could almost forget that she'd cast a host of insults at him in the four days he'd known her, and he felt a stirring of charity toward the girl. After all, despite her best efforts, they'd finally reached Rouen on the day he'd appointed from the beginning. Aye, for once he'd made it plain that he'd brook no further delay, she'd ridden as well as any man in his train.

His eyes traveled lower to the gown she wore. Gone was the stained traveling dress, replaced with an embroidered sendal gown of brightest blue shot with fine golden threads that shone in the sun. The woman Hawise had laced it tightly beneath the full sleeves to show the contour of Catherine's breasts, making it difficult for a man to remember she was so young. Were it not for her sharp tongue and her obstinance, Guy could almost envy Robert of Caen, but as it was, he told himself he pitied him instead. Aye, he sighed regretfully, but Catherine of the Condes was beautiful enough to enslave a man and termagant enough to make his life miserable ever after. And somehow he did not think a heavy hand would improve her in the least.

"Art insolent to stare," she snapped in annoyance.

"I ask your pardon, Demoiselle. I was but thinking it a pity that your tongue comes with you," he answered, grinning. "Aye—mayhap I should warn Robert that 'tis the other daughter he should take."

"The next time you see him, I hope you are lying on the ground vanquished, my lord."

"Thankfully that is in the hands of God alone."

"And you think He favors you, my lord?" she demanded scornfully. "Nay, he does not. If you stand with Duke Robert, you will find 'tis otherwise."

"Mayhap, but I have done naught to offend God so far as I know it," he answered easily, his eyes still reflecting his smile.

"Well, you have offended *me*," she retorted.

"Ah, but you are not God."

She looked up sharply and met the gold-flecked eyes. " 'Tis blasphemy to jest of such things," she reminded him evenly. "You would mock me."

"I have asked your pardon once—I'll not ask it again this day." His voice was quiet, his face older than his years from fatigue, but despite his aching body, he maintained his humor under her scrutiny. His cheek moved as his smile broadened again and the gash she'd given him bore witness to how close she'd come to getting his eye. As it was, the faint scar that divided his eyebrow seemed to be a part of the red line that continued below. When it healed, it would look as though it had happened in one blow and people would marvel that he still had the eye. She felt shame for what she'd done, and then she reminded herself that he was, after all, Curthose's man, and he brought her here to an uncertain fate. Bitterness crowded all else from her mind.

Their progress through the streets was slow, owing to the intense bustle of a city crowded beyond its means, and her sense of ill-usage increased with each plodding step. They were bunched together so closely in the narrow lanes that when a cart would have passed them, Rivaux's leg pushed against hers.

"Jesu, but you take liberties with my person," she complained irritably.

" 'Twas not my intent, Demoiselle."

The knowledge that he was right did nothing to improve her temper. She fought back angry tears that irrationally welled in her eyes, turning away so that he would not see them. She might as well have come to the Conqueror's city in chains, something that he failed to understand, and Rivaux's indifferent manner was infuriating.

The gates of the palace swung open before them without a challenge, another reminder of the young lord's standing with Robert Curthose. The red-and-black banner of Rivaux hung limply above them in the heat of an airless day, a symbol of the wealth and power that gained him a voice in the duke's own council despite his youth. A symbol of the power that had enabled him to come to the Condes for her.

Ostlers rushed to take the reins from the riders, yet another sign of Curthose's favor, and the duke himself, in the company of his duchess, several ladies, and an assemblage of barons, waited to greet them on low steps. It was as though he felt relief at Rivaux's arrival, Catherine decided as she openly studied the Conqueror's eldest son. He was aptly called Curthose, the name that had stuck since he'd been but a boy, for his legs were disproportionately short to his body, making him overall a head shorter than the men around him. He must've had those legs of his mother, she supposed, for her own mother had said the Duchess Mathilde had been very short also. He turned dark eyes on her and, forgetting her promise to her mother, she swore softly under her breath. God willing, 'twould soon be her godfather King Henry in his place, and Normandy would once again know peace and justice.

Guy eased his weary frame from the black horse and turned to Catherine. Reaching upward for her, he was unprepared for the vehemence in her voice as she hissed at him, "Take your hands off me, Guy of Rivaux—I can get down myself." She raised her whip as though to strike, and the memory of her last blow came to mind.

"Conduct yourself as a lady, Catherine. You are in the presence of your duke," he reminded her coldly, his hand still on her waist. "Your father's suzerain," he added in warning.

She raised her hand higher. "Unhand me, my lord, else I'll mark your other cheek," she gritted out between clenched teeth.

For answer, his other hand snaked out to grasp her whip and wrenched it away. Then, throwing it on the ground, he pulled her from her saddle and pushed her down against the dirty paving stones, soiling her rich gown and sending a nervous titter of amusement through the crowd. The muscle in one jaw twitched and his eyes glittered angrily. "You make your obeisance to Duke Robert from there, Demoiselle," he gibed over her. Bending down to pick up the discarded whip, he leaned closer until his face was but inches from hers and spoke low. "And we are done, Catherine of the Condes, for you would try me once too often. Not even your lady mother would expect me to bear what I have borne from you these three days past." Straightening, he nodded to Robert Curthose, announcing clearly, "I give you the Demoiselle Catherine, Your Grace, in answer to your writ. You will find her ill-tempered, overbold, and given to violence, but she is here."

Humiliated by the laughter around her, Catherine considered making her disgrace complete by flying up at Guy and opening his face wound again with her fingernails, and then she thought better of it. Instead, she bent her head low to the stones and murmured, "My lord duke. Duchess Sybilla."

"Rise you, Demoiselle," Robert Curthose acknowledged briefly. "My duchess would make your stay in Rouen a pleasant one." Beckoning her forward, he nodded to the pale woman beside him. "You have prepared a place for her, have you not?"

For answer, the duchess reached a cold hand to touch Catherine's chin. "We bid you welcome, Demoiselle." A faint smile did not warm her pale eyes at all as she added, "You have the look of your mother, child."

The duke's attention turned to Guy of Rivaux as he asked, "Have you heard aught of Belesme, my lord? I had expected him ere now."

"We met the other side of Froilyn. I believe he is scarce an hour's time behind me."

Curthose's face lightened. "Aye, I knew he would come. He's not like to fight for my brother since Henry banished him from England. And you, my lord—do your vassals heed your call?"

"Some of them. I would return to Rivaux by your leave, your grace, that I may raise my levies from there."

Catherine's heart sank unexpectedly and a sense of desolation stole over her as she listened to him. Despite what had passed between them, she was afraid to have him leave her alone in the strangeness of Normandy's court. In front of her, the duchess saw the stricken glance Catherine gave Guy and she frowned in disapproval. "Come, Demoiselle, that we may see you are settled. Your maid will be shown where to put your things whilst we explain your tasks.''

With a swish of her gold-banded hem against the stone steps, Sybilla turned to go inside. Catherine hesitated, wishing now she'd not provoked Guy of Rivaux and hoping he would look her way. Instead, he was surrounded by barons intent on discussing the impending war. Reluctantly she brushed the dirt from her gown and followed the duchess, telling herself that she would survive—that he'd not forget his promise to her mother no matter what he had said.

It did not take long for Catherine to discover the duchess's penchant for needlework. There had scarce been time for Hawise to put her things in the narrow cupboard she shared with another of Duchess Sybilla's ladies, a younger daughter of the Count of Meulan, Bertrade by name, before she was summoned to join all the ladies in the bower. To her dismay, she found the day's occupation to be the embroidery of priests' mantles for the city's cathedral. To her further dismay, a discreet inquiry garnered her the information that this was how they spent most of their days, the chief variance being the pieces worked. And after pleasant introductions amongst the dozen or so ladies, Catherine was presented with an alb and told to embroider the design along the hem.

She stared a long moment at the snowy linen garment before seeking the duchess's attention. ''Your pardon, Your Grace,'' she began tentatively, ''but my stitches are too poor for this.''

Sybilla's pale blue eyes took in the alb before resting on Catherine. ''Demoiselle—Catherine, is it?—false modesty will gain you faint praise here,'' she warned.

''But I would not ruin it.''

''I have seen your mother's work, Demoiselle, and 'tis quite pretty.''

''But she learned it at Fontainebleau, Your Grace, and I've not the skill.'' She reddened as the other ladies turned to stare at her. "And needles make my fingers sore."

"You have not been taught to sew?" the duchess demanded incredulously.

"My father said my lord could pay to have his clothes made, and I spent my days learning to write and cipher," Catherine defended.

The older woman's mouth drew into a thin line of disapproval while she considered the newest of her ladies. "Then you will learn to ply your needle here, Demoiselle."

"But . . ." Cat's protest died on her lips at the scandalized looks she received from the others. Dropping her eyes modestly to hide the chagrin she felt, she murmured apologetically, "I will be obedient, madam, but I would not ruin this."

The duchess's brow furrowed as she contemplated Catherine. If it was as the child told her, Eleanor of Nantes had sadly neglected her maternal duty. Finally she took one of the silken cushions from behind her back and placed it on the clean-swept floor, gesturing to Catherine to come forward. "Sit you here, Demoiselle, and I will show you myself how 'tis done." Lifting the priest's gown onto her lap, she selected a needle threaded with purple silk and deftly began stitching. "You must take care to keep them fine, Catherine, taking but a thread or two between, so 'twill be smooth." She held the material closer for Cat's reluctant inspection. "Work this small place whilst I watch, and we will see how 'tis."

Despite the mutiny in her breast, Catherine settled onto the cushion and began making the tiny stitches as directed. The duchess, satisfied for the time, turned her own attention back to the beautiful golden design she'd marked on a silk altar cloth and did not notice the set of the girl's jaw.

The day dragged slowly as Cat sewed and the duchess picked out her stitches, admonishing her to repeat them with more care. From time to time the girl looked up to see the curious stares of the others, some openly admiring and some quite envious. Finally Bertrade of Meulan edged closer when Cat was close to tears. '' 'Tis not so bad, Demoiselle, when you are used to it. Here, let me see if I can aid you.''

"Why would you wish to?'' Catherine asked suspiciously.

"Because we are to be bedmates, Demoiselle, and I'd not have you weeping all night.''

The girl was as plump and white as a turtledove, with great blue eyes, yellow hair, and skin as pale as fine linen, but there was no guile or animosity in her face. With a sigh, Cat handed her the well-creased alb and shook her head. ''By the time I am finished, 'twill be so unraveled that 'twill look old before 'tis worn.''

Bertrade examined it closely in the late-afternoon light from the high window behind them. ''The pattern is too difficult for you to learn at once, Demoiselle. You should be working something simple first, I think.'' She leaned to pick up the chasuble she embroidered and held it up. ''Even this requires skill, but 'tis easier than that. I will ask the duchess if I may show you on a bordered scarf first.'' The girl's smile was disarming. ''How are you called, Demoiselle?''

"My parents and sisters call me Cat.''

"Cat?'' Bertrade cocked her head sideways to study her. ''Aye, the name becomes you, I think. Everyone here save Duchess Sybilla addresses me as Berta.''

"Berta.'' Catherine looked up to see the others watching them, and some were openly hostile.

"Pay them no heed, Cat,'' Bertrade murmured low. "They are but envious of your beauty, and they begrudge you the time you have spent with the Count of Rivaux.''

"Sweet Mary, but they cannot know him then,'' Cat whispered back.

"Nay, none of us can claim the honor. Roland says that he is more monk than man, but I'd not listen to him.''

"Roland?"

Bertrade wrinkled her nose in distaste and sighed. "Roland de Villiers—I am betrothed to him and will wed when Curthose returns to Rouen after King Henry leaves."

"And you like him not."

"I scarce know him." She cast a furtive look at the duchess, who had moved to the other end of her bower in search of better light, before adding, "He is but seventeen and serves Count William of Mortain as squire yet, but my father dared not speak against the marriage because Curthose wills it. Aye," she admitted with another glance at Sybilla, "I like him not."

"So 'tis with me." Cat dropped her voice even lower to confide, "My father would give me to Robert of Caen."

"The king's bastard?" Bertrade colored and she looked away to the floor. "Your pardon—I should not have said that, for there's none to say anything against him. Indeed, when he was here last, he was much admired by the younger ladies, and even the men seemed to like him."

"Oh, I care not that he is bastard-born. You mistake the matter—'tis but that he is the wrong bastard, Bertrade." Cat's eyes flashed defiance for a moment, and then she shook her head. "Nay, but I would have Brian FitzHenry."

" 'Berta,' " the plump girl reminded her. "And I do not know this FitzHenry, but then, there are so many of them that . . ." Her voice trailed off suddenly and she flushed anew. "I should not have said that either, but . . ."

"But 'tis true," Catherine finished for her. "Aye, everyone notes it, so why should you not also?"

"He must be very handsome to gain your favor."

Catherine cocked her head and considered the boy she'd known most of her life and tried to decide how best to describe him. The image of the dark-eyed, brown-haired boy with the smile that won all the ladies came to mind, but she could think of nothing that would give Bertrade a sense of what he was like. "Aye," she sighed finally.

"Is he as comely as the Count of Rivaux?"

"Nay," Cat admitted.

"Well, 'tis of no matter if he is not—I can think of none who are. Alas, we can but dream of one like that, Cat, when we will go to Robert and Roland whether we will it or not."

"Nay, I'll take none but Brian."

Guy had barely had time to cross-garter his chausses after his bath before Curthose's summons came. The message had been terse—the duke wanted a council of war and he wanted it immediately. Traversing nearly the length of the ducal palace, Guy entered the narrow chamber thinking to take his place in one of the carved high-backed chairs that were fitted into the wall. Already most of Normandy's loyal barons were there, and Belesme's usually cold face was heated with anger as he raised his voice to his suzerain.

"Nay, but she is of more use to us at Belesme, I tell you! If the battle is lost, she will have value to us yet if she is in Mabille's hands. As 'tis now, Henry could march unchallenged to Rouen and we have nothing with which to treat for peace."

"You forget yourself, my lord!" Robert Curthose snapped.

"Nay, I forget nothing! Can you not see that even if we fail, we may offer the Demoiselle to save our skins? My mother can hold Belesme against Henry, Your Grace, and he will know that she will blind Catherine of the Condes if I am harmed—nay, she will *kill* her! For the love he bears her parents, he will not let that happen—he will not! But if you leave her here, he will think her safe, and we are doomed!"

"You speak as though we have already lost," Guy broke in.

All eyes turned on him and a strained hush spread

over the room. The duke, whose temper was strained by Belesme's outburst, muttered irritably, "You are late to council, Lord Guy."

"Your pardon, Your Grace." Guy edged into the room, aware now of a crackling undercurrent of hostility, but uncertain as to the reason. "Had I known you meant to convene so quickly, I'd not have bathed," he murmured apologetically.

The Count of Mortain, Curthose's cousin and ranking baron in the room, leaned in his chair to whisper in the duke's ear, and the quarrel with Belesme was forgotten. Guy watched uneasily as his bitterest enemy gestured toward him, and knew instinctively something was very wrong. Even as he waited, he heard de Mortain whisper the words "whore's whelp." Curthose leaned back and studied him from beneath hooded lids that made his dark eyes little more than slits. "Froisart is in my brother's hands," he said finally, waiting for the younger man's reaction.

"King Henry took Froisart?" Guy echoed in disbelief.

"Nay, Herluin of Braose threw open his gates." Curthose's voice was cold now, his eyes suddenly intent. "Your liegeman betrays me, Guy of Rivaux."

Guy's worst fears about de Braose confirmed, he could but stare at his own suzerain. The hairs of his neck prickled under the duke's almost malevolent gaze, and he realized he himself was in danger, that Robert Curthose could accuse him and execute him now and repent of it later. He sucked in his breath and met those dark eyes squarely.

"I did not know, Your Grace, but he never answered my summons to arms. Aye," he added slowly, " 'twas why I would return to Rivaux to raise my levies from there. I thought to go to Froisart myself and remind Herluin of his oath to me."

"You did not know?" The duke raised a disbelieving eyebrow. "You would have me believe that you did not suspect his treachery?'' he demanded, his voice rising.

"Think you I would be here if I knew?'' Guy countered. "That I would have brought the Demoiselle of the Condes to you, knowing one of my vassals would betray me? Nay, but I am not a fool, Your Grace.''

"God's blood, but he would lie to you!'' de Mortain exploded.

Guy ignored his old enemy, his gaze never wavering from the duke's. "Where had you the news of this?'' he asked with a calm he did not feel.

"This hour past, de Braose's own chamberlain rode in, saying his lord had gone over to Henry. Since his son serves here, he feared for the boy and hastened to tell me.''

"Taillefer?''

"Aye.''

Guy knew Taillefer well and knew he would not bear false tales. With a deep sigh he nodded. "Then I ask your grace's permission to raise Rivaux's levies and march on Froisart.''

"To join your vassal?'' de Mortain gibed venomously.

Robert of Belesme, who had been strangely silent, his face back to its usual impassivity with those cold green eyes fixed on Guy, moved suddenly to confront him. Guy's flesh crawled beneath his stare, but he willed himself not to flinch or quail as he'd seen so many others do, for any observable weakness always earned Belesme's contempt rather than his mercy. Coming to stand between Guy and Robert Curthose, Belesme effectively blocked any appeal to the duke, and Guy, who had learned to fear few things in his nineteen years, was afraid now. Belesme was so close that the younger man could see the fine stitches of gold thread that formed the leaf design on his green silk tunic. The whitened dent of his caved-in cheekbone was but inches away, and for a moment his famed blood lust shone in his eyes. Then his mouth twisted into that sensuous half-smile of his.

"You deny that Herluin de Braose acted on your orders? That you knew his intent? That you wished to leave Rouen before 'twas discovered so that you could join your vassal in his rebellion?" His voice, though deceptively soft, carried throughout the totally silent chamber, its delicate sarcasm more devastating than a shouted accusation.

"Aye. I deny it all," Guy answered evenly. "Had I known of Herluin's treachery, I'd have gone there rather than bringing the Demoiselle here." His own gold-flecked eyes met Belesme's soberly. " 'Twould have been foolish of me to deliver Roger de Brione's daughter to Rouen if I meant to go over to King Henry, would it not? He'd scarce thank me for the service to his goddaughter, I think," he retorted.

"Nay!" de Mortain protested. "He lies as he has ever done!"

"Nay." Belesme shook his head. "If you brought her here, 'twas that I followed you until many leagues after Lisieux."

"You followed him, Robert? Why?" Curthose asked sharply, his surprise evident.

"Aye. I mistrusted him to bring her here. I expected him to take her to Froisart or Rivaux."

"Nay, you did not, my lord," Guy disputed evenly, fighting to keep his temper in check. "You met me outside the Condes and demanded custody of Catherine de Brione for your own revenge on her father. If you would charge me now, 'tis because I would not yield her." The gold flecks spiked across his hazel eyes as he continued to meet Belesme's. "Were I plotting with King Henry, I'd not take her anywhere else, Robert, for she'd be safer in the Condes than at either of the places you would name."

Curthose leaned half out of his high chair, now more disturbed by Guy's revelation than by Herluin de Braose's treachery. "I charged Count Guy to deliver the Demoiselle of the Condes to me for hostage, Robert. I gave him my writ—you had no right to interfere with my wishes."

"A mere boy!" Belesme scoffed. "And he had but thirty men to keep her safe."

"And you had but twenty," Guy reminded him.

"I needed no more."

"Would you have brought her to Rouen, Robert? Or would you have used her for her own revenge on her parents?"

A murmur of unease rippled through the assemblage as memories of the struggle between Robert of Belesme and Roger de Brione came to mind. Robert's green eyes flashed as he defended himself. "I would have kept her safe! I am no boy sent to do a man's task."

"And Eleanor of Nantes would never have yielded her daughter to you, Robert," Curthose snapped. "Nay—'twas not your place to interfere."

"So you bring her to Rouen to leave her in the company of women before we go to meet Henry! 'Tis folly, I say! Nay, but she should be held where she can be used for our purposes if the need arises."

"You would send her to Mabille?" Guy's lip curled in disgust. "And you would have us believe her safe there? God's bones, but what fools you must think us, Count Robert! You would deliberately provoke her father against us and ensure that we lose! Nay, but you would use her for your own ends rather than Normandy's."

"He'd not dare to come to Belesme!"

"But he would join King Henry then."

"And be forsworn!"

"Jesu! I never thought to call you fool, Robert, but 'tis folly, what you would propose! Do not destroy Normandy with your hatred for Roger de Brione!" Guy realized suddenly that he was shouting in Belesme's face. Dropping his hands, he stepped back and lowered his voice. "There's none here who would save his patrimony more than I would, my lord, but harming a child will not further our cause.''

Curthose looked from one to the other and realized it served no purpose to have two powerful barons quarrel in council. Despite his own anger over de Braose's defection and Belesme's challenge to his authority, he knew he had to have the support of both of the men before him if he were to keep his duchy, for without Belesme's leadership and Rivaux's levies, he had no hope. "Nay, sit you down, both of you," he cut in tiredly. "If my lord of Rivaux will but renew his feudal oath to me, I am prepared to hold him blameless for his vassal's actions." Then, to placate Belesme, he added, "We will discuss what is to be done with the Demoiselle later. For now, we are better occupied defending Normandy."

8

The ducal court displayed a festive air despite the underlying tensions of a duchy preparing for a fratricidal war. And judging from the crowded passages and overflowing hall, Catherine found it difficult to believe the rumors of daily defections amongst Normandy's baronage. Indeed, the crush of nobles, knights, men-at-arms, and household servants made tempers short and strained even Rouen's usually well-filled larders, and she did not see how Robert Curthose could stand the expense much longer. And yet the duke played the lavish host, providing grand banquets, lively entertainment, and rich gifts to those who had answered his call to arms.

Following Duchess Sybilla and her ladies through the crush of bodies that pressed for admittance to the hall, Catherine found herself cut off from the others as the surging crowd closed between them. Fearing the duchess's displeasure, she tried vainly to slip through, only to be forced back despite her cries of, "Let me pass—I attend your lady! Let me pass! I pray you, my lords, let me by!"

Several young men waiting at the edge of the crowd turned to survey her with interest, taking in the richness of her gown. One, emboldened by her isolation, insolently swept his eyes over her, allowing them to linger suggestively on the swell of her breasts beneath the metal-shot samite. His lips curved into a leering smile as he reached to touch her shoulder with a finger that slipped to trace downward to her breast.

"Ho," he announced loudly to his companions, "a beauty among crones, my lords. And you said there were no comely wenches to be had in Normandy's court, Frambert. Come closer that we may see you, little one."

His fingers closed on Catherine's shoulders and he leaned forward, his wine-breath in her face. She tried to shake his hand away. "Unhand me, sir, that I may pass," she told him coldly. " 'Tis no peasant wench you touch, and well you know it. I am Catherine of the Condes."

"Catherine of the Condes," he repeated, jerking his head toward the others. "D'ye hear her—'tis Catherine of the Condes! Nay, Demoiselle, but you are in Rouen now, and your sire's run to England."

"The duchess will hear of the insult you offer, sir. I demand you let me pass."

"She demands!" he chortled. "Nay, little maid, but 'twill take a kiss for toll."

To her horror, he bent even closer, his eyes scarce inches from hers, and then his leering grin froze. Suddenly someone gripped both her elbows from behind and pulled her back against a decidedly hard and muscular man's body so tightly that she could feel the metal of his belt in her spine. His fingers cut into her flesh through the sleeves of her red-and-gold samite gown as he barked, "Make way for the Demoiselle! Make way!" Her tormentor drew back as though struck and shrank against his companions, while the crowd surged and ebbed as everyone sought to get out of the way. In front of her, a young man in a richly brocaded tunic shouted, " 'Tis my lord of Belesme! Make way for Belesme!"

An involuntary shiver traveled the length of her spine and her skin turned to gooseflesh as he thrust her forward through the press of men's bodies that had blocked the double doors of the duke's hall but a moment before. Those who stood inside the door parted, melting away as ice before fire.

"Sweet Mary!" she breathed with relief when Belesme released her into the open air of the hall itself. "They are more like beasts at the trough than people come to dine."

"Aye. Well-said, Demoiselle," Belesme murmured behind her. "You would do well to remember that we are all beasts, the difference between us being that some are better broken to saddle and bit than others."

"Even you, my lord?" she asked without thinking.

"Nay—I was born to ride them."

His eyes flicked over her as she looked up in surprise, and a slow smile spread across his twisted face, sending another shiver coursing through her. To hide the sudden stab of fear she felt, she looked to where the duchess was taking her seat at the raised table. He reached out to turn her head back and force her chin up with his knuckle.

"What were you born for, Catherine of the Condes?" he asked in a low voice. "Will you achieve for me what I could not?"

The green eyes burned intensely, boring into hers as though seeking some answer. For a moment she was drawn to him, strangely fascinated by him. Then she remembered what he'd done to her mother. "Nay," she answered coldly, jerking her head away.

"Curthose is a fool, Demoiselle—he will serve my ends rather than his in this." Dropping his hand, he nodded toward the dais. "You'd best take your place if you would sup, little Catherine. And you must remember you are not in the Condes now. An army of men pours in, swelling the court with those who have left their women behind, and 'tis not safe to be unattended."

"I am under the duke's own protection, my lord," she reminded him.

His strange eyes traveled to where Curthose sat at

the high table, and he shook his head. " 'Tis no protection at all, Demoiselle—do not place your hopes on
one who cannot rule. I'd keep you safer than he can."

His words echoed in her ears as she made her way
across the crowded hall to sit several places below
Curthose and his duchess. Sybilla frowned her displeasure and turned back to her lord, while Bertrade
of Meulan leaned close to Cat and whispered, "Sweet
Mary, but how came you to be in the Count of Belesme's company? Our duchess likes him not."

"With reason, I'll warrant," Cat muttered dryly.
"Nay, he did but help me through the crowd when I
became separated from you."

Bertrade eyed the count as he took his place on the
other side of Robert Curthose, furtively signing the
Cross across her breast as she did so. "Well, I'd not
want to speak with him," she added with conviction.

Guy of Rivaux, seated according to his rank, occupied the low bench just below Robert of Belesme and
shared his trencher. His only recompense in the matter
was that it was Belesme rather than de Mortain, for
the latter had absented himself from supper. More than
once he'd had the unhappy distinction of eating with
the man who'd sought so bitterly to take Rivaux from
him, and the meal had been ruined by the rancor between them. Glancing cautiously at his trencher part-
ner, he realized that this night there was scarce
improvement, and he could curse himself for intervening where Catherine de Brione was concerned. He'd
gained himself two powerful enemies instead of the
one he'd always had, and he'd been a fool to do it.

Belesme's green cabochon emerald ring flashed in
the torchlight as he reached for a dish of fruit and
selected an apple. Biting into the fruit, he leaned back
against the wall behind them and chewed, his strange
eyes distant and thoughtful. Curthose's servants carried in great wooden platters of carved pig, beef, venison, and mutton, followed by peacocks, swans, and
herons, all dressed, roasted, and glazed before being

refeathered for showy display. Fishes boiled in ale and stuffed with almonds gave off steam from plates placed next to bowls of stewed onions, peas, and beans, puddings and frumenties, while breads and cheeses were set on boards in front of Curthose's guests. At one side of the hall, musicians played lutes and pipes above the din of voices raised by those who would converse.

Guy poured wine from a golden pitcher and swirled it idly. He'd watched Belesme come in with Catherine de Brione, had seen the girl blanch at whatever had been said, and knew instinctively that Belesme had threatened her. Well, it was no business of his, he told himself defensively, for he'd washed his hands of her. Or had he? The nagging memory of his promise to Eleanor of Nantes came unbidden to his mind. That Catherine de Brione had tried his patience, made mockery of his chivalry, and scarred his face without reason bore not at all on his responsibility to keep her safe. Setting his cup on the long trestle table, he rubbed his cheek where the whip had cut it. It was sore still, scabbed in a long thin line that would heal like a knife wound, marking him forever. Someday it would appear to be one with the earlier, higher scar, but for now it was a reminder of Catherine of the Condes. He leaned forward, his elbows resting on the table, and looked past Belesme to where Catherine sat next to one of the duchess's younger ladies. Her dark hair gleamed, streaming unbound over her shoulders like a mantle, rich and warm in the flickering torchlight. The flame of one of the large wax candles set on the table for illumination cast a rosy glow to her fair skin and played off the gilt threads in her gown. Jesu, but she was a feast for a man's eyes.

"I have heard you bear the little Cat's mark."

Belesme's words interrupted Guy's disjointed musings and brought him up with a start. Realizing that one of his men must have told the story, he reddened slightly and nodded. "She thought to escape, and I was fool enough to reach for her before I took the whip,'' he admitted frankly.

''You should have beaten her backside.''

''Had she been mine, I would have, but as she is the Demoiselle of the Condes, I did not.''

Belesme's attention turned to Catherine for a long moment as he studied her soberly. ''She is more Eleanor's daughter than his,'' he observed half to himself. Abruptly he straightened, his face bitter. ''By rights, she should have been mine.''

Guy was uncertain as to whether he meant that Catherine should have been Belesme's daughter or if he referred to Eleanor of Nantes herself, but he was not fool enough to pursue the matter. Instead, he reached for the wooden board that held an elaborately prepared peacock, its lovely fan of feathers spread out behind its glazed body.

''She'll go to Belesme ere I am done.''

Guy's hand stopped in mid-reach. ''I thought your countess in Ponthieu, my lord,'' he reminded him. '' 'Twould be unseemly to send her where your lady is not.''

''Nay, she must be in Mabille's care, else she serves no purpose to me.''

Guy's flesh crawled at the thought of Catherine de Brione in Mabille of Belesme's hands. ''Care'' would scarce be the word for what that witch might do, since she'd poisoned more than one, mayhap her own husband even, for her son. Indeed, 'twas oft said they were so alike, mother and son, that both were the creation of Satan rather than God. And it was whispered that the reason Robert's countess was not at Belesme was she feared Mabille. Not that the count would have made any concessions to his wife's feelings in the matter—he made no pretense of affection for her—quite the opposite, in fact. Nor did he appear to care for his children either. Once Eleanor of Nantes had been denied him beyond hope, he'd wed an heiress, gotten his heirs on her, and gone his own way, an even more violent, embittered man.

"Nay, the child can gain you naught, my lord. If she is harmed, Holy Church will take Henry's side." Almost by afterthought, he added, "And I am sworn to protect her."

"You?" Belesme regarded him for a moment lazily and then straightened. "Nay, but I have mine own plans for the Demoiselle, and you'll not interfere."

"What can a child bring you now, my lord?" Guy asked, trying to fathom Belesme's reasoning.

"She can still bring Nantes." The green eyes warmed slightly as Guy stared into them. "Aye. Gilbert has no sons and Eleanor has no sons."

"And you have a countess," Guy retorted, his very being revolted by the thought that came to mind. Surely Belesme did not mean to take the daughter for revenge on the mother.

The older man made no answer, but reached for a heron leg. Wrenching it off, he broke it between his thumb and forefinger like a dried twig. Laying the broken bone on Guy's end of the trencher, he wiped his fingers fastidiously on the cloth before noting soberly, "Aye, but life is uncertain, is it not? And women are weak creatures."

A chill stole over Guy. Normandy had been torn asunder fourteen summers before in the quarrel over who had the better right to Eleanor of Nantes, a quarrel that had ended with her return to her rightful lord. That Belesme would think to open the festering wound again in these troubled times defied reason, for this time he might well ensure Curthose's loss of Normandy with his folly.

"Curthose will never send Catherine of the Condes to Belesme, my lord."

"I'd not wager against me, Rivaux—Normandy will lean where I push."

Down the table, Catherine moved her food around on the trencher she shared with Bertrade and pondered both Robert of Belesme's strange manner and his words to her. What did he think to get of her? She could give him nothing that he did not have, she reasoned as she tried to make sense of what he'd said. He'd wanted to wed her mother once, but now had taken another, and that could scarce touch her—unless he meant to draw her father back from Wales. Nay, but he could not wish to fight him again—not after so many years. Her brow furrowed and then cleared. He had but wanted to frighten her, she declared to herself forcefully.

"You'd best eat, Cat, else you'll hunger later," Bertrade whispered. "And the duchess keeps naught but wine in her bower."

Knowing that the other girl spoke the truth, Catherine cut off a small piece of mutton and forced herself to take a bite. Homesickness swept over her like nausea as she remembered the way it would have been prepared in the Condes, stewed rather than roasted, and surrounded by vegetables in a thick, rich sauce spiced with mustard and ginger.

"Demoiselle Catherine." The duchess leaned behind Bertrade to address Cat. "My lord husband tells me your grandsire comes to Rouen. Mayhap you would wish to sew him a fine purse for his belt to practice your stitches."

"Gilbert?" Cat's eyebrow rose in surprise at the news. Of all who would take up the duke's banner, her grandfather would be expected the least. Even now, she could remember her shame when Rivaux's men had spoken of Gilbert of Nantes's cowardice and voiced the opinion that he would not come. Shaking her head, she managed aloud, "Nay, but I scarce know him, Your Grace."

"'Tis a pity you do not, Demoiselle, for he holds Nantes for you."

"He'd not have it were it not for my father."

The duchess's manner chilled perceptibly and she eyed Catherine narrowly. "As suzerain to Nantes, my husband confirms the inheritance, Demoiselle. If your mother would keep it, your father had best fulfill his oath to Normandy instead of cowering in Wales.''

"My father keeps all his oaths, Your Grace. Unlike those who would rule, his word is his honor.'' Bertrade gasped beside her, bringing home to Catherine what she'd said, and she knew she should beg pardon for it. Instead, she met the duchess's outraged expression mulishly. She had but voiced what everyone said behind Curthose's back anyway, and she'd not listen to anyone insult her father.

Sybilla's face stared in astonishment, and then a slow flush crept upward into her pale cheeks. "You will leave this table, Demoiselle, and return to my bower, and you'll not eat again until you learn to hold your tongue," she managed levelly.

"Your Grace, she did not mean . . ." Bertrade's voice trailed off under the older woman's quelling look and she dropped her eyes to the food on her trencher.

Catherine rose hastily, nearly upsetting her narrow bench, and drew Curthose's attention. He looked up in surprise, his knife halfway to his mouth. "God's blood, Billa! Let the child eat!"

"Nay, I'll not have her at my table."

His eyes traveled to where Catherine stood, stiff and proud. "Sit you down, Demoiselle," he ordered.

"Nay." Sybilla shook her head. "I punish her for her insolence."

"Mayhap you mistook her words," he soothed. "She is but a little maid, after all."

"Nay, but I am not hungry." Catherine spoke with a coldness that matched the duchess's manner, and, head high, walked toward the open doors. Behind her, she could hear Robert Curthose still protesting Sybilla's harshness to a child, but she didn't care. She neither wanted nor needed defense—she had but spoken the truth.

Beside him, Guy heard Robert of Belesme murmur low, "He has not the time to waste on a child, Rivaux.

Mark my words, he'll yield her yet. And he needs me.''

"He needs me also." Abruptly Guy rose. "Your pardon, my lord."

Belesme looked up, his face betraying faint amusement. "Do you think to set yourself against me? 'Twould be like a pup thinking to take the boar in the hunt."

Catherine walked quickly, partly out of fear and partly out of anger. If life in Rouen had been unbearable, she had no doubt that she'd made it doubly so now, for Sybilla would not easily forgive the insult she'd offered. Sweet Mary, but would she never learn to hold her tongue?

"Demoiselle."

She spun around defensively, ready to fight any fellow who thought to accost her. She'd borne enough insults herself this night. Then, seeing it was Guy of Rivaux, her anger faded. "What do you want?" she asked sullenly.

"God's blood, but you would make your life unpleasant, Demoiselle," he chided as he caught up to her.

"I am naught but a prisoner here," she reminded him bitterly. "Aye, you may say I am one of her ladies, but I am not. She does not even like me."

"You do not even try to please her."

"And you would not know if I did, my lord," she spat back. "Nay, but you promise my mother you will keep me safe, and yet you would leave for Rivaux without a thought for me."

" 'Tis not so, Demoiselle." A rueful smile curved the corners of his mouth as he shook his head. "I cannot be shaved and not think of you."

Her eyes took in the reddened cut on his cheek, and she colored. A sharp retort died on her lips. "Oh . . . aye. Does it hurt very much?"

"Nay—not now."

"Well, I am sorry for it, but you should not have stopped me."

Refusing to argue with her, he moved to take her arm. "Come—you must not be unattended with so many strangers about, Demoiselle. I will take you back to the duchess's solar." When she would have pulled away, he tightened his grip and pushed her ahead of him. "Your disgrace was noted by nearly everyone, and I would not have you followed."

"As you have done?" She bristled at his tone and tried to break his hold on her arm. "Release me, my lord—I can walk unaided."

"Jesu, but you are an ill-tempered little maid," he complained as he continued pushing her down the narrow corridor. "If you do not hold your tongue, Curthose will think you more trouble than you are worth to him."

"Then he can send me home."

"Nay, he could send you to Mabille of Belesme, Demoiselle, and you'd learn that Duchess Sybilla is far the kinder lady."

"He would not dare!" She stopped so suddenly that he nearly collided with her. "My father—"

"Is in Wales," he finished for her. "Aye, and Robert has asked for custody of you. Think, Demoiselle— do you wish to go to Belesme?"

"Of course I do not wish it! Count Robert frightens me, if you would have the truth, my lord."

"I saw him speaking with you earlier."

"He spoke in riddles, asking if I would give him what he could not get himself or some such thing, but I made no sense of his words." Looking up, she noted Guy's frown and nodded. "Aye—he did but mean to frighten me, I think."

"Nay. Robert neither threatens nor boasts that which he will not do. He takes pleasure in foretelling his plans. 'Tis what makes his power over men, Demoiselle—they wait in dread for him to move, knowing full well he will when he is ready. Nay, but Belesme does not boast idly.''

"Well, Curthose is not such a fool that he would risk my father's wrath, I think,'' she maintained with a confidence she did not feel, knowing even as she spoke that he'd already dared her father by taking her hostage.

"You mistake the matter—sometimes he is the greatest fool in Christendom, Catherine.''

"Then why do you fight for him?''

"I told you—because I must. I am so sworn.''

"As you were sworn to protect me, my lord?'' she gibed. "How is it that you can forget one oath and not the other?''

"I hold my lands of him.''

"Jesu!'' Her face was flushed and her dark eyes bright with challenge as she stared up at him, reflecting the rosy glow of the spitting pitch torch suspended above them. Her thick, dark mane of hair fell away, exposing the fine brow, the delicate face, and the perfect skin. With an effort, he resisted reaching out to feel the silken strands, to smooth it down over her shoulders, to touch where it lay against her back. "I did not think you wished my protection, Demoiselle,'' he murmured softly.

His manner had changed so suddenly that she was taken aback. An odd thrill traveled down her spine as blood rose to her face. Looking away, she managed lamely, " 'Twas my mother you promised, Guy of Rivaux.''

Disappointed, he dropped his hand and stepped back, the heat fading from his body as quickly as it had risen. For a moment he'd wanted her to tell him that his help would matter to her, but she had not. "Aye"—he nodded finally—"I keep my word in all things, Demoiselle.''

They walked in silence the rest of the way, stopping at the foot of the narrow stairs leading to the ladies' bower. Another pitch-dipped torch sputtered and popped in an iron ring that hung from a lion's head, catching the gold-embroidered talons of the hawk on his chest. "You are safe enough now, Catherine," he told her. "Here." He reached for her hand and pressed a linen-wrapped chunk of cheese into it. "Mayhap 'twill fill your stomach for now." Then he did what he'd wanted to do earlier, and brushed the shining hair back with his fingertips, savoring the silk of it. The faint odor of roses floated up in the warm night air. "Sweet Mary, but I've not seen another like you," he half-whispered, drawing away. "God keep you until the morrow, Demoiselle."

She waited until he'd gone several steps before daring to speak. "Wait—when do you leave for Rivaux, my lord?"

He stopped and turned back to her. "I am not going." His mouth twisted wryly. "Curthose does not trust me to leave again, so I have issued my call from here."

"Oh." She formed the word almost silently, unable to control the sudden rush of gratitude she felt. "Then I will see you again."

9

"My lord of Rivaux, I would be private with you."

Robert Curthose's words carried across the dissolving council meeting, prompting curious stares from Normandy's disgruntled barons. It had been a hotly disputed session, with Belesme, de Mortain, and Guy even goading the duke into taking action against King Henry's further incursion into the duchy. And it had been called after news arrived that Walter de Clare, warden of four ports and lord of a dozen fiefs, had declared for the king and raised Henry's standard over Beauville.

Guy waited warily as the others filed out. And as Robert of Belesme passed him, he leaned to mutter for Guy's ears alone, "Do not let him waver, else we'll all winter in France this time." And Waleran of Theroux hissed low, "Aye, but he cannot tarry now, my lord."

"You may close the door," Curthose directed a parting page with a wave of one beringed hand. Motioning Guy closer, he rose to stare out one of the tall arched windows into the busy courtyard outside. Silence settled over the room as the footsteps in the corridor grew fainter, and Guy wondered what new disaster was to befall him. Did Curthose mean to chastise him for his outspoken words in council? And if so, why had he not done so before the others? But he'd meant what he said—if they did not fight, and fight now, there'd be no Normandy left for those loyal to their duke. He sucked in his breath and waited, ready to argue again if necessary.

"I have decided to bestow Catherine of the Condes on you for wife." The duke turned around as he spoke, his dark eyes sober as they met Guy's. "Aye." He nodded, taking in Guy's stunned expression.

"Jesu!" Guy gasped, exhaling in shock. "Sweet Mary!" he whispered as he attempted to assimilate Robert Curthose's words. Disordered thoughts crowded his mind, making rational response impossible. For an instant he wondered if the duke had gone mad—or if he himself were dreaming.

"She is a pretty child," Curthose added, his face breaking into a smile. "And 'tis rare to find such wealth and beauty in one bed. With Gilbert of Nantes having no sons, and his daughter not like to have one, the little demoiselle can make you lord of lands vaster than Belesme's."

Numbly Guy tried to follow the duke's words, but the image of Catherine as he'd last seen her flooded his consciousness suddenly, blotting out all else. He could see those dark eyes, feel the silk of her hair beneath his fingertips, and smell the rosewater she'd worn. Sweet Jesu, but he'd not even dreamed . . . With an effort, he forced himself to listen, his body tense and his mind wary. For Robert Curthose to make such an offer, he had to want something very badly.

"You appear surprised, my lord," the duke observed with satisfaction. "Aye, but I would give her to you—on condition. You have not renewed your feudal oath to me, and—"

"You do not need to reward me for what is yours, Your Grace," Guy cut in, drawn away from thoughts of Catherine. "Nay, but I would place my hands between yours now if you will it."

" 'Tis a public display of your support that I need now, my lord," Curthose snapped, and then caught himself to add in a more conciliatory manner, "I want you to swear to me in the presence of all Rouen. You would have me fight my brother, would you not?" he demanded as a faintly querulous tone crept again into his voice. "Then you must be prepared to give me more than your feudal dues, else I cannot."

The duke had not wasted time with the subtleties of his strange offer, Guy thought wryly—he would trade Catherine of the Condes for men and arms when all was said and done. "Your Grace, there is no need to bribe me—all I have, I hold of you. What would you have of me?"

"Rivaux is a rich fief," Curthose mused aloud, "and provides you with great wealth—enough perhaps to pay mercenaries from Italy . . ." His voice trailed off as he appeared to consider the possibilities.

"Aye." Guy waited to see what the duke meant to ask in exchange for Roger de Brione's daughter.

"I need men." The older man's eyes met his steadily. "With each day bringing word of those who would follow my brother, I must have men who will fight for me. How many do you owe me?"

Guy would wager that Curthose knew to the last battleax what he owed, but he answered anyway, "Two hundred mounted knights, five hundred footsoldiers, and twenty-five arbalesters, all equipped to do battle."

"How many of that number were Herluin de Braose's?"

"Not many—I had but twenty knights, fifty foot, and five bowmen of him."

"Buy me what you lost of him and one hundred mounted mercenaries, and I will give you the Demoiselle of the Condes."

A low whistle escaped Guy at the price. God's bones, but Curthose would sell the girl dearly. "Nay, but I'd not wed her against the will of her family," he answered slowly as he counted the cost. "She is promised to Robert of Caen."

"And she is not betrothed," Curthose reminded him

impatiently. "Nay, but as her father's liege lord, I would bestow her where I may, and I'd not give a Norman heiress to one of my brother's bastards."

"You sell her."

"I need men. God's blood, but I had thought you pleased to have her—aye, I have noted the way you look on her."

"She is but thirteen and small-boned."

"And old enough to wed and bed." Curthose turned away to look again into the courtyard. "I need men," he repeated. "Now, do you take the Demoiselle and give what I ask? Or do I offer her elsewhere? There are others who would count the price cheap for what she will inherit."

"You would beggar me," Guy stalled, his mouth dry at the thought of Catherine de Brione in his bed. Jesu, but if he found her too small to lie with now, there would always be later.

"Scarcely that, my lord. You have the gold and you will gain much through the girl—nay, you are one of those who can afford the offer."

"I'd not make an enemy of her father."

"I have the right to give her." His back still to Guy, the duke shrugged, indicating he tired of the discussion. "But if you would wish," he conceded, "after you swear to me again, I will have Gilbert confirm your heirs as his once you are wed."

"And if I do not take her?"

"You are not a fool, I think." Curthose turned back slowly, his eyes measuring his liegeman. A slow smile formed at the corners of his mouth. "You want the girl, do you not?"

"She has the temper of a termagant."

"Beat it out of her."

Somehow the thought of beating Catherine repelled Guy. As much trouble as she'd been, she'd but tried to escape an injustice. And for all her tongue, she'd showed more courage than most girls. His senses reeled even as he thought of the feel of her when he'd pulled her from her horse that night at Froilyn, of the smell of her rose-scented hair, and he knew he'd take her if he had to beggar Rivaux to get her.

"When will you have the banns cried?" he asked finally.

"There's not the time. Gilbert comes today or tomorrow, and we will move toward meeting my brother. As Belesme and William de Mortain are certain that Henry means to capture Mortain before coming further, we'll go to the relief of that fortress." The irony of the situation was not lost on the duke. "Aye—'tis strange for you to be aiding de Mortain, is it not?"

"I'd not fight beside him."

"You'll not—Belesme asks to flank you. But we wander—you will wed the Demoiselle ere we leave, that you may take her with you."

"Nay—"

"Sybilla has taken the child in dislike and would not keep her. I think she blames the daughter for what the father will not do, and the little demoiselle's tongue does not improve her lot."

"An army is no place for a child," Guy protested.

"Nay, but her safety cannot be certain, and I promised her mother . . ." He halted mid-sentence, aware of Curthose's frown.

"We will take her."

It was final—he would wed Catherine of the Condes without so much as a crying of the banns and without the pomp and ceremony due their rank. And he would take her with him in an army's train. Jesu, but it was a mixed gift Curthose would give him, an heiress whose temperament would cut up his peace, an heiress whose family had promised her to King Henry's son. If Curthose lost, Guy did not dare think of the consequences. Banishing that possibility from his mind, he sighed heavily. "Do you seek the mercenaries or do I?"

"I have already sent for them." The duke smiled, his expression that of a man who had gotten exactly what he wanted. "Would you have me tell the little maid?"

"Nay. I will tell her—she'll not be pleased."

Curthose's smile broadened as his eyes traveled over Guy. "Art a comely fellow, Guy of Rivaux—Sybilla tells me all the maids think it—so I'd expect Catherine of the Condes to be no different."

Still shunned by all but Bertrade for her intemperate remarks at supper several days before, Catherine sat apart and plied her needle with indifference, scarce caring to remove the knots she made in her grandfather's purse. Her stomach growled, reminding her again of her refusal to beg the duchess's forgiveness, and she stabbed viciously at the heavy silken cloth. Sybilla had banned her from meals pending her apology, and she'd had naught but bits of bread and cheese smuggled to her by Bertrade. Sweet Mary, but what she would not give for a slab of venison or some salted herring just now.

At the other end of the bower, a girl worked the shuttles of a loom while others visited over their needlework, their soft voices carrying across the narrow room. From time to time Catherine looked up to see if anyone was watching her. Her hunger gnawed at her insides until she could scarce think of anything else, but she'd not apologize. Not when the duchess would insult her father. Reaching the end of her thread, she bent to bite it apart and knot the strand.

A page in Normandy's colors entered to approach the duchess, went down on one knee, and murmured something to his mistress. Nodding, Sybilla motioned Guy of Rivaux in from the threshold, and a hush spread through the bower as the ladies turned their curious attention to him.

Even as he knelt in obeisance, the duchess raised a disbelieving eyebrow. "So you seek speech with the Demoiselle, do you?" she asked, mild disapproval in her voice. "You will find her down there."

Guy frowned. He'd not considered that he'd have to tell her in the presence of so many others, particularly not since he expected her to be displeased with his news. He glanced furtively to where she sat, her head bent over the silk purse. Her dark hair fell forward, touching her knees, and her fine profile was marred by an expression of utter disgust, warning him that she was not in the best of tempers. Sybilla followed his gaze and nodded. "Aye—you'd best walk apart with her, my lord. Demoiselle!" she called sharply to Catherine. "Count Guy is come to see you."

Catherine almost dropped the purse and then caught herself. As glad as she was to see a friendlier face, she'd not let him know it. Instead, she carefully folded the silk pouch and stuck her needle through it. Laying it aside, she rose and moved forward, hoping he would not hear her stomach. Her eyes darted to the ladies of the duchess's court and she noted with satisfaction that their expressions ranged from chagrin to outrage. Behind her, Bertrade whispered, "How you are envied, Cat—don't dawdle—'tis Rivaux!"

Light-headed from lack of food, she did not trust herself to curtsy before him and instead inclined her head. "My lord."

"Jesu, but she forgets herself," came a disgruntled mutter from the other side of the duchess.

Ignoring Catherine, Sybilla turned to Guy. "The day is warm and the herb garden empty, my lord, if you would take her there."

"Aye."

Catherine's heart quickened at the thought of leaving the bower for even a short time, and her pleasure was mirrored in her dark eyes. She took the arm he offered, flashed a small smile of triumph at those who would shun her, and nodded at the duchess. Sybilla smiled frostily and turned back to the gold-and-green stole she'd been working.

"My thanks, my lord," Cat whispered as she escaped into the stairwell.

"For once, Demoiselle, I could almost think you glad to see me."

"I am," she admitted openly. "I tire of sitting for hours and hours with naught to do but stitch this piece or that." She held up her right hand to show him her reddened fingertips. "They are so sore that I have taken to pushing the needle with my other hand, my lord. Sweet Jesu, but I would be away from there." Peering down the steep and winding steps, she swayed slightly. "I'd not go first, if you do not mind it."

He opened his mouth to remind her of her words at the Condes, and then thought better of it. If they were to wed, it would be better to strive for pleasantness. He edged past her and started down, staying close enough to feel the skirt of her gown at his back. She tottered dizzily, swayed again, and lost her balance, stumbling into him. He half-turned to brace himself, and caught her against him. Even on the shadowed stairs he could see she was very pale.

"Jesu, Demoiselle, but what ails you?" he asked as he steadied her. "I would get you back."

"Nay!" She clutched at his tunic for balance and shook her head. "I am all right."

"You are shaking, Demoiselle—we'd best go back."

"Nay, I would but have food," she protested. "I begin to think of naught else."

"Food!"

"Aye—food. My lord, I am so hungry I cannot sleep."

"Jesu. You have not eaten?"

"If I had, would I be like this?" she snapped. "Nay, but I am not given so much as a crumb until I beg her pardon for saying he is an oath-breaker! Yet she would not beg my pardon for what she says of my father! Nay, but I'd not do it!"

"She starves you?" he asked incredulously.

"Have you seen me at supper?" she countered hotly. "Nay, but you have not!"

"But you are given food surely—"

"Nay."

"God's teeth! Curthose said . . . But I'd not thought . . ." He caught himself and shook his head. " 'Tis no matter—I'll get you food," he decided grimly. "Can you walk down or would you have me carry you?"

"I can walk, I think."

He half-carried, half-walked her the rest of the way down and then pulled her after him toward the kitchen buildings that lay to the back of the ducal palace. Pushing her ahead of him through a heavy oak door, he gestured to a scullery wench who stood stirring a bubbling pot in the stifling heat of the kitchen. "Get her some bread and some of that if 'tis done," he ordered harshly.

Catherine sank onto a stool drawn up to one of the preparing tables and leaned her head in her arms while the girl scurried to do Rivaux's bidding. She did not even care what it was in the pot.

"Here." Guy thrust a bowl of stewed mutton and vegetables heavily seasoned with cloves and thyme in front of her. "A spoon also—and the bread," he reminded the kitchen girl.

It was so hot it burned her tongue, but Catherine didn't care. The first bite scalded all the way to her stomach. In the absence of wine, he tore off a chunk of bread and handed it to her. "Sop it until 'tis cooler."

The scullery maid stared in fascination as the richly gowned girl stuffed herself with the abandon of a peasant while the young gentleman in embroidered tunic watched. Reluctantly remembering her stew, she tried to stir it with one eye on them. And when Catherine was done, the bowl was wiped clean from the sopping bread.

"My thanks, my lord," Cat murmured gratefully after the last crust was swallowed.

"Mayhap you should be starved more often, Demoiselle," he told her, grinning, "for twice this day you have thanked me."

She looked up from the rough-hewn table and managed a rueful smile. "Aye, and I've eaten like swine at the trough, have I not? I'd begun to think I could not survive much longer."

"It would have been better to have begged her pardon."

"Nay—the fault was hers first."

"Art a stubborn little maid. Come, I'd not talk here." He grasped her hand, pulling her up. "You can tell me which herb is which."

"If I know."

His scarred eyebrow rose and his strange gold-flecked eyes were alight with humor. "If you know? Demoiselle, if you cannot sew and you are unskilled in simples, what can you do?"

"I can read and write, cipher and tally," she responded haughtily. "And just because I may not know every herb does not mean I am not skilled in simples. I have learned to make balms and soothe wounds in case Brian should ever be hurt. Aye," she added proudly, " 'twas my salve that cured his arm when he was dragged by his horse."

He sobered. He'd not thought of Brian FitzHenry. He tried to keep his voice light despite the sudden misgivings he felt. "Then you do have some housewifely skills at least."

"I mean to be of use to Brian, my lord, for he has not the inclination to his letters that he ought. Despite his father's learning, he says such things are for priests rather than knights."

"Well, he is wrong, Demoiselle, for how is a man to know he is not cheated if he cannot study the accounts himself?" he asked dryly.

"Aye—so my father told him, but he would not listen. So 'tis important that I can read them, is it not?"

He opened the gate to the walled garden and waited for her to pass. Shutting it securely behind him, he murmured, "Have you never considered that you may not get this Brian for husband?"

"Nay. My father and my mother will be brought to see that I will take no other. 'Twill take time, but I'll do it."

Her naiveté touched him, making him reluctant to broach the matter of her marriage to him. Instead, he dropped to a low stone bench and leaned back against the wall. She eyed the bench with disgust.

"Nay, I'd not sit, my lord—not when 'tis all I do the whole day in the duchess's bower. Sweet Mary, but I know not how they stand it, the carding and spinning, weaving and sewing! In my mother's house, 'tis the serving women who do such!"

"Then what does your mother do?"

"She has the ordering of my father's castle. She plans all that we will make or buy, whether 'tis salted herring or candles or iron for the armorer, my lord," she answered with pride. "And she keeps my father content." She caught the gleam of amusement that lit his green-gold eyes and shook her head. "Nay, but you do not understand—he trusts her to rule rather than serve—they are of like minds, my mother and my father."

"Eleanor of Nantes is a rare woman, Demoiselle."

"Well, did not your father value your mother?"

The light faded from his eyes and his face grew suddenly harsh, the healing scar accentuating the set of his jaw. "I know not what he thought of her, Demoiselle, for she died birthing me. But, as little as I knew him, I do not believe he ever liked anything in his life. If he bore her any love, it died with her, and he spoke not at all of her."

"Oh, I did not mean—"

'I know you did not." He straightened and pointed to the neat herb beds as they lay in geometric patterns between cobbled walks. "Tell me what you know of them."

"Well . . ." She glanced down at the plants nearest

her and with a toe pointed to fuzzy stalks. "This is pennyroyal—'twill sweeten your breath if the leaves are chewed—and 'tis sometimes used to bring the flux in women." She colored as she realized what she'd said, and added lamely, "Well, 'tis supposed to keep the number of bastards down. But considering it was given to Agnes and Tyra and they both had their babes, I do not think it works." The memory of how she'd learned it was Brian's bastards they bore came to mind, paining her still. She closed her eyes for a moment.

Her sudden change of mood was not lost on him. Bending forward to snap a stem, he plucked leaves from it and handed her one. "I am supposed to chew it?" he asked as he popped another into his mouth. "Mary, but 'tis strong," he murmured as he worked it between his teeth.

Giggling in spite of herself, she touched the tip of hers against her tongue and sucked lightly. "Aye, but none will know what you have eaten this day. I think there are places where 'tis brewed with water and drunk," she added.

He leaned over and spat the leaves on the ground. "I think my mouth is as sweet as I want it." Pointing across the narrow walk, he directed her to another bed. "What's that?"

"Fennel."

"And that?"

"Dill."

"I thought you said you did not know them," he teased lightly.

"Nay, I meant but that I might not know all of them. See those over there? I've no notion what they are." She walked across the small garden to inspect the plants more closely.

He leaned back and studied her lazily. She was far more beautiful than a man had a right to expect in his marriage, and the knowledge that Curthose meant to give her to him was almost too new to grasp. She was small, but not nearly so small as her mother, and her body was slender yet well-formed. Aye, he could span her waist with his hands, he decided as he watched her move about gracefully. If her temper could be borne, there was naught else about her that was unpleasing to a man. She pulled up a plant and sniffed it before turning around triumphantly.

"Tis sweet marjoram!" she crowed.

"Is there a sour one?" he asked, grinning.

"I know not," she answered truthfully. "Is there anything else you'd know, my lord?" She returned to stand before him, her hands on her hips. "Or would you do naught but stare at me?"

"Mayhap I like watching you." Without thinking, he reached to pull her onto his lap, settling her against him and closing his arms around her. The softness of her body made him forget she was but thirteen. "Thou art a beauty, Catherine of the Condes," he murmured softly into her hair.

Shocked by the suddenness of his action, she sat very still for a moment. "Even if I am out of favor, my lord," she told him stiffly, 'I doubt the duchess would approve of your touching me." But even as she spoke, she was intrigued by the strength of his arms and the hardness of his body against hers. "Nay—release me ere you are seen."

She was lighter than he'd expected, and smaller than any of the whores he'd had. He moved his hand to stroke her hair where it fell forward over her breast, and felt as well as heard the sharp intake of her breath. He bent to nuzzle the shining crown of her hair. Both of her hands caught at his and she tried to push free of him. "Nay, but I am no castle wench to be fondled at will. I demand you release me now, my lord, else I shall cry out." Twisting her head to look up at him, she tried to keep her voice calm despite the racing of her heart. Jesu, but even Brian had not been so bold.

"One kiss for toll first."

He bent his head down, thinking to brush her lips lightly, but the smell of roses and mint made him forget everything save that she was to be his. Her lips parted in protest beneath the pressure of his, and he could taste the sweetness of her mouth. His tongue traced the edge of her teeth and his free hand stroked the silk of her hair. She squirmed beneath his touch and struggled to sit up. Reluctantly he released her.

She lunged forward to stand, her eyes wide, her color heightened with anger. "A kiss for toll? God's bones, but you are like that lout who would have accosted me at supper, are you not? Nay, you forget yourself, Guy of Rivaux! I thank you for the food, but I'll not stay to be ravished!"

She was almost to the gate when he caught her from behind and held her while she kicked backward against him. "Sheathe your claws, Cat," he murmured above her ear. "You've not heard why I sought you out."

"And you are disrespectful—my name is Catherine!" she spat out. When he would not release her, she bent her head to sink her teeth in his knuckle.

"God's teeth! I'll turn you loose if you will but stay to hear what I came to tell you." So saying, he dropped his arms and stepped around to bar her path to the gate.

"Nay!" She was breathing heavily from her struggle, and her dark eyes flashed defiance. "If you so much as attempt to touch me again, my lord, I will claim Normandy's protection, and I'll tell him why!"

"He gives you to me."

She blinked and stared, too stunned for speech at first. Then, watching him nod slowly, she echoed in disbelief, "Curthose gives me . . . to *you?*"

"Aye—we wed ere the army moves." He stepped closer but did not touch her. A crooked smile lifted one side of his mouth, and his eyes were almost gold. "Come—'tis not so terrible, Catherine. I'll not beat you—nay, but I'd treat you gently."

"Nay!" She backed away, her eyes still wide with the shock she felt. "Nay." Her voice dropped low and she looked away. "Sweet Mary, Lord Guy, I'd not wed

with you." But even as she spoke, she realized she
was but a prisoner of Robert Curthose's and there was
none to listen to her in Normandy's court. A tight knot
formed in her stomach and threatened to rise as she
swallowed back tears. "Nay, I'd not," she whispered.

"You'll have no choice in the matter," he told her
gently, reaching for her.

"Don't touch me!" she hissed as she broke away.

"You'd not get the FitzHenry anyway, Demoiselle."
He tried to think of the means to console her. "Your
father would give you to Robert of Caen, but his suzerain gives you to me."

"And I am no better than a serf in the field," she
complained bitterly. "Nay, I am no better than an ox
to be sold!"

"I said I would treat you well."

Infuriated by the even way he spoke, she turned on
him viciously, spitting out, "You! Think you I am a
fool, Guy of Rivaux? 'Twas you who brought me here!
Aye, and you knew—you *knew* when you came to the
Condes, did you not? You listened to me speak of Brian
and you knew what Curthose planned!"

"Demoiselle . . . Catherine . . ."

Fed by rising anger, she completely lost control of
her temper. Her body shook and hot tears scalded her
eyes, spilling over onto her cheeks. "You promised
my mother I'd be safe when you knew 'twas false!"
she charged hotly. "Jesu! And Curthose dares to think
my father forsworn!" She moved to face him, her body
scarce inches from his, and raised her hand as though
to strike.

"Nay, I am not twice the fool, Demoiselle," he told
her as he caught her wrist painfully and forced her arm
down to her side. "You'll not open the wound you
gave me."

" 'Twas why you asked if I were betrothed, was it
not? You think to be Lord of the Condes and to have
Nantes and Harlowe!"

"Lower your voice, Catherine," he ordered sternly.

"You'll have every man in Rouen come to hear you. And, nay, I did not know what he meant to do, else I'd not have brought you here." Releasing her hand and stepping back, he strove to control his own temper. The muscles of his jaw were so tight they ached as he reminded himself she had a right to be angry and that she was, after all, scarce more than a child.

"I do not believe you!" she spat at him. "Jesu, when I think I was beginning to like you! To believe you were not so bad as the rest of those who serve Curthose!" The tears coursed freely now, streaking her face, and her lower lip quivered as she fought for control. She reached to wipe her cheeks with the back of her hand, and gulping for air, she stopped to stare balefully at him.

"Cat . . . Catherine . . ." He paused to gain her attention and nodded. "Aye, whether you believe it or no, 'twas never in my mind to wed with you until Curthose offered. And then 'twas to me or another he would sell you for men and arms." She met his eyes silently, her face set in mulish defiance. "You may believe what you will," he repeated, "but I would not lie to you."

The garden hummed with late-summer sounds around them, and the fragrances of a dozen herbs intermingled as the sun beat down, its brightness a sharp contrast to the bleakness in Catherine's heart. His strangely beautiful eyes were intent on hers, his face solemn. The anger ebbed from her body slowly, the last vestiges exhaled in a heavy sigh.

'It does not matter, does it?'' she asked finally, her chest aching with the emptiness she now felt.

Relieved that her fury was spent, he took her elbow and tried to lead her gently back down the cobbled path. "Walk a pace with me, Catherine, and tell me what you would have for bridegift—I'd give you what you want."

While she did not shake him off, she shook her head. "I am no whore to be bought with a pretty bracelet, my lord." Looking up at him, she spoke tonelessly. "I would go back now."

10

"Unhhhhhhhh?"

Catherine bent to poke him cautiously again, and Guy rolled over to cradle his head in the crook of his arm. The straw pallet rustled beneath him as he repositioned his body, his bare shoulder visible above his red cloak. "My lord," she whispered furtively, her hand touching his warm skin, her eyes warily on the door.

He came awake suddenly, groping to pull the cloak to cover his nakedness. Squinting in the semidarkness of the curtained-off chamber, he tried to adjust his eyes to the flickering torchlight. "Jesu! Demoiselle, what are you doing here?"

"Shhhhhhh," she hissed. "I would speak with you."

"What time is it?"

"I do not know," she answered truthfully, "but everyone is still at supper."

"You should not be here—'tis but a common sleeping room." He sat up, one hand clutching the cloak while the other rubbed the sleep from his eyes. His dark hair was rumpled and his face shadowed with the day's growth of beard.

"You were not at the duke's table," she pointed out as though that should explain everything.

"I was too tired to eat." He combed his hair with

107

his fingers and eyed her irritably. "God's bones, but what cannot keep until the morrow? And how is it you are here? 'Tis no place for a maid, and well you know it. Jesu!"

" 'Tis all right—I complained of the stomachache and 'tis believed I am in the garderobe. And nay, it cannot wait. Had you been at supper, I'd have asked to speak with you after, but you were not there."

"I was tired," he repeated. "And we wed on the morrow, so you could have spoken then."

"Nay." She shook her head. "Then it would be too late."

Even in the dim light, he could see the determined set of her jaw, and he realized that to her, at least, whatever she had to say was important enough to risk further censure from Sybilla. "You are fortunate you leave the duchess's household," he muttered, "else you'd never eat again. 'Twas all I could do to get you back to table tonight."

"I care not." She leaned closer, her dark hair falling forward to spill onto his bare shoulder, its soft fragrance floating over him. For a moment, desire flooded his consciousness, testing the rigid control he'd learned to keep over his mind and body. Resolutely he drew away and rolled to sit with his back to her. His voice strange, he ordered her, "Wait outside and I will dress."

"Think you I have never seen a man before?"

"Where?"

"Well, when I was a little maid, Linn and I were used to watching from the tower as the stableboys ran from the bath shed after old Herved doused them with cold water." Smiling, she added truthfully, "But they were quick and we did not see much from the distance." Her expression sobered as her dark eyes met his. "And I cannot wait outside, my lord, for I would risk discovery."

"Sweet Mary, but with you nothing is simple, is it?" he complained as he reached for his chausses.

"Look, then—'tis no more than you will see later anyway, I suppose." Drawing the hose over his legs, he stood, his bare buttocks exposed. She stared curiously for a moment and then averted her eyes out of fear that he might turn around. He hastily pulled up the chausses, tied them at his waist, and reached for the embossed leather garters, cross-wrapping them so quickly that he did not take the time to smooth the light woolen hose against his calves. "You can look now," he murmured, his voice suddenly warm with amusement.

He was still bare above his waist, and his hose bulged over his sex, but he was covered after a fashion. Fascinated, she studied the expanse of his chest and unwittingly compared it to Brian's, noting that three years in a boy's age seemed to make a great difference in how he looked. Either that or the muscles that rippled with movement across his shoulders and upper arms were the result of considerably more practice with broadsword, lance, and battleax. And whereas Brian's chest boasted but a few scattered reddish hairs, Guy of Rivaux's had a triangle of black curls that began just below his neck.

"Well, am I pleasing to you?" he asked, grinning at the flush of embarrassment that diffused through her cheeks. His voice muffled as he pulled his discarded overtunic over his head, he told her, "You may speak whilst I take you back to the duchess's bower, and hopefully, if we are seen, 'twill be said that you were but overeager." Feeling on the floor with his toes, he managed to discover and slip his feet into his soft leather shoes.

"Overeager? *Overeager?*" Her voice rose in indignation even as her color deepened. "Nay! If I am here, my lord, 'tis because I would not have you!"

"Keep your voice down then, Cat, or you will be found."

"I'd not have you call me Cat," she sniffed haughtily.

"Catherine then."

"And not that either."

"All right," he murmured as he took her arm and pushed her toward the door. "What would you that I call you?"

"Demoiselle—I would stay unwed."

Ignoring the gibe, he eased the door open and peered into the darkened corridor. "Jesu, but how did you find me? 'Tis black as the pits of hell out here."

"Aye. I came in on the curtained side."

"Where the men-at-arms pallet? God's bones, but 'tis a wonder you are still whole."

"I told you—they are all at supper."

He grasped a pitch torch from a ring suspended above them in the sleeping chamber and slipped past her to lead the way down the black passage. "Aye—I had thought to get some sleep before the snoring starts, but 'tis not likely now. All Rouen is filled, until Curthose has naught to give any but a pallet."

"But you are a count," she protested.

"Aye, and so are Gilbert and Mortain, and yet they sleep here also. Only Belesme brought his own bed." He stopped to transfer the torch to his left hand, holding it out so that the popping pitch sparks would not make holes in his fine tunic. "He offered to share it with any who wished, but there were none who dared sleep with him. Not that I did not consider it," he admitted, "since tomorrow is my wedding day." Laying his free hand on her shoulder, he guided her toward the end of the corridor. " 'Tis not every day that a man renews his feudal oath, marries, and gets fleeced at the same time."

"Fleeced?" She stared up at him, unable to see much in the darkness.

"Aye." He dropped his hand to catch hers and began walking rapidly, pulling her after him. She nearly had to trot to keep up with his long strides. "You come dear to me, Catherine of the Condes—'tis an army he would have from me for you."

"Wait!" She pulled back, grumbling. "Sweet Mary, but you would walk me so quickly that you would have me lose my shoes." Balancing against him, she lifted a foot and adjusted her slipper over her heel. "My legs are not nearly so long as yours, my lord."

"All right." He peered into the silent darkness ahead to be satisfied they were alone. "Then you can tell me now what 'tis that is so important you must needs wake me."

"Here?"

"There's none to hear you save me."

"Aye, but . . ."

"But what?" he prompted impatiently. "I am awake enough to listen now."

"Nay, I would not speak here . . ." Her voice trailed off in uncertainty.

"Jesu! Where, then?"

"Mayhap the garden . . ." she suggested tentatively.

He brought the pitch torch down to illuminate her face, and even in the flickering yellow-orange light he could see her eyes were enormous, betraying her agitation. "All right," he decided finally, "but I would warn you, Demoiselle, that my temper is not the best. I am tired unto death, half of my vassals have not answered my call to arms, and I prepare to fight a war. And, above all else with which I must contend, I am wedding you within a matter of hours now." Feeling her hand tense in his, he relented and sighed. "But if 'twas important enough to wake me, then I will hear you out, Catherine."

The oak door at the end of the passage groaned and creaked on heavy iron hinges as it swung outward into the duchess's herb garden, the same garden where four days earlier he'd told her she came to him. The night breeze was cool in comparison with the stale air in the corridor, prompting her to shiver slightly. Above them, the moon showed but half its face, sending only a faint silvery light over the plant beds. Guy released Catherine's hand to lean over and push the stem of the torch into the soft earth.

"Sit you down, Demoiselle, and tell me now what keeps me from my bed." Straightening, he wiped his hands on his wrinkled tunic and waited. "Well?" he asked finally when she made no move toward the stone bench.

"My lord . . ." She eyed him uncertainly now, working her damp palms against the fullness of her skirt, her heart thudding. He was but a foot or so away from her, but his face was deeply shadowed, giving it a harshness she'd not expected. The flecked eyes that stared back at her reflected the faint light eerily.

"Come, there's naught that cannot be said between us, Catherine. As husband and wife, I would hope to achieve a peace and understanding, else we shall both be the most miserable of people." His voice had gentled, dropping to a softness that surprised her. "What would you have of me?" he prompted. "Is it some favor you would ask? Or is it your bridegift mayhap? Curthose beggars me, but I'd not have it said I could not buy you what you wish." He was at a loss, his mind searching for reason in her sudden appearance at his pallet. His experience with women was limited, having mostly consisted of brief encounters with willing whores or camp followers eager to please in exchange for a small coin, and it had not mattered if he saw any of them again. But the girl before him was Catherine of the Condes and therefore different. This was the girl who would grow to womanhood as his wife, the one who would bear his heirs for him, and somehow it was important that he please her insofar as was possible. He reached to touch a strand of hair that strayed over her face, lifting it and brushing it back with a fingertip. "What can I give you, Catherine?" he asked softly.

She sucked in her breath, afraid now to tell him. It had seemed so simple, so reasonable even, when she'd thought it out earlier, but now she realized it for a foolish hope. Exhaling heavily, she looked away and gathered her courage to blurt finally, "My lord, I cannot wed with you—I cannot."

There was a desperation in her voice that took him aback. "Cat . . . Cat . . ." he soothed, reaching out again to her.

"Nay!" she cried, backing away from him. "You have not heard all I would say! Curthose's cause is doomed—you admit your vassals will not fight for him, and . . . and he has no right to give me to you . . . and . . ." The words tumbled out almost incoherently, mirroring her disordered thoughts. "Aye—and you cannot wish to wed with me without my father's consent, can you? You said yourself that Curthose asks too much for me, and . . . and I'd not be a very good wife to you—I swear I would not. I mean, I cannot sew or weave or spin . . . or card even." To her horror, a smile twitched at the corners of his mouth and then broadened. Hastening to finish her proposal before he touched her, she continued, "As you know, King Henry is my own godfather, my lord. Take me to him and you shall be rewarded, I promise—aye, you'll keep your lands and . . ."

His smile vanished as he stared incredulously at what she asked of him. "You would have me take you to King Henry? To flee Rouen in the middle of the night, leaving my vassals behind to Curthose's wrath? You would ask me to be forsworn—to forget my oath to my suzerain?" he demanded. "God's bones, Demoiselle!"

"And what of your oath to my mother?" she retorted without thinking. "Aye, you promised on the Cross to keep me safe! And that, my lord, is the oath I would have you keep!"

"Jesu!" he muttered. "You could not ask for anything I could give you, could you? Nay, but you'd have me damned before God as an oath breaker if 'twould free you from me."

He was not reacting as she had hoped. "Oh, nay—

'tis not you, my lord,'' she cut in quickly. "Nay, but you are greatly desired as a husband—indeed, the other ladies would have me most fortunate, but . . .''

"But I am not Brian FitzHenry,'' he finished for her. "Well, I am sorry for that, but you'd not get him anyway.''

"I might! But if I am wed to you, then there will be no hope—can you not see that?'' she pleaded. "As long as I am unwed, I can hope to change my father's mind! Can you not see how 'tis for me?''

"Cat . . . Catherine . . .'' He took a step closer.

"Nay, do not touch me!''

" 'Twas not my intent—but I would have you listen to me.''

She backed away again, this time losing her balance against the low bench, stumbling, and falling over it. "Oooooooph!'' she gasped as she landed in a sprawling heap, the skirts of her chemise and overtunic billowing out from her legs.

"Are you unhurt?'' he asked as he extended his hand to pull her up. She nodded and tried to brush dirt and twigs off her expensive gown. "As I was saying before you fell,'' he continued while she smoothed her skirts, "you've not considered how it is for you. None was more surprised than I when Curthose offered you to me—aye, you can believe that or not—but do you know what he wanted for you? One hundred mounted mercenaries, twenty knights' service, fifty footsoldiers, and five bowmen—all above what I already owe him for Rivaux.'' He watched her eyes widen in shock at the cost. "Think on it, Demoiselle—there's not many who can pay such in these troubled times: myself, de Mortain, Belesme, and a few others I'd not care to name. So if I refused Curthose's *generous* offer,'' he emphasized sarcastically, "think you he would have stopped with me? God's bones, Catherine, but his duchy's the prize now—he either keeps it or loses it—so your wishes are of small concern to him. He will use you to gain what he can and hope it will be enough to help him win. He cares not for you—he cares not for me. Nay, but I would not seek to talk me out of taking you, Catherine of the Condes, lest you be given to the likes of Belesme.''

''Belesme is wed.''

''Aye, but ask your lady mother how much marriage bonds mean to him.'' He watched her recoil visibly and lowered his voice to speak more kindly. ''And if not Belesme, then to whom would he give you? Let us consider. De Vere mayhap? Aye, now there's a widower for you—with three wives buried yet. At least I am young and vigorous and you'll not have to watch four men lift me into my saddle. But mayhap he might consider Brittany's young sons—the oldest cannot be above ten—but what's that to say when an heiress is being sold?''

''Stop it! You would mock me,'' she hissed furiously.

''Nay, 'tis the truth I tell you. Take me, Catherine of the Condes, and make the best of what you are given. I at least am sworn to protect you, and I'll not beat you without cause.'' He paused, waiting for her further response, and was disappointed when her shoulders sagged and she looked away, her defiance gone in the face of reality. A disheartening silence settled over them as she digested what he'd told her. Finally, when he could stand it no longer, he picked up the torch, its flame burned down to an orange glow on the hardwood limb. ''Come on—we'd best get back while we can still see a little. You will have a tiring day on the morrow and you will need your strength.''

''So you can climb on me like a rutting beast when 'tis done?'' she asked bitterly.

He stood stock-still for a moment, his eyes bleak as they contemplated her. ''Is that what you think I mean to do, Catherine? Whether you choose to believe it or not, just because I take what Curthose offers me does not make me an animal.'' He grasped her shoulder and turned her back toward the doorway. "Come on—you've got to get back undiscovered."

"I care not if I am seen."

"I care. I'd not have it said my countess lacked modesty or was free with her favors."

She stared up at him a moment and then sighed, nodding. "Aye." His fingers squeezed her shoulder and then he released her. Falling in beside him, she walked back, her mind occupied with the realization that she could not stop the marriage—that by the time the sun set on the morrow, she'd be Countess of Rivaux. It had been foolish of her to think it could be otherwise, she chided herself, and now she would have to force herself to give up her dreams of Brian FitzHenry. As she kept stride with him, her thoughts strayed to the inevitable and she stole a sideways glance at him, wondering what lying with him was going to be like.

He stopped at the bottom of the stairs leading to Sybilla's bower. As she turned to him, he tried to hide his disappointment by telling her lightly, "I'd ask a kiss for escort, but I'd not be like just any castle lout."

"Nay, you could not be," she managed. For a moment her heart pounded at the thought that he might kiss her again anyway, but he merely lifted her chin with his knuckle and studied her beneath a torch ring. His green-gold eyes were sober.

"God grant you a good night, Catherine," he told her finally.

"Where have you been, Demoiselle?"

Both of them spun around at the sound of the duchess's cold voice, and Guy instinctively reached a protective hand to Catherine. "She was ill, Your Grace, and would have me bring her back."

Sybilla's eyes traveled over Catherine first and then Guy, with open disapproval taking in the girl's soiled gown and his bagging chausses. Without acknowledging Guy's explanation, she addressed Catherine. " 'Tis well you wed, Demoiselle, for I'd not keep you in this house. The ladies who serve me are chaste.''

Catherine took in the shocked faces of the women behind the duchess and reddened in embarrassment. ''Nay, but I fell on the way,'' she tried to explain lamely.

''Get you to your bed. Your woman awaits you, Demoiselle, and you will need your sleep.''

Thus dismissed, Cat had no choice but to climb the steep stairs up to Hawise. Her head held high, she turned her back and started up. Behind her, she could hear Sybilla bid Guy of Rivaux good night, the censure in her voice still evident. And as his footsteps faded on the stone floor, one of the duchess's ladies sniffed, ''And 'tis well rid of her you are, Your Grace, for I'll warrant the little demoiselle is virgin no more.'' ''Aye,'' another agreed, ''there'll be no blood in her marriage bed.''

Cat briefly considered running back to confront them, but then realized it would serve no purpose other than gaining her further censure from Sybilla. As it was her last night under the duchess's protection, she would simply go on up to bed. On the morrow, her things would be moved to the Archbishop of Rouen's palace, where she and Guy would share their marriage bed in more privacy than Curthose could provide. She had Guy to thank for that, at least, she grudgingly admitted to herself, for surely the bedding ceremony could not be overly bawdy in such a place.

In the hallway below, Guy left the duchess and started back, tired now in spirit as well as body. He'd not expected Catherine of the Condes to be overjoyed to wed with him, but neither had he expected her to cling to her childish passion for Henry's bastard son. God's bones, but could she not see that he could make her Countess of Rivaux whilst all FitzHenry could do was wait to gain what she inherited at some later year? And what made her think herself so different that she should have a choice in the matter? Did not all daughters of noble houses wed where they were given, accepting husbands old, young, fat, thin, violent, overly pious, or given to vices too secret to mention, and meekly become vessels for their husbands' seed? Nay, but he could not see Catherine of the Condes doing anything meekly, he admitted. A wry smile curved his mouth as he thought of her. In the short weeks he'd known her, she'd not gone tamely to her fate, but rather had struggled every step of the way, and he could not but admire her for it.

It was strange that he could think of her as his lady already when scarce four days before he'd not even considered taking a wife. Aye, he'd never had the time or the inclination to dally with fair maidens, preferring instead the simple relief of an occasional whore who knew what she was about. Would the spoiled and pampered Cat be repelled by what was expected of her? Would she cringe and cry in her marriage bed—or would she fight? That gave him pause. He'd no wish to ravish a woman, whether he had the right or not. He stared unseeing, trying to imagine in his mind what she would look like without her fine clothes, her slender body pale, her dark hair spread out on his pillow, and the very thought made his mouth dry with desire. Would her eyes, already a deep brown, darken with passion, or would they stare at him in horror? Somehow he could not think of Cat being afraid of him. Cat. Aye, but she was rightly named, his Cat.

"My lord?"

He looked up, startled by the sound of William de Comminges' voice, and realized he'd come all the way back to the common sleeping area, where a space had been curtained off for the more notable of Curthose's guests. He'd walked darkened corridors unseeing, his thoughts on Catherine of the Condes, and yet he'd somehow managed to find his way. God looks after all fools, he supposed.

William, having known Guy from his birth, sensed his introspective mood and fell silently into step beside him. The boy was a puzzle to him, a complicated person whose great prowess in combat was matched by an almost unbecoming gentleness despite all William had done to toughen him. That he could dispatch his enemies with savage thrusts of his broadsword and yet save a cat from those who would torture the creature was almost beyond comprehension. Eyeing his young master from beneath heavy brows, the grizzled old warrior tried to make sense of the boy. It had been a task of pride to take the child of ten and teach him the art of war so well that Guy of Rivaux's prowess surprised enemies eager to dispossess him. Aye, but the boy was cunning and strong, his savagery tempered and checked by years in the monastery. God's blood, but if the old count had waited much longer to relent, it would have been too late to make him a warrior.

"What think you of the Demoiselle?" Guy asked finally, breaking the silence.

"I think her overyoung, my lord."

"Aye."

"And too small to bed," William added significantly.

"She is already bigger than her mother."

"She is but thirteen."

As much as he'd said the same things to himself during the four days past, Guy was reluctant to part with his dreams of Catherine. Part of him realized the truth of what William said, but part of him wanted her in spite of it. "Holy Church accepts that a girl of twelve may be bedded," he reminded William.

"Aye, and Holy Church buries them also, my lord. If you would keep the little demoiselle long enough to bear your heirs, you'd best not lie with her." The older man cocked his head for a better look at Guy. "But she is yours to do with what you will," he added with a shrug, knowing that he'd touched the young man's conscience. "She is, after all, a beauty, and she'll be all fire, I'll warrant."

"Aye."

"Your mother wed at thirteen."

"And died at fourteen—is that what you would remind me?"

"It is something to think on, is it not?" William retorted. "Why wed an heiress if you would not have what she brings you? And a dead girl brings nothing, my lord, for the lands go to the next daughter if she has borne no babe."

"Do you remember her—my mother, I mean?"

"Aye."

"What was she like?" In all of his years, Guy had never heard much about the child bride of his elderly father, and he suddenly wanted to know of her now.

"She was a beautiful child." William shook his head and sighed. "Aye, and a very foolish creature who paid for her sins."

"You do not think I should have taken Catherine of the Condes, do you, William?" Guy asked suddenly.

"I think you have a war to fight, my lord. And I think you have made too many enemies. There's not many—nay, not even Curthose when he thinks on it—who will like the looks of Rivaux, Nantes, Harlowe, and the Condes together." His eyes met Guy's soberly and then he nodded. "Aye, and that is what your son may one day have—if Curthose wins."

"I know. I hear the grumbling already," Guy admitted, "but there's not many as would pay what I pay to get her."

"Except Belesme."

"Aside from his first protest, Count Robert has said little—'tis de Mortain who would howl as though stuck. Now Curthose would have it that I must wed the demoiselle first and renew my fealty after, so 'twill not look as though he sold her. Jesu! As though none will suspect when all know! We fight for a fool, William."

"Aye. And you'd best seek your pallet, my lord, else you'll be unfit for your marriage bed." William reached affectionately to clasp the boy's shoulder.

"Aye, and whether you bed her or not, you'd best look ready for the task."

"And you?"

"I go back to the hall, my lord. Curthose provides wine and jongleurs, and I'd not miss them. I did but come to see how you fared."

"I am all right."

All was quiet after William left, and Guy once again eased his tired body onto his pallet, taking the time only to remove his shoes. Rolling on his side, he cradled his head and tried to sleep. Jesu, but never before in his life had he found the task so difficult—not when he was but a child sent to a monastery or a boy come out to fight for his patrimony. And now he had even more to lose—his life, his lands, and Catherine de Brione. Never in all his years had he risked so much with so little hope of success, for this time all that he had depended on the feckless Robert Curthose's ability to keep his duchy. Trying to banish troubled thoughts from his mind, he closed his eyes and thought of Catherine.

𝕖𝕤 11 𝕖𝕤

Bells pealed throughout Rouen, signaling the plighting of troth between Catherine of the Condes and Guy of Rivaux. It was to be a day of ceremonies, the first being the marriage, followed by the renewal of Guy's oath of fealty, and then a wedding feast. Necks craned and eyes strained for a glimpse of the bride when she came in on the duke's arm. If any considered it strange that 'twas not Gilbert of Nantes that gave her in marriage in the absence of her father, there were others who considered it further evidence of Curthose's favoritism toward his young vassal. A hush descended over the assembled baronage and clergy as the duke placed the Demoiselle of the Condes' hand in Guy of Rivaux's and stepped back. She was very pale but otherwise composed, a picture of regal beauty to all who'd come to admire, to witness, and to grumble over Guy of Rivaux's good fortune.

She stole a sideways glimpse through the gold tissue veil that covered her hair and flowed down over her shoulders from beneath a simple circlet set with uncut stones. Beside her, Guy stood, his rank splendidly displayed in a tunic of red silk, heavily embroidered and crusted with winking jewels that caught the colors of the ornate stained-glass windows above them. The tunic, which nearly touched the floor, was split on the sides and laced with gold cord past his hips, falling open below to reveal bright blue hose that fit smoothly over his calves and disappeared into gold-embossed red leather slippers. His black hair was freshly barbered and hung in a fringe over his brow, flattened by the narrow gold circlet that proclaimed his ranking amongst the baronage. His flecked gold-green eyes were somber as he faced the premier cleric of the duchy. But without looking at her, he must have sensed her eyes on him, for he squeezed her fingers briefly.

It was morning still and therefore yet cool, but Catherine felt suffocated by the closeness of the air within the cathedral. Closing her eyes momentarily, she fought the panic rising in her breast. In a matter of minutes she would belong to Rivaux forever, she would be his to do with as he willed, and her fate would irrevocably be tied to his. She felt his hand tighten again and became aware that the archbishop had begun to speak, challenging any who would stand against the marriage. A low rumble spread through the crowd, but no one spoke out openly, and then Guy, in response to the question of whether he would take her, spoke loudly and clearly for all to hear with an "aye" that seemed to reverberate off the walls, the pillars, and the vaulted ceiling, echoing again in her mind, an audible reminder that she was to be his. As Guy repeated the age-old vows, she found herself oddly calm now, her panic receding with acceptance of the inevitable. There was a pause and she suddenly realized that the archbishop addressed her, asking if she would take Guy of Rivaux for husband. Sucking in her breath, she released it slowly and nodded. "Aye," she answered low. In what seemed almost to be a dream, she repeated the words spoken before her, matching the archbishop's cadence.

It did not take long, the ceremony that bound people to each other, and as Catherine knelt beside Guy to receive the blessing of Holy Church on the union, she resolved to make the best of what she had been given.

Guy of Rivaux was neither old nor fat nor stupid nor cruel, and for that at least she could be grateful.

As soon as the Cross was signed over their bent heads, Guy leaned closer to whisper through the golden veil, "Art lovely, Catherine—fairer than a man dare expect." His breath was warm and his voice soft against her ear.

Coloring, she struggled to her feet, encumbered by her flowing gown with its layers of chemise and undertunic twisting about her ankles. Supporting herself on Guy's arm, she lifted the full skirts away from her legs and straightened them. Sybilla, under Curthose's orders, had spared nothing in the making of the wedding finery, and despite the haste of its construction, the gown was truly beautiful. Smoothing the rich green samite down over the undergown with her free hand, Cat caught the edge of the hem and slid it over a hook on her golden girdle to expose the banded undergown of purple sendal.

Taking a deep breath, she nodded. "I am ready, my lord."

Later that day, Cat would be hard-pressed to remember much of the Mass that followed. As she sat between Guy and Gilbert of Nantes, her attention wandered, first to covert glances around her and then to the beautiful patterns of rich blues and reds and greens created on the stone floor by the light that filtered through the windows above. The image of Brian crept unbidden into her thoughts, but she resolutely pushed it away. That part of her life was past forever.

The press of bodies, some unwashed, heated the air and made it close. Cat closed her eyes and told herself that it would soon be over, that she had but the renewal of Guy's oath and dinner to survive before she could rid herself of the hot veil and voluminous gown. Aye, but then would come the bedding, she remembered suddenly, and her stomach tightened at the thought. Well, she would survive that also, for she had a fair notion of what would happen, and while it sounded distasteful in the extreme, she could be comforted in that she'd have the satisfaction of proving she came virgin to her husband. Guy's hand moved to cover hers on the carved armrest, and his fingers stroked hers. She closed her eyes but did not pull away.

When at last the priest pronounced the final benediction, Guy released her hand and stood, ready to give his public avowal of support for his embattled duke. Cat nudged her grandfather awake, and he lurched from his seat, thinking it finished, only to fall back, glowering from beneath full gray brows. A few more minutes, she told herself, and they could go out into the air.

In full view of everyone, both Curthose and Guy walked forward. People shifted uncomfortably in the hard seats and craned to watch as Guy of Rivaux knelt to place his hands between the duke's. Cat leaned forward, straining to hear Curthose ask, "Do you wish without reserve to be my man?"

"Aye—I wish it," Guy answered clearly.

The archbishop stood behind the duke with a small casket believed to contain a relic of the martyred St. Stephen, ready for the swearing. He stooped to whisper something to Curthose and then nodded to Guy.

Clearing his throat, the young count began, calling out to the assemblage, "I promise, by my faith, that from this day forward I will be faithful to Robert, Duke of Normandy, and will maintain toward him my homage, entirely and against every man, in good faith and without deception, so help me God."

Curthose released his hands and took the casket, holding it out, asking, "Do you swear on these bones of St. Stephen that all you have said is true and binding, now and forever?"

For answer, Guy placed his right hand on the box. "I so swear."

As Curthose raised him to bestow the kiss of fealty on each cheek and to receive it in turn, Catherine turned to see Robert of Belesme watching her, his strange green eyes cold, his face impassive. Suppressing a shudder, she wondered what he thought now, now that he'd lost in his bid to send her to Belesme. Her eyes met his briefly and his expression did not change. Jesu, but one could not tell what was in his mind. Abruptly he turned to look at Guy, and an odd smile crossed his face, sending a shiver of foreboding down her spine. She was certain that her marriage had not ended whatever plans he had for her and that Guy could now consider the Count of Belesme an enemy.

The feast, which began in late afternoon, lasted for hours. Bones littered platters, bowls stood empty save for congealed sauces that were left, and the cloths were stained from spilled food and wine, and still the merriment continued as jongleurs performed their tricks and troubadours sang of heroic men and beautiful ladies. Cat's neck ached from sitting straight on the high dais with a smile fixed on her face. From time to time, the frequency increasing with the drunkenness of the revelers, someone would lurch to his feet and call out a toast to her, and everyone would lift his cup again. Her ears already burned with the bawdy comments of the men, but she pretended ignorance and continued to smile.

Guy, more than a little drunk himself, lazed back on his bench, his back braced against the wall, and studied her from beneath heavy lids. God's bones, but she was the most perfectly made female he'd ever seen, he decided as he took in her fine profile, those eyes so dark that pupil and iris often appeared as one, and that shining hair. Impulsively he leaned to lift the circlet that held the gold tissue veil over the crown of her head. She recoiled from the suddenness of his movement, and he mistook the reason.

"Nay—I would but see your hair."

"You would have the duchess think me overbold, my lord, for I must leave it covered now."

"Not if your lord wills it." Even as he spoke, he

drew off the gossamer fabric to expose the shimmering waves of rich, deep brown that cascaded over her shoulders and down her back. "You should always wear it thus."

"I think you have partaken of too much wine, my lord, else you'd know 'tis unseemly to have it unbound after today," she retorted.

"You are free to use my name now, Cat."

"I would, but it sounds strange to mine ears yet."

"When we are alone, I give you leave to practice saying it." He straightened suddenly and handed her the veil. "Churchmen retire early, it would seem, and by the looks of it, our host of the night means to leave."

She looked up to see the archbishop rise, still conversing with Robert Curthose, and then he nodded toward Guy of Rivaux. One of the duchess's older ladies, Marguerite of Chalon, came to whisper in Cat's ear, "Would you have me go with you for witness, Lady Catherine?"

A chill of fear gripped her for a moment and then passed. Somehow she'd not expected to be bedded so soon. "Aye."

"We are fortunate that not many will leave to walk so far," Guy murmured low. "But I cannot give you long, else the gates will be locked for the night." Rising, he pulled her up after him and held her hand high to signal the final toast. Obscene advice accompanied by raucous laughter was hurled at them, until, in full view of everyone, he bent to kiss her full on the lips. A cheer went up from those still sober enough to pay attention.

"Run, Lady Catherine," Marguerite urged. "Now!"

"Sweet Mary," Cat breathed, still shocked by the public kiss.

"Go on." With a playful push, Guy directed her into the older woman's hands.

It was no short run to the archbishop's palace, but

Cat, discovering that some of the younger men meant to follow her, gathered her skirts up and ran with the abandon of a child through the corridors of Curthose's palace, the narrow streets of Rouen, and into the walled house. Servants in Bonne Ame's colors barred the gates behind her and promised that none but the archbishop and her husband would be admitted.

Hawise met her and led the way to the chamber William Bonne Ame had so generously offered for her wedding night. Even as the door closed after them, both Hawise and Lady Marguerite began stripping her, removing her girdle, pulling her gown over her head, and removing her undergown. As she stood in her snowy cambric chemise, Hawise began plaiting her hair, suggesting it would tangle less if it were bound, while Sybilla's lady tried to advise her on what would be expected. "You must not weep or cry out, for 'twill give him a disgust of you," she offered. "And if you but lie still, 'tis soon over." Her eyes traveled over Cat's slim body as though measuring her. "You are small yet, to be sure, but mayhap you will not conceive soon." To Hawise she directed, "Remove the chemise that all may see she is unblemished."

"Nay!" Cat recoiled. "I'll not!"

Hawise grasped the chemise firmly at the waist and pulled it upward, drawing it over her head so swiftly that Cat stood naked before she could stop her. Already the clamor of those at the gates could be heard. In panic, Catherine broke away from the two women and tore open the bed curtains, scrambling inside and wrapping her bare body in the sheets. Even as Marguerite chided her for being foolish, Cat held the top of the cover tightly under her chin and listened to the running footsteps in the corridor. She swallowed hard and shut her eyes when the door burst open.

"Where is she?" someone demanded drunkenly.

To her horror, the bed curtains were pulled and her eyes flew open beneath the curious scrutiny of a half-dozen men. She must've looked as embarrassed as she felt, for Guy's man William pushed everyone back, saying, "Nay, but she's where she ought to be, my lords. Have done, else you will scare her wits from her."

Behind him, she could see that Guy was being stripped of his clothes amid earthy comments about his body. "Aye, and if you cannot keep her pleased with that, there's something wrong with you." Someone laughed.

"Would you see her before witnesses, my lord?" Lady Marguerite felt compelled to ask.

"Nay—I accept she is whole," he responded quickly, his eyes on the red-faced Catherine.

Cat bit her lip and willed herself to watch. The dark hair on his chest converged to the middle and continued downward in a line past his navel and below. As they pulled his chausses down to his ankles, she stared at his face and realized he was as uncomfortable as she was. He stepped out of them and then literally dove into the bed beside her, his face flaming, and she wondered momentarily if he were virgin also.

"God's bones, but you are wrapped in the sheet," he complained. "Loose your hands and let me cover myself."

"Nay."

His fingers pried hers off the cover and he rolled under, his body touching hers. Pulling the sheet up over both of them, he slid his leg against her calf and crossed her ankle with his. William de Comminges leaned his head in between the bed curtains and announced solemnly, "They are bedded, my lords—let us go back and drink more of Curthose's wine to celebrate."

Catherine lay as still as stone, afraid to move under the weight of his leg. His naked body was harder and heavier than she'd imagined. As the noise outside the chamber died away, Hawise pulled the bed hangings shut and then dragged her pallet into a small alcove.

Alone at last with the man she'd wed, Cat steeled herself, expecting him to throw his whole body over hers.

Guy lifted his leg off hers gingerly and rolled over on his back to stare upward into the darkness. He was acutely aware of her, so much so that every inch of his body was sensitive to her nearness. Even her sharp intake of breath when he'd touched her had sent his pulses racing. But she was so young and so delicately made that he feared to take her. Struggling to master his desire, he willed himself to think of the mother who'd died bearing him, who had died because she'd been too small, and slowly, ever so slowly, the heat ebbed from his body.

"You've naught to fear from me, Catherine," he told her when he finally dared to speak. "Turn over and try to sleep."

Having prepared herself, willed herself even, not to cry out when he lay over her and took possession of her body, she could not believe what she'd heard at first. Relief flooded over her, easing her mind and body. He wasn't going to take her maidenhead—he wasn't going to tear her asunder to plant his seed—he wasn't going to touch her at all. And even as she began to realize exactly what he'd said, he rolled to lie on his side, his back to her.

Her relief faded, replaced with indignation. "Do you mean you are not . . . that you . . . ?" Words failed her for a moment.

"Aye. You have naught to fear of me, Catherine," he repeated.

The thought of Sybilla and the others smirking when it became known she'd not bled made Cat furious. "You are not going to lie with me?" she asked incredulously. "Nay, I'll not be insulted thus! 'Tis my right, my lord—if you wed me, you'll bed me!"

"Catherine—"

"Do not speak 'Catherine' to me! You would shame me, Guy of Rivaux, and I'll not let you! D'ye hear me? I had no wish to wed with you, my lord," she hissed in a lower voice, "but since 'tis done, you will not make me scorned for what is not my fault!" Pushing herself up to sit in the bed, she stared down at him.

"God's bones, but what ails you, Cat?" He rolled back over and tried to focus on her in the darkness. "Jesu!"

"And I'd not be called Cat either!" In her fury, she let the sheet drop as she reached to poke him with her finger. "I prepared myself to accept what must happen between us, my lord, because I would not have it said I came not a virgin to you."

" 'Tis more like that they'll know you were too young to bed." He caught her hand and held it.

"Nay, they will not! Already there are those who sneer at me and gibe that I am unchaste!"

"Cat . . . Cat . . ." He sat up also and tried to make out her features, but all he could see of her was the flash of her eyes. Groping for the pull cord with his free hand, he opened the bed curtains to let in the light from the sputtering tallow candles that stood impaled on tall iron spikes. "There's none to say you are unchaste if I do not complain. Look at me—I am your husband now, Catherine, and 'tis only I who have the right to say how you came to me. Lie down and get your rest—the day has been overlong for both of us."

"Nay!" Hot, angry tears welled in her eyes and spilled over. "That 'tis not important to you makes no difference, my lord—'tis my honor you dismiss so lightly!"

Despite her anger, she appeared very pale in the flickering yellow light. Guy's eyes traveled from her face to where she held the sheet clenched below her breasts. She was small and yet the tipped peaks were firm and well-formed. His mouth went dry and his senses reeled. He sucked in his breath sharply and fought rising desire. With an effort, he released her hand and reached to pull the sheet up. "Cover yourself," he ordered harshly.

"Why? Do you find me displeasing?" she demanded. "Sweet Mary, but you have done naught but stare at me since first I saw you! And now you would not even lie with me!"

"I do not find you displeasing, Catherine," he answered with a sigh. "But you are overyoung—how long have you had your courses?"

"Nearly a year."

"Jesu!" He'd not expected her to act thus, and he knew not how to appease her. His body, at war with his mind, warmed again to the nearness of hers, and yet he feared to risk getting her with child so young. Resolutely he shook his head. "Nay, 'tis not long enough—my own mother died in childbed when she was older than you."

"I am bigger than my mother," she maintained stoutly.

She leaned closer and her fragrant hair, which had come loose from its unfinished plaits, cascaded over him like a silken curtain, brushing against his bare skin and trailing fire in its wake. Her face was but inches from his and he could feel her warm breath as she spoke. The pupils of her dark eyes were large in the faint light and her lashes were like black smudges against her fair skin. Despite his resolve, he reached to twine his fingers in the silky mass of hair to draw her closer. As her image blurred from nearness, her lips touched his, tentatively at first, as though she didn't know what to do. The taste of her was enough to send liquid fire through his veins. Somewhere in the recesses of his mind he argued with himself that he could touch without taking. He leaned back, pulling her down with him.

His body was lean and hard, the muscles of his upper arms and shoulders moving beneath her as his hands eagerly stroked her hair against her back. His mouth, which had been soft and pliant against hers, hardened also and demanded more than her lips, and as his tongue teased hers, a tremor of anticipation trav-

eled downward, warming her. She wriggled against
him, suddenly feeling his aroused body.

"Jesu!" He pushed her off him and rolled to sit on
the edge of the bed. "I did not mean . . . Nay, you
know not what you ask, Cat." With an effort he heaved
himself out between the curtains and groped for his
clothing. Cursing as he half-stumbled over a low
bench, he found his discarded chausses and began
drawing them on. Behind him, Catherine blinked in
bewilderment and disappointment, uncertain if she'd
done something wrong.

"But where are you going? Nay, but you cannot
leave me now, else I shall be doubly shamed, my
lord."

"I will be back."

He dressed quickly, not bothering to garter the hose,
and pulled on his tunic with such speed that his head
seemed to pop out of the neck. Fear gripped Catherine—surely he did not mean to sleep apart from her
on their marriage night. It would be bad enough when
Lady Marguerite and the others came to see proof of
her maidenhead on the sheets, but if her husband was
not even with her . . . She dared not think what would
be said of her. Too many would point and laugh—or
pity, and that would be worse. She hung her head and
managed to mumble, "If I have offended you, my lord,
or given you a disgust of me, I am sorry for it—'twas
but that I feared what everyone would say . . ."

"I said I would be back. Lie down and try to sleep."
He slid his shoes on and bent to straighten the points
over his toes. Straightening, he started toward the
door.

"Sleep?" Her brief lapse into humility forgotten,
she sat upright and cast about for a weapon. "God's
blood," she muttered, "if I were a man I would kill
you for the insult you offer me."

His scarred eyebrow rose in amusement as he turned
back to her. "Ah, Cat, the day will come when I will

remind you of your eagerness—I only hope you are as willing then.''

"Leave me, then! 'Twill give my father the means of breaking this marriage!'' she flung after him. Pounding the pillow behind her, she flopped back down. As his footsteps grew fainter, she lay there seething, certain that Brian FitzHenry would not have left her.

Willing herself not to think about it finally, she wriggled and burrowed until she made herself a place within the feather mattress and tried to sleep. Her eyes grew heavy from the fatigue of the day's celebrations, and she was nearly asleep when he returned. He shook her awake, pulling her upright.

"Get out, that I may tend the sheets.''

"Unhhhh? Jesu, you are back,'' she muttered irritably as she struggled to come fully awake.

"Aye. Stand up.''

Before she'd scarce had time to roll off the edge of the bed, he was pouring something from a small metal container onto the middle of the sheets. ''Are you daft?'' she grumbled. ''Nay, but I'll not sleep in a wet bed.''

"Aye, you will. Get in there and smear it around— 'tis pig's blood from the slaughterhouse, but 'twill have to do.'' As she stared in horror at the red splotches, he examined them. ''Do you think 'tis enough?''

"Sweet Mary—do you not know?''

"I never lie with virgins.'' He stepped back, grinning at the skeptical look she gave him. ''Aye—'tis true. Whores know their business and expect naught but a coin or two in return. Virgins, I am told,'' he added wickedly, ''scream and cry or else lie like stone.'' Gesturing to the bed again, he added, ''Well, would you have some more? By the looks of it, even Sybilla ought to pity you tomorrow.''

"You expect me to sleep with pig's blood!''

"It won't hurt you—the pig's dead,'' he told her reasonably.

"Sweet Mary.''

He peeled out of his clothing with his back to her and then slid between the soiled sheets. "You can stand there freezing if you wish, but I mean to get some sleep whilst I can. Curthose expects to leave Rouen later in the week, and you will find straw pallets hard and uncomfortable. You'd best enjoy the luxury of a bed now." Turning on his side and propping his head on his elbow, he looked up at her. "And do not despair, Cat—you'll grow and give me fine sons yet."

❦ 12 ❧

Even though it was misting rather than raining outside, the day and the circumstances were dreary enough to dampen spirits in the small tent. Hawise sat in one corner, mending a rent in one of Guy's tunics, while Catherine plied her needle determinedly, taking small careful stitches as Hawise had shown her earlier. The piece was simple enough, an undertunic of fine cambric with a blue diamond pattern embroidered at the neckline to show beneath an outer garment. Pricking her finger, Cat muttered a mild oath and sucked at the tiny drop of blood. Hawise looked up, a secret smile on her plump face.

"Be careful that you do not stain the fabric, Cat," she reminded the girl.

"Aye." Catherine held up the piece, turning it in the dim light provided by a tallow candle on a spiked stand beside her. "Do you truly think he will like it?" she asked skeptically. " 'Tis not perfectly done, but neither will most of it show."

"Aye, he'll like it—if for no other reason than 'tis your own work." The older woman's eyes twinkled as she added slyly, "Methinks, Cat, that you are not as displeased with your young lord as you once thought."

"Because I make him something to wear? Jesu, but there's naught else to do, is there? I can scarce go about with hundreds of men outside, and besides, 'tis

136

raining." Laying aside the undershirt, she stretched her hands toward the small brazier that smoked beneath the chimney hole. "And even if it were not, 'tis cold for September. Jesu! Tinchebrai!" She spat out the name of de Mortain's keep contemptuously. "It shows who has Curthose's ear now, does it not? Guy says there are better places to fight, but because 'tis de Mortain, we come here."

Hawise smoothed the mended tunic and nodded complacently. In the fortnight since Catherine's marriage, there'd been a subtle change in the girl, and it was a change that made the older woman proud of her little mistress. When the girl had seen that defiance would serve her ill, she'd capitulated and accepted her marriage with a grace that was obviously winning her the love of her young lord. Not once had Catherine spoken of Brian, putting aside her childish passion instead and making the best of what she'd been given. And from what Hawise could see of Guy of Rivaux, he appeared enormously proud of his beautiful little wife and valued her well. There were not many secrets when one traveled with an army, and more than one night, she and the others who shared the tent with their lord and lady had been kept awake until early hours listening to Guy tell Catherine of the day's happenings. De Comminges, who appeared to have an almost fatherly relationship with his lord, had grumbled good-naturedly that "Catherine of the Condes knows more of Curthose's plans than half the Norman baronage." Aye, but Cat was far better off with the young Count of Rivaux than with the likes of Brian FitzHenry.

"At least Curthose and his brother talk now," Hawise reminded Catherine. "Mayhap it will be as before and Henry will go back to England with naught but more of Curthose's gold and another piece of Normandy."

"Sweet Mary, but I begin to care not about either of them," Cat complained restlessly as she paced within the narrow confines of the tent. "Whilst they parley and posture for each other, I have naught to do

but sit and sew and sleep. I would that I were a man,''
she finished irritably.

"That would leave me little to wait for, would it not?''

She spun around at the sound of his voice and her
face flushed. He was standing at the raised door flap,
his silk tunic wilted from the mist and drizzle, his
black hair clinging damply to his forehead. Even as
she saw him, he ducked low to enter, and her heart
thudded at the look on his face. He bore ill news, she
was certain, and she feared to hear it. To cover her
feelings, she thrust a piece of unused cambric at him.
"You'd best dry yourself, my lord.''

His divided eyebrow shot up in surprise at the sudden tartness in her voice, a tartness at variance with
the fear in her eyes, and he made no move to take the
cloth. Instead, he walked over to pick up the undertunic Cat had been working and held it up to his shoulders, looking downward at the tiny blue stitches.

"You do this for me?'' he asked quietly, raising his
eyes to hers.

"Aye.'' She colored again, embarrassed by the
warmth that had sprung into those strange eyes. "That
is . . . well, there's naught else to do, and . . . I
thought I would try . . .''

"I thank you for it.'' Folding the shirt carefully, he
placed it on a closed clothing box. "God's bones, but
I am weary, Catherine, and there's so much to do ere
we sleep,'' he muttered as he dropped his tall frame
onto one of the small benches they'd brought with
them. Closing his eyes for a moment, he leaned his
head back against a sturdy tent pole.

"Where's Alan? Hawise, see if you can find Alan,''
Cat ordered. "We've got to get my lord out of his wet
clothes ere he takes a chill.''

"Nay, he and William are counting men and equipment for me to ensure all is ready on the morrow.''
Opening his eyes again, he nodded to the maidservant.
"But I would have you leave us—I'd be alone with my
lady for a while.''

"But it rains," Cat protested. "Where is she to go?"

"Nay, not now. Even the mists clear—'twould seem God grants us a good day for battle."

"I will bring supper from the pots," Hawise cut in quickly. Packing away her mending, she bobbed a hasty obeisance to him, her own heart heavy at the sound of his words.

Catherine stared blankly. "For battle," she echoed as what he'd said sank in. "Oh . . . nay!" she gasped in consternation. "Nay!"

"Aye."

Guy waited until the maidservant had left before he dared to look again at Catherine. And when he did meet her eyes, conflicting emotions warred in his breast, with part of him wanting to know if she cared and part of him wanting to reassure her. Given the circumstances of their marriage, it seemed almost too much to hope that she could someday come to love him, and not . . . His thoughts trailed off, his mind unwilling to admit the likely outcome on the morrow.

"They talk no longer, then?" she asked finally.

"There was little to say," he admitted wearily. "They met outside the keep, Henry with Anjou and Maine at his side, the duke with Belesme, the Atheling, de Mortain, and myself. 'Twas pleasant enough at first as each asked after the other's wife and spoke of nothing to the point. Then, at Belesme's prompting, Curthose dared to ask what Henry expected to gain from making war in Normandy. The king blustered about, saying that the Church and the baronage were tired of misrule, and then finally offering to let Curthose keep half the revenues of Normandy during his lifetime, with Henry ruling the duchy, and then 'twould all go to Henry and his heirs on the duke's death."

"Sweet Mary! Jesu! He would make no provision for Sybilla or William the Clito? Nay, but . . ."

"Aye. Curthose has no choice but to fight."

"What did Belesme say? And de Mortain?" she

wanted to know, her eyes still wide with the shock of Henry's insult to his own brother.

"What could they say? Neither of them would fight for Robert of Normandy if they had the choice, but if Curthose loses, they lose all they have. Henry made it plain enough in England that there's no place in his kingdom for them—and they know 'twill be the same in Normandy if he rules."

"But Curthose cannot win! We cannot win!"

She'd come to face him, standing above him, her skin gone pale next to her dark braids. Gone were the gibes about Henry's power and Curthose's folly that she'd once cast at him, and Guy realized with a start that she'd said "we" instead of "you." Despite the awful fatigue from hours of arguing in the duke's council, he felt a sense of elation. Pulling her onto his lap, he folded his arms around her and brushed the top of her hair with his cheek. She stiffened briefly and then settled against his chest, and he reflected wryly to himself that two weeks and more of lying naked in the same bed had at least given them an easier relationship. " 'Tis not of Curthose or Henry I would speak," he murmured aloud above her head. " 'Tis you."

She was very still in his arms, fearing to hear what he would say, savoring the strong feel of him as he held her, knowing that battles left men dead or maimed on both sides. When he made no move to speak further, she turned her head into his shoulder and felt the cold dampness of his ruined silk tunic. His arms tightened, holding her closer as though to both take and give comfort. His heart beat beneath her ear, and she knew suddenly that she feared to lose him, this new husband of hers. Irrationally, the memory of how they'd stood back that morning in the archbishop's palace and watched as Lady Marguerite and others had examined the blood-smeared sheets came to mind and she suppressed a giggle.

"It amuses you that I go to war, Cat?" he asked above her.

"Nay—I was but thinking how they all pitied me for that poor pig's blood—even William looked displeased with you."

"Aye, he gave me to know that I was not to use you thus again." His voice, which had been somber, betrayed a shared amusement. "Jesu, Cat, but what made you think of that?"

"I do not know—I suppose it is that I would not think of the other."

She was too near to him, and the warmth of her small body, the soft fragrance of her rosewater-rinsed hair, reminded him anew how much he wanted her. Her braids, neat and shiny and twined with gold thread, lay against his arm, and he had a nearly irresistible urge to unplait them that he could once again see that rippling mantle of dark hair spread out over her shoulders. But one thing could well lead to another and he dared not allow himself the thoughts that would crowd his mind. She was soft and pliant in his arms now, but somehow he knew she'd be all fire when he took her. But she was overyoung, he reminded himself. He closed his eyes to blot out the nearness of her, and still reeled from the effect of his thoughts on his senses. It was as though he could feel her lying beneath him, hear her moaning as her body opened to his. His own body tempted his mind until he argued within himself that he might die on the morrow and never know the pleasure of coupling with her.

She stirred and tried to look up at him. "Art silent, my lord," she chided. For answer, he opened his eyes and betrayed his desire. He felt rather than heard the sharp intake of her breath, but it was enough to bring him to his senses. Priding himself on the rigid control he had over mind and body, he pushed her gently off his lap. "I have to get out of these clothes, else I am like to take a fever from them," he explained in a voice that was strained even to his own ears. "I would have you warm me some wine whilst I get dry."

Having both sensed and seen the effect she had on

him, Cat was more than a little disappointed to have been pushed away so abruptly. She had more than a fair notion of what happened between men and women, particularly after listening to Lady Marguerite's rather daunting advice, and she felt an intense curiosity as to how it actually would feel to be possessed by a man. Besides, Guy of Rivaux was her husband, and she had to admit that she felt a very real attraction to him. Every night, she lay on their shared pallet, drawing warmth from his naked body, knowing he wanted her, and it was a heady feeling. More than once she'd thought that he would have given in to his desire had they not shared their small space with Hawise, William de Comminges, Alan and Arnulf.

Reluctantly she crossed the open area to pick up a wineskin and an empty cup. After pouring the red liquid into the metal vessel, she thrust a poker among the coals in the brazier to warm it. While she waited, she turned to watch him. He'd already shed both his tunic and his undertunic and was reaching for the shirt she'd made him.

" 'Tis not finished, my lord."

"I mean to wear it in hopes 'twill bring me good fortune. Besides, I doubt any will note whether 'tis done or not."

The poker sizzled and smoked when plunged into the cooler wine, and the pungent smell of hot metal permeated the tent. Cat waited until the cup itself was warm before withdrawing the poker and laying it aside. Carrying the heated wine to him, she held it out. "There's honey or a small sugar loaf if you would sweeten it."

"Set it down." Turning his back to her, he peeled off his braichs and his chausses, discarding them in a heap at his feet. Pulling on dry hose, he tied and gartered them while she waited patiently. Finally he straightened and gestured to the bench where they'd been. "Sit you down that we may talk, Catherine."

His flecked eyes studied her over the rim of his cup

as he drank deeply to warm himself. But even as she sank gracefully to the seat, he was at a loss to put into words what had to be said. "I have made my will," he announced with a suddenness that startled her.

"My lord, there is no need—"

"Jesu, but I would hear you call my name once before I die. I am Guy—Guy of Rivaux—canst you not say it?" he flared harshly. "Nay, I am sorry, Cat— I've no reason to complain of you since we wed. If you cannot care for me . . ." His voice trailed off and he looked away.

"My lord . . . Guy . . ." She groped to put into words that which she felt. "For good or ill, whether I chose you or not, you are my lord husband, and there's naught to change that now, and . . . and I would rather be wife than widow."

Turning back, he stared at her. Her eyes were like dark pools that reflected the firelight in the dreary tent, and they met his squarely. "Jesu," he breathed, feeling anew the intense longing. "Why could you not have been older . . . why could you not have been fifteen or older?"

"It doesn't make any difference."

"Aye, it does. But you will grow." He moved to stand over her, his reason reasserting itself. "What I wanted to say to you, Cat, is that I cannot leave you much if I should fall, regardless of which brother wins. There are no males heir to my lands, so they will go either to Curthose or to Henry anyway. But it doesn't really matter, for you are an heiress in your own right. I do not think Henry will fault you for this marriage, but if he does, you will have your father to stand for you still."

"Guy—"

"Nay, let me finish. What I am saying to you, Catherine, is that you can carry none of Rivaux with you, as you are not with child—and even if you were, 'twould make little difference to Henry, for he'd want to punish my heir for what I have done. And what money I have had is gone to buy Curthose's mercenaries, so there's not much left for you, but William will see you have my mother's jewels ere we leave in the morning.''

''Nay!''

''Mayhap they will add to your dowry—though I doubt Robert of Caen will care what you bring him once he sees you.''

''Nay—you'll not die! You'll not! I would not speak of this!''

''I hope I do not—nay, I mean to do my best to live, Cat, but I fight beside Belesme, and who is to say what may happen? He's not forgiven me for taking you, you know.'' A crooked smile twisted his mouth, and his eyes spiked green and gold. ''Nay, but I have lived longer than mine enemies ever thought possible. And 'tis one way to shed an unwanted husband, if you think on it.''

''You are not an unwanted husband!'' she blurted out, and then, realizing what she'd said, she reddened. ''Sweet Mary . . . that is to say . . . I'd not have you dead for what you could help no more than I—nay, I'd not.''

''My lord?'' William de Comminges lifted the tent flap and peered inside. ''Curthose calls his council yet again.''

''Again? God's bones, but what can be said that has not already been heard?'' Guy grumbled.

Not daring to look at Catherine, William stared at the woven reed mat that covered the packed-earth floor. ''Gilbert,'' he muttered succinctly. ''He does not want to fight in a lost cause.''

Catherine sat motionless for a long time after they left, her thoughts warring with her loyalties. All of her life, she'd considered King Henry the best of the Conqueror's sons, and deserving of Normandy as well as England, but now it was brought home to her that there would be good men sworn to die in Robert Curthose's cause also. And one of the dead could well be Guy of Rivaux.

13

Neither Catherine nor Hawise spoke much while they waited anxiously for news of how the battle went. Guy had been so restless in his sleep that Cat had slept very little also, and yet her anxiety was such that she was not tired. As the sun waxed higher in the sky, she forced herself to remember it had been but a couple of hours earlier when she'd helped Alan lace Guy's padded gambeson and fasten his mail coif at his neck. He'd been different then, preoccupied with the task that faced him, and he'd scarcely spoken to anyone. There had been a grimness, a determination, and yet a fatalism about him that had made him seem so much older than his nineteen years. She clasped her hands tightly in her lap and tried to pray. Sweet Mary, but to have seen him ride out in full battle dress, his face obscured by his polished helmet so all that she could identify was the scar that sliced down his cheek, and to know that he might well never ride back again.

Mary, Mother of God, watch over this son of Normandy and keep him safe. . . . Her lips formed the words silently, but her mind insisted in straying yet again to her memory. He'd seemed so tall, nearly as tall as Belesme, sitting astride his destrier with his long battle shield, its black hawk swooping across the red field, hung over his arm. And even now she could feel the coldness of the metal links in his mail as they'd pressed into her flesh

145

when he'd leaned to clasp her as she bade him Godspeed.
Holy Father in heaven, grant that he be spared. . . . She
tried to will herself to pray, but the possibilities of what
could happen to him were too terrible to share even with
God. Had she met Guy of Rivaux in another time and
under other circumstances, she had not a doubt in her
mind now that she could have loved him as much as she
loved Brian. Brian. With a start, she realized that she'd
not thought of him in days.

In the distance, there was the sound of horses, battle
horses pounding the earth hard. Cat looked up to see
Hawise make the sign of the Cross over her breast and
murmur her own swift, unintelligible prayer. "Please,
Father, I beg you that my husband lives," Cat whispered aloud as she grasped her skirts and ran outside.

Climbing to the small hill where the supply wagons
sat unhitched, she shielded her eyes against the sun
and tried to see. At first the glare was too great, but
as her eyes adjusted she could make out the green pen-
non of Belesme coming straight back through Curthose's camp. On the horizon behind, mounted knights
broke to pursue.

Belesme himself was in the lead, his green surcoat
unmistakable, and he was slashing his way through
any who dared stand in his way, ally and foe alike.
Horrified, she watched as a green-shirted man ran out,
begging not to be left to Henry's mercy, only to be cut
down with a swift swing of Belesme's sword. She stood
transfixed, disbelieving what she saw, until she realized the count was riding for her. Her first thought was
that he meant to kill her before he fled, but he lowered
his weapon and reined in. A tremor of fear shook her
and the hair on the back of her neck prickled in warning as he shouted at her.

"Catherine! You must flee—Curthose is taken!
Come on—there is no time!"

Even as he spoke, he nudged his horse closer to her
and reached down, his mailed and gloved hand grasping for her. She stood transfixed, paralyzed and numb,

until his words sank in. "Wait! What of my husband?" she cried. "What of Rivaux?"

"I saw him not—come on!" he urged her. "De Mortain is down, and Gilbert runs for his life." He was breathless, casting quick glances at those who pursued to catch the hapless ostlers and cut them down. "Come on!"

"Nay! I'd not go with you, my lord!" she defied as she backed away.

"Do not be a fool! 'Tis not safe to wait!"

He leaned further and tried to grab her arm. His mailed glove brushed her shoulder and caught in her gown. She felt the fabric tear even as she dropped to the ground and rolled beneath one of the supply wagons, and she heard him curse loudly. Praying to St. Catherine, she begged that he would not stop to come after her, and her prayers were answered. Mounted knights in the colors of Count Elias of Maine, one of Henry's allies, called to Belesme to surrender. Shouting defiance, he wheeled his horse so sharply that it reared, spurred the huge animal viciously, and broke for the open ground beyond the camp. As Catherine crouched behind heavy wooden wheels, the horsemen thundered by in determined pursuit. By now, footsoldiers of the English fyrd were running toward Curthose's camp eagerly, ready to divide the spoils of war, and the screams of panicked female camp followers mingled with the cries for mercy of Norman stragglers.

Catherine knew if she was caught out in the open, she risked being ravished by those who would take first and identify later, and she realized her only hope lay in reaching King Henry's more noble allies. Even as she hid herself, she was numbed by the quickness of the defeat and the dull fear that Guy had fallen made her heart like lead in her breast. How could it have happened so soon? It was not possible that the husband she'd helped arm scant hours earlier could be gone already. A sense of hopeless rage rose, supplanting the numbness. She wanted to flail her arms and shout that there was no justice when a Guy of Rivaux had to fight for the likes of Robert Curthose.

The screams of a woman drew her, and to her horror, she saw one of the camp whores pinned down, held by leather-jerkined men, her skirts hiked high to reveal thrashing white legs, while a common soldier grunted and thrusted, his buttocks bared above hastily dropped braichs. The raucous laughter echoed and died suddenly, and the soldier let out a cry of pain rather than release as a mail-clad knight leaned from his saddle to strike him with the flat of his sword.

"Pursue the enemy! There's time for that when we are done!"

Recognizing Maine's colors, she scrambled from beneath the wagon and ran pell-mell for the knight's horse. "I am Catherine of the Condes, sir, and I crave protection! Sweet Mary, I pray you aid me!"

Startled, the knight looked down from beneath his helm. His eyes narrowed above his nasal, taking in her torn gown and her panicked expression, Nodding, he reached down to her and pulled her up in front of his saddle. "God's blood, Demoiselle, but what are you doing here?" he demanded.

"I was Curthose's hostage. Please, sir, but I would find my godfather—I'd find King Henry—and I would know if Rivaux lives." The words tumbled out of her mouth breathlessly. "I'd know if my husband lives. I pray you, help me!"

Wordlessly he slid a mailed arm around her, balancing her on the huge battle charger, and turned back toward the battlefield. Bodies of the dead and dying, those cut down in flight, littered the open area below the town of Tinchebrai. Catherine closed her eyes and reeled from the sight of the maimed, sightless corpses and the sounds of the wounded.

"Ho, Evrard, you found one!" someone called out.

Cat opened her eyes to see a contingent of mounted men, their noble prisoners lined single file behind them, riding toward Curthose's camp. At the front rode the king himself, flanked by Count Elias and the bare-headed and bowed Robert Curthose. They reined in and waited.

"Cat! Sweet Jesu! 'Tis Cat!"

One of the squires behind the king swung down from his horse and started toward her on foot. The knight who'd rescued her eased her off the charger, leaning to set her down in the muddy road, and turned to the king. "I found her beneath the supply wagons, sire—she says she is Catherine of the Condes."

"Cat! God's eyes, but you are a welcome sight!" the boy before her cried out joyfully as he enveloped her in his arms.

The smell of metal and leather and sweat commingled, but Catherine didn't care. She clutched him gratefully and burst into tears. "Oh, Brian!" she sobbed into his woolen surcoat. "Is there any word of Guy of Rivaux? Does he live?"

The mounted prisoners watched from behind Henry's guard, dispossessed and disheartened. Guy stared bleakly to where Catherine stood locked in a boy's embrace, and felt heartsick and empty. Beside him, William de Mortain watched and grumbled, "God's blood, but there's a bastard who'll get what Henry takes of us," and Guy knew without asking that he spoke of Brian FitzHenry.

The king's prisoner, Guy lay on his pallet and contemplated his bleak future. De Mortain had already been sent to England, blinded and condemned to a life of imprisonment, Robert Curthose was in confinement at an undisclosed location, and Henry had begun the task of dealing with those who'd remained loyal to Duke Robert. In Guy's case, what passed for the king's justice had been swift and severe. In a brief audience, he'd accused Guy first of treason, then of treachery in supporting Curthose. Unrepentant, Guy had reminded him that he'd have been forsworn to have done anything else, and Henry had grudgingly ceded the point. Not that it mattered ultimately, for he'd stripped Guy of Rivaux of all his lands and revenues, and ordered him to repudiate his marriage to Catherine of the Condes.

Guy shivered and pulled his cloak closer as he remembered the king's anger over the marriage. He ought to have obeyed, he supposed, but Cat had been forced into one alliance not of her choosing, and he'd not let Henry force her to take Robert of Caen also. Instead, he'd maintained the legitimacy of the union despite the king's ranting that he'd break the marriage by papal decree. Cursing himself for a fool, Guy wondered why he'd done it—it was plain from watching that she loved Brian FitzHenry—it pained him still to remember her in the boy's arms. What difference could it make to him if she were given to Robert of Caen or to the Fitz-Henry? Either way, she'd not warm his bed. But for some unfathomable reason, he'd refused to yield to Henry in this, and now he faced an exile in England. Shifting his arm to cradle his head better, he corrected himself—not England, really, but Wales. He was being sent to redeem himself by subduing the wild Welsh, something the English had been trying to do for centuries, something that only the ruthless Robert of Belesme had done before his expulsion from the country.

There was no justice in what Henry would do with Curthose's vassals, Guy reflected bitterly. The faithless Gilbert of Nantes was allowed to keep his lands and his revenues for merely giving his oath to the king, and Belesme, who had fled when de Mortain's line crumbled, sat unmolested at home in Belesme—not that the count could rely on Henry's pardon, Guy knew. Nay, but once the rest of Normandy was pacified, Guy had no doubt that Henry would once again turn his attention to destroying Belesme with as much tenacity as he'd used against the count in England.

Beside him, William de Comminges lay wide-awake, staring at the tent ceiling. It was hard on a man his age to have to start over, but he'd sworn to the Lady Alys that he'd see to her son—and now it looked as though he'd have to follow the boy into Wales. His bones still ached from the blows he'd taken at Tinchebrai. Tinchebrai—a battle that had changed their fortunes all too swiftly.

"Lord Guy?"

One of the sentries posted outside stepped in to shake Guy awake, not realizing that he did not sleep. Guy rolled over and sat upright, hoping that he was not being summoned to another stormy session with King Henry. "Aye."

The soldier, his hand still closed over the precious silver mark she'd given him, glanced furtively at William before leaning closer to murmur, "You have a visitor, my lord."

"Jesu," Guy muttered. "There's not many as would still seek speech with me. Who is it?"

"The demoiselle—the Lady Catherine."

Guy sucked in his breath and shook his head. Behind him, William sat up also, and his squire, Alan, rolled to stare up at the sentry. Guy's heart raced at the thought of seeing her again, but he forced himself to remember her as he'd seen her last—in the comfort of Brian FitzHenry's arms. "Nay, 'twould serve no purpose."

"She begs but a few minutes . . ." The man hesitated, knowing he risked his king's displeasure by even allowing the visit.

"Nay." Guy was definite. "Tell her that King Henry forbids it."

"Aye, my lord." The sentry retreated, hoping she would not demand her coin back.

"I never thought to call you a fool, my lord," William snorted in disgust.

"William . . ." Guy's voice lowered in warning. " 'Tis not your place to discuss her."

Unmollified, the older man shook his head. "Nay, but you would cause her pain. She is your wedded lady, no matter what any dare say, and I'd not have you send her away."

"Jesu! What aid can I give her now? You forget she

has a father well able to hold for her, whilst I am naught but disinherited. Besides,'' he added glumly, ''she can seek help from the FitzHenry. I doubt not she already has.''

''My lord—''

''Nay, but I'd not speak of her,'' Guy cut him short.

Outside, Catherine stared at the sentry in disbelief. ''Did he say why he would not see me?'' she demanded. Tears welled in her eyes and threatened to spill over onto her cheeks. ''Did he say nothing of *why?*''

''He said that King Henry forbids it, Lady Catherine.''

''I . . . I see.'' She stood, nonplussed for a moment, and tried to reason his rejection in her mind. Unaware of the man staring at her, she groped for an answer and found none—unless her usefulness to him had ended, unless the king had made it plain that he'd not inherit from her, regardless of the marriage. Somehow, she'd thought he was different, that he cared beyond dynastic ambition, but he would have been a rare man if he had. The lowering thought that she had been used—by Curthose, by Henry, and by Guy—that she was but pawn to be moved for advantage, defeated her.

''Lady, are you unwell?''

She blinked back tears of humiliation and stared up at the soldier. Gathering her dignity about her like a cloak, she straightened, squaring her shoulders. She was, after all, Catherine of the Condes, daughter to Roger de Brione and Eleanor of Nantes, and nothing could change that—nothing, she told herself fiercely.

''Nay, I am cold only. And you may keep the money.''

❧ 14 ❧

March, 1111

Unable to sleep, Eleanor of Nantes stared pensively out the narrow slitted window into the garden below. The air was crisp and the hoarfrost covered the dormant beds with silver that glistened in the faint dawn light. The pungent odor of wood burning in the main hearth and the numerous braziers throughout the keep mingled with the smell of bread already in the ovens. After a week of entertaining Henry and his royal retinue, even the Condes found its resources strained.

But it was not so much the royal visit that troubled her, rather the fact that Henry had brought Brian with him. There was no question in her mind after seeing the young man in Cat's company that he was more attracted to the girl than ever. And Brian FitzHenry was well on his way to equaling his father in the number of bastards he left behind, if even half the stories could be believed. He had such an easy charm with women that Eleanor worried about her eldest daughter, for Cat was becoming more restless as months and years passed with her situation still unresolved. The girl ought to be wed, Eleanor mused, and then caught herself—aye, there was the problem.

Nearly five years had passed since Cat had come home after Tinchebrai, and in those five years neither Henry nor Roger had been able to break the girl's marriage to Guy of Rivaux despite the pressure they'd

brought to bear on the old archbishop before he'd died.
Nay, he'd told the both of them, there was no cause—
it could not be claimed that the couple was related
within the bounds of consanguinity, nor could it be
claimed the marriage had not been consummated. In
a deposition sent to Rome, the old man had maintained stoutly that ''if ever there was evidence of con-
jugal union, it is so in this case, for the girl bled
heavily, owing to her small stature and her youth.''
Finally, Henry had given in gracelessly, finding the
heiress of Gloucester for his son Robert instead. And
Cat, her poor Cat, had been left at the Condes, a wife
without a husband.

"Come back to bed before you chill yourself, Lea,"
Roger murmured behind her.

With a sigh, Eleanor closed the tall shutters and
padded barefoot over to stare down at her husband.
His blond hair, now lightened with strands of silver,
was rumpled from sleep, but his blue eyes were awake
and studying her. A thrill as intense as any she'd experienced in her youth traveled down her spine, sending a shiver of excitement through her when he patted
the soft mattress beside him. After nearly nineteen
years of lying with him, of loving him body and soul,
she still found herself alive with anticipation. For answer, she let the loose robe fall away from her shoulders and slip to the floor.

He reached up, catching her hands and pulling her
down. "Jesu, Lea, but you are nigh frozen," he chided
as he warmed her with his body. "What ails you that
you must needs sit and worry before 'tis even light?"
Even as he spoke, his fingers stroked her hair, smoothing it out on the pillow.

He was warm, he was safe, and he was going to
love her the way she liked it, slowly savoring the pleasure of union between them, building intensity until
neither could stand the fire that would consume them.
His palm brushed her breast lovingly, nearly blotting
out all else from her senses.

"Sweet Mary," she whispered, turning against him, "but I would that Cat could know even one-tenth of what is between us."

His hand stilled as he craned his neck to look at her. "All right," he sighed, " 'tis best to speak of her now, since she plagues your thoughts. What is it this time, Lea?"

"She grows restless, Roger, and I fear for her. Have you not noted how Brian looks on her? He knows what ails Cat, and he would satisfy his lust." Her hand crept to push back an unruly lock from his forehead, and her eyes met his. "He would make her his leman."

"Nay, he would not—they are but as brother and sister, Lea."

"As we were?" she reminded him.

"That was different—I knew I could wed with you."

"Aye, but if it had not been possible, would you have lain with me anyway?"

"Nay, I'd not have let you bear my bastards."

"Ah, but in that, Brian is different from you—can you not see it, Roger? How many bastards has he sired already?" Even as she watched him, she could see him mentally reviewing Brian's many conquests. "Aye," she pressed her advantage, "and Cat is truly beautiful. As much as it shames me to think it, I believe she would know what she does not have—can you not see where that will lead her?"

"Cat is chaste," he muttered, wondering where Eleanor meant to lead him.

"For now," she agreed readily. "For now. But she is flesh-and-blood woman—she is a child no more, Roger—she cannot but wish to be loved by a man."

He pulled away to prop his head with his hand and watch her. "Aye," he admitted finally. "But there is no answer. The Church—"

"But there is! Roger, she is wed already, is she not? Has not Holy Church said her marriage is binding—that she belongs to Guy of Rivaux? Yet she is here and he is in another land. It makes no sense, Roger!"

"Nay, but he has nothing now, Lea. Would you give your daughter to one who is disinherited? Nay," he answered his own question. "Have you forgotten that he wed her without our consent and knowing she was all but betrothed to another?" His ardor cooled, he threw back the covers and sat up. "I'd not speak of him," he muttered.

Eleanor clasped his shoulder determinedly and shook her head. "Roger, I know you think to put me off with your anger in this, but you will not do it this time. I cannot sleep for worry over her, and I'll not let you turn me aside. Listen to me," she reasoned with him, "and think on it—Guy of Rivaux is of higher birth than the man you would have given Cat to, and if he has lost all, 'tis through no fault of his own. He did but what you yourself would have done—he fought for Curthose because he was Normandy's sworn vassal and owed no other liege."

"He has no lands!"

"Because Henry took them!"

"Jesu!"

"Aye, and from what Cat said to me when she first came home, he had no choice in the marriage, either—had he not taken her, Curthose would have given her to another. If anything, he risked all he had in taking her, Roger. Why must he pay for that with his lands? Now he has neither Rivaux nor Cat—and 'tis not right!"

"You want her to live as wife to Rivaux?" he asked incredulously.

"Better that than dishonored. Aye, there's little to dislike in the boy—he is young and handsome and honorable, and—"

"And you've not seen him in five years," he interrupted. "If he had wanted her, he'd have taken her with him."

"You cannot know that! He faced an angry king, Roger, and we both know Henry has hardened in these last years—and we both know he knew we wished to give her to Robert of Caen! Then you and Henry sought to break the marriage! You do not know—mayhap 'twas all Rivaux could do to keep his life in the face of the king's anger.''

Grudgingly he turned back toward her, and she pressed her argument further with the skill of a counselor in royal court. ''Think on it—Rivaux was but a boy called to a man's responsibilities, and he discharged those responsibilities with honor—when Gilbert laid down his arms and Belesme ran, 'twas Rivaux that stayed and fought until Curthose was taken.''

''Why have you not spoken of this before, Lea? God's teeth, but it has been five years and you've said little of this—why does it weigh so heavily on you now?''

''Because I can see my daughter yielding to Brian's lust, and the result cannot be happy for any of us. 'Tis time she was given to her own husband.''

Roger could see that she felt very deeply about the matter, but he was loath to think of parting with his firstborn, and particularly not to a man he scarce knew. To him, Catherine was the most precious of his children, his heiress, the culmination of his love for Eleanor. ''He has no lands now,'' he repeated defensively.

''Then enfief him yourself—give him land for Catherine's dowry,'' she argued reasonably. ''Make him your vassal, if need be, for we are rich in land and likely to gain more. Sweet Mary, but Cat will have Nantes and Harlowe and this also one day, anyway.''

''You do not even know if he wants her.''

''Have you not seen how men look on her?'' Eleanor countered. ''Nay, but he'd be a blind fool not to want Catherine of the Condes.''

Lying back down beneath the warmth of the covers, he stared upward, his expression distant and preoccupied. There was so much to be considered beyond what she asked. His hand found her arm and stroked it absently as he pondered the problem. If Guy of Rivaux had loved Cat as he himself loved Eleanor, he could have accepted the marriage easier, but there'd not even been a word between them in nearly five years. Who could know what had happened to him in those years? Mayhap he had a leman, or several even, and mayhap he was content to leave Catherine where she was. And certainly Henry would not want him back. Finally, he mused aloud, "I doubt it could be done, Lea, even if I willed it. It was one thing for Henry to wed her to his own son, for he would have been providing for one of his bastards, but 'tis not likely that he'll want to see Cat bear a child not of his blood who can hold Harlowe, Nantes, and the Condes. He would fear too much power coming to one person."

"He allows you to do it."

"Aye, but I've not inherited all of it yet. Think on what he did to de Mortain—he said one earldom was enough and he pushed him into rebellion. Now de Mortain lies blinded and castrated somewhere in one of Henry's keeps and no doubt prays to die."

"But Henry loves you, Roger."

"Aye, but he is no fool, Lea—he may fear my heirs."

"But would you accept Rivaux for Cat if Henry could be brought to allow it?" she persisted.

"If I do not, you'll give me no peace." Reluctantly he nodded and sighed. "Aye, I suppose I would have to, wouldn't I? But I doubt 'twill happen." His brilliant blue eyes met hers and warmed anew. "Now that you have won in this, I can think of things I would rather do." Turning to envelop her in his arms, he nuzzled her hair, murmuring softly, "Ah, Lea, but you've not changed in all the years I have known you— thou art soft and small, but you have a soul of fire and a will of iron." Sliding a hand down over her bare back to trace the outline of her hip, he murmured, his breath warm and intimate above her ear, "If I knew

not you'd carried ten babes, I'd not believe it, for you
are as slender as a young girl.''

Her pulse quickened at his touch and she clung to
him, moving closer to mold her body to his, feeling
his body come alive with a desire to match her own.
"This time," she whispered into his shoulder, "I'd
not have you spill your seed—I'd bear a son for you
still.''

"Nay."

"But the Church teaches 'tis not right."

"I'd not risk losing you—and it grows harder for
you with each year." To stifle her protest, he bent his
head to possess her mouth, knowing he could make
her forget for a few moments at least that she'd given
him no son.

"Sire, I would speak with you, if 'twould not dis-
please Your Grace.''

The king looked up from scanning writs prepared
for his seal, to find Eleanor of Nantes in the doorway
of the bedchamber. Her hands were laden with fresh
linens for his chamber, carried before her like a shield.
Involuntarily his mind harked back nearly twenty-six
years to when he'd first seen her, a young girl of twelve
standing in the field at Nantes. He'd wanted her then
for wife, and the wanting had not abated in the intervening year. Even as he watched, she laid aside the
folded cloths and approached to kneel at his feet. Her
braids, interwoven with gold threads and fastened with
embroidered silk, brushed against the hem of his long
robe, and he could remember how her hair had once
looked, rich and dark, cascading like a heavy silken
curtain down her back. Despite four live girls and six
dead babes, she was beautiful still, so much so that
she could yet take his breath away.

"Nay, do not kneel to me, Eleanor." He spoke
softly.

"Sire, I would crave your aid."

He rose, the fur border of his long gown touching

the floor beside her braids, and leaned to raise her. "Nay, but between us there is no need for such cere- mony," he told her as his hands clasped hers. "And there is naught that you can ask that I would not will- ingly give to you." When she did not proceed imme- diately to explain what she wanted, he turned to his chamber servants, ordering, "Leave us."

Her eyes widened and stories came to mind of the many women who'd betrayed husbands to lie with him in exchange for royal favor. Her concern must have been evident when he turned back to her, for he shook his head. "Nay, I am not one to place no value on a loyal vassal, Eleanor. But if it worries you what any will think, we may walk apart below, where all may see but not hear us."

"I'd not have Roger know I am here unless you grant what I ask," she admitted quickly.

His eyebrow lifted, betraying curiosity, and his brown eyes were suddenly intent. "It must be a matter of some import, then."

"Aye." She hesitated, uncertain how best to ap- proach him, knowing that her daughter's future might well lie in her words.

She was close, so close that the smell of the per- fumed oil he'd brought her as a gift wafted upward, intoxicating his senses. Of all the women he'd known, she was the only one he'd wanted desperately and yet had never lain with. And she stood before him a sup- plicant now. For the briefest moment he considered the risks, and once again his head ruled his heart. She was Roger de Brione's wife—and she belonged to her husband heart and soul and body. Reluctantly he turned away to master his emotions.

"You must not fear to ask, Eleanor," he spoke fi- nally. "For twenty-six years your life has been en- twined with mine in one way or another, and I'd not like to think you unable to speak your thoughts to me."

"I am come to you, Your Grace, to seek justice for a man."

Without looking back at her, he straightened the rolled writs on a low table. "You would accuse me of an injustice then?"

"Nay, but I think he has been punished long enough."

Turning around, he met her steady gaze and sucked in his breath. "Who is the man?" he demanded.

"Guy of Rivaux."

His eyes narrowed suspiciously. She was the last person he would have expected to come to Rivaux's aid in anything, but she stood before him with a determined face and waited. "Why do you concern yourself for him? He is naught to you."

"He is my daughter's husband."

"He wed her without your consent or mine."

"Aye."

"Then why do you care what happens to him?"

Eleanor clasped her hands together and pressed them into the folds of her skirt to gain courage. "Because Holy Church says Catherine is his wife, and naught we have done can change that, Your Grace. While he yet lives, she cannot be given to another, and she would have a man, I think."

Henry thought of Catherine de Brione for a moment, bringing her image to his mind and seeing her as he'd once seen Eleanor. They were much alike in looks, and none could dispute that the girl had grown into a beauty to rival her mother. Only last evening he'd watched her tease and laugh with his son and had seen how Brian touched her when they'd danced to the pipers' music, brushing close to murmur something that had made her blush. Somehow, he doubted that Cat of the Condes would welcome her husband back. He stroked his brown beard as he considered the problem. "Have you said aught of this to the girl?" he asked after a time.

"It would not serve."

" 'Tis a pity that she cannot come to my son, for I think them well-suited," he mused slowly. "I should

have bribed Bonne Ame to say she was never bedded.''

"Nay, I would have for her a constant husband.''

As his own lack of fidelity to his queen was well-
noted by the number of bastards he'd gotten since his
marriage, he chose to ignore her last words, turning
instead to the matter of Guy of Rivaux. "I can scarce
afford to recall him to Normandy, Eleanor. Of all those
who fight for me in Wales, he has been the most suc-
cessful. Aye, but the marches are safer now than
they've been since my father first took England.'' He
moved to stare out the tall window into the courtyard
below, watching for a time the ostlers leading horses
out to be exercised in the fields beyond the walls.
"Why can you not be as other women?'' he complained with a sigh, his eyes still on the bustle beneath
them. "Most will trade their bodies willingly for the
favor of a royal fief for their husbands or a jewel for
themselves. But you come to me offering nothing and
ask for something I would not give. Have you not
thought that I have enjoyed the revenues of Rivaux
these past years? If I allow him to come back, he is
like to sue for the return of his lands.''

"Sire, he did no wrong—he did but fight for his
sworn liege. Let him swear his loyalty to you and come
home, I pray you. And if you will not return the honor
of Rivaux to him, then Roger will enfief him with
something. Or you can confirm him as Gilbert's heir,
if it pleases Your Grace, and keep what you have taken
from him. My father grows old and cannot live forever.''

"You bring Nantes to your husband,'' he reminded
her. Turning suddenly to look at her, he considered
what she asked. "Have you spoken to Roger of this?''

"Aye.''

"And?''

"He said that you would not do it,'' she admitted.
"But I cannot accept that you would punish a man who
fought honorably, refusing to break his oath to his duke

at the risk of his life. If you will not grant me this now, Your Grace, I pray you will think on it.''

"Eleanor, you scarce know Rivaux," Henry chided gently. "What care you whether he is here or there?"

"I fear for Cat," she answered simply. "I would not have her dishonored by Brian or anyone else. I have watched them together and can see that he would have her."

"I can send Brian back to England, if 'twill please you."

"Nay." She shook her head. " 'Twould not end the problem for my daughter. Cat nears eighteen, Sire—would you deny her the love and comfort of her own lord because they once were forced to wed? As 'tis, she is neither wife nor maid whilst her sisters wed. And do not suggest the convent, I pray you, for she has not the temperament to be content in such a place, and I would not send her away."

"Aye, and she is heiress to much." Already Henry's mind worked, turning over the fact that neither Eleanor nor her mother had borne any living sons. If Catherine of the Condes gave Rivaux none, Henry could control the disposal of Rivaux, Nantes, Harlowe, and the Condes. At worst, he would have a say in the marriage of any daughters, and at best, he would see some of the lands revert to royal authority. Rivaux's revenues had declined steadily in the young count's absence, making it not nearly so profitable as it had been at first. Exhaling heavily, he nodded. "I will think on it," he promised her, knowing that he would sign the writ on the morrow. If he could not give Catherine of the Condes to his own son, then he'd see to it that he at least gained the loyalty of young Rivaux. "And if you would not have Roger know of this, you'd best go," he added regretfully.

After she left, he stared unseeing at the pile of writs on the table. No matter what she'd asked of him, he knew in his heart that he would have granted it. Aye, but if fate had given him Eleanor of Nantes, he was certain he'd have had no need for any other. And there was a time when he could have gotten her for wife, a time when he'd mistakenly let his reason overrule his heart's desire. But that was long ago, and he'd gambled right in the matter, he told himself, for he'd gained England's crown with his quick thinking and the loyalty of the English people with his marriage to his cold Saxon princess.

Resolutely he reached to unroll a parchment and forced himself to read the grant of a small fief to the family of Monthermer. When his clerks returned, he'd dictate the return of Rivaux to its count.

❧ 15 ❧

"Art Guy of Rivaux?"

Guy, still astride the big black horse he favored for traveling, looked down at King Henry's messenger and nodded, leaning to receive the parchment case the fellow held up to him. God's bones, but it was mere chance that he'd been found, for in the past week he'd come from Chester all the way to Chepstow, stopping in between at Belesme's old keep in Shrewsbury and at Ludlow to rally the marches against another Welsh rising. Laying his metal-scaled gloves across his saddle in front of him, he wrenched off his helmet and tossed it to Alan. Tired unto death nearly, he tapped the parchment from the cylindrical case and unrolled it, scanning it quickly while those around him fell silent at the sight of the king's seal affixed to the end.

William de Comminges watched anxiously as Guy read the writ, and saw his jaw tighten ominously. Nay, but there could not be ill news—not when Guy had been in his saddle day and night for months on Henry's behalf. Finally, when Guy muttered an oath that bordered on blasphemy under his breath, William could stand it no longer.

"By all saints, my lord!" he exploded. "There's none to serve him better than you have done!"

Guy looked up and shook his head. "Nay, he summons me home for reward—I am to go to the Condes for Catherine and then to mine own lands.''

''And you are displeased?'' William asked incredulously, his own face breaking into a broad smile at the news. ''God's eyes, but I'd not thought to ever see Rivaux again, my lord.''

''Aye,'' Guy agreed grimly, ''but I'll warrant there's more to tell than is written here, for 'tis not like him to give anything for nothing.''

''Mayhap 'tis his conscience,'' Alan ventured.

''After five years?'' Guy's eyebrow rose skeptically and he favored his squire with an ironic smile. ''Nay, 'tis more like that he's bled all there is from my people and would give me back what he cannot use,'' he decided cynically.

Even as well as he knew his master, William was nonetheless surprised by his lack of enthusiasm for Henry's sudden generous gesture. Shaking his grizzled head, he could make no sense of it. But then, the Guy he'd known in Normandy had changed, becoming harder and harsher after the loss of his lands and his child wife, and that troubled William more than he dared to admit even to himself. With a warning look to Alan, he reached to lay a mailed glove on his count. ''Aye, but Rivaux can be rebuilt even if 'tis gutted, my lord, and the king recognizes your marriage to the little maid.''

''Aye.'' For a moment, Guy stared absently, seeing again Catherine as last he'd seen her, clasped tightly in Brian FitzHenry's arms, her head pressed against the other man's bloody surcoat. His eyes bleak, he collected himself finally and sighed. ''Aye, I am bidden to take my unwilling bride.''

''When do we depart England?''

''He commands my presence in Rouen by Whitsunday, that I may take my oath of fealty there and be enfiefed anew with Rivaux.''

Whitsunday. The fiftieth day past Easter. William calculated the date in his head and nodded. God willing, they would be home at Rivaux with a summer for rebuilding whatever was needed, and hopefully they would have time to see that at least part of the crops were paid before winter came.

"But I would not leave here ere the Welsh come to terms," Guy continued, musing aloud. "There are almost times when it could be wished that Belesme yet held Shrewsbury, for his very reputation kept the Welsh peaceful."

"Aye," William agreed dryly, "and he robbed and ravished both sides at will. Would you have that again?"

"Nay, I would not," Guy admitted, "but I'd know peace ere I go."

One of Chepstow's ostlers claimed his attention with an insistent tug of the reins. Guy rerolled the writ, taking care not to tear off Henry's seal, and slid it back into its case before handing it down to Alan. "Keep this that I may answer it." Even as he leaned to dismount, he became aware of how very tired he was. His joints were stiff from days spent in his saddle, and his muscles ached with fatigue. He needed a bath, he needed food, and he needed a bed. And mayhap he needed a woman to blot out the memory of Catherine de Brione in Brian FitzHenry's arms.

"He's in Satan's temper," Arnulf complained to William as he emerged from the chamber allotted to Guy. Word had spread quickly through the keep that Henry was restoring Rivaux's lands, and the result had been obvious when the castle's tenant gave Guy a bed rather than a pallet in the main hall. "You'd think him displeased to regain his lands," he muttered.

"I'd think him overtired," William retorted. Grasping the elbow of the wench he'd found, he thrust her before him through the door. "There were not many to be had, my lord, but this one is clean enough."

Guy turned around to see her, a young girl of perhaps fifteen or sixteen, still slender, with dark hair and dark eyes. She eyed him openly, obviously pleased with what she saw, and her mouth curved into a smile that

revealed white, even teeth. For a moment his breath
caught in his chest as he remembered Catherine. He
moved forward to stare hard into the girl's upturned
face and then reached to lift the dark hair that fell over
her shoulders. Unlike Catherine's, it was coarse and
heavy as he let it slide through his fingers, and it
smelled of strong soap rather than roses. And a closer
look revealed her to be older than he'd first thought.

As if she knew his mind, she shook her head.
"Nay—I belonged to my lord of Hereford's son as
leman until he took Lady Bertrille to wive, but since,
I've lain with the others." Her dark eyes solemn now,
she reached to loosen the gold cord that girded her
waist and let it fall at his feet. Unlike the whores he'd
known, she moved with fluid grace, lifting her arms to
remove her gown and letting it slide down to join the
girdle. She wore no undergown, and her flesh gleamed
white and pink against the flickering fire in the brazier.

He stood transfixed, his mouth suddenly dry with
desire, his body alive despite its earlier fatigue. "I
would you left us," he ordered William before he bent
his head to possess her lips. Behind him, he heard the
door close, and then the warmth of the girl's response
blotted all else from his mind. He would puzzle over
King Henry's summons and Catherine and Rivaux on
the morrow, but for now he would seek ease, satisfy-
ing the hunger of his body.

It was a quick coupling, lusty and intense, one that
left him satiated and sleepy. His passion spent, he
rolled off the willing girl and lay quietly, staring upward in the darkness while he caught his breath. Beside him, she gasped for air.

"How are you called?" he asked finally.

"Giselle."

"God's bones, but you are a greedy wench, Giselle—I vow you've scratched my back till 'tis raw. I
wonder that Hereford's son kept his skin."

"He said I was a cat," she admitted with a giggle

while her hand crept to rouse him again. To her surprise, he pushed her away and sat up.

"Nay, 'tis enough."

His voice had grown harsh and she wondered what she'd done to anger him, for none other had reacted so. "You are displeased with me?" she asked, betraying her hurt.

"Nay." He felt nothing now except an eagerness to be rid of her. To hide his disgust with himself and her, he slapped her rounded rump and pushed her to the side of the bed. " 'Tis sleep I would have, for I ride out on the morrow. Seek me out in the morning and I will see you are well-paid for this night's work."

"Your man paid me already." She rose quickly and groped for her clothes, pulling the gown on and tying the girdle about her waist. "My thanks, my lord," she murmured as she turned toward the door.

He lay back, still and silent within the curtained bed, his thoughts faraway on another Cat. For nearly five years he'd fought to put her from his mind, and now 'twould seem that even Chepstow's castle whore conspired to bring her back. Damn King Henry! Why had he not kept his vow to break the marriage? Why had he waited so many years, ignoring the matter, and now decided to send Catherine to Rivaux? Guy closed his eyes, willing his thoughts away from her, but she would not leave him. The image of her in Brian FitzHenry's arms was still there, as fresh and hurtful now as then. He didn't even want to see her again.

The sound of William's pallet scraping across the floor as it was dragged into the room drew Guy from his reverie. "Nay," he called out as he pushed himself up in the bed. "You are as tired as I am—I'd have you share the mattress. Your bones are more than twice the age of mine, after all, and I'd not see you too stiff to sit your saddle."

"My bones are as good as yours, my lord," William responded gruffly. Bending to reroll the pallet, he pushed it against the wall. "I thought you'd keep the wench most of the night," he added. "Aye, I paid her to stay."

"I sent her away."

"Jesu, but the monks had you overlong, I fear."

"I was weary—and once was enough."

"Aye," William conceded, "I heard her thrashing about and I'll warrant that full half of the keep did also." The ropes creaked as he sat on the edge of the bed to unwrap his chausses. " 'Twill be good to get back to Rivaux," he sighed.

"So we can cease fighting the wild Welsh to fight mine neighbors?"

"Nay—Henry rules Normandy with a firmer hand than Curthose did."

"And leaves Church offices unfilled whilst he weds his bastards to his minor wards—aye, he is stronger, but at what cost? He let Belesme escape at Tinchebrai, and now he's as powerless as Curthose to stop Belesme's raids in Normandy."

"He drove him out of Normandy," William reminded him as he eased his body into the depths of the feather mattress. "Now 'tis only France that succors Belesme. And the day will come when he raids too far and is caught." Turning his back to Guy, he lay on his side and contemplated the spitting fire in the brazier grate. "I worry more about how we are received by Roger de Brione than about Henry or Belesme," he admitted as he stifled a yawn. "God's blood, but I am tired, my lord."

"I'd not go there save for the king's command."

William was silent for a time, and Guy began to think he'd slipped into sleep, but then the older man observed insightfully, "Nay, Catherine of the Condes is your lawful wife, and you cannot take another. If you would get heirs, 'twill have to be on her. And I'd not think the task unpleasant, for she is the comeliest little maid I have ever seen."

"I would not speak of her."

"But you would think of her."

"I think of her as I saw her last, William, and 'tis not a pleasant thought. Aye—'tis strange King Henry gives her back to me now, is it not? Mayhap he seeks to cover her dishonor with a husband," he mused aloud, finally putting into words his nagging suspicion.

"I think he gives her to you because Holy Church says he cannot give her to anyone else," William declared flatly. "And I did not get in bed to speak all night when I must ride all day. God rest you now, my lord."

"And you also."

Guy turned away. His body felt heavy and his mind was weary beyond words. His problems would still be there on the morrow, he told himself, but then mayhap he'd be better able to face them. The room was chilly despite the fire, but the covers lay thick and warm over him. Slowly, ever so slowly, he let his mind wander, and as he drifted off toward sleep, Catherine of the Condes was bending over him, her rose-washed hair enveloping him.

It was some time before William slept. Long after Guy's breathing evened out, the old man lay beside him listening and remembering the time when he'd hidden Lady Alys' son under his cloak and ridden two days with the hungry, sodden babe to the safety of her father's keep. It had taken the power of her family to save the child from the old Count of Rivaux's rage, but the boy had proven himself worthy, and William had no regrets. Aye, and when Count Eudo had grudgingly ordered the boy brought out of the monastery to thwart Curthose, none had thought he could be made into a warrior—none but William. Aye, William remembered with pride, it had been a privilege to train one with such inborn skill. And now he only hoped that he would live long enough to see Guy's own son come into this world, for the blood on both sides ought to make one of the best fighting men ever born.

❧ 16 ❧

The warm May breeze blew in across the wall where
Cat walked to cool her temper and sort out the problems that plagued her. Belowstairs, she could hear
Brian FitzHenry calling to her, his voice rising in anger. Well, she'd not go back, she muttered to herself,
for he had not the right to press her as he did. "Lie
with me—lie with me now," he'd begged as his hands
sought to unlace the sides of her gown. Well, she was
no leman to be taken and left—nay, she was Catherine
of the Condes, and she demanded more than a quick
tumble in some dark and dank storehouse. Her face
still burned with the humiliation of what he'd expected. Aye, she'd gone willingly enough with him,
she admitted, but she had not thought he meant to lay
her like a common wench. "You've had a man before," he'd whispered hotly, his breath rushing in her
ear, his fingers teasing her breasts through her gown.
Even now she recalled the glitter of passion in his eyes,
and a shudder of disgust made her shoulders shiver.

Turning to look out over the peaceful fields, their
green rows lying in neat patches below the wattle-and-
daub houses built in the shadow of the fortress, Cat
breathed deeply of the clean air to rid herself of the
moldy grain smell of the storehouse. Slowly her rage
abated to mere anger, anger that Brian had dared attempt such a thing, and then to reason. Aye, the fault

172

was not entirely his, she remembered guiltily, for had she not gone with him? And had she not laughed and teased with him, happy to have diversion again from her sister's wedding, eager to show Aislinn and the others that she was desirable, that she held some power over men? Aye, and what power it was, for she'd gotten naught but Rivaux's coldness and Brian's furtive offer of passion despite her much-admired beauty. Let Aislinn and Pippa and Bella go forth from the Condes with husbands, contentedly facing lives in their own keeps, looking forward to bearing their husbands' heirs. Cat would go on as always, daughter rather than mistress of her house, punished for the childish pride that had demanded proof of her virginity in the face of Sybilla's censure.

A horn sounded beyond the fields and she wondered briefly who had obtained her father's permission to hunt. And then she was distracted by footsteps on the stairs behind her. Thinking that sentries came to watch, she turned back to face Brian. His face was sober now, his brown eyes serious in his rounded face, and for once she could see the resemblance to his royal father.

"Art unwelcome here!" she snapped.

"Cat—"

"Did you think to ravish me in my father's keep?" Her rich overgown billowed out from her underchainse as she paced angrily before him. "Aye, and what if I'd conceived of you? Would you ride out and leave me to my shame? God's bones, but I'd expected more of you! You grew to manhood here—you lived in this keep and ate at my father's table these many years past, Brian! And yet you would tumble me as you did Agnes and Tyra, would you not?"

Her wind-tangled hair blew across her flushed face and her eyes flashed indignantly, reminding him anew that she was the most beautiful creature he'd ever been privileged to see. He stood passively and waited for her to spend her anger. When she paused to catch her breath, he dared to meet her eyes.

"I did not think, else I'd not done it," he admitted openly. "But before you would cast me into the pits of hell for wanting you, I'd plead my defense."

"Nay—"

"You think I had no reason? Aye, I have lived here since I was but a small boy, Cat, and there's none I admire and love so much as I love your father, but . . ." He could see her mouth open to interrupt him, and he shook his head. "Nay—let me say my piece ere you rail at me again. I have seen you grow from child to woman here, and I have seen the way you look at me also. I am but a man, Cat, and I'd have you—aye, I admit I have strong appetites—I am my father's son in blood if not in birth." He paused, scanning her face for some sign that she understood, and found none. Sighing heavily, he looked away. "What I would say to you, Catherine, is that 'tis not right to tempt where you would not. When I took you to the empty granary, I thought 'twas for what we both wanted. You let me kiss you and—"

"And you thought I would give my honor for a kiss," she finished for him, her voice low. "Sweet Mary, but I'd not meant . . . I'd not thought . . . You knew I was not free to wed." Mortified, she moved to touch his sleeve. "Brian, even if I wanted to lie with you, I could not. I have loved you these six years and more, but I am my parents' daughter and I'd not shame them."

"*Do* you love me, Cat?"

Uncertain now of the answer, Catherine stared into the plain tunic that covered his blocky shoulders. "Do *you* love me?" she countered. "Or would you be as your father and take me for leman, knowing what pain that would cause *my* mother and father?" Even as she watched, she could see him flush guiltily, and she knew the truth.

"There's none to compare with you for beauty,

Cat,'' he answered slowly, admitting, ''Aye—I'd take you for leman if I dared.''

''I am of better birth than that, Brian. I am heiress to this and Nantes and Harlowe, and there was a time when I thought to bring them all to you.''

''But you wed Rivaux and lay with him in the marriage bed,'' he reminded her. ''I would have wedded with you but for that.''

''Nay, you would not—you would not have defied your father's wishes,'' she accused. ''I know now I was a fool to have expected that.'' Her voice bitter, she turned away to stare unseeing into the distance. The horn sounded again, nearer this time, as a long column of mounted men came over the horizon. The sun caught the row of polished helms and glanced off them as from a line of mirrors. Cat squinted against the brightness, her attention caught by the red banner that waved stiffly in the breeze above them, disbelieving what she saw. As recognition dawned, her mind spun in shock, forcing her to grip the stone ledge for balance.

Brian watched the blood drain from her face and her eyes widen in horror. ''God's teeth, Cat, what ails you?'' he demanded. Their quarrel forgotten, he reached to steady her on the high wall and followed her line of vision. ''Are you all right?''

Still staring, she appeared not to hear him. ''Holy Mary!'' she breathed, her eyes on the knight at the head of the approaching column. '' 'Tis Rivaux!''

''Jesu! Are you certain?'' He tried to make out the figure on the red banner, straining his eyes until he saw the black hawk, its wings spread for the kill. ''Nay, it cannot be.''

''Aye, but it is,'' she muttered grimly. As she pushed away from the wall, her manner changed abruptly. Her face set, she started for the stairs purposefully. ''I know not why he is here,'' she muttered under her breath, ''but I'd have Papa send him away.

God's blood, but he cannot just ride in with no word after these many years."

Eleanor faced her angry daughter across her solar and knew the task of placating Cat would not be an easy one. For once, Roger leaned back, his shoulders braced against the stone wall, his blue eyes watching as though he would say: I would watch how 'tis you mean to contend with what you have wrought.

"You *knew* he was coming?" Catherine demanded incredulously. "And you did not tell me?" She paced furiously, her color heightened ominously. "Nay, I'll not see him!"

"Lower your voice else everyone hear you, Cat," her mother ordered calmly. "And, aye, 'twas I who asked that he be pardoned."

"But why, Maman—*why?*"

"Think you I have not eyes?" Eleanor responded, her voice still quiet. "Think you I do not love you too much to see your disgrace?"

"I know not what you mean!"

"I have seen what passes between you and Brian, Cat, and it cannot be."

"Because of Rivaux!"

"Aye, because of Rivaux," Eleanor agreed gently. "Holy Church rules you are his, and 'tis time you went to your husband."

Catherine stared and the color drained from her face. "You . . . you would send me *away?*" she asked as her mother's meaning sank in. "Nay, I'd not go." Turning to her father, she held out her hands in appeal. "Papa . . . Papa, tell her you'll not let me go."

He straightened his tall frame and met his daughter's eyes soberly now. She was willful and she was spoiled, but he loved her beyond all save Eleanor, and it was going to pain him deeply to part with her. "Cat," he began, groping for the words to explain, "you are a woman grown now—"

Sensing he meant to agree with her mother, Catherine whirled on Eleanor. " 'Tis your doing, is it not?" Tears welled and spilled from her dark eyes. "And how, pray, did you achieve this?" she asked spitefully. "How did you persuade the king to pardon him? You may speak of how I look at Brian, my lady mother, but it cannot be any worse than the way King Henry looks on you! Think you I have not seen that also?"

"Cat!"

"I care not, Papa—'tis true!"

"Catherine, you will beg your mother's pardon for the insolence," Roger told her coldly. "You know full well that 'twas no such thing." He moved forward to clasp her by the shoulders, forcing her to look at him. "I've not beaten you once in the nearly eighteen years you've lived, but afore God, if you do not ask her pardon now, I will."

"Roger, leave her be—she is but angry with me," Eleanor cut in.

"Nay."

Cat knew she'd gone too far even for an indulgent father, and she also knew her accusations were untrue. Swallowing hard, she looked at the floor and nodded. "Your pardon, Maman," she managed low. " 'Tis my accursed temper again. But I would not leave you and Papa—and I'd not go with Guy of Rivaux."

"Did he mistreat you when you were with him before?" Roger asked in a gentler tone. "Tell me why 'tis you should not be given to your husband."

"Because I've not even seen him in five years, Papa! Can you not see—he's not sent so much as one message to us! And now he comes to claim me? Why? Because King Henry bids him take me? Because my mother thinks I should go?" she argued passionately. "Papa, I am flesh-and-blood woman, not a castle or a piece of property that can be left sitting until its lord returns!"

"Aye, but he had much to trouble him ere he left Normandy, Cat," Eleanor reminded her. "He lost his lands when Henry won, and there was naught for him but exile. And Henry openly challenged the marriage, as you remember, so 'twould have been foolish of Rivaux to ask to take you with him.''

"Nay, he did not ask."

"You cannot know that."

"I know he would not even see me." Catherine closed her eyes against the memory of the humiliation of that last night. "Aye, he wed with me at Curthose's bidding, but when the duke lost, Guy of Rivaux left me," she admitted bitterly.

"Cat . . . Cat . . ." Eleanor sighed, and met her daughter's eyes with sympathy. "You are his, whether you will it or not—and whether he wills it or not also. Put what is done in the past and live for now. See him as he is now rather than as you remember him." Moving closer, she laid a comforting hand on Cat's shoulder, murmuring, "You cannot wish to live your life here as neither wife nor maiden, growing older without the comfort of a husband and children. 'Tis time, lovey, to accept Guy of Rivaux." Slipping her arm about her daughter's stiffened body, she advised gently, "Learn to love what God gives you and do not yearn for what you cannot have. There's naught to dislike in Lord Guy, Cat."

"Cat, I have not the power to keep you from your husband if he wants you," Roger spoke finally, "but if he beats you without reason or if he otherwise mistreats you, I will come for you. Aye—and with an army at my back, if need be."

"Has he said he comes for me?" Catherine asked suddenly. "Mayhap . . ."

"He comes for you. Henry has commanded that he take you with him to Rivaux."

"The king has commanded, and I am moved as a piece on the chessboard. Jesu, Papa, but what if Rivaux does not want me? What if he does but come because he must?"

"Then 'tis your task to make him content with you." Roger scanned his daughter's face for some sign of understanding and found none. "Would you that I spoke with him first—would that ease your mind?" he questioned.

"Roger, he awaits his bath, and I have said I will send Cat to him," Eleanor reminded him.

"Then you bathe him!" For a moment, Catherine's temper flared, but the seriousness of her parents' expressions told her it was no use to argue further. "Please, Maman," she added in a meeker tone.

"Nay, 'tis not my place, when he has a wife for the task. 'Tis fitting that you go to him now and make your peace with him. Go on," Eleanor urged.

"Nay, but—"

"Cat, you will not disobey your lady mother."

The sternness in her father's voice killed her protest before it was uttered. Looking from one to the other of her parents, she realized that both were agreed. "Where is he?" she muttered.

"Since you have your own chamber, 'twas decided to put him there," Eleanor answered. "You will need to get soap from your mother's maid."

Without answering, Catherine stalked for the stairs. Aye, she told herself as she stomped angrily down the narrow steps, she would bathe him if he insisted, but 'twould be a bath he'd not soon forget.

... as ... She stood ... ... at him. ...
her breath
far the ... ...
...

⟨² **17** ²⟩

Catherine held the towels close to her as though to
hide her thumping heart, and called out, "Open the
door—'tis Catherine of the Condes!" She could hear
the scraping of benches and muffled voices from
within. Impatient with the delay and yet loath to see
him, she shifted the towels and reached to turn the
iron door handle, and to her dismay it moved in her
hand. The door swung open, almost causing her to
lose her balance.

"Sweet Mary, but you would . . ." Words failed her
as she stared upward at him. There was no mistaking
that black hair or those strange eyes or the faintly
mocking eyebrows that rose above them. And there
was no mistaking the scar, the thin white line that divided his cheek below the bone. But the man before
her was a stranger, a dark giant come to take her away
from the Condes. It seemed to her that he blocked the
whole doorway with his tall body, looming over her
like an animal over its prey. She clutched the towels
tighter, pressing them against her breasts.

The first thought that crossed his mind as he returned her stare was that his memories of her did her
no justice. Aye, but he'd never seen the like of the girl
who stood numbly outside the door. For a moment his
senses reeled from the mere sight of her and his pulse
raced. In defiance of custom, her head was uncovered

and her thick braids fell over her shoulders like gold-threaded ropes that reached almost to her waist. She'd changed her gown from the shining blue one he'd seen her wearing on the wall and was clad now in a plain thing of coarse wool, something more suited to a nun than an heiress, but the shapeless dress could not hide her beauty.

Recovering first, she blinked to break the spell between them and managed to observe lamely, "Art bigger than I remembered."

The flecked eyes traveled over her, lingering on the swell of her breasts, and his mouth curved in a faint smile. "As are you, Cat."

His voice was richer, deeper than she remembered it, and his meaning was unmistakable. She looked away to keep him from seeing the confusion she felt, muttering, "I am sent to bathe you."

He stepped aside, still holding the door open for her to enter the chamber, and she had to duck beneath his arm, brushing past him so closely that she could feel the warmth of his body. Wrinkling her nose, she complained, "And 'tis no wonder—you stink of horses." To avoid looking at him, she peered behind him to see Alan and William de Comminges staring at her in openmouthed admiration. Out of the corner of her eye she could see that someone had already filled the bathing tub. Laying aside the towels on one of the benches, she walked over and dipped her fingers into the water. " 'Tis cold."

"I waited for you."

She spun around, unable to control her temper any further. "Jesu! And why could not one of them do it? You have no right to come here and demand aught of me!"

"Leave us," he ordered curtly, nodding to the men.

Alan looked from his master's set face to her flushed one and suppressed a grin, while William murmured as he passed her, " 'Tis a right welcome sight you are to these old eyes, Lady Catherine."

Cat waited until she heard their footsteps on the stairs before turning again to her husband. "Why did you send them away? They could have undressed you."

"Aye, but I'd not have them hear your carping." He walked to face her, stopping but a pace away. "And mayhap I favor a woman's gentle touch." Reaching out his hand, he caught her chin and forced it upward until she had to meet his eyes. "As for having any right, I have every right—Holy Church and my overlord are agreed that you are my wife."

His eyes were more green than gold and utterly devoid of warmth as she stared into them. A chill descended over her at his words. "I have done naught to deserve this, my lord," she told him finally, "and I'd not be wife to you."

" 'Tis too late. I am here at the bidding of my king, told to take you to Rivaux." A harsh laugh escaped him as her eyes widened. "Aye, but covering your honor with my name is a small price to pay for my lands, is it not?"

"I do not know what you mean," she retorted.

"Nay? Then how is it that Henry left me to fight in Wales, a landless knight with naught but my sword arm to sustain me for five years—five years, Cat—and now he bids me come home to you and gives me back the patrimony he took from me?" The bitterness in his voice was unmistakable as he continued, "I lost my lands for this marriage, Catherine of the Condes. The lands I gain now for taking you are mine own."

"I did not ask you to come here—take your lands and leave me be! Aye, and bathe yourself, my lord, for I'll not do it!" She whirled, her body stiff with anger, and started for the door, but was caught before she'd taken but a few steps. Wrenching her back painfully, his hand gripped her arm so tightly that she thought he meant to break it. "Unhand me!" she snapped.

"Nay. I'll put up with your airs and your tempers no longer, Catherine. Try me and I will beat you—do you understand?'' He released her with a shove toward a bench. "Now, I'd have my bath ere we sup."

She met his eyes defiantly, staring into the green depths until he looked away, muttering, "One day I will treat you as you deserve, Cat."

For a moment she considered running again for the door and calling for aid, but then the whole keep would know how things stood between her and Guy of Rivaux, and she had too much pride to endure the pity of Aislinn and the others. Not when Geoffrey of Mayenne came in less than a fortnight to wed with her sister—nay, but she'd not listen to Linn crow over her sweet-tempered lord. And she'd not be routed from her own bedchamber by Guy, anyway. If anyone must leave, it should be Rivaux, she told herself. Collecting her dignity, she nodded. "Very well, my lord, I will bathe you as is your right, but I take leave to warn you that I am unskilled in such things. In this household, 'tis my mother who tends to her guests."

Her quick capitulation somehow disappointed him, mayhap because he was spoiling for a fight to clear the air between them, mayhap because he wanted to goad her into admitting what he already suspected. With a sigh, he dropped to a bench and extended his foot toward her.

"God's blood, but can you not even remove your own boots?"

"It pleases me for you to do it."

Casting him a look of utter loathing, she knelt by his leg and grasped the heavy boot with both hands, giving it a rough twist before pulling it off. When he made no complaint, she did the same with the other, wrenching it even harder.

"Now I know what 'tis I have missed about you, Catherine—'tis your gentleness," he murmured sardonically above her head.

Ignoring him, she reached to unfasten his leather cross-garters and unwound them. The calves of his legs were hard and well-muscled beneath her fingers, an unusual thing for a mounted warrior. Discarding the garters, she rose. "You will have to stand, my lord, if you would remove your chausses."

"Aye." He came to his feet and waited expectantly. "But 'tis custom to take the tunic first—unless you are overeager to see the other."

"I would not know of that, my lord," she answered sweetly despite the rush of blood to her face. "I do not undress men. And you will have to lean over if you'd have me aid you." When he complied, she lifted his overtunic from beneath his arms and pulled it upward over them, deliberately catching his hair while his arms were immobilized. Yanking it roughly, she brought the tunic off over his head with a quick jerk that elicited a wince of pain from him.

"Hold up your arms if you would have me do this," she ordered as she reached for the plain cambric undertunic.

"I pity your poor babe when you have one," he told her with feeling as he lifted his arms. "Art rough, Cat."

"Aye—if you like not my gentle touch, you may do this for yourself. And I told you to bend over." Hastily she yanked the undergarment, making sure she gave his head a twist as it came off. He was bare to the waist now, and despite her anger, she eyed him curiously, noting an ugly scar that came down nearly to his left nipple. "Sweet Mary, but you never had that before."

"Aye, 'tis where a Welsh arrow was cut from me— you were nearly a widow without knowing it." His eyes met hers soberly now, the green and gold once again intermingling in them. "And you are nearly done."

Despite the thudding of her heart and the sudden dryness of her mouth, she took a quick breath and reached for the ties at his waist. Her fingers hesitated but briefly and then pulled, making a knot instead of releasing the ends. She bent her head to hide her embarrassment and worked determinedly, feeling the tremor of his stomach muscles beneath her hands.

He closed his eyes at her touch on his bare skin, sucking in his breath and holding it as her fingers sought to undo the knot she'd made. When he could bring himself to look downward, her head was but inches from his chest, its shining crown divided by the neat, even part of her braids. For a moment he thought he could smell the rosewater again, but he decided his mind played tricks on his senses. Despite his effort at control, he could feel the tautening in his loins.

The ties gave way, freeing him, and he grew before her eyes. She stepped back hurriedly, her face aflame, mumbling, "You'll have to do the rest, my lord."

" 'Tis nothing you have not seen before, Cat—a man is a man, after all," he gibed. "Even Brian Fitz-Henry."

"I would not know of that either, my lord," she responded woodenly. "And your water grows colder as you tarry."

Again he felt cheated. If she had but screamed that he accused her falsely, if she had but denied loudly, he would have felt less a loss. But as it was, he lifted his hands and then dropped them, not knowing how to bridge the chasm between them, not wanting to show her how much of him would have her still. Instead, he pushed his chausses down and stepped out of them.

She did not want to bathe him—she did not want to touch his naked body—for she feared to rouse him further and she had no wish to lie with the cold stranger he'd become. Fighting her own bitterness, she gestured toward the oak-and-iron tub. "Try not to slop water on my mats—it took Hawise a week to weave them."

He eased his tall body into the water, shivering as he did so. "Try not to soap my eyes." But when she picked up a cloth and began washing his back gently, he shook his head. "Nay—you begin with the hair.

God's bones, but you'll never get me clean like this,''
he complained.

"I never wash men," she muttered through clenched
teeth.

" 'Tis apparent, but you will learn.''

Her anger flared anew at the injustice of her lot and
she forgot her brief fear of him. If he thought to treat
her no better than a servant, she would make him pay
for his insolence. Reaching for one of the pitchers
placed by the tub, she emptied it over his head, letting
it pour over his face, and while he still strangled from
the deluge, she grabbed the chunk of soap and rubbed
it so hard against his hair that pieces broke off. Then,
before he could duck away, she pulled his head back
by yanking the hair so roughly that he let out a yelp
of pain.

"God's bones!" he spluttered as he tried to free
himself.

" 'Tis not my intent to harm you," she assured him
sweetly while she dug her nails into his scalp and raked
it. "Aye, you were right—'tis so dirty that I wonder
you do not have to be deloused, my lord.''

"Jesu! Have a care. I—'' His words were cut off as
she grasped his head firmly with her forearm, imprisoning it against her, and poured another pitcher of
water straight in his face. "My eyes—" he managed
before choking.

Warming to her task, she held him tighter while he
floundered to clutch at the sides of the big tub. With
his head now locked in her elbow, she assured him,
"I will wipe it out," and then swiped a soapy cloth
across his tightly closed eyes. Releasing him while he
yet groped blindly, she pushed him forward in the water and grabbed a stout brush that Gerdis used for
cleaning the tub. Soaping the stiff bristles, she began
to scour his back, leaving red streaks on his skin.
"Aye, the water's so dirty you will have to be rinsed
twice, my lord," she murmured above him, now en-

joying herself thoroughly. "I can quite see the bath was needed."

She'd caught him unguarded and he knew it. His eyes burned so unbearably from the lye-and-tallow soap that he could not see, and his back was being shredded with God only knew what. In defense, he caught her skirt and tried to dry his eyes, but she yanked his head back and doused him again. To his chagrin, he could hear her giggle above him. With an effort, he grasped the sides of the tub and heaved himself upward, sending a shower of water over her and onto the floor. "It amuses you to blind your husband?" he growled as he made a swipe for her.

She stepped backward but was not quick enough to elude him. His wet hand closed over her wrist and pulled her closer as he stepped from the tub. Taken aback by the fury in his face, she tried to twist away, fearful that he meant to harm her. And before she could fathom his intent, he lifted her and plunged her headfirst into the soap-scummed water. She choked and came up coughing as her braids dripped and her skirts sank. Grabbing the side of the tub, she righted herself and tried to rise, sputtering, "Look what 'tis you have done! You have ruined my gown!"

"Nay, we are not done, Catherine," he told her, holding her shoulder down with one hand and side-stepping her clawing hands.

She looked up through the rivulets of water that coursed down from her hair, to see him standing over her, wiping his burning eyes with a towel. "You . . . you hateful beast!" she spat at him.

"Beast? *Beast?* 'Tis you who have blinded me!"

Ducking from beneath his hand, she lunged forward and tried to get up, only to be pushed back roughly and dunked again. This time, when she came up, he leaned over and tugged at the ends of her neat plaits, loosening the gold thread that bound them and combing them out with his fingers. Still choking, she gasped in pain as the wet tangles gave way. Her dark hair floated out from her shoulders, gathering the soapy film from the water.

"Stand up," he ordered curtly.

Thinking he meant to let her out finally, she raised herself and her wet gown bagged heavily against her legs. But before she could step over the side, he grasped the shoulders of the loose gown and pulled it upward so forcefully that her head jerked back. The gown made a slapping sound as it landed against the hard floor. "Nay!" she gasped in alarm, her hands clutching at his as he reached for the waist of her undershift. "Nay!"

Twisting free, he ignored her protests to lift the clinging material away and pull it off. "Holy Mary," he heard her whisper as he stared at her. For a moment he forgot his anger. His eyes traveled hungrily over her smooth pale skin, taking in every detail of her slender body. Her breasts were fuller now and the curve of her hip more rounded, but her waist was narrow and her belly flat. His mouth grew dry and his blood pounded at the sight of her until pain brought him to his senses.

"God's bones—you bit me!" he accused, dropping the undershift to rub his bleeding hand. "Art a cat in need of taming, I think."

She scrambled out of the tub to face him, her wet hair clinging like dark strings over her bare breasts. "If I were a man, I'd kill you for the insult you offer me!" she shouted. Looking around for something she could use as a weapon, she picked up the soap and hurled it at him, missing him by inches. He bent to retrieve it and advanced on her. "Stand back," she warned, "else I'll break this pitcher over your head." For emphasis, she waved the empty metal ewer at him.

"Nay, Cat—I think not." He circled her, waiting for her to raise her arm, and when she did, he lunged and caught the hand that held the pitcher. "Drop it," he ordered sternly.

"Nay!"

"God's bones, but you are a stubborn wench!" Still holding her against him, he forced her back toward the tub. This time he pushed her backward over the side, wrenching the pitcher away from her as she fell, and then held her under the water until she ceased clawing. When he let her up for air, he soaped her hair roughly.

"Stop it—else I'll scream!"

Ignoring her, he pushed her underwater again and her hair floated around her. When she came up, he emptied the last pitcher of clean water over her head. "Where is the brush you used on me?" he demanded, turning around to look for it.

She pulled up and struggled out of the tub. "Have done! Sweet Mary, but what right have you to . . . to . . . ." she sputtered furiously. Hot tears of impotent rage spilled over onto her cheeks, mingling with the water that dripped from her hair. "How dare you come to my father's house and treat me so?" she panted, brushing at her wet cheeks angrily. "You have no right to come for me—no right, do you hear?" Her voice rose almost hysterically as he turned to stare at her. "And I meant it when I said I'd not be wife to you! I care not what King Henry says, I care not what Holy Church says—I'll not have you!"

" 'Tis too late for this! God's bones, but why did you not speak up when they sought to annul the marriage then?" he demanded, his own voice rising. "Aye, I even expected it!"

"Because they would have wed me to Robert of Caen!" she shouted back.

"That was years ago—he has Gloucester's heiress now," he reminded her. "You could have said something once he'd wed."

"Nay, but I could not! Jesu, but you are a man and cannot understand! When they asked at first, I swore I'd lain with you—how could I have recanted later? Do you know what proof they'd have—do you? They would have looked!" Reddening even as she said it, she nodded. "Aye, I would have been stripped and examined before witnesses, my lord, and I am no whore to be seen like that!''

"So you lay with Brian FitzHenry until your shame reached King Henry's ears! Jesu, but did you think I'd have no pride? That I'd take you back without question? Nay, Cat, but I am not such a fool." He moved closer as she watched in stunned disbelief. "I swear to you that if you are delivered of a babe too early, I will kill Brian FitzHenry."

"Afore God, 'tis too much!" she spat out when she found her voice.

Before he realized her intent, she reached out and slapped him with such force that she feared she'd broken the bones in her hand. He stood like a rock in the face of the blow, too surprised to react. Slowly he reached to rub the reddened palm print on his cheek. "I suppose I should be grateful you had no weapon, else you would have marked me again," he spoke finally, his anger strangely gone.

"You have no right to come back after five years and accuse me of such baseness, my lord. Five years it has been—five years when I have sat here as neither wife nor maid! But I have never dishonored myself or you, Guy of Rivaux!" Her voice had dropped to a near-whisper, but her words hung between them as if she'd still shouted. "Aye, I know not why you are come home, but I know 'tis not because of me."

"You swear to me that you have lain with no man?"

"Swear to you? *Swear to you?* Nay, I'll not swear it! Not when I have already said it! Sweet Mary, but 'tis I who should have you swear to me! For all I know of you, my lord, you have had a dozen lemans since last you left me. Aye, but then, you are a man, are you not? And 'tis expected of a man," she added bitterly.

He wanted to believe her, but the pain he'd carried since Tinchebrai would not go away—not when he'd seen them this day on the Condes' wall. "There is but one way to prove the truth, is there not?" His flecked eyes took in her naked body and then her face, watching the blood rise in her cheeks. "Come here."

"Nay."

"You are old enough now, I think."

"Nay." She wet her lips nervously and backed away.

" 'Tis my right, Cat." Following her as one would a skittish animal, he waited until he'd backed her almost against the wall. Then, leaning forward to rest a hand on either side of her, he closed in. "Prove your honor to me, Cat," he murmured, lowering his mouth to hers.

Her eyes widened as his grew closer, and then closed when his face blurred before hers. Her protest died under the pressure of his lips as they moved on hers, and his tongue teased, tasting the salty tears and bathwater that mingled there. An instant heat sprang between them, nearly blotting out rational thought. His hands came up to twine in her wet hair, imprisoning her, and her hands, which had sought to push him away, slid around his waist instead. It was as though all the pent-up anger and bitterness turned into a different fire that warmed their still-wet bodies and ignited a need of such intensity that Cat neither cared nor wanted to fight anymore. Telling herself that he was her given husband, she clung to him, savoring what she'd been too long denied.

He'd expected her to fight, to claw and scratch at him, so much so that he was unprepared for her response to him. His mind urged him to go slowly with her, but every fiber of his body demanded hers to slake his need and release the terrible tension he felt. His hands slid from her hair to her back and then down to her hips, his palms moving over her wet skin with such urgency that he could feel her body tremble beneath them.

Her rational mind was under siege from her senses—she knew he meant to take her and that her pride ought to make her resist him, but his very touch sent a thrill cf anticipation through her. "Sweet Mary!" she breathed in wonder when his lips left hers to trace their fire down her neck. His touch was light as it moved, but her flesh came alive beneath his mouth and his hands. Her head arched back to give access to the sensitive hollows of her throat. A low moan rose from deep within her as his palms cupped her hips, pressing her against his aroused body.

When he lifted his head to whisper, "I would have you, Cat—I'd wait no longer," his hot, ragged breath rushed against her ear and sent shivers of excitement down her spine. And when he lifted her suddenly, she clasped her arms around his neck and turned her head into his shoulder to hide the eagerness she felt as he carried her across the room to her bed.

Still holding her, balancing her weight against him with one arm, he leaned to pull back the embroidered coverlet, twitching it off to one side, and then lowered her among the banked pillows. Her hair spilled onto the silk cushions in tangled confusion, spotting them with wetness, and her pale body glistened damply as she half-rolled to make room for him. For a moment he stood above her, mesmerized by the dark pools of her eyes as they stared upward at him. Her chest rose and fell, her breasts rising with each rapid breath, and his heart pounded until he could scarce breathe from the sight of her. She was the most beautiful girl he'd ever seen, and she was his.

Her gaze traveled from his face downward until it reached his aroused manhood, and she felt a stab of fear. Her breath caught sharply and she wondered what she'd done. She closed her eyes tightly, bracing herself against the pillows, and felt the bed give with his weight as he stretched his long body beside hers.

He'd seen her sudden fear and knew he ought to go slowly, but for once his steel will failed him. The feel of her, the heat that rose between them as he took her in his arms, touched off as intense a need as he'd ever felt, and blotted out all else. He'd thought to take the time to caress, to wait until she was ready for him.

Instead, he explored her breasts eagerly, drawing his palms over the rose-tipped mounds until the nipples hardened beneath them, eliciting a soft moan from her as she sought to move closer. He brushed lower with one hand, feeling the rapid beating of her heart beneath her rib cage and the tautness of her stomach, until he reached the silky down below. She gasped and drew back momentarily as his fingers explored the wetness there, but he could wait no longer.

He rolled her onto her back and eased his body over hers, separating her legs with his knee, forcing them outward, pinning her down with his weight. Her eyes flew open and her hands pushed at his shoulders. Her hips thrashed against his, drawing away as his body sought entrance to hers. With one hand he cradled her head for his kiss, and with the other he grasped her hip, holding it steady. She tensed as his tongue teased, and then gave a cry that faded to a moan as he took possession of her mouth and her body at the same time. He felt the resistance and then the tear, and somewhere in the recesses of his mind, he knew she'd spoken the truth.

Despite her own desire, she'd been unprepared for the final culmination of his. Her body had been alive and, as though it had a mind of its own, it had sought eagerly the release of the tension he'd created within her, but at the last moment, her reason and fear had reasserted themselves, and she'd tried to draw back. She felt speared and torn asunder by him when he entered her, but then the heat returned as he moved within her, slowly at first and then deeper and harder, setting her on fire again and erasing her pain with her own need. Her hands left his shoulders to move restlessly, stroking the hard muscles of his back as he strained against her and drove himself rhythmically toward release. She twisted and writhed beneath him, striving ceaselessly to reach an unknown ecstasy, until she heard him cry out and she felt the warm flood of his seed. He collapsed above her, his breath coming in great rasps by her ear, and lay quietly, his weight resting on his elbows. She closed her arms around him and held him tightly, still savoring the feel of him.

"Cat, you are fire itself," he managed when he finally caught his breath and rolled away. "Jesu, but I've not known your like before." Twisting his head to look at her, he could see the beads of perspiration that dampened her face, and he reached to brush back the dark tangles from her forehead. Her eyes were still closed and she was swallowing to master her own breath. "I did not mean to hurt you," he added softly.

"Nay—the fault was mine also," she murmured beside him. "Brian always told me to tempt not where I would not." The instant the words were spoken, she could feel him tense beside her, and she cursed herself for a fool, wishing for all the world that she could call them back. Dismayed, she turned to watch him, hoping he would somehow understand. He lay on his back, staring upward almost bleakly, and his strange eyes, gold with passion moments before, were now heavily flecked with green. Impulsively she reached to touch him, her fingers lightly stroking the hairs on his chest.

"Nay." He spoke abruptly, brushing her hand away. "There is no need for that." Rolling to sit with his back to her, he leaned to brace his elbows on his knees. It seemed an eternity before he could bring himself to speak further. "I know I am not what you would have, Catherine, but I am what you are given. If 'tis I and no other who lies with you, I will try not to fault you for wanting Brian FitzHenry."

"Guy . . ." She pushed herself up and would have touched him again, but he ducked away from her hand.

"Nay—there is no need to say what you believe I would hear."

Before she could think of what else she could do, he rose from the bed without looking at her again, and she was conscious that the chasm between them was as wide as it had been earlier. Dropping her hands in defeat, she rolled out on the other side and padded to a cupboard to get a cloth to clean herself.

"I ask your pardon for one thing, Cat—I know now you were true in body if not in heart," he added in a strained voice as he bent to pick up the clothes that Alan had laid out for him.

She opened her mouth to speak and then closed it. At this moment she knew not what was in her heart, and she knew that nothing either of them would say could ease the terrible confusion she felt.

❧18❧

"Your food grows cold, Cat."

"Hmmmm? Oh, aye, I suppose it does," Catherine answered her sister absently. Drawn back from her still-disordered thoughts, she picked up her knife and speared a piece of meat.

"And if Guy of Rivaux came for me, I'd be staring at him rather than the wall," Aislinn whispered. "Sweet Mary, but what ails you, Cat? King Henry gives you back a handsome husband, and you do naught but ignore him."

"Eat your own food and leave me be," Cat retorted, unreasonably cross at the way Linn and Pippa flirted with Guy, smiling at him and listening raptly to every word he chose to utter to them.

"If 'tis Brian, you are yet the fool," Aislinn hissed furtively, keeping her eye on Guy's back. "Aye, were Rivaux mine, I'd think I had the better man."

Cat halted her knife in midair and turned furiously on her sister. "Well, he is not—and 'tis not your concern anyway," she snapped. Then, realizing how jealous she must sound, she added. "But I wish he *were* yours—then you'd know of what you speak."

Linn leaned forward until her head nearly touched her trencher, to gain a better view of Guy of Rivaux. He still faced away from her, but she could hear snatches of the polite conversation between him and her father. His black hair shone beneath the torchlight, and the flickering yellow flame played on the rich gold embroidery that decorated his red silk tunic. "God's blood, Cat," she murmured under her breath, "but he is far bigger than either Geoffrey or Brian."

Catherine mentally compared him to them and grudgingly conceded the truth of that. In size at least, Guy of Rivaux was of taller and stronger build than most men—aye, he was bigger than her father now, and mayhap he was even as tall as she remembered Robert of Belesme, the tallest lord of her memory. She felt a stab of disloyalty at the thought, as though she should find Brian to be the best of everything.

"And I've seen none comelier, sister—art fortunate, I think," Aislinn persisted.

"And one would think you wanted to lie with him, the way you speak, Linn," Catherine muttered dryly.

"Cat!" In her shock, Aislinn forgot to whisper, and to her horror, Guy of Rivaux turned around. Her face reddened as she hastily bent her attention to the food before her.

Catherine looked up, realized that he was watching her instead of Linn, and wondered what he'd heard. It did not matter, she told herself, for he'd been as cold to her as she had been to him, preferring to discuss the fighting in Wales with her father rather than seeking speech with her. It was as though he were a stranger—that he'd forgotten what had happened between them but hours earlier.

But she could not forget. Even now, she could not meet his gaze for the shame she felt. She'd let him take her—nay, she had *given* herself to him, responding to his touch like a wanton whore, thrashing and bucking beneath him, moaning and panting for his seed. He reached to cut a bite of venison from the chunk on the trencher they shared, and the stiff samite of his sleeve brushed against her arm, sending a shiver of remembered passion deep within her. She drew back as though from a fire, and her face flamed from the thoughts that came to mind.

To him, it was as though she recoiled in disgust from him, and he felt again the resentment he harbored for Brian FitzHenry. Had it not been for King Henry's bastard son, Guy was certain he could have won Cat's heart as well as her body. But he had something that Brian did not—he had Catherine of the Condes in his bed and he meant to keep her there. He stared, seeing again the way she'd looked lying beneath him, and he felt anew the warming of his blood. She might think she preferred the other man, but afore God, Guy meant to make her forget him. Then, barely half aware of her father's polite attempts at conversation, he tried to will himself to listen. His ears heard Roger de Brione speak of the need for more stone castles in the Welsh marches, and his head nodded in appropriate agreement, but his mind lingered on Catherine. Stealing a look at her from beneath lazy lids, he studied her proud profile and thought her the most beautiful creature he'd ever seen. And over and over he told himself that she was his—whether she wanted him for husband or not, she was his wife.

"What thought you of Chepstow?"

"Chepstow?" Reluctantly drawing his thoughts from Catherine again, Guy forced himself to consider the keep FitzOsbern had built after the Conqueror's victory before answering. "It is well-defined by nature, with that steep gully on one side and that deep drop to the river on the other," he mused. "Aye—and it sits on solid rock right in the bend of the Wye. I doubt 'twill ever fall to the Welsh or to any others, but if it does, 'twill have to be because of treachery from within." His flecked eyes met Roger's warily. "Why do you ask?"

"To hear you say what I have thought. If there were many Chepstows, we'd have control of Wales now."

"Nay, but there is more to it than that," Guy disputed. "The Welsh are too warlike to bow for long.

'Twill take a strong leader, one with the courage and ability to fight them into the mountains, one with the will to do what must be done. When Belesme had Shrewsbury—''

''Belesme ruled through violence and treachery,'' Roger cut in curtly. ''Aye, and there's naught to say that he could hold what he won for long.'' Then, realizing how he must sound, he added in a more conciliatory tone, ''But I know of what you would say— there's none to compare with Robert on the field. 'Tis an advantage to have a name that strikes fear in all but fools.''

''You bested him.''

''Once.'' Roger's expression grew distant, as though he saw again the day he'd dared to meet Robert of Belesme in single combat. ''Aye,'' he sighed finally, ''I did it but once—never before or since—and I'd not want to try again.''

''Men still sing the tale,'' Guy reminded him.

''It sounds better in verse than it was. We were both overtired in the end, so much so that I doubt either of us had the strength left for the kill. But there have been times that I regretted I did not strike him the fatal blow—many times,'' Roger admitted. ''Now I look on the ruin and death he metes out in Normandy when he raids, and I think I should have killed him nineteen years ago.'' His blue eyes met Guy's soberly. ''Had I the chance again, I would do it.''

''He is mine enemy also.''

''Then you'd best pray you are well-fortified, for unless I mistake the matter, he will raid again into Normandy. Every year since Tinchebrai, he has come with the French king's backing, raiding and burning, wreaking vengeance on all who stood against him, and then returning to hide in France ere the snow falls.''

''So I have heard. I pray that King Henry leaves me enough at Rivaux to defend myself. My keep had but a timber wall and one stone tower finished ere I left it—I had thought to raise it again in stone, my lord, but the work was scarce begun.'' Guy's gaze swept the great hall around him and he shook his head. "I fear Cat will think it poor when compared to this.''

"I'd always heard you were a wealthy man," Roger countered.

"Aye—in land and vassals, I was, but what Curthose did not levy from me, King Henry took," Guy answered, his bitterness betrayed in his voice. His eyes, more green than gold now, met Roger's steadily. "I inherited of my father at sixteen, my lord, and my duke nearly beggared me with my father's death dues, and then de Mortain thought to take Rivaux from me, burning my unfinished wall to the ground and slaying my men in their beds. Had it not been for William"— he nodded toward where de Comminges sat among Roger's men—"I should have perished also. But, as it was, I escaped to fight again—and again, and again— with no aid from my duke, until 'twas all mine once more. And when the tallies were all collected and counted, I was said to be a wealthy man, but then my gold was needed to buy Curthose more men to field against his brother. The battle between them lasted but an hour, and when 'twas done, I was but one of the vanquished. My lands were taken and I was banished—for my treason, King Henry said. For my treason," he repeated for emphasis. "I fought for my liege lord against one to whom I had not sworn, but 'twas the excuse given for my banishment from this land."

"Aye, there were others who went unpunished for greater wrongs," Roger sympathized.

"But they had not wed Catherine of the Condes, my lord." Guy's jaw worked as he sought to control the anger he felt at the memory. "But I swear afore God that before I am done, I'll have every hide and every mark that I ever lost—and more. Nay, but I'll not leave my son as my father left me."

Surprised by Guy's bitterness, Roger wondered if they'd been wrong to bring him back to Catherine. If he blamed her for his losses, he was not likely to make a kind or loving husband. But when he spoke, such thoughts were veiled. "If you know not what you will find at Rivaux, Guy, mayhap you would wish to leave Cat here until 'tis safe. Aye—go to your own lands and see to your defenses, and then come for her. Lea will be glad for her company when Aislinn is gone."

Without answering, Guy cocked his head back to look at his wife. She'd turned again to her sister and now disputed whether she would wear her red gown or her purple one to the younger girl's wedding. She was so lovely to look on that it made him ache almost, and even her soft baudekin veil could not hide her rich, dark hair. Instead, the light of the torch above them caught the many silver and gold threads in the silk tissue and made the braids beneath shimmer. As she inclined her head closer to her sister, the gossamer veil cast iridescent shadows on her white neck. Desire flooded over him as he watched her.

"Take her to Rouen with you when you swear to Henry, if 'tis your will," Roger persisted, "but bring her back to the Condes until you have had the time to rebuild Rivaux."

"I have other castles," Guy murmured, his eyes still on Catherine.

While she yet argued her point with Aislinn, she reached absently for a comfit on the serving platter in front of them, and this time, it was her hand that touched his arm. Startled, she looked up into his face and saw his thoughts mirrored there. Her expression froze, but not before he'd heard the sharp intake of her breath. Her heart pounded, sending blood rushing to her head and forcing her to look away. He picked up one of the pitted sugar dates and bit off half of it, chewing almost lazily, and then held the rest in front of her mouth. Her fingers plucked it from his as though she feared he would burn her, and she popped it into her mouth quickly.

Aislinn leaned around her to address him, "What

think you, my lord—is it red or purple that favors Cat best?''

His eyes still on Catherine, he answered almost too softly for Linn's ears, ''I think her comelier than anything she could wear.''

''Aye, but . . .'' Aislinn's voice trailed off as she became aware that he was not speaking to her at all.

His voice was low and husky, and his eyes had warmed almost gold, betraying what he would have of her. Catherine swallowed hard to maintain her composure under his gaze. The pulse in her neck was visible where the filmy baudekin fell away, and when his eyes dropped to the swell of her breasts, she could feel the heat spread through her body.

Roger's voice sounded far away as it penetrated Guy's consciousness when he repeated his suggestion that Catherine remain at the Condes. ''Nay,'' Guy answered finally, his eyes still on her. ''I take her with me by King Henry's command.''

As the servants began removing platters from the tables and refilling wine cups, jongleurs tumbled into view from behind a screen at the end of the great hall. Roger leaned back reluctantly, knowing that Guy had the right to do with Cat what he would. Mayhap before it was time for them to leave for Rouen, he would have a better opportunity to discuss the matter. Eleanor, who had been keeping Brian FitzHenry away from her daughter with a determination that made her husband marvel, turned to whisper in his ear, ''He does not look to be one to brook interference in his affairs, my lord.'' Reaching to tweak an errant lock of blond hair made lighter by strands of silver, she teased to lighten his mood, ''On the morrow, 'tis the barber for you, lord husband, else you'll look more English than Norman.''

The household began to clap in rhythm as the tumblers performed their feats of agility, rolling, leaping, and springing across the open area of the hall, contorting their bodies to form platforms for those who would run, bounce, and cartwheel into the air. The girls' shortened skirts fell away from their lithe legs, revealing the modesty cloths they wore beneath them. To Guy, it was as though everything conspired to heighten his desire—the rhythm, the wine, the dancers, and, above all, the girl at his side. Even though he'd drunk very little, he felt intoxicated, his senses reeling with the very nearness of Catherine.

"Eleanor would have you come to her solar when we are done here," Roger leaned to murmur behind Guy's ear. " 'Tis our custom to play at tables or dames—or chess, if you prefer it—ere we retire."

"I am overtired, I fear," Guy answered. "Mayhap tomorrow . . ." His voice trailed off, his thoughts racing ahead to when he would again be alone with her.

"Oh, but you must come!" Aislinn urged. "If you do not, I shall be left with Brian, who is a poor player at best. You do play chess, do you not?"

"Aye, but I have not the will for it tonight. I—"

"Brian is *not* a poor player!" Cat felt compelled to argue. "For shame, Linn—I never win against him."

"Because you do not try. God's blood, Cat, but if you ceased watching him with sheep's eyes and did but watch your game instead—"Aislinn halted and her hands crept to her stricken face when she realized what she'd said in Rivaux's presence. "That is . . . well, you never were a very good player anyway," she added lamely. But stealing a look at her sister's husband, she knew her barb had struck the wrong mark.

Guy felt a surge of anger that everyone knew of Catherine's preference for another man, and his ardor dissipated. "I would play him," he muttered grimly.

"But I . . ." Aislinn fought to hide her disappointment, realizing that he meant to challenge Brian on any field he could now.

"Leave him be, Linn," Eleanor ordered hastily. "Can you not accept that the man is tired and would not play?"

"Well, I would," Cat decided. "Aye, let him retire,

and I will best you at tables, Linn. Then Brian can sing and you will be spared his game.''

''Nay, I would play him also.'' Brian, his face flushed from too much drink, stared past Eleanor and Roger to Guy. His animosity evident, his courage bolstered with Roger's wine, he challenged, ''I will play you at anything, my lord, if the wager is sufficient.''

''Done,'' Guy growled.

Eleanor and Roger exchanged uneasy glances before Roger signaled the end of the meal. As serving maids sopped up spilled wine and began removing the covers, men-at-arms and other household members rose to bid their lord and lady good night. Ten-year-old Isabella complained loudly of the injustice of letting thirteen-year-old Philippa accompany their parents whilst she had to follow Hawise to bed, but both Pippa and Aislinn ignored her in their efforts to gain Guy of Rivaux's attention.

''When you have beaten Brian, would you play tables with me?'' Pippa begged him.

''Nay, 'tis my right as the elder,'' Linn insisted. ''If Cat will not play with him, then it should be me.''

''Stop it—both of you,'' Cat hissed at them.

''Jesu, but you are cross, sister,'' Pippa noted.

''With good reason.''

Roger's chamberlain lighted the way up the narrow, winding steps, pausing at the top to hand his master the torch, and then pressing his body back against the cold stone to let everyone pass. The night was cool for late spring, and the fresh fire in the central brazier was warm and inviting. Impulsively Eleanor turned back to Guy to ask, ''Do you sing, my lord?''

''When I was a squire,'' he admitted with a rueful smile. ''Now I doubt I know above one lay from beginning to end.''

Brian, with the ease of one long accustomed to life at the Condes, crossed the room to find a wineskin, and Catherine followed him to whisper, ''Have you not had enough? Nay, but you'll be no match for him.''

"Leave me be." Dismissing her with an unsteady wave of his hand, he found a cup and filled it, spilling the red liquid onto the woven mats that warmed the floor. "I do not need you to tell me how to play the game."

"Linn, see if there is any honey in the pot," Eleanor ordered her second daughter. "If there is, offer Lord Guy some sweetened wine. Would you have it mulled for you?" she asked, turning to him. "There is some ginger for it."

"Aye."

"Pippa, get the lute for Lord Guy, that he may play for us."

"Maman, 'tis Brian's lute," Cat protested. "And Guy did not say he would sing, anyway."

"Lea . . ."

Eleanor turned back to her husband, a mischievous smile playing at the corners of her mouth. "Ah, did you wish to sing for me, Roger?" she asked innocently, knowing full well that there was little chance of getting him to do it.

"Nay."

"I did not think so. And while the pieces are found and the board is set, Cat may mull the wine and Guy may sing to us. Linn, see if you and Pippa can find the dice for tables, if you will." Passing close to Roger, she leaned to murmur for his ears alone, "I would not have Brian play when he is half gone with drink—else he may force a quarrel. If you can but keep them apart for a little while, I doubt not that he will just go to sleep." Aloud, she directed Philippa, "Get the cushions, that we may sit around the fire, sweeting." Taking the lute from the girl's hands, she thrust it at Guy. "I would hear your one lay, my lord, and mayhap 'twill remind you of others. There's not a knight I know that cannot sing enough to entertain me."

Philippa dragged a long bench up closer to the fire and then banked silk-covered cushions against it. "If it would please you, my lord, you may sit here,'' she offered with uncharacteristic shyness. Tossing another cushion at the end, she nodded to her sister. "Cat?"

"Nay, 'tis too hot. And you heard Maman—I am to mull the wine. Do you want yours heated with the rest, Brian?"

"Nay." He slumped heavily to sit, his back braced against the outer wall of the solar, and drank deeply.

"I have the bones," Aislinn announced triumphantly, straightening up from where she'd been rummaging in a chest for the dice. "If Brian is to drink and Lord Guy is to sing, then I will stand you in tables, Cat." Then, noting her sister's chagrin, she added impishly, "And I get the first toss."

"Nay—play with Papa, Linn." Cat removed the cooling poker from the pitcher of heated wine and stirred in the honey and ginger. Satisfied with the sweetness of the mixture, she began pouring it into cups. "Here—see that everyone has some."

"Even Brian, sister?" Aislinn asked with feigned innocence. With a toss of her still-unbound chestnut hair, she nodded toward where he sat pouring himself yet another cup of Roger's wine. " 'Twould seem he has found his own." Even as both girls watched, he let the skin slip to rest against his leg and turned to cradle his head against the solid rock, and it was obvious that he was very drunk. Cat walked over to shake him awake, and his eyes opened briefly, tried to focus on her, and then closed as she turned away in disgust. His cup rolled, spilling its contents into a pool beside him.

Behind them, his back settled against the cushions, Guy strummed Brian's lute softly, his fingers seeking the feel of the instrument, while he hummed a tune under his breath and tried to remember the words. Eleanor set up the chessboard and motioned to her husband to play, and Philippa picked up the dice from where Aislinn had laid them and began casting them aimlessly onto the floor, waiting for a challenge from one of her sisters.

Wishing fervently that Brian had not chosen to drink himself into a stupor, Cat finished pouring the warm, sweetened wine and handed the cups to Aislinn for distribution. Taking a seat on the other side of the fire, she looked across the circle to where Guy tightened a string on the lute. The flames glowed red and orange on his face, illuminating the scar she'd given him, and his eyes, when they met hers, reflected the flickering firelight eerily. Apparently satisfied at last, he stopped humming and began testing his voice with a short verse of the sort the guards chorused on long watches. Aislinn handed him a steaming cup and he paused to take a sip, setting it down on the mat beside him. Cat hunched forward, clasping her arms around her knees and resting her head on them, telling herself she hoped he got as drunk as Brian.

An intimate hush settled over the room, broken only by the popping and spitting of the logs in the brazier, when Guy self-consciously began the lay he knew best. His voice, warmed by the wine, was deeper than Brian's, but his delivery was clear and pleasant, gaining in richness as he relaxed and gave himself up to his song.

Roger, who had been about to move one of his knights on the chessboard, stopped to listen again to the story of how he had been the only man to lay Robert of Belesme on the ground and live. There were as many versions of the song as there were singers in Normandy, he reflected as he sat, his piece still in his hand, and heard Guy sing the old tale. Pippa dropped her dice and edged closer to listen, and Aislinn dropped down beside Guy to sip her wine.

The lay was long, its verses having grown with the intervening years, its story embellished until Roger was no longer merely a man, but rather a symbolic hero of epic proportions who had taken on evil and vanquished it. And Guy's delivery of the song was

compelling, drawing everyone's rapt attention. Even
Catherine found herself under the spell of the story
she knew by heart, and as he bent his head down in
concentration, she could picture again the way it must
have been the day that her father fought Robert of Belesme for her mother.

Eleanor pushed aside the chessboard and leaned to
rest her head on her husband's shoulder, savoring again
the strength of the man she'd wed. Aye, for most of
her life, he'd been her sword and buckler against a
violent and treacherous world. His arm cradled her,
stroking her silk sleeve against her shoulder, and she
felt again the thrill of knowing he was hers. Guy
paused, his throat parched from singing, and washed
his mouth with the warm liquid, swallowing it slowly
before returning to his song. His eyes met Eleanor's
warmly and he nodded as he began again with a verse
that described her incredible beauty.

She sucked in her breath and stared in that moment,
feeling for all the world that time stood still. An awful
stab of recognition hit her, sending a shiver to the very
core of her being, and then it passed. She forced herself to look again, but he'd bent his head to the lute.
The fire played off the glossy black of his hair and off
the shimmering embroidery on his tunic. Her heart
hammering fearfully, she willed him to look up again,
and she prayed she would not see the resemblance
again. But this time, when he turned to Catherine,
Eleanor studied his profile, taking in the high cheekbone, the chiseled, slightly aquiline nose, and the firm
chin, and her frightful suspicion returned. The song
forgotten, she argued within herself, chiding herself
for foolish fear, telling herself that it could not be,
and yet wondering what she had done to her daughter.
Then, shaking off what her rational mind told her was
impossible, she tried to listen to the part about Belesme coming for her at Fontainebleau and taking her
prisoner.

Catherine cast a disgusted look at Brian and then

turned her attention to her husband. Even she, who
professed not to want him, had to own that Guy of
Rivaux was everything that Aislinn had said of him—
handsome beyond any other she'd seen, big and dark,
with those strange eyes of his, his handsomeness
marred only by the two scars that appeared as one on
his face. Her thoughts ended abruptly when she realized he stared back, and the blood rushed to her head.

He missed neither words nor cadence despite the
sudden rekindling of his desire for her. Her unguarded
admiration of him gave him a headier feel than the
wine. This night she would be his, this night she'd
think of no other, he promised himself. Even his fingertips that strummed the strings were sensitive to the
anticipation that surged anew within him. His mind
raced ahead of his words, discarding verses, in his
haste to be done.

He'd reached the place where "Lord Roger threw
down his gauntlet" when she looked away. At his side,
Aislinn refilled his cup with the now cool wine and
whispered that he'd forgotten part of the story, but he
shook his head and went on to tell of the battle itself.
"And when 'twas all done, 'twas Belesme that lay vanquished in the dust, his green plumes lying in his
blood," he finished, strumming the lute strings rapidly to signal the end of his song. There was silence
for a moment, and then the sound of Brian's snoring
broke the spell.

Roger pulled himself up by a low bench and reached
a hand to Eleanor. Yawning, he stretched sleepily. "If
'tis the only lay you know, my lord, you have managed
to remember it well," he murmured to Guy. "Aye, if
you could not earn your bread with your sword, I'd
warrant you could do it with your song." Putting an
arm about Eleanor's shoulders, he yawned again.
"Jesu, but I am tired tonight."

Eleanor stared upward at Guy, seeking some sign of
what she'd thought she'd seen, and was relieved to discover it had passed. 'Twas but a sign she was getting

older, she decided finally as she told herself that her mind had but wandered from the song he'd sung. "I'd not heard the story told in a long while—I thank you for it," she managed.

"Aye—I learned it in Wales, where his enemies still sing of Belesme." Guy grinned. " 'Tis a favorite there." Turning to look across to where Catherine gathered the empty cups, he addressed her, "And I am tired also—I would retire, Cat."

Her heart thumping against her ribs as though it would jump from her chest, Catherine averted her head and nodded. She knew she had no right to refuse him if he wanted to lie with her again. Placing the cups on a shelf for Hawise to tend to on the morrow, she tried to quell her own rising desire, denying even to herself what she wanted. But despite everything, she could not control the traitorous trembling she felt when he took her hand.

"Well, Lea," Roger murmured against Eleanor's hair after everyone had left, "what think you of the boy now? Think you he can please our Cat?"

"I think him a man grown," she decided softly. "And 'tis Cat who will have to please him."

"Nay—I had thought him angered with her, but now I can see he is besotted instead."

❧ 19 ❧

Guy sat on a bench near the bed while Arnulf removed his shoes. Behind him, he could hear Hawise humming as she brushed out Cat's hair, and he tried to hide the eagerness he felt by staring into the small fire before him. His back still smarted where his linen undertunic rubbed against the scratches she'd made but hours before, and his eyes were sensitive from the soap and the smoke, but his body, rather than being tired, was acutely alive as he thought of her.

"Sweet Mary, but you would make me bald," Catherine complained, ducking her head and pulling away from her serving woman. "Jesu!"

Unperturbed, the plump woman stepped back to lay down the brush. Having just remade the bed with clean sheets, she had a fair idea of what ailed her young mistress—Cat sought to cover her nervousness with ill temper. Aye, it could not be an easy thing on the girl's conscience to lie with one man when she thought she loved another.

Rising to pour herself a cup of wine, Cat kept her back to him, not knowing that the firelight shone through her thin undershift, outlining her body. "I think you have had enough." He spoke behind her as he stood.

"Nay, you'll not tell me—" Her voice trailed off with the realization that he had moved toward her. Her

211

mouth went dry and her heart beat wildly in a curious mixture of dread and anticipation.

Hawise, looking from one to the other, realized that her services were no longer needed. With a quick little bobbing bow, she excused herself and made for the door. They were either going to battle or breed, by the looks of it, and she had no business watching either.

Guy followed her to bar the door and then turned back to Catherine. Padding almost silently across the rush-matted floor, he reached to take the still-full cup from her nerveless fingers. "I favor my women sober, Cat," he murmured. Setting it down on the shelf where she'd gotten it, he watched the color drain from her face. "Nay, I'll not hurt you this time," he told her softly as his fingers stroked the bones of her shoulder through the thin fabric.

Her eyes widened at his touch and an uncontrollable shiver shook her as she waited. "God's bones, but you are cold," he whispered, taking her into his arms. She closed her eyes to keep him from knowing it was not cold, but heat that coursed through her body. But she willed herself to stand stock-still within his embrace—she'd not play the wanton for him this time.

He felt her stiffen in his arms and released her. He wanted her desperately, but he also wanted her willing. He waited until she turned away, and then he came up behind her. She had too much pride to let him see her give in, he reasoned, but an old whore had taught him once that there was more than one way to arouse a woman. Sliding his arms around her, he pulled her back against him, folding his arms across her waist and bending to nuzzle her hair with his cheek.

"I remember the smell of roses in your hair," he whispered.

"Well, tonight it stinks of lye soap," she snapped. "As well you should know, my lord."

"Aye, but 'tis still a smell headier than wine, Cat." Pressing his body more closely into her back, he held her with one arm and began brushing lightly over her breasts with the other, and as she leaned her head away, her hair fell back to bare her neck. His lips sought the sensitive place where her neck met her shoulder, and he was rewarded with the sharp intake of her breath. Her body trembled against his and her skin turned to gooseflesh as his lips moved upward to the shell of her ear.

His breath sounded like a gale as it rushed across her ear. She closed her eyes again and swallowed hard. "Sweet Mary, but I'd not have you do this to me," she whispered in near-anguish.

"Your body tells me a different tale," he murmured against her. He felt her nipples tauten beneath his palm and sensed he had half the battle won. Both of his hands moved to cup her breasts through her undershift and his thumbs teased the peaks that strained against the thin cambric.

She caught at his hands to stop them with her own, but she could not still the waves of desire that threatened to overwhelm her. He was rubbing against her back, letting her feel his aroused manhood through their clothing, and when his hands moved from her breasts, they skimmed over her rib cage and then lower to smooth the fabric of the undershift over her hips. And it was as though even the light touch of his fingertips had the power to awaken an ache deep within her. Her pulse pounded so loudly in her ears that she was unaware he eased her shift upward until she felt his hand on the bare skin of her thighs, and suddenly she didn't care anymore. Every nerve, every sense in her body was tuned now to his touch and was centered between her legs. She didn't even hear him whisper soft love words as his fingers found the wetness there and slid inside. A low moan escaped and rose to an animal cry while fire spread and engulfed her. She tried to turn in his arms, twisting against him, wanting the feel of him, wanting him to feel her need of him.

He lifted her by her waist and backed toward the bed, and then when he reached it, he brought her shift up over her shoulders, pulling it off even as he laid her down. Fleetingly, somewhere in the back of her brain, she wondered where he'd learned to do that, and then she watched wide-eyed as he stripped himself of his clothes.

She'd expected him to cover her with his body, to take possession of her and give her what she wanted now, but he eased into the bed beside her and began exploring her body leisurely with his hands, watching her with those strangely beautiful eyes of his until she thought she could stand it no longer. She wanted to tell him she was ready, but could find no words. Her body arched as his fingers found her again, and she thought surely he meant to come to her now. Instead, he bent his head to kiss her, brushing her lips with agonizing slowness and then taking full possession of her mouth as though to savor the taste. Her legs opened invitingly, her desire making her shameless, and still she waited, wanting his body to release hers from its mindless need.

He probed and stroked and teased until she forgot all else save the exquisite sensations her body gave her. With her eyes tightly closed again, she was in another world of intense pleasure where everything centered on what he was doing to her. Her body thrashed, bucked, and moved ceaselessly beneath his hand, and still he would not take her. She felt her senses heighten to where the aching desire built into pulsing, throbbing waves that spread outward from where he touched her, consuming all of her. No longer caring what he would think, she cried out in great gasps of ecstasy until the intensity ebbed and she floated finally, breathless and at peace.

He'd not meant to take so long, but as he'd watched her, seeing her woman's response to his touch, he'd wanted her to feel what he knew whores only feigned. And now, as he saw the fine mist of perspiration on her forehead that made tendrils of hair cling to her temples, he knew he'd wanted to make it good for her, to make her want him even as he wanted her. Moving his hand to stroke the smooth, satiny skin of her belly, he waited for her to open her eyes. And when at last she stared up at him, he bent to kiss her again, to blot out the embarrassment that brought a rush of blood to her face.

"Nay, Cat—'tis how 'tis supposed to be between us," he murmured softly when she would have turned away. And the feel of her lips beneath his sent a thrill of renewed passion through him, reminding his own body that it had yet to be satisfied. His hand cupped her breast and the rosy tip budded anew. Lowering his head to rest on her chest, he licked the hardened nipple, teasing it with his tongue and then sucking, and he felt her tremble as her hands grasped his hair.

"Have done . . . I cannot . . . ohhhh . . ." Her fingers caressed the thick black hair restlessly as desire rekindled deep within her.

"Sweet Cat . . . my sweet Cat," he whispered as he eased his body over hers.

He awoke to the early morning sounds of a castle rising, and turned to ease Catherine off his arm. He'd slept with his arms wrapped around her, his body curled to draw warmth from hers, and now the limb tingled almost painfully from its cramped position. She slept the deep sleep of the sated and her face betrayed none of the night's passion. He propped himself up on an elbow and rubbed his aching arm while watching her. A slow, almost tender smile curved his mouth and warmed his eyes. Her dark hair lay tangled between them, spreading out from a face that would have made a sculptor proud of its perfection. God's bones, but there could not be another like her anywhere, he thought to himself, and yet she was his. Pride surged through him as he gingerly lifted the covers to look again on her body, a body that had given him more pleasure than any other, a body that, while still as stone now, had moved beneath him with such abandon but hours before. Whereas whores were paid to moan and pant and cry out their pleasure, Cat of the Condes had responded to him with such fire that she'd made his desire her own. He let the coverlet fall and smoothed her tangled hair back from her temples softly to avoid waking her.

A cock crowed somewhere in the outer bailey, breaking through his reverie and reminding him he was hungry. He rolled away from her to sit on the edge of the rope-hung bed and collect his thoughts. She moved behind him, adjusting her position to the shifting of the mattress, and sighed heavily in her sleep. Rising, he reached for his discarded chausses that lay in a heap at the bottom of the curtained bed. Jesu, but he'd wanted her like nothing he'd ever wanted before, he remembered. Aye. That thought gave him pause.

He'd managed to survive twenty-four years by the sheer strength of his will and his acknowledged fighting skill. There'd never been any softness, any ease in his life—not his earliest years, spent unwanted in his grandsire's house—not in the lonely isolation of the monastery—not when his father had grudgingly brought him out as heir to his patrimony—and certainly not since he'd inherited. Had it not been for William, he'd not have been valued at all. Memories of aching loneliness, of wanting his cold father's acceptance, washed over him. Nothing he had ever wanted had come to pass—or if it had, it had not lasted.

He turned back to stare at the sleeping Catherine. Aye, she'd given him her body with abandon, but even in that, he'd had to make her want him. He could lie with her every night, he could get his heirs of her body even, but his rational mind had to admit that he might never possess her heart. He could be her husband, her lord and master, but he wanted more of her than that— he wanted her to be what no one else had been to him.

The cock crowed again. With a reluctant sigh he pulled on his chausses and sat to garter them, wondering how early Lord Roger broke his fast. But even as he wrapped the leather bands about his legs, his thoughts went back to Catherine. God's bones, but in those years since Tinchebrai, he'd thought he'd ended his foolish dreams of her—and yet he'd had but to see her again to rekindle them. Absently he leaned to pick up his undershirt and pulled it over his head. He'd allowed himself to be at no man's mercy, he'd kept his distance from his fellow magnates out of wariness, and now he was hostage to a mere girl—a girl who did not even reach his shoulder. Well, he could never let her know—'twould give her too much power over him if she even suspected how much he yearned to be everything to her.

His feet found his leather shoes and he tugged them on, straightening the points beyond his toes. A man ought to wear boots rather than such silliness, he told himself, for what good was something that extended so far that some men stuffed the long points while others rolled them? He never favored such nonsense, but it had gotten to where it was impossible to buy a pair otherwise. As it was, his were shorter than most, and still he thought of them as fool's shoes.

His overtunic was wrinkled and in need of pressing, but he had only two others suitable for wear at the Condes. Aye, that was another thing—as Count of Rivaux, he outranked Roger de Brione in title, but he was a pauper in comparison. While Lord Roger had kept his lands by not fighting, Guy had lost Rivaux and its revenues for five years in one battle.

Idly he wondered what Catherine would think of him when she realized he did not even have sufficient money now to pay for lodgings for her in Rouen. Nay—he'd not tell her. Mayhap when he got to Rivaux, he would find things were not so bad as he expected them, and after fall crops, mayhap he'd be a richer man. Before Tinchebrai, he'd had numerous estates throughout Normandy, and now he did not even know if Henry meant to restore more than just Rivaux itself to him.

His boast to Roger that he had other castles had been made recklessly, because he didn't want Cat's father to think him unable to provide for her. Under other circumstances she would have been dowered when she came to him, but since he'd wed her without her family's blessing, or even consent, he could scarce expect anything—nay, he would not take it even were it offered.

"Art wake early."

He spun around guiltily at the sound of her voice and found her propped up looking at him. Her tangled hair fell about her shoulders in wild disarray, spilling over the covers she clutched to her breasts, and her great dark eyes were serious, as though they would know his thoughts now. And whatever she saw sent a rush of color to her face.

"I did not mean to waken you," he apologized.

"Nay—you did not. Most days I am up before this."

"I thought you'd be overtired."

Her blush deepened, sending desire through him again, and he had to look away to master himself. He ought to be sated—able to go days without her after the night past—and yet he wanted her now. It was as though the more he had of her, the more he would want of her. Resolutely he reached for the wrinkled tunic and laid it across one of the benches. His back still to her, he rummaged in a box for another one. Finding a relatively plain blue overtunic, he shrugged it over his head before he dared turn to her again. And when he looked back, she'd already risen and pulled on her undershift. He breathed a sigh of relief that she was covered at least.

She walked to the narrow slitted window and threw open the shutters to breathe deeply of the fresh spring morn. "When do we have to leave for Rouen, my lord? I'd—"

"I leave on the morrow. I am commanded to give my oath on Whitsunday."

At first she's not thought she heard him aright. "To-

morrow? But I . . .'' Her voice trailed off in consternation. "You leave on the morrow," she repeated,
swallowing. He did not intend to take her with him,
she realized incredulously, scarce able to believe it.

"Aye."

She felt a sense of shame that threatened her composure. Hot tears of humiliation welled in her eyes as
she realized that he'd used her as he would have a
castle whore—he'd come to the Condes and bedded
her, not once, but twice and more in the same day—
and now he meant to leave her to the certain pity of
her sisters. And, Sweet Mary, but she'd let him—nay,
she'd lain willing for him, giving him what she'd denied Brian. The fear that she'd been a fool made her
furious.

"Nay! I am neither whore nor leman, Guy of Rivaux, but rather your wedded wife! If you did not want
me, then you should have stayed in Wales!''

"I am come to do my liege's bidding," he reminded
her. "I will be back, I swear."

"Nay! If you leave me now, I'll not go with you
later, my lord. How do you think 'twill look to others
come to my sister's wedding when 'tis told that you
bedded me and left?'' Her voice rose angrily as she
choked back her tears. "D'you think I *wanted* you to
come back? Nay, but I did not! And did you think I
wanted to lie with you? Nay, but I did not! And if you
think that you can come and take and leave, you are
sore mistaken, Lord Guy!'' she hissed furiously.

"Cat . . .'' He took a step nearer and stopped, not
wanting to touch her for fear his resolve would col-
lapse.

"And do not cry 'Cat' to me!'' She looked around
her helplessly for a weapon to wound with. "Jesu! 'Tis
not any maid you would take for wife—'tis Catherine
of the Condes! And I'll not be insulted by the likes of
a man lately come from exile—I'll not!'' Her fingers
closed around an iron candle spike and she hurled it
at him, missing his head by a hairbreadth. It clunked

against the stone wall, breaking the candle and exposing the pointed spike.

"God's bones, Cat! You could have put out my eye!"
To his horror, she'd spied the dagger William had laid
on a table, and he lunged to intercept her. "Nay—'tis
enough of this!" He caught her at the waist and held
her at arm's length while she kicked and clawed at
him. Releasing her, he took possession of the dagger.
"I'd not thought you wanted me so badly, Cat," he
murmured as she faced him, panting.

" 'Tis your hide I would nail to the wall!" she spat
back. " '*I am come to do my liege's bidding,*' " she
mimicked. "Well, you can go back to King Henry and
tell him I'd rather be Brian's leman than *your* wife!"

The smile that had begun to form at the corners of
his mouth faded, and the gold in his eyes gave way to
cold green. She backed away, suddenly frightened of
the temper she saw in them. "Nay, I am all you are
given, Cat," he told her evenly as he advanced on her.
"If ever I think you have lain with anyone else, I will
kill him. You are mine to take and no one else's, Catherine of the Condes, and so long as blood flows in this
body, I will not hesitate to defend mine honor—do you
understand me?" His hand reached to cup her chin
and force it upward until her eyes met his. "*Do* you?"

"And what of *my* honor?" she cried. "Do you not
even care that I will be pitied—that 'twill be said that
you tire of me already!"

"In two days' time?" he asked incredulously. "Nay,
'twill not." He looked into the depths of her dark eyes,
trying to understand her, and he felt a surge of desire.
Dropping his hand as though burned, he exhaled
sharply and tried to think of what she was saying.
"Yesterday you shouted at me because I came, and
today you would shout because I must leave. Jesu, Cat,
but I cannot understand you. Which would you have
of me—that I go or stay?"

It was not fair of him to make her choose between
two things she did not want, she reflected bitterly.

"Since we are caught in this marriage neither of us willed, and since Holy Church says we cannot break the bond between us, then I would go with you to Rouen," she answered finally. "I'd not be left to pity, my lord."

His pride would not let him tell her that he had not the money to take her to King Henry's court as befitted Catherine of the Condes. And as much as he wanted her even now, he'd not give her such power over him. His anger gone, he shook his head. "Nay, Catherine, but I cannot take you with me now. And you cannot wish to absent yourself from your sister's wedding, after all." Not daring to touch her again, he nodded toward her dress. "Put on your gown and comb your hair, that we may go down to eat."

"You have ended my appetite."

"Catherine . . ." He walked to pick up the dress she'd worn the night before and handed it to her. "I have an accursed temper—so much so that it has taken me all my life to master it even poorly. I would not try me further this day were I you."

"I cannot help that I—that we—cannot like what we are given, my lord."

His gaze traveled past her to the rumpled bed and a slow smile formed again, curving his mouth. "Nay?" he questioned with raised eyebrow. " 'Twould seem we were content enough in each other last night."

"But I would have more than that," she replied, turning away in shame.

He sobered. "Even that is more than many get, Cat."

"Mayhap, but 'tis not enough for me—I cannot but want what my parents have, my lord. I would be valued as my mother is by my father."

"Cat . . ." He raised his hand to reach to her and then dropped it.

"And if you think it but a foolish wish, Guy, then there can be naught but this between us."

"I can be no Roger de Brione, Cat—there is but one

of him on this earth.'' He reached out again and turned her back to face him, holding her shoulders and looking into her tear-sparkled eyes. ''But I can give you children of your body—we can found a house together, Cat.''

''And you think that is what I want? That I want to live my life as naught but mother to your sons? Sweet Mary, but there is more to me than that!''

He knew not how to answer her—he could not bring himself to say what he wanted of her. He would not let her see what she had the power to do to him—not until he knew for certain that he could make her forget Brian FitzHenry. Finally he drew her into his arms, where she stood rigid and unyielding. ''I would that I could take you to Rouen with me, Cat, but I cannot.''

❧ 20 ❧

Brian FitzHenry felt the toe of Aislinn's slipper when she kicked him awake. Rolling over in his pallet, he blinked against the morning light and shielded his eyes with his hand. His head ached as though it had been split with a battleax and his mouth was sour with the taste of last night's wine.

"Get up and send your whore away," she ordered him coldly.

"Wha . . . ?" He shook his head as though to clear it and winced from the pain. "Oh . . . 'tis you," he mumbled, drawing his blanket to cover his head. But even as he turned away, her foot hit him again in the small of his back. "Jesu! Why are—?" He didn't get a chance to finish his question before she poured the pail of drinking water over his head. Beside him, Tyra came awake with a shriek of outrage.

"Whore," Aislinn repeated contemptuously. "You ought to be tending to your babes rather than getting more of them, Tyra."

The serving woman clutched Brian's blanket to her bare chest and stared insolently at the younger girl. Brian, sensing even through the cobwebs of his mind that Linn was angry, slapped Tyra hard on her thigh and pushed her off his pallet. "Nay—go on." Sitting up, he wiped his face with the corner of the blanket

223

and looked up balefully at the girl who stood over him
with her hands on her hips.

"Get up—else I'll douse you again."

"God's beard, but you are cross," he complained
as he struggled to sit and the blanket fell away, exposing his nakedness all the way to his lap. " 'Tis no
place for you, Linn."

"Nay, it is not, but I would speak with you about
Cat, Brian. Get up and get dressed and come down to
the field—I will meet you where the quintains are set."

"Jesu, but you cannot just wake a man and—"

"The sun is already high and everyone has eaten
but you. Maman already meets with the butler and the
chamberlain to speak of the guests, Papa has gone
hawking with Geoffrey, as you may remember if you
were not too drunk to note it, and Cat practices with
Pippa and Bella, showing them how they are to com-
port themselves at my wedding. Now, do you get up
or do I have to go to Papa with the tale?"

"What tale?" he asked warily. "God's beard! Make
sense, will you?"

"Are you getting out of that pallet or not?"

"Aye, but—"

"Then I will see you at the quintains—and do not
stop to eat on your way."

The skirt of her embroidered overgown brushed
against him as she twitched it behind her and marched
from the room. With a sigh that pained his aching
head, he groped for his clothes, wondering how it
could be thought that she was the sweet-tempered one.
He stood naked to relieve himself in the chamber pot
and then hastily pulled on his chausses. If Linn meant
to carry some tale to Roger, he must have done something ill, but his memory failed him. Jesu, but he could
not even remember taking Tyra to his pallet. Not bothering with his undertunic, he pulled on a plain brown
wool overshirt and belted it over his chausses to cover
himself. Cross-banding his legs to smooth the hose
over them, he tried to think. Aye, he'd drunk far more

wine than he should have, but he'd done nothing beyond that, surely. He leaned over to pull on his slippers and tied the long toes back.

He had to balance himself against the stones with one hand and hold his head with the other to negotiate the narrow steps down from the old square tower where the unmarried men slept. Passing the old chapel, a relic from when the Condes was but one tower and a wall, he paused, wondering if he ought to ask God's pardon for whatever he'd done ere he faced Aislinn again. But for what? "I would speak to you of Cat," she'd said. Jesu, if he did not have enough on his mind there, for Cat had been behaving strangely to him ever since Rivaux had left nearly a week before.

"It took you long enough," Aislinn greeted him sourly when he let himself through the gate and into the practice field. She stood waiting beneath the tall wood-and-straw targets used to train squires on horseback in the arts of lance and mace.

"You did not want me to empty a full bladder?" he retorted. "Or did you want to watch?"

"Sometimes you make me glad I had no brother," she shot back. "You give me a disgust of men."

"Then 'tis well that you wed Mayenne, for he's more maid than man."

"I did not come here to speak of Geoffrey—'tis Cat who worries me."

He moved to lean against one of the quintains. Squinting in the sun, he passed his hand over his face and wished for all the world that he had some wine to ease his pain. "What of her? God's blood, Linn, but you have changed," he grumbled with feeling. "There was a time when you were the gentle little sister, but I vow you've cracked my ribs with your foot."

" 'Tis no more than you deserve, Brian Fitz-Henry."

"Jesu!" He looked skyward, shaking his head, and blanched from the sun's brightness in his eyes. "And what is it that you think I have done this time?"

"I'd not see my sister dishonored, Brian."

"Dishonored? I know not of what you speak," he muttered. Then, meeting her eyes, he sobered. "But that's what you think I want, isn't it?"

"Aye, and only a blind man could not see where you would lead her."

"Aislinn, I swear to you—"

"Do not waste words with me, Brian. I saw you and I heard you last night."

"Then you mistook what you saw."

She shook her head. "Nay, but I did not, and I swear to you that if ever again I hear you tell her how Guy of Rivaux will not know of it if she lies with you, 'tis to my father you will answer."

He colored guiltily, remembering vaguely that he'd shared Cat's trencher the night before and wondering if he had said such a thing. She'd been in high temper, and her determined gaiety in the face of those who came to witness Aislinn's wedding had made her even more beautiful. Aye, he could have said something, he supposed. "It must have been the wine," he conceded, "for I remember it not."

"You remember it not. You have no memory of how 'twas that you stroked her hair and then her shoulder, and then, when she did not draw away, you leaned to whisper, 'Come to me, Cat—he will not know now.' God's blood, Brian, but if any had heard you but me, you might as well have branded her your leman in front of everyone! And had Papa not been on the other side of Maman, and had they not been speaking with Geoffrey's father, he would have heard it! As it was, I had to convince my betrothed husband that *his* ears deceived him!"

"I swear I—"

"I care not what you swear, Brian—I heard you with mine own ears. You sought to use my sister's anger with her wedded husband to get her in your bed. What a fool you are—what a fool!" She paced furiously before him. "If Guy of Rivaux even suspected what you have said to Cat, not even King Henry could save you from his wrath—do you not know that?''

"If he cared for her, he'd not have left.''

"Jesu! And that makes it right? Nay, but it does not! There is the matter of her honor, and her husband's honor, and my father's honor—and my honor even. I would not have Geoffrey or his father discover such a thing, else they might think *me* unchaste. Just because you would lie with anything from hag to wench to . . . to . . .'' Words failed her at that point.

"To Cat,'' he cut in. "Aye, I admit it, but who would not? Think you Rivaux did not bed her when he was here?''

"He had the right, Brian. He had the right. He is her wedded husband, lest you would forget it.''

"Why did you not speak of this last night?''

"I had not the chance, and I would not have wanted anyone to note it, but if she'd not shared my bed whilst Geoffrey and the count had her chamber, I'd have gone to Papa.''

"Well, it never happened—I took Tyra to my pallet, as you saw.''

"Not because you did not wish it,'' she answered. "Cat said 'twas not for me to interfere, but I'll not stand and watch you bring dishonor to my sister and my family, Brian. I'll not let you turn her anger at her husband against her. She may be blind to your lust, but I am not.''

"The blame is not mine alone,'' he replied. "She has teased and enticed me since we were children, and well you know it.''

"She thinks she loves you, but I'll warrant 'tis but that you were the only boy we knew then, for I cannot think her foolish enough to really want a man who lies with anyone who will spread her legs for him.''

"Linn, I meant her no dishonor last night, I swear. I do not even remember what you say.'' He met her eyes ruefully and shook his head. "I had too much wine to remember anything.''

"Aye, you had too much wine—you have had too much wine ever since Guy of Rivaux came to the Condes. Look at you—look at yourself, Brian Fitz-Henry!" she challenged. "Are you proud of what you are? Can it be that you want naught but to live at my father's table?"

"My father gives me not the means to live at any other," he answered bitterly. "This is my home as much as it is yours, Linn. I fostered here almost as long ago as you were born."

"Aye, but you are a boy no longer."

"I have not the means to go anywhere else," he repeated.

"You have a good sword arm and a horse, Brian. Do as my father did and take service with a great lord. Earn a place for yourself and do not seek to be that which you are not." Seeing the slow flush that crept to his face, she added in a gentler tone, "You can never be my father's son or my sister's husband, Brian, but that does not mean that you cannot be lord of your own lands one day. Go to your father . . . offer him your service. He knows what it is to have naught—the old Conqueror left him no land, but only a few silver marks. If he is king now, 'tis because he used his wits." Her dark eyes met his soberly and held them. "If you think to do naught but drink and wench, you'll be but a drunken sot, fit for nothing but sitting with your head in your trencher."

Stung, he stared hard at her, seeing her not as the child who had followed him and Cat about when they were children, but as a woman grown and ready to be married, a woman not afraid to speak the truth to him. "Why do you tell me this, Linn? Why do you care what happens to me?" he asked finally. "And why did you choose not to tell your father?"

"Because he'd send you away."

" 'Tis what you would have me do, is it not? You are telling me to leave, Linn."

"Brian, you are as a brother to me—can you not

understand that? I want you to go of your own will, and not because you are sent in disgrace,'' she answered simply. "I'd have you use the skills my father taught you, and I'd see you return someday as lord of your own lands.''

"You would have me trade wenching for warring, Linn.''

"I'd have you make your own way.''

"My father gives me nothing. I am but one of his bastards and nothing more. And I am not one of his favorites like Richard or Robert, so he finds no heiress for me. God's blood, Linn, but 'tis Earl of Gloucester he makes Robert of Caen! And yet when I asked him, he would not give me Catherine of the Condes!''

"Be glad of it. How long do you think Cat would tolerate your bastards if you were to wed to her? You'd have to learn constancy or you'd need a taster for your food.''

Even through the pain that pounded in his temples and throbbed behind his eyes, he knew she spoke the truth. He'd known even before he came back to the Condes that Cat was lost to him. And he'd sworn to himself long ago that he'd do nothing to harm Roger. Aye, not even Cat was worth the cost if he lost the love of her father. Mayhap that was the reason he hated and feared Guy of Rivaux so much—not because he had Catherine, but because he now shared a bond of blood by marriage with Roger de Brione.

"Brian . . .'' She reached to lay a comforting hand on his shoulder, knowing she'd spared him no pain.

"Nay—if you are going to tell me again what a sot I have become, I'd not hear it,'' he told her wearily.

"You are not a sot—'tis that I fear you will become one. I'd see you rise before the world as my father has done.'' She dropped her hand and sighed. "Come on, I had the cooks save food for you.''

He pushed off from the quintain support and tried to ease his aching neck. Falling in beside her for the walk back, he felt a sense of loss.

Finally, after several minutes' silence, she spoke. "Why do you need so many women, Brian? Is it because you cannot have Cat?"

"Mayhap I am my father's son."

"But you do not have to be."

He reached for her hand and held it as they walked. "You should not worry over me or Cat when 'tis you who are to wed this week. You should think of happier things."

"Aye, but I'd not see either of you unhappy."

"Do you wish to wed him?"

"He is my father's choice for me. And we have been betrothed since I was twelve." She stopped to look up at him. "I am almost seventeen, Brian, so I have stayed here longer than most girls stay at home."

"Aye." He'd heard his father complain that Roger de Brione valued his daughters too highly, refusing to send them to husbands until he could delay no longer. But in Geoffrey of Mayenne's case, he'd warrant there was more to it than that. The boy who'd showed such promise when he was twelve had proven to be pleasant enough in a gentle, almost girlish way. And he'd grown no taller than Brian, and without the huskiness necessary to wield a broadsword. Aye, if Mayenne had not pressed the matter, Brian doubted Roger would have ever honored the pledge between them. And Brian thought it a pity that he had, for while she did not have Cat's breathtaking beauty, Aislinn was far too comely for the likes of Geoffrey of Mayenne. But it was not his place to say anything that would make her dissatisfied with the husband she had to take.

"Art silent."

"What would you have me say? You have called me a sot and a lecher and have said I am too lazy to earn my bread with my sword arm."

"I never said you were too lazy—do not give me words I did not speak."

"Your pardon—I am but a sot and a lecher, then." In spite of everything, his face broke into a grin.

"God's blood, Linn, but you keep a man from his own conceit, do you not?"

She looked up, surprised by his sudden lightness. He was not a handsome man like Guy of Rivaux, but there was something about him that made women like him. And she was, after all, a woman. "Aye," she answered with a smile that crinkled the corners of her brown eyes. "In your case, Brian FitzHenry, 'tis most necessary that someone do it."

❧ 21 ❧

Unable to sleep, Guy spent a restless night contemplating his meeting with the man who'd sent him into exile nearly five years before. Some things were different now: Henry was the acknowledged lord of all he'd coveted, holding both England and Normandy as his father had done; and some things were the same: the Norman barons still fought among themselves and resisted ducal rule to the extent that England's king spent more than half his time being Normandy's duke. And this year had been worse than most, for despite Henry's determination to rule both lands, he'd not been able to keep the old Saxon custom of wearing his crown in England on the major feast days because of the unrest in Normandy.

It had begun this time when Maine had gone to the warlike Count of Anjou upon the death of Elias of Maine, and even Henry dared not leave the duchy—not when the age-old rivalry with Anjou threatened again. And unless he mistook the matter, Guy expected France to take advantage of the growing strife. Already he'd heard in Rouen that Robert of Belesme, bolstered by French gold, had crossed from his sanctuary in France into the Vexin to burn whole villages and destroy the crops before they'd scarce begun to grow. Amid the growing violence, it was speculated that Henry would ask Roger de Brione to take the field against the Devil of Belesme once again.

But the strife that brewed boded well for Guy, he'd decided as he lay awake among the snoring men who shared the common room in the ducal palace. Aye, the more he thought on it, the better he felt about coming home. With Elias dead and de Braose, Malet, and Bainart deprived of their lands, there were few, other than the Lord of the Condes, strong enough to combat either Anjou or France—and certainly none other who would willingly pit himself against Belesme. But if Guy had nothing else to offer, he had acknowledged skill as a fighter, both as a knight and as a leader of men, and he meant to make use of his own reputation to redeem his lands of Henry. Nay, Henry needed him now.

Rising early, he endured the combined ministrations of Arnulf, Alan, and William, even submitting to a fresh barbering, to make himself presentable for court. But when Arnulf thought to give him a liberal sprinkling of rosewater, he'd had enough. "Nay," he told him, pushing him away, "I'd not go smelling like a maid going to her marriage bed."

William looked at him from beneath grizzled brows and shook his head to hide his pride. "There's naught about you to be mistaken for a maid, my lord—not when you stand a full head taller than Henry and half a head taller than most. Aye, and not with that face of yours—'tis more like to turn a maid's head than be mistaken for one."

Guy instinctively felt the thin scar that divided his cheek, rubbing it ruefully. "There are those who prefer shorter men with rounder faces."

"Art a fool if you would believe that," William snorted.

Arnulf smoothed the front of Guy's best tunic, a long overshirt of gold cloth that would reach well past his knees. Holding it to the light of the window, the body servant inspected it for spots and found none.

The design was magnificent—the black hawk of Rivaux, its talons studded with glittering cabochon stones, spread across his chest as though it swooped for prey. The design had been chosen for political reasons as much as anything else. Guy meant to go before his suzerain with the full trappings of his patrimony, for he intended to gain more than Rivaux if all went well for him. When dealing with Henry, he suspected that he'd need a show of strength rather than weakness. He stooped slightly to allow Arnulf to draw the rich garment over his head and straighten it over his trunk. For once, he was glad he'd not sold it, for now he could face Normandy and his court without anyone knowing just how straitened his circumstances had become.

Alan stood ready with Guy's stamped and studded sword belt and waited for Arnulf to lace the exposed undersleeves of Guy's red silk shirt with gold cord. His lord stood the almost ceremonial dressing patiently, knowing all too well that he needed to make Henry think he was still possessed of some wealth if he were to gain what he wanted. The irony was not lost on any of them—a poor man was likely to be rewarded poorly and a rich man stood to be given more to buy his loyalty. When Arnulf was finished, Alan buckled the heavy belt and stepped back to get Doomslayer, Guy's prized sword. William knelt to fasten to his ankles the spurs Guy had earned on knighthood.

Guy took the sword, balancing it as before a battle, testing its weight and admiring the intricate chasings that decorated the polished steel blade. He'd won it from a knight returning from the Holy Land, a fellow who'd told him the design was an incantation that protected whoever wielded it. His hand closed over the tall forged hilt. It felt good—it embodied the warrior in him. Satisfied, he slid it into the scabbard that hung almost to his feet.

"God's bones, but you look more ready for war than

peace, my lord,'' Alan murmured. "Had you come in mail, they'd think you meant to fight."

Guy nodded grimly, acknowledging the truth of it. He and William had discussed how to approach Henry and had decided that a martial appearance would serve him best, for he meant to remind his duke of his value as a fighter. Already in Wales there were those who had compared his ability to that of Robert of Belesme, and Guy meant to remind Henry of it. If Anjou threatened and Belesme raided, Henry had need of Guy of Rivaux.

Arnulf shook out the short cloak of green brocade and stood on tiptoe to fasten it at his master's shoulder with a large round brooch. He'd scarce managed the clasp before a page in Normandy's colors knocked lightly and entered the chamber.

"My lord of Rivaux?" he asked respectfully.

"Aye." Guy slid a sheaf of documents under his tunic.

"His Grace would see you now." His eyes wide in admiration, the boy took in Guy's tall frame, noting the exquisitely stamped scabbard and the hilt of Doomslayer. "Is it true, my lord, that you slew twenty Welshmen unaided at Wigmore? We had a fellow sing the story when we were at Shrewsbury," he blurted out suddenly.

"Nay." Guy watched the boy's face fall in disappointment and relented, grinning. " 'Twas but eight."

There was a buzz of whispers as they passed into Normandy's audience chamber, the same chamber where Curthose had first given him Catherine of the Condes, and Guy knew much of the talk was of him. For effect, he elbowed back his cloak to rest his hand on the hilt of his sword as he walked past the first group of courtiers. "Sweet Jesu," he heard someone utter, "he comes armed."

The knot in his stomach eased when he saw King Henry sitting in the carved chair of Norman dukes. He had his chance now, and it was as good a chance as he'd had on any battlefield. He walked slowly, savoring the swell of anticipation that followed him. Robert of Belesme had once gained much through his fearsome reputation, Guy remembered, and he himself was not above reminding everyone of his own military prowess—after all, he not only had to get Rivaux back, but he had to keep it. He stopped a short distance from the youngest of the Old Conqueror's sons, Henry, the first of his name to rule both England and Normandy.

The duke conferred with a clerk, giving Guy the opportunity to stake his ground first and to observe the man who would become his liege lord. Had he not met him before, Guy would have been disappointed, for there was little in the man's dress or appearance to distinguish him from any other. He wore but a plain gown slit at the sides to expose his hose where it fell away at his knees, and his head was bare. Then Guy noted dispassionately that he'd abandoned the Norman custom of being clean-shaven for a Saxon beard. But when Henry's brown eyes turned to him, Guy was almost arrested by the shrewd, calculating way the duke assessed him. They watched each other warily while the chamber grew quiet. Finally Henry beckoned him forward. Guy swung his scabbard backward as he knelt on one knee in obeisance and then rose unbidden.

"God's blood, but he's arrogant," one of the clerks whispered to another, drawing a barely discernible twitch of amusement in Guy's otherwise impassive face.

"How left you Wales?" Henry asked without preamble.

"Mayhap better than I found it, Your Grace," Guy responded easily.

"You are overmodest, my lord. I am told you have served me well there—Hereford was loath to have you leave him." Henry's eyes rested on Guy's sword hilt speculatively. "But then, my father believed a warrior is a warrior wherever he may be."

"If he has the inclination."

His eyes narrowing, Henry knew that although there was nothing disrespectful in the younger man's words, he was not returning as a penitent begging to be given what was already his. And the duke was enough of his father's son to appreciate what Guy of Rivaux could mean to him. Silently he was grateful that Eleanor had asked for his return, for now that he saw him, he instinctively saw a man capable of balancing Normandy's fractious barons. Aye, with Guy in Rivaux and Roger in the Condes, Belesme would find a duchy ready to stand against his raids. Even though Rivaux was young for the task, Henry had heard and seen enough to know that he'd not give an inch of what he held without a fight, something that could not be said for Gilbert of Nantes and a host of other barons. Aye, he'd have the inclination.

"Well-said." Henry nodded. "You will serve me well in Normandy, I think, if you are properly rewarded."

"I ask for but what is my birthright, Your Grace."

"Rivaux is yours—give me but your oath to keep it."

"And I will swear freely for it," Guy answered solemnly. "But there is the matter of my other estates—those I hold of my mother's dowry and as my grandsire's last heir." His eyes met Henry's squarely and held them. "If there is a dispute as to who should hold them, I am prepared to sue to determine my rights in ducal courts, Your Grace."

Henry stiffened, knowing full well that any hearing that touched on a man's birthright could stir others to follow the example. God's blood, but Guy of Rivaux was shrewd for one so young, almost as shrewd as he himself had been. The initial surge of anger he felt at the young man's audacity turned to grudging admiration—a dispossessed lord with naught but his sword arm to recommend him dared demand restitution in veiled terms. Waving vaguely to where the clerks sat behind long tables, he delayed, murmuring, " 'Tis a complicated matter, Lord Guy, and will take some time to determine which lands would bear a claim.''

Guy reached into the bosom of his overtunic and drew out a packet of writs that bore seals dating back before the Conqueror's time. ''If you will acknowledge receipt, Your Grace, they have my leave to examine these. I think they will find that my claim is primary in every case.''

Henry, who fancied the appellation of Beauclerc because it reminded people that he could read, took the writs and scanned them silently, noting the seals affixed at the bottom of each. The one pertaining to Rivaux itself predated Henry's great-grandsire. Nodding grimly, he handed them back to Guy. ''Give them to the clerks,'' he directed. ''They will be confirmed. You will do me homage and meet your feudal obligations for each.''

Guy gave an inward sigh of relief. Henry would no doubt exact a stiff price for what he grudgingly confirmed, but Guy was once again a landed magnate, possessing enough to carry weight in Normandy's council. ''Whenever Your Grace wills it,'' he managed aloud.

''You were with the monks, were you not?'' Henry asked dryly. '' 'Twould seem they taught you well.''

''Aye.''

''What think you of Sunday next?''

''If 'twould please Your Grace, I stand ready to swear to you now,'' Guy countered, his eyes still on Henry's. ''I'd return to mine own lands as soon as may be and look to my defenses before Belesme reaches Rivaux.''

''Aye, he burned it last year, and I doubt it has been repaired since. And, as 'tis Whitsunday, you will be well-witnessed.'' Henry stood, still looking upward at Guy, taking measure of him. ''You have my leave to swear now.'' Turning to the table of clerks, he ordered that the oath-taking be recorded for the marks of the magnates present.

Belesme had burned Rivaux. Guy's face never betrayed the anger he felt, but he silently vowed revenge on Robert of Belesme. Let other men boast of what they would do—he would do it.

Henry waited while the clerk's pen scratched carefully across the parchment. Impatient, he nodded to Guy. "You will go to Rivaux when you leave here?"

The image of Catherine as he'd left her floated before his face unbidden. "Nay," he decided, "I return to the Condes for a wedding first. Then I will go to Rivaux."

Grasping Isabella by the shoulders, Catherine propelled her after Philippa. "Go find Maman," she ordered the two youngest girls. "I would look to Linn."

"But I would watch her dressed," Bella protested
loudly.

"As would I—'tis not fair of you, Cat," Pippa added
with feeling. "How is it that you are sent?"

"Because I am a wedded lady. Now, be gone, both
of you, else I shall tell Papa you've no wish to attend
Linn at her wedding."

Bella hung back mutinously, but her sister clasped
her hand and pulled her toward the courtyard. "Have
done—Gerdis needs to straighten your sleeves anyway."

"Cat!"

Catherine turned back from watching the girls, to
find Brian waiting for her on the stairs. She'd scarce
seen him since that first night that Mayenne and his
retinue had come to the Condes, and she was surprised
to see him now. He was already dressed for the wedding and looked especially fine in a new blue tunic
that hung just past his knees, but she was almost too
angry to notice. He'd blown hot and cold since Guy
rode out to Rouen, first making a fool of himself over
her at supper and then ignoring her ever after. Her
sense of ill-usage grew at the sight of him.

"Oh, 'tis you," she muttered silently. "I cannot tarry for speech, for I am expected to aid Hawise in readying Linn, and I am overlate." She started to brush past him, but he caught her arm. "Nay, unhand me," she told him coldly.

"I am come to tell you that I am leaving after the wedding, Cat."

In spite of her anger with him, she stared, her eyes widening in surprise. He met her gaze soberly and nodded. She leaned against the rough-hewn stone and tried to comprehend what he was telling her. "You are leaving me also," she echoed slowly. Her anger gone, she felt nothing—not the wrenching anguish of his earlier parting from her, not the terrible pain of loss she'd expected. Instead, there was but a sense of emptiness when she looked at him, an emptiness that left her baffled.

"There's naught for me here, Cat," he told her gently.

" 'Tis your home."

He shook his head. "Nay. I thought I could return and we would be as we always were—you and me . . . Roger . . . the girls. But 'tis not so, Cat. You are Rivaux's wedded lady, and I can never be your father's son. Linn told me that but a few days ago, and I've thought of naught else since. She is right, you know." His brown eyes never wavered from her face. "If I stay here, I'll never know if I can make my own way or not."

"But what will you do? You have no lands . . ." Her voice trailed off as she remembered she touched on his bitterness.

"I mean to go to my father. I'll offer him my service, but if he has no place for me, then I will turn to another landed lord. There cannot but be one who would welcome a man trained in the skills of war by Roger de Brione, I'd think. Aye, and if none will take me, I'll return to my mother's house."

"But 'tis *Wales*, Brian."

"Aye, and there is always fighting there. Mayhap the husband my father gave my mother will welcome me, if not for my blood, then for the sword I bring him." He scanned her face, disappointed that she did not even protest her love for him. "Rivaux managed to come back from there with my father's favor—mayhap I could also."

"Brian—"

"Nay. Do not feel the need to say what is not in your heart, Cat. 'Tis time for the truth, I think."

"Do you not love me even a little?" she managed to ask.

"Aye, but not as we have thought. Linn made me realize that what I really feel for you is but the love of a brother. Oh, I admit that I have wanted you—who could look on you and not think the thought?—but 'tis your father's love I have sought. Mayhap I believed I loved you because I wanted to be his son. God knows, but my own father loved me not."

"Sweet Mary!"

"And 'tis not all my fault if things are different between us, Cat. You were not the same Cat who came back from Tinchebrai, I think. I did not see it then, but I see it now as I look back to then."

"Nay, I . . ." She halted numbly and looked away. "I was glad this year when you came back to the Condes."

"I know. But have you thought that 'twas because you sought diversion from your life here? Your place is with Guy of Rivaux, Cat, and I think you already know it."

"You do not have to leave because of me, Brian."

"There's naught here for me—you will go to Rivaux, Linn will go to Mayenne, and your father has a full household. If I stay, there is but wenching and drinking to occupy my time. Your father is at peace, and there's none foolish enough to challenge him. If I stay, I will become but a drunken sot too willing to take any woman to my bed." He reached to lift her chin with his knuckle. "Linn made me see the truth, Cat."

Brian was leaving her. Oddly, the pang of sadness turned to relief: she need not feel guilty for lying with Guy of Rivaux. And then a different, deeper sense of loss struck her, leaving a dull ache in her breast. Rivaux did not want her either. To him she was but a mother for his sons. But she had too much pride to let anyone know how deeply Guy's leaving her had stung. Gathering her dignity, she managed to smile at the man before her. "Wheresoever you go, whatsoever you do, Brian FitzHenry, I wish you Godspeed." Tears brightened her eyes as she leaned to kiss his cheek. "God keep you safe."

"God's teeth, Cat, but I think I like your claws better," he told her gruffly. "Aye, I shall miss you."

Aislinn stood in the center of her mother's solar while Hawise straightened the glittering gown over her plain chainse. The fabric, called "flames of fire" for its iridescence, caught the light from the window, and its interwoven threads of red, green, and gold seemed almost to glow. Chafing her cold hands, the girl felt a sense of panic. She was overold to wed and she went to a kind and gentle lord, she told herself to bolster her flagging courage. Aye, there was little to dislike in Geoffrey. Surely he would use her gently. Maybe too gently. She'd watched him these last days since Brian had said he was more maid than man, and what she'd first thought but gentle courtesy she'd begun to see as a flaw. Indeed, even her father had remarked that the Geoffrey who came to the Condes seemed little like the boy he'd met years earlier. But who could envision what changes time would bring? Mentally she compared him with Brian FitzHenry and Guy of Rivaux and found him sadly lacking in manly appearance. But Brian wenched, she admitted, and Guy made Cat unhappy. And somehow she could not see Geoffrey taking another woman to his bed, nor could she see him quarreling with her as Guy did with Cat. In truth, she could not see him doing *anything*.

"Sweet Mary, but I hope you do not mean to greet your guests with such a face, Linn," Catherine chided from the doorway." 'Twill be remarked that you appear to mourn rather than rejoice in your marriage." Coming into the room, she plopped on one of her mother's cushions to watch Hawise weave strands of thread taken from the gown's fabric through Aislinn's thick chestnut hair. Then, sensing her sister's agitation, Cat ordered Hawise away. "See to her chaplet— 'tis in my chamber—and I will finish this." Rising, she picked up several shiny threads and moved to start a new tiny braid at Aislinn's crown. "Go on."

"Jesu, 'tis well you are a countess, Cat, for you speak as though you were born to be obeyed," the younger girl observed.

"Mayhap I was. Stand still, Linn." Separating the hair with her fingers, she began almost conversationally, "Now, what is it that ails you?"

"Nothing. God's blood, but you are rough, Cat— you'll have me sore-headed before you are done."

"Nay, and do not think to turn me from my question. You are as pale as cow's milk. Is it that you fear to be bedded?"

Aislinn pulled her head away and walked to the window to stare into the courtyard below. "I know not what I fear," she admitted. "Mayhap I fear that I will never have what you and Maman have."

"No one has what is between Maman and Papa, Linn. And you are mistaken if you think that there is aught between Guy of Rivaux and me but the marriage bed itself." Cat moved closer and touched her sister's shoulder. "Come, 'tis time you were ready."

"At least you and Guy have words. Geoffrey does but smile at me!" Aislinn burst out. "Aye, I know not what I am getting!"

"Geoffrey is kind, Linn—he will use you far more gently than I am used."

"And you think that is what I want? Nay, I want . . . Jesu!" she cried, unable to put it into words.

Catherine remembered the fiery coupling between her and Guy and wondered if Aislinn could even guess how it was. "Do you understand what is to happen? Mayhap you are but overset, Linn."

"If you are asking if Maman has said aught to me—aye, she has. And I am not so ignorant that I have not seen the animals do it. 'Tis but that I cannot see Geoffrey do it! But then, I'd not expect you to understand—you who have Guy of Rivaux in your bed! Even Brian says Geoffrey is more maid than man, Cat," she added in a softer voice.

"You know not how it is. Aye, there is that between us, but when we are not in bed, we can do aught but quarrel." Catherine sought the means to make Linn more satisfied with her husband. "Aye, Geoffrey is not like to treat you as I am treated, and for that you may be grateful. In the time I have known him, Guy has pushed me in the dirt, threatened to beat me, turned me upside down in the bathing tub and nigh drowned me, bedded me, and left me. And you are a gentler soul than I am—you'd not like it."

"You cut his face," Aislinn reminded her. "At least you are well-matched in temper, Cat."

"Nay, we are not."

"Well, I would rather have your husband than mine. I'd even rather have Brian than Geoffrey." Turning back to Cat, Aislinn managed a rueful smile. " 'Tis unseemly of me, isn't it?"

Catherine shook her head. "But what would you do about Tyra and the others? You always chided me for a fool for saying the same thing."

"I'd do nothing about *them*," she decided. "But were he mine, I'd tell him that I'd castrate *him* if any more wenches claimed to bear his babes." Sobering, Linn asked Catherine, "But what of Guy? Do you think he warms his bed with others?"

"I know not." But then Cat remembered how he'd

touched her, and the now-too-familiar longing came over her. He'd learned that somewhere, after all. Putting it from her mind, she sighed. "I suppose he does."

They were interrupted by Hawise returning with the chaplet, a delicately woven crown of spring flowers and gold ribbon that Cat had worked earlier. Lifting the gossamer veil of soft baudekin over Aislinn's head, the woman nodded to Cat. "She is the prettiest bride wed in the Condes, do you not think?"

"Aye, she is that."

"And as well you both know, I am the *only* bride ever wed here," Aislinn retorted.

"Well, then you will be the prettiest one ever to be wed here." Cat laughed as she hugged her.

The chapel was hot as the small crowd come to witness the marriage took their seats and waited. From the side door Catherine watched her father escort Aislinn to the altar railing and step back. Leaning over, he straightened out the long train of the shimmering gown and whispered something to his daughter. How very like her father, Cat thought with a pang. He had loved each of the girls Eleanor had borne him without reservation, taking pride and pleasure in all of them. It was as though he never admitted wanting the son Eleanor had tried so hard to bear for him. Aye, and even King Henry chided him for not marrying them early where it would give him the greatest gain. And now, when he could delay no longer, he was sending Aislinn from the Condes regretfully. Soon Catherine herself would also be leaving. Thinking how little she would see of them after she left, she felt a lump form in her throat and she had to turn away.

When she could bring herself to look again, Geoffrey of Mayenne had joined her sister before the altar rail. Even though he was half a head taller than Aislinn, he looked pale and frail beside her, his pallor accentuated by the bright blue tunic he wore. Invol-

untarily Cat gazed across the small chapel to where
Brian sat in a tunic of the same color, and she could
not but note how vital and alive he looked in compar-
ison with Geoffrey. How she could have ever envied
Linn's gentle, sweet-tempered lord was beyond her.
She almost pitied her sister for her marriage bed now.

The clear, high-pitched voices of the small boys'
choir floated through the air as people shifted on their
hard seats and watched Geoffrey take Aislinn's hand.
Cat's mind harked back to the day in Rouen when she'd
wed Guy of Rivaux with as much pomp as Duke Robert could manage in such haste. Sybilla's ladies had
envied her so, showing their jealousy in petty ways,
for there'd been not a maid among them who would
not have willingly changed places with Catherine of
the Condes that day. Aye, and Guy would have nearly
made two of Geoffrey even then.

The singing ended and the Condes's chaplain began
by asking who gave Aislinn in marriage. Roger's voice
was low, almost muffled in answer, and Catherine had
to strain to hear him. Her eyes traveled to where her
mother sat, still and pale, beside the Count of Mayenne. There'd once been such hope of the marriage,
this union between powerful families, but the wedding
had been postponed more than once, first with Geoffrey's father pleading the boy's illness, and then with
Roger's growing reluctance to give his daughter to the
slender, almost delicate boy. But in the end, under
pressure from Henry and Mayenne both, he'd given in
and sent Linn's dowry to Mayenne. Cat watched her
mother struggle to hold back tears as Geoffrey repeated his vows to Aislinn.

Outside in the courtyard there was the sound of a
late arrival, probably someone who'd traveled far and
encountered trouble on the way. Cat glanced toward
the door curiously and then shrugged it off—whoever
it was had all but missed the wedding anyway. Aislinn's voice rang clear in the chapel, drawing Cat back
to her. Sweet Mary, but there'd be none to know of

her sister's misgivings, Cat reflected with pride: Aislinn was a de Brione through and through.

Their vows taken, the couple knelt for blessing, and the priest signed the Cross over them. Catherine was absorbed in watching and did not hear Guy come up behind her until he laid a hand on her shoulder and whispered, "I'd thought to be here earlier, but my horse was overtired." Nodding dumbly, she dared not turn around for fear he would see just how very glad she was to see him. She'd not have him know what his touch, the sound of his voice, could do to her. Instead, she leaned against the doorframe and tried to master her racing heart. Stealing a look upward, she could see he was still dressed for traveling, in dusty woolen tunic, braichs, and boots. His black hair was in windswept disarray above those flecked eyes of his, but to her he was the handsomest man in Christendom. As if he read her thoughts, he grinned, exposing those fine, even teeth. "I forwent the mail so I would not embarrass you—I thought surely if there was a safe place in Normandy, it would be in Roger de Brione's lands." Turning her back to the ceremony with his hands on her shoulders, he pulled her against him and breathed deeply of the rosewater scent in her hair. "I'd not forgotten how delicious you smell, Cat."

❧ 23 ❧

The sounds of men cheering loudly somewhere in the field beyond the keep slowly penetrated Catherine's consciousness. She came awake reluctantly, stretching lazily, savoring how good she felt, and reaching to touch her husband. "Sweet Mary, but . . ." she murmured, stopping with the realization that he wasn't there. Rolling over, she scanned the room curiously to find he'd already gone. She sank back against the pillow with a sense of disappointment—she'd wanted to watch him waken, to see those strange, beautiful eyes of his open, to ruffle that black hair back from his face, and to trace that straight profile of his as he'd done hers the night before. Aye, she admitted with a satisfied smile, and she'd like to do more than that with him.

A flush crept into her cheeks as she remembered how little attention either of them had paid to Aislinn's wedding feast, or to her bedding with Mayenne, as the anticipation had built between them until, when at last they were alone, there'd been no need for words. Sweet Jesu, but she knew not why it was thus—there was no love between them—but she'd not imagined it could be like that with a man. Aye, it was not until they'd both found release from all-consuming desire and had collapsed in each other's arms that he'd whispered sweet words to her. Looking down at the swell of her breasts beneath the covers, she remembered anew how his mouth had felt there, and she felt the tautening of desire. There was no mistaking it—she was the wanton wench he'd called her. But instead of chastising her for it, he'd seemed immensely pleased.

"Lady Catherine?" Gerdis peered apologetically into the room. "Lord Guy said I was not to wake you, but—"

"I am awake." Regretfully Cat gave up her memories of the night before and sat up. " 'Twould seem I have overslept." Stretching to ease sleep from her bones, she added, "Where is Hawise?"

"She tends your sister."

Aislinn. She'd scarce spared a thought for Linn, and yet now she could remember her lying silently in the bed while Guy and Brian had undressed Geoffrey. Even Brian had appeared to pity her sister, leaning to whisper encouragement rather than his usual bawdy comments, and Guy had murmured for Cat's ears alone that "I pray he is not as ill as I think him." She'd taken a second look at Geoffrey then and wondered if Guy were right—that it was illness that gave the boy his pallor. Certainly when the betrothal had been arranged, Cat's father had not noted anything amiss, but that had been years before. Aloud she managed to ask, "How fares Linn, then?"

"God willing, my lady, there will be an heir born to them."

Cat wished it were Hawise come to tend her—Hawise would not spare the earthy details of what had happened, but Gerdis, as Lady Eleanor's serving woman, considered it beneath her to gossip with the daughters of the house. Sighing, she rose. If she wanted to know anything, she'd have to ask Aislinn herself, she supposed. At least Geoffrey had managed to consummate the marriage, though, or Gerdis would not have mentioned children. Holding her arms out for the woman to slip her chainse over, Cat wondered aloud, "I do not suppose you have seen my husband?"

"Nay, but if you listen, you will hear of him," Gerdis responded as she pulled the undergown down over Cat's body. "There's scarce anyone left inside since 'twas said that your lord father and your lord husband would share their skills with Mayenne's squires. Aye, even your lady mother watches them."

She should have remembered. One of the boys in Hugh of Mayenne's retinue had begged to see Guy wield Doomslayer, and Guy had reluctantly agreed on the condition that her father would show his skill with Avenger, the famed sword he'd used against Belesme. How very like men, she reflected wryly: they would take any opportunity—even a wedding celebration—to demonstrate the violent arts of war. The noise outside took on meaning; apparently quite a crowd had gathered to watch two of the most skillful knights in Normandy.

Gerdis selected one of Cat's older gowns, saying " 'Twill leave your good ones to impress your husband's people in Rivaux," and held it out for her approval.

"Nay." Her thoughts on Rivaux himself, Cat shook her head. He'd been back but one night, and she meant to make sure that he looked at none but her. "I'd wear the purple one."

Shrugging, the woman shook out Cat's favorite gown and held it up to her. Catherine pulled it on while Gerdis lifted her hair from inside and let it fall over her shoulders. " 'Tis lovely hair, Lady Catherine," the woman murmured as she reached for Cat's comb. "More's the pity that it must be bound."

"Nay. Take the tangles and be done—I'd wear it down."

" 'Tis unseemly for a wedded lady," Gerdis reminded her.

"I'll cover it," Cat promised. The cheers grew

louder, making her impatient. "God's blood, but I'd not stand here all day whilst you do my hair."

"Then sit."

"Where's Hawise?"

"She still tends your sister."

As far as Catherine was concerned, there was none but Hawise who could please her, and the thin-faced Gerdis considered herself too important to minister to her lady's daughters unless told to do so. Most probably she'd chosen Cat this day because Cat was now a countess. Aye, but even in the Condes, there'd been a subtle change amongst the servants and men-at-arms once Guy of Rivaux had come for her. She was no longer "Cat" or "Lady Cat" as she'd been called as long as she could remember, for now even the seneschal, the bailiff, the butler, and the chamberlain addressed her as "Lady Catherine." The comb caught in one of Cat's tangles, almost bringing tears to her eyes. "Give it to me—I'd see Linn, anyway, and Hawise does not pull so much."

Shrugging imperturbably, Gerdis handed her the comb. "Do not forget your shoes, then. I'd not have you shame your mother with both your hair unbound and your feet bare." Her birdlike eyes met Cat's as she added, "Lady Catherine."

Comb in hand, Cat made her way to the chamber Aislinn had shared with Pippa and Bella before last night. For her second daughter's marriage night, Eleanor had moved the two younger girls onto pallets in her solar, and left the bed to Linn and Geoffrey. The image of Linn as last she'd seen her, quiet and composed, watching her new husband, floated before Catherine. Poor Linn. Fate had not been kind to her in her chosen husband. And yet Cat could not but be proud, for there was not the least public display of distaste for Geoffrey—Aislinn was their parents' daughter, above all.

She found her sister seated on a bench having her waving chestnut hair plaited. If anything was amiss, she gave no sign, gesturing instead to Cat to come inside. "Ah, I have stolen Hawise, have I not? God's blood, Cat, but what will you do when you go to Rivaux?"

"Maman says I may take her with me. *You* may take Gerdis, sister."

Aislinn made a face and shook her head. "Nay, 'tis Tyra who goes to Mayenne with me." Her brown eyes held Cat's. "The fortune is all yours, 'twould seem."

Cat eyed her curiously for a moment, seeking some sign of unhappiness, and thought she saw and heard a hint of wistfulness. "I'd not have Tyra if Maman told me to take her, Linn," she told her. "If I could not have Hawise, I'd ask for Gerdis—or mayhap Agnes. I'd as lief not bear Tyra's insolence—I'd have it beaten out of her."

"Mayhap I am not so unforgiving as you, Cat."

"Aye, mayhap you are not." Noting that Hawise had finished with her sister, she sat down and held out her comb. Then, watching as Aislinn rose to look out the window, she added casually, "Where is Geoffrey?"

"With everyone else in the Condes—watching men play like boys with the quintains. I wonder that you are here when 'tis your husband they would see."

"I came to see how you fared."

"I am neither content nor discontented, Cat. My husband is kind and pleasant, and I managed to please him, I think." Aislinn's chin quivered as she turned back, and the expression on her face prompted Catherine to send Hawise away hastily.

" 'Tis plain all is not well with you, lovey," she murmured sympathetically. "If he has mistreated you, we will go to Papa and—"

"Oh, 'tis no such thing, I swear to you. 'Tis . . ." Aislinn's face contorted piteously as she fought for control of herself. Sniffing back tears, she wailed, "Oh, Cat, I pray I may bear his heir while yet he lives!"

Catherine was at her side in an instant, enveloping her sympathetically. "While he lives . . . ?" she echoed faintly. "But surely it cannot be as bad as that—why would you say such a thing, Linn?"

"Aye, it is. After . . . when 'twas done last night, Geoffrey told me how it is with him, Cat." Aislinn spoke haltingly and then mastered herself. "He held me and . . . and said it sorrowed him that I would not know him as he once was." Tears sparkled in her eyes but did not brim as she bit her lip to calm its trembling. "His limbs are wasting. He has less use of them now than even a few months ago, he tells me. The physicians Count Hugh brought from Bologna cannot aid him and offer no hope that he will improve. 'Tis why his father pushed for the marriage—he feared he would have to return my dowry to Papa and he'd have no heir if Geoffrey dies—'twill go to Anjou. But if I bear Geoffrey's babe, Mayenne may yet stay free of Maine and Anjou."

"Holy Mary," Catherine breathed. "Does Papa know?"

"I am certain he does not."

"Oh, Linn, I am so sorry. I—"

"Nay. Do not waste your pity on me, Cat. 'Tis Geoffrey who bears the pain of dying." Aislinn broke away and stepped back.

"And you are not afraid—do you not fear to contract his malady?"

"He says he has had it some years now, and no others have gotten it."

"But can he . . . ? That is, is he able to . . . ?" Cat's voice trailed off.

"Can he get a son?" Aislinn supplied for her. "I know not, but he can try."

"And you can accept that?" Catherine asked incredulously.

"I gave my pledge before God and Holy Church, Cat. And now that I know what is wrong, I understand how it is for him. I mean to be a good wife to him if his father will let me, and when 'tis over, I will return to the Condes.''

"Oh, Linn!"

"Nay, do not weep for me. God willing, my son will rule Mayenne so that it does not go to the Angevin." Her eyes met Catherine's soberly now as she added, ''Aye, and I will choose for my next husband a man strong enough to hold Mayenne if I am given a son.''

"I do not care about Mayenne, Linn, I care about you. You cannot—"

"I will do anything to thwart Anjou, Cat. So long as he threatens King Henry, he threatens the Condes. Besides, Geoffrey needs me." Cocking her head to listen to cries of "Rivaux! Rivaux!" outside, Aislinn reached for Catherine's hand. "By the sound of it, they salute your husband. Come, 'tis time we saw what 'tis he does.''

Catherine followed her almost numbly, wondering how her sister could accept what had been given her. Had she been the one to wed Geoffrey, she doubted she would have managed to be so calm, but then, Aislinn was the sweetest-tempered of Roger de Brione's daughters. But that was not saying much for the tempers of any of them. For a fleeting moment she wondered what her father would do if he knew how Hugh of Mayenne had cheated them, but then she realized there was naught he could do now. She thought of going to her mother. But Eleanor would only be heartsick for Aislinn, a bride going forth from the Condes with a doomed husband, and there was nothing she could do about it. Catherine decided that if Aislinn thought herself able to accept Geoffrey, then she should hold her tongue.

Every guest, every man-at-arms, every idle servant stood gathered along lines drawn through the grass on either side of the practice field. At one end a group of younger men, squires from the Condes, Mayenne, and Rivaux's retinue, gathered to admire the sword that had bested Belesme nineteen years earlier, while older men of the household examined the famed Doomslayer as William de Comminges explained the strange inscription on its blade. After the stories of Guy's Welsh campaigns, there was considerable curiosity as to whether it bore peculiar powers. Catherine shielded her eyes and scanned the field for her husband.

· Hugh of Mayenne saw them and stepped over to greet them. It took all of Catherine's will to keep from spitting in his face for what he'd done to Aislinn. Through his deceit, he'd knowingly given her sister a husband who would die.

"Ah, but you are late. Rivaux has made twelve passes at the quintains, striking true every time." He gestured to where boys set up the revolving target used to practice two squires at once. "He split it in two the last time and they have had to put another in its place. God's blood, but I've lived forty-four years and seen a blow like that only once before. Aye, and that was when Belesme was in the Old Conqueror's train—he wagered his horse he could shatter the one we kept at Bayeux. One blow, he said, and we were fools enough to doubt it." His black eyes were intent on the memory. "He came down the field spurring so hard the ground shook beneath our feet before he hit his target in the center. There was such a noise that we thought he'd been unseated and trampled, but when the dust cleared, the board had been shattered, broken off the iron bar that held it, and straw was everywhere. I've not forgotten the sight, nor the horse I lost over it."

He turned to stare where Catherine saw Guy astride his horse. "I'd not thought to see such force in a man ever again, but methinks young Rivaux might rival him. Sweet Jesu, but he may even be as tall as Belesme."

"Aye, Guy Longshanks, I have heard him called," Roger's bailiff murmured. "But he'd never have beaten my lord even ten years ago."

"Mayhap aye, mayhap nay, but I'd not try to match

either of them." Cat turned at the sound of William
de Comminges' voice. "Every fifteen or twenty years,
there is born a man to rival the best one born before, "
the older man observed. "In my time, 'twas argued
whether 'twas Lord Roger or Robert of Belesme."

"And now?" someone behind Catherine asked him.

"Now 'tis Rivaux."

"Nay, 'tis still Belesme," someone else argued.
"When he fights, you can see Satan in those green
eyes of his."

The two-armed quintain was in place, sending a hush
of expectation through the crowd. Catherine stared to
where Guy sat at the end of the field. He was bare-
headed, but his body was protected by a stiffened
leather hauberk visible over a plain linen tunic. Even
as she watched, he took the lance from Alan and adjusted it for balance in his hands. He saw her and lifted
one hand in salute.

"Sweet Mary!" Aislinn gasped beside her.

Reluctantly Catherine tore her eyes away from her
husband to follow her sister's gaze. There, at the opposite end of the field, Brian FitzHenry hoisted himself into his saddle and took a lance from Roger's
squire. Laying it across his saddle, he leaned down for
his helmet. Catherine's heart rose to her throat as she
realized what he meant to do: he'd challenged Guy of
Rivaux on the quintains. Done right, it was an exercise
of skill to be appreciated, with one man coming at the
target from one side, hitting hard enough to spin it,
and the other man catching the other side as it spun.
But Brian was no match for Guy—he was nearly a head
shorter and his arms lacked Guy's reach by a full hand-
breadth. Mutely Catherine turned to appeal to her father.

Aislinn was not so silent. "Nay, but Brian cannot—
Papa, do not let him! 'Tis too dangerous!"

"Aye," Roger agreed grimly. "But as it was Brian
who issued the challenge, I can scarce interfere. And
'tis not as though they meet each other in combat."

" 'Tis but sport," Hugh of Mayenne assured her. "They do but hit different sides of the quintain. Aye, if he were to cross swords with Rivaux, I'd fear for the bastard, but as—"

"His name is Brian FitzHenry," Catherine informed Mayenne evenly. "And he bears the blood of the Conqueror, lest you forget it." Turning back to her father, she urged him, "You can stop it, Papa— this is the Condes and you are lord here. I'd not see Brian try this."

"I'd look at the quintain—walk apart with me," he responded, ignoring her appeal. Drawing her arm through his, he started toward the target. Leaning closer, he shook his head. "You must not interfere in this, Cat, nor can I. If there is a dispute between two men, 'tis better settled here with a quintain between them than with weapons directed against each other. Brian challenged Guy, Cat, daring him to try—even calling him a coward when he demurred—nay, but 'tis time Brian learns he cannot stand behind me and taunt."

"But—"

"But nay," he silenced her. "Let him be a man." Reaching the heavy wood-and-straw target, he checked the iron bolts that held it to the center post. His hand rotated the cross-piece carefully. "Aye, I'd not see him do it either, but mayhap he will learn to hold his tongue and cease idle boasting." His blue eyes were serious when they met hers. "And do not think that being your father makes me blind, Cat, for I know why he does it. And I know why Guy accepted."

"Papa—"

"You cannot tempt two men who would have you, Catherine, without making them rivals."

"You do not think 'tis for me they do this, surely not, when . . ." She stopped, aware now that Guy had jammed on his helmet and waited impatiently for the field to clear. "Papa, 'tis not so. Brian leaves the Condes for you. It is your love he would have."

"He has it." Looking down the lines drawn in the grass, he shook his head. "Unless I mistake the matter, that is not what Rivaux thinks." He grasped her elbow and directed her to the side. "Come on, I'd not be trampled."

Guy of Rivaux and Brian FitzHenry faced each other across the wide expanse of the practice field and waited for the signal. Catherine had watched the squires do this dozens of times, missing their targets more often than not, but she had an awful foreboding about this meeting. Aislinn caught up to them, her own face creased in concern. She did not like contests of violence and she doubted she ever would, but she too was uneasy about Brian's challenge. He had not the skill of Rivaux, and it was far too easy to miss the quintain. The thought of a lance carried too close made her blood run cold. An accident or misdirected blow might well kill one of them. What if Brian thought to gain Cat through treachery? Or what if Rivaux thought to dispose of a rival?

Directly across from them, Cat could see her mother's white face and she knew Eleanor did not like this contest any better than she did. Hugh of Mayenne stepped out for better visibility and waved the red cloth for both men to see. When they nodded, he lifted it and released it to float gently downward.

Guy lowered his lance, positioning it for the hit, and spurred his big black forward. He'd not wanted to do this—he had no need to prove himself, he knew, but FitzHenry and Count Hugh had been determined. He was going to reach his target first. Leaning slightly to brace himself, he hit the crossbar, and as it spun from impact, he wheeled aside.

Brian, faced with a spinning bar, drew off and made his pass, to the jeers of Rivaux's men. Stung, he reined in short and prepared for another run. This time, he would be the first to hit his side of the quintain. He kicked his horse so viciously that he was nearly unseated, and then leaned forward, intent on the hit.

Both men reached the target at the same time, but Guy of Rivaux's greater strength gave him the greater impact. The quintain shuddered and split with such force that Brian was hit by the rebound. For a brief moment it looked as if his lance were hung up, and he raised in his saddle, reeling from Rivaux's blow on the other side, and then, pitching sideways, he thudded to the ground as Guy thundered on down the field.

"Brian!" Both Cat and Linn screamed at the same time, and before Roger could restrain either of them, they were running onto the field.

Brian lay motionless in a heap, oblivious of the collective gasp of horror from the assembled crowd. Catherine reached him first and dropped to the ground beside him. Rolling him over, she tried to cradle his head, while Aislinn knelt to chafe his hands.

"Make way, both of you," Roger ordered as he too knelt. "God's teeth! Will not everyone stand back?"

Guy reined in at the end of the long field and looked back to see what had happened. Nudging his horse forward, he came up to where Brian lay. The younger man's face was ashen and his eyes were closed. "Jesu!" Guy muttered, dismounting. Grasping Catherine, whose eyes were brimming with tears, he pulled her away by her shoulders. "Let me see to him."

"Haven't you done enough?" she cried. "I think you have killed him!"

Aislinn, her own cheeks wet, leaned to rest her head on Brian's chest. "I do not hear him breathe."

For a moment Guy wasn't attending. He stared in disbelief at Catherine, his hazel eyes almost green. To him, it was as though she accused him of trying to murder Brian FitzHenry. "Make no mistake, Catherine," he told her coldly, "had I wished him dead, he would be. Nay, he has but lost his wind."

"You could have passed! You saw he would hit it!"

"I saw naught but my target, Catherine." Pushing her aside, he bent to look over Aislinn's shoulder. "Get up," he ordered her curtly. Roger, seeing he meant to assist Brian, pulled Linn off. Guy dropped to one knee and lifted his opponent's head. Removing his leather glove with his teeth, he reached his free hand to raise one of Brian's eyelids. Roger moved closer to ease the steel helmet off Brian's head. "I think him but stunned," Guy murmured. "Mayhap he hit his head when he fell."

"I did not see it."

Guy pulled Brian's inert body up further and turned him over across his knee. His palm open, he gave several sharp blows to the man's back. He was rewarded by a sudden gasp, followed by a gurgling sound, and then Brian began to retch violently. Guy pushed his head down to keep him from choking, and waited as the color came back slowly. Brian's ashy clamminess receded, to be replaced with a flush. Guy nudged him off his knee and rose, letting him fall clear of his vomit. Meeting Catherine's eyes coldly, he announced, "He lives. Tend him if you will." Then, brushing past her, he walked from the field.

As Catherine stared after him, she saw him pull his helmet from his head and throw it on the ground. His black hair shone like a raven's wing in the sun, and he held his tall frame stiff and straight. He'd mistaken her meaning, and he was angered with her, she knew, and she wavered. She ought to go after him—her best instincts told her to do it—but she was de Brione. She had too much pride to run after a husband whose very coldness had sent a shiver down her spine. Brushing the tears she'd shed for Brian aside, she turned back. She'd wait for Guy's anger to abate before she sought him out.

❧ 24 ❧

Summoned to her mother's solar, Catherine was surprised to find only her father there. He was standing, his hands clasped behind his back, watching the ostlers help Rivaux's men ready their horses in the courtyard below. The Roger de Brione who turned to face her looked older than she could ever remember seeing him, and his blue eyes were reddened as though he had been crying.

"Maman?" she asked fearfully.

"Lea is seeing to food for your travel to Rivaux, Cat."

His voice was husky also, having that quality of suppressed emotion. Catherine knew something was terribly wrong and yet she dared not speak until he told her of it. The sunlight caught in his ruffled blond hair, reflecting off the silver that mingled there. He was but forty-two and still strong. Cat stared at his handsome face, discovering new care lines about his mouth and eyes that she could have sworn had not been there yesterday. His eyes appeared to study her as though he sought to remember her forever.

She could stand it no longer. "Papa, 'tisn't as though we shall never meet again. You will come to Rivaux, and I will come home."

"Aye, but we do not know what God's mercy will bring us, Cat." Clearing his throat of the huskiness, he sighed. "Word has but come from Harlowe this day—your grandsire Richard of Harlowe lives no more."

"Oh, *Papa!*" she gasped. It seemed but lately that she'd seen him, the last time he and her grandmother had been in Normandy. Instinctively she made the sign of the Cross over her breast and murmured a silent prayer for the repose of his soul. "But how . . . ?"

"His horse reared, throwing him against his pommel. What he injured, I do not know, but my mother's confessor writes that he suffered three days ere he died."

"Sweet Mary."

"Aye. He was a good father to me once we were met," he mused aloud. "I have oft regretted that I knew him not when I was a boy. 'Tis impossible to compensate for all those lost years, Cat." He turned back to the narrow slitted window. "I go to Harlowe with a heavy heart, little one, not knowing how you or Linn will fare in your new homes. I would to God that you'd make your peace with Guy ere you leave here."

"Papa—"

"You are my eldest born, Cat—my most precious child—your flesh is made from mine and Lea's. You are the triumph of our love over Belesme, over Gilbert, over Curthose, over everything, Cat. When you go forth from the Condes, you take part of me with you. I cannot aid Linn in what she faces now, but I'd try to make your life easier."

She swallowed hard. "Nay, Papa, but you've naught to worry with me," she managed through the ache in her breast. "I am your daughter in all things."

"Are you? I have never been too proud to acknowledge when I have been wrong, I think, but you have set yourself against your husband over what happened yesterday. The fault was Brian's—or perhaps mine for allowing it to happen—but there was naught Guy of Rivaux could have done to prevent what befell Brian."

"I . . ." She stopped, remembering how cold Guy had been since the accident. He'd lain rigid and distant in the bed they shared, too angry to speak. And for once, she'd been sorry that he had such control over himself. Aye, if he'd railed at her, or even beaten her, she could have found the means to explain, to apologize for her hasty accusations. But in the face of such coldness, she was afraid he would not listen. "Nay, I cannot. He—"

"Catherine."

He seldom called her Catherine save in anger, but he did not appear angered so much as saddened. She wished he would turn around and look at her so that she could try to put what she felt into words. Instead, she stood numbly and waited for him to go on.

"I was displeased with Guy of Rivaux—I admit the fault," he continued after a time. "I wanted to wed my eldest daughter, my heiress, where I willed, and Robert Curthose and Guy of Rivaux robbed me of that privilege. When Eleanor argued that you were neither wife nor maid and that you needed your husband, I reluctantly agreed to it, but I was prepared to hate him. Not because he is young and I grow older, not because he is strong and men sing of him as often as of me, not because he is a count and I am not—but because he would take you from me, Cat." He stopped again and leaned against the stone, his eyes intent on the black-haired young man who paced the cobbled yard. "Aye, but I had not seen him then, Cat. Come here," he commanded. "Stand beside me and tell me what you see."

Curious, Catherine moved next to him and peered down. The yard was filled with red-shirted Rivaux men. She scanned the mesnie until she saw him. He was unmistakable with that black hair and the long red overtunic blazoned with the black hawk of Rivaux across his chest. Even as she looked down on him, he raised his head, and she felt her heart lurch in her chest. "I see my husband and his men, Papa," she sighed.

"Aye." Roger slid his arm around his daughter's shoulders. "Your husband, Cat—the man who will protect you and give you your sons and daughters, the man who will hold your fate in his hands. And what hands they are, sweeting, what hands they are. You see down there a man capable of holding all I will leave you for you and your heirs."

"He . . . he did not want to wed me, Papa. He came back to me because Henry willed it."

"I do not know what was between you ere he returned, Cat, but I have seen what passes between you since. God's teeth, but there's not above a dozen women in all of Normandy who can claim to have anything like it with their husbands. Aye, I recognize the way he looks on you—'tis as I have ever looked on Lea."

"You mistake the matter, Papa." She looked down at Guy, then back at her father. "There is no love between us."

"There is fire, Cat—there is *fire*. It gives you the means to make him love you, if you will but be just." His voice lowered and he nodded. "Aye, and you know he did not mean to harm Brian. Believe me, if he had, Guy of Rivaux would not have knocked the wind out of him—nay, he would have knocked the life out of him." He squeezed her shoulders encouragingly. "Your sister would have counted herself fortunate to have been given to Guy. As it is, she leaves the Condes to do her duty to a husband whose life ebbs from him so slowly that he is prisoner to his poor body."

"You knew?"

"Nay. I would have found the means to delay until he was dead if I had even suspected. But once I saw him, I knew he was not the boy I met before the betrothal."

"Linn did not want me to tell you."

"I spoke to her of it yesterday after Brian took his fall. I have promised her that she shall have the choosing of her next husband—'tis all I have the power to do for her." Roger looked down at Catherine's upturned face and gave her a twisted smile. " 'Tis strange, is it not, that I can amass lands and wealth, but I cannot give your mother a son, nor my daughters happiness? I have prayed to God for the one, to no avail, so mayhap he will take pity on me and grant the other."

"Oh, *Papa!*" Catherine turned into her father's arms and buried her face in his plain linen tunic. His strong arms closed around her and he held her silently, smoothing her dark braids against her back. All of her life, he'd stood for her, cared for her, and loved her. Now her fate rested in another's man hands. Sniffing back tears, she sought solace one last time from her father. "I will make my peace with Guy—I swear," she promised against his hard chest.

"Good." He stroked errant strands of hair back from her temples. "I'd not worry about you while I am in England." Releasing her reluctantly, he gave her a gentle push toward the door. "Now, be gone with you before I weep also. Your husband waits."

Catherine paused on the first landing and wiped her face with the back of her hand. She knew not how she'd regain Guy's goodwill, but she'd not do it with red eyes and a wet face. Resolutely straightening her shoulders, she started on down.

"Cat . . ."

"Sweet Jesu, Brian, but must you always lurk on stairs lying in wait for me?" she complained even as her face broke into a tremulous smile.

"I'd wish you Godspeed, Cat, but I'd not make matters worse for you with your lord. God's blood, but he is a man I'd not want to anger."

Her eyes searched his face. "You are unhurt from yesterday—truly?" she asked.

"Aye." He caught both her hands and held them.

"I got what I deserved, Cat—the fault was mine. When I heard everyone jeering at me for the first pass, I was determined to hit it the next time rather than pass again. It was a foolish thing to do." Leaning closer, he planted a chaste kiss on her cheek. "Godspeed, Cat. God willing, I will be a lord in my own right when next we meet."

"Come down with me."

"Nay, I'd speak to your father. He goes to England to see to Harlowe, and I'd not have him go alone— Earl Richard was like a grandsire to me also. And while I am there, I will go to see my mother and seek her blessing. Too long I have hated her for what she made of me."

"And after that?"

"I have already written to my father. I suppose much will depend on what he would have me do." He managed a faint smile. "Aye, and I told him that I did not mean to hang on his purse, either, but would have a chance to earn my way."

Already Catherine could hear the sound of the huge iron grate creaking upward as the bridge strained downward. She knew she dared not tarry longer, for Guy and his men were impatient to leave the Condes. She gave Brian's hand a quick squeeze and stood aside to let him pass her. "Godspeed," she repeated softly to his back.

"Catherine! Catherine!"

She could hear Guy calling to her from the yard, and she hastened on down. When she emerged into the open area of the yard, most of the men were already mounted. Her mother, who had been standing beside Hawise's horse giving the maidservant last instructions for Cat's comfort, hurried across the courtyard to bid her daughter farewell. Blinking back tears, she kissed Cat on both cheeks, murmuring, "God love and care for you, dearest child. Mayhap we will meet again at Christmas, if Henry keeps the feast in Normandy this year also." Stepping back, she shepherded

Philippa and Isabella, both solemn-faced over the news of Richard of Harlowe's death, forward to say good-bye. "God be with you, Cat," Pippa whispered, kissing Catherine on the cheek. But Isabella was curious about what would happen now that their grandsire was dead. When she leaned closer to make her farewell, she whispered, "Gerdis says that one day you will be a countess three times over—Nantes, Harlowe, and Rivaux. Will you truly?"

In spite of her heavy heart, Catherine could not hide a smile at Bella's childish curiosity. "Aye, I suppose I will."

"Well, 'tis most unfair of you—you should let me have one of them." Then, brightening at a new thought, she asked, "Since you are gone, and Linn leaves on the morrow, may I have your bed? I tire of sleeping with Pippa."

Catherine turned her youngest sister toward the pack animals and pointed. "See that one? It carries my bed with me. Now, kiss me, you greedy creature, and have done before Maman hears you."

"We have to leave, Catherine."

Her pulse raced at the sound of his voice as he came up behind her, and she could not suppress the shiver of excitement she felt in his very presence. Aye, she'd make her peace with him if he'd let her. Looking up at his impassive face, she could see he was already helmeted and ready to ride.

"Aye," she managed through suddenly dry lips. "Will you mount me?"

There was a faint quiver at the corner of his mouth at the remembered phrase. "I take leave to warn you, Catherine, that I do not tarry on the way this time. Alan!"

The squire took the reins of Catherine's bridle from an ostler and led her horse to her. Guy leaned to cup his hands courteously and waited for her to step in them. She caught at her pommel and put her foot in his hands just as Bella blurted out, "But where is

Brian? You cannot leave ere you speak with Brian, Cat—you cannot!'' Catherine could have cursed as Guy's body went rigid for a moment. He threw her up unceremoniously and turned to William de Comminges.

''Is all in readiness?''

''Aye, my lord.''

Guy's eyes met Eleanor's briefly and his face softened slightly. ''I did but hear of the sudden death of Earl Richard, my lady, and I am heartily sorry for it. Please convey to Lord Roger that I stand ready to aid him should he need an ally to claim his patrimony.''

''I thank you, my lord. We do not expect any difficulties, since King Henry confirmed the inheritance when he ascended England's throne.'' With a significant glance at the keep around them, she added, '' 'Tis Normandy I fear, for Roger will be gone much of the time now.''

''Nay, there is none to challenge Roger de Brione in all of Normandy,'' Guy protested. ''And the Condes can withstand nearly any assault.''

''There is Belesme.''

''He has not the means anymore,'' he reassured her. ''Aye, he is but a tool of France and would not attempt the Condes.''

''I pray you are right.'' Eleanor smoothed the silken fabric of her gown against her legs and looked away. '' 'Tis foolish of me to fear him yet, is it not?''

''Nay, not foolish, but you must not think of him now. If ever you fear for your safety when your lord is away, send word to me, Lady Eleanor, and I will come.''

She studied his face intently again, as though she sought to see what she'd fleetingly thought she saw before. ''You fear him not, do you?'' she asked soberly.

''All men fear him, but I think he can be taken.''

''You are very like him.''

His divided eyebrow disappeared beneath his helmet

as he raised it, and the scar Catherine had given him tightened visibly. Eleanor, seeing the stunned looks around her, hastened to explain, "Nay, I did not mean you were cruel or ungodly, my lord. Even I, who fear him greatly, admit that his very presence strikes fear in his enemies and emboldens those who stand with him—that is the quality that I see in you, my lord."

"We are enemies," he managed curtly. "I'd not be like him in anything."

"Maman, it grows late." Cat leaned between them to kiss Eleanor one last time. "Tell Papa I will be his daughter in all things."

"Aye, I suppose you will," Eleanor sighed. " 'Tis but your looks you have from me."

"Art ready to sound the horn, my lord?" William asked.

"Aye." Guy waited for Alan to bring his black horse closer, and then, one hand on the pommel, the other on his reins, he swung into his saddle. A boy scarce older than Philippa put the horn to his lips and blew the signal for everyone to fall into line.

"Godspeed, Cat!" the younger girls chorused.

"Wait!"

Guy reined in as Aislinn ran into the yard. She caught her skirts up from her ankles and made her way to where he sat his horse. "I'd have you take care of Cat, my lord," she told him seriously. "Aye, and by your leave, I'd visit Rivaux when I may."

"I'd make you welcome—and Geoffrey also."

"Linn, 'tis I you are supposed to bid Godspeed," Cat cut in.

"You know I pray you go with God, but he does not," Aislinn shot back. Then, her lip quivering, she grasped Catherine's hand. "Oh, Cat! I'll not know how to go on without you."

"Nor I without you, Linn. Godspeed—sweet Jesu, but I cannot do this! Linn . . .''

Guy was watching them curiously, his own emotions sharply divided. He'd never had a loving parent, nor a sister, and his brothers when alive had not bestirred themselves to even speak to him. Despite his anger with Cat, he felt both a stab of jealousy and one of sympathy, knowing he would have given all he had to be loved by his family. Seeing her anguish, he leaned to take her reins. "We have to leave, Cat," he told her gently. "God care for you and yours, Lady Aislinn."

25

The air was heavy with unshed rain, making his gambeson and undertunic damp and uncomfortable. Reining in to scan the hillocks ahead with a sense of foreboding, Guy leaned forward in his saddle and frowned. For the last several miles there'd been naught but destruction, with the remnants of burnt villages and idle fields to remind him that Belesme had been there wreaking his awful vengeance on Henry's Normandy. It made Guy afraid to think of what he'd find at Rivaux.

"He did not leave much, did he?" Catherine observed quietly.

"Nay."

"The poor people—to be left with naught. Jesu, but how could he do this?"

"He did not leave them, Catherine. I'll warrant there's not a living man in this valley," he answered grimly.

"Would you rest the horses, my lord?" Alan asked him.

"Nay, I'd reach Rivaux ere it rains." Clicking his reins, he nudged his horse forward with his knee.

Catherine stole a glance at him and sighed. In the three days since they'd left the Condes, she'd not had an opportunity to make her peace with him. And now she was in a strange place, an eerie place almost, with

naught but him for succor, and the thought of living
with a cold, angry man was almost more than she
could bear. It was as though the fire between them had
been banked, and she did not know if she could rekindle it. Four nights now, he'd turned his back to her
to lie still and silent even when awake. Oh, there was
that cold courtesy between them, as when he'd asked
her ever so politely to move her leg off his, but nothing
more. She, on the other hand, had lain beside him,
her whole body aching with the wanting of him. How
could he have desired her so intensely but days before,
when now he all but ignored her? Her pride demanded
the answer, but her heart was afraid to know. With
every plodding step of her horse, the chill inside her
deepened.

They crested a hill that formed part of a half-circle
above a small river-fed valley. Cat stared at the ruined
clusters of burned-out hutches that looked like blackened stumps amid greening grass. The fields around
them were brown and untilled.

"My lord, 'tis Rivaux!" Alan shouted.

His pointing hand drew Cat's attention to the re-
mains of a fortress, a grim, broken shell that had been
pulled down around a single square tower. Too stunned
for speech, she sat, disbelieving what her eyes saw.
This, then, was Rivaux, seat to Norman counts since
the time of the Viking Rollo. This was her home. She
barely heard the string of blasphemous oaths that escaped her husband as he too stared at the cornerstone
of his patrimony. The first splat of raindrops came like
pebbles from the sky, further dampening her already
low spirits and increasing her misgivings about the
place.

"Holy Mary," William muttered behind her. " 'Tis
unfit for occupation. We'll have to press forward to
Belvois this day."

Guy stared bleakly at the ruins of his ancestral home
and shook his head. "Nay," he decided, heaving a
heavy sigh. "We rebuild it."

"Surely you jest, my lord," Catherine protested as the chilly rain beat down on them. " 'Tis but burned sticks and broken stones! Nay, but I'd not stay in such a place."

"Aye, you will," Guy told her grimly. "Aye, you will." Spurring forward, he left her to follow him.

"But there is noplace to live there!" she shouted after him.

"There is the tower!" he flung back over his shoulder.

Tears of impotent fury mingled with those of humiliation as she stared after him. No matter how she had angered him, no matter what he might have thought she'd done, he had no right to treat her so. He had no right to bring Catherine of the Condes to this ruin and expect her to live in it. She raised her whip to strike blindly at her horse's flank, but William de Comminges leaned across the pommel of his saddle to stay her hand.

"Let him go on, Lady Catherine," he advised. "He needs to ride out his own anger at what Belesme has done."

Her lower lip trembled and her voice quavered. "But I . . . I cannot . . . I would not . . ."

The old man still held her wrist, but the eyes that met hers were not unkind. "Aye, you can—you are Catherine of the Condes, lady," he chided gently. "Think you your father—or your lady mother—did not face adversity? When he was thought to be naught but Roger FitzGilbert, your father made his way." He released her wrist and unfastened the rolled blanket behind his saddle. "Lord Guy will rise again also. Here . . ." he told her gruffly, handing her the blanket, "wrap yourself, that you do not get chilled."

I would be your daughter in all things, Papa, her mind echoed. *I will make my peace with Guy—I swear.* Straightening her shoulders, she sniffed back her tears and reached for the blanket. What right did Guy have to bring her here? He had every right—he was her husband. Her dark eyes, still sparkling with unshed tears, met William's solemnly. "My thanks," she managed, nodding.

William's face softened as he watched her pull his blanket around her soaked shoulders. Aye, she was a beauty, but there was more to Catherine of the Condes than the perfection of her looks. She was as unlike the Lady Alys as night unto day, he reflected with a sense of pride in Guy's wife. Her hot temper had the power to reach into her lord and melt the icy bitterness that chilled him—she had the power to help Guy become what William knew he could be. She would be the fire that would temper his steel. Jiggling his reins to signal his mount to move, he gave Catherine that grudging smile of his. "Come on, let us see if we can but make the place livable."

Catherine moved about Rivaux's remaining tower, supervising Hawise's cleaning. The place was little better than a swine wallow, she told her woman with feeling, and it could not all be blamed on Robert of Belesme. Whoever Henry had given captaincy of the place had left it filthy. Taking a broom herself, Cat pushed a pile of rotten rushes into a corner while she waited for one of Guy's soldiers to bring up limewater for washing down the floor.

But it was Rivaux himself who carried the bucket. Setting it just inside the doorway, he stood to watch Catherine's determined sweeping, and for a moment his face betrayed his hunger. She stopped to mop her brow and push back wisps of hair that fell over her forehead. "Sweet Mary, but I'll warrant they fed the dogs here," she grumbled under her breath as she leaned on the broom. "Put the water over there and help us get this stinking pile out of the way," she ordered over her shoulder.

"Aye."

She spun around at the sound of his voice. Her hands flew to straighten her braids behind her, a gesture designed to hide the sudden confusion she felt. "How long have you been here, my lord?" she asked as the slow flush crept into her face.

"Long enough to know I'd not have you doing this, Catherine."

"And who's to do it? Hawise is but one poor woman, my lord, and I'd not sleep among such filth. I'd have the floors swept and washed to purify them, and I'd have the walls cleaned of the soot.

"I'll send you some of the men."

"Nay. I'd not listen to them complain of women's work," she retorted. "Besides, I've not a doubt but that there is much to do everywhere. My mother taught me 'tis better to help do something right than to complain of it when 'tis done wrong." Bending over, she began lifting armfuls of the stinking rushes into woven baskets. "But you could have someone wash a tub—I'd have a bath when I am done. Otherwise," she announced as she straightened up, "you'll not be able to sleep for the stench of me."

He'd not been able to sleep well since his last night in the Condes, but he'd not let her know of it. He'd not have her know she disturbed his peace so much that he lay stiff beside her, holding his body almost rigid, to check the raging desire that threatened to make him a slave to her. His mouth was dry now at the sight of her. "You'll get your tub," he told her, keeping his voice steady for fear that it would betray him. "Here . . ." Dropping to kneel beside her, he scooped up more of the foul-smelling mess and deposited it into another of the big baskets. "Jesu!" he muttered. "I wonder that you can stand it."

" 'Tis like an unclean garderobe—your nose finally gets used to the smell while you are in it."

She stood back and watched him finish gathering what she and Hawise had swept. Despite her misgivings, she had to admit the solar looked better already. A little limewater, a little whitewash, some rush mats, and it would be almost habitable. Looking down on his mud-spattered tunic and his filthy hands, she also had to admit that she was fortunate at least to be inside. Although the rain had stopped, it was still damp and muddy out, and Rivaux's men, all soldiers unused to such labor, worked to salvage enough wood to begin rebuilding a makeshift stockade below the tower.

"Nay, 'tis enough," she told him finally. "If you will but pour the bucket, Hawise and I can do the rest. You did find some lime, did you not?"

"Aye. You should have more than one woman to do this for you—I'd not have you sicken from this." Without thinking, he reached to pull himself up by her hand, and as her fingers closed over his, he heard the sharp intake of her breath. As soon as he was on his feet, he let go as though burned. Turning away, he groped almost blindly for the bucket of limewater. "How much of it do you want?"

"Half here and half across the room. Hawise will take that side and I will take this one, I think." She reached for the broom and waited. "Go on—there are rags enough to sop up what does not dry."

He lifted the bucket, sloshing the limewater over the sides, and poured it where she directed. "I have sent to Belvois for more men and provisions. 'Tis my intent to bring villeins from there to here, as I am lord to both. Mayhap there will be some girls among them suitable to learn from you."

"From me? Nay, but I am no better seamstress now than I was at Rouen."

"By your leave, I will train them," Hawise spoke up.

"Well, we will have to see what Alan brings back." His task done, he picked up the empty pail and started for the door. "William and two other hunt the forest in my name, that we may eat. I'd not expect you to cook for us, Catherine." For the first time since the Condes, a glint of humor crept into his eyes, warming them slightly. "Now you will see how an army eats when it forages."

"Wait—is there any whitewash?"

"I know not. It is five years since I was last here, Catherine, but you have my leave to look for it. As chatelaine, whatever you find is yours to use."

Even Catherine was surprised by the results of her and Hawise's labor. Her hands on her hips, she surveyed the cleaned and whitewashed solar critically. It was, she decided, a small corner of civilization amongst ruin. The first people from Belvois had arrived, bringing two girls who possessed some household skills, and Cat was not hesitant in putting them to work immediately. One she set to helping Hawise weave reed mats from rushes gathered by soldiers glad enough to escape work on the stockade wall. The other she directed to help her unpack all she had brought with her from the Condes.

From time to time she stopped her own labors to watch the men work below. There was so much to do that she marveled any knew where to begin, but in half a day a wide ditch was started and measurements were marked for the setting of stakes for the palisades above its banks. By the looks of it, Guy meant to make Rivaux bigger than it originally was, for the burnt stumps of the earlier stockade stood well back from where flags marked the new ones. And Guy himself paced among his men, stopping here and there to help villein and soldier alike, directing them and taking the pickax even to show one how to hew into rocky ground. Swinging it as though he pounded an enemy with his mace, he managed to break a place for a stake as Cat looked on.

"Where would you that I put this, my lady?" the girl called Beda asked.

Reluctantly Catherine turned around to see what it was and found the girl held a neatly folded pile of Guy's clothing. "You'll have to empty one of the boxes—take the plate from that one over there. I do not know where we will put it, but it does not belong here.''

''Your pardon, my lady, but where would you that we set this?'' a strange man asked as two more strangers dragged pieces of her bed in from the stairs. ''My lord said 'twas to be put up.''

But Cat wasn't attending. Her eyes caught the irregular blue embroidery on one of Guy's undertunics and she recognized the shirt she'd made years before. It could not fit him still, and yet he'd kept it. How very poorly it was worked, she thought as she touched again the blue threads. And yet he'd kept it. It must have meant something to him, after all. She could even see places where he'd had it mended before he'd outgrown it.

''Would this please you, my lady?'' the fellow tried again, indicating a place on the other side of the empty brazier.

''Hmmm? Oh . . . aye,'' she answered absently, still staring at the undershirt he'd worn that last day she'd seen him before he went to fight at Tinchebrai. He'd been different from the bitter man he'd come back. She closed her eyes and tried to remember what he'd been like, the nineteen-year-old husband she'd help arm for war. He'd been kinder to everyone then—oh, he'd had his pride and his temper even then—but he had been gentler—aye, that was the word: gentler. Laying aside the folded clothes, she looked again to the scene below. He'd pulled off his tunic and his undertunic both, tying them at his waist, and he wielded the pickax again, striking the rocky ground over and over with a rhythm that rippled the powerful muscles in his arms and his back. He was lord of lands, but he was not too proud to work like a villein.

Chewing her thumbnail thoughtfully, she stepped back. If his arrogance, his anger, and his pride were more directed at her than anyone else, then perhaps the cause of his change was her also. Perplexed by her own reasoning, she sat on a bench but moments after it was carried in and stared unseeing, trying to make sense of it. He'd kissed her farewell, holding her and comforting her while she'd cried, and then he'd ridden into battle. And when it was over, when he was King Henry's prisoner, he would not even see her. All these years she'd thought it was because of King Henry— that he'd left her by Henry's command—that he'd returned to her by Henry's command.

And then she remembered the fire between them. It had leapt like a great flame, so intensely it burned. *"You are old enough now, I think,"* he'd said. Her face reddened at her thoughts, at the memory of being taken by him, and she was weak all over, trembling almost, as she remembered the feel of him. Well, she knew not all of what ailed him, but she bore responsibility for accusing him of trying to kill Brian. That, at least, she could speak of to him.

"Hawise . . ."

"Aye, my lady?"

"I'd have my bath brought up."

Hawise looked to where they still worked on putting together Catherine's bed. *"Now,* my lady?"

"As soon as they are done. And I'd have you smooth the wrinkles from my purple gown."

26

Guy made but a brief appearance at supper, staying just long enough to address his men, telling them he meant to rebuild Rivaux in stone and he meant to plant crops despite the lateness of the year. He asked, nay he demanded, their help in doing both. To the peasants he had brought from Belvois, he spoke of protection, promising that he would see to their safety and would forgo their rents in return for their work on his castle and in his fields. And when he was done, there was not a man among them unready to begin the tasks.

Catherine sat beside him in the barely habitable hall and counted Rivaux's people—there were thirty men-at-arms other than William de Comminges and Alan, two menservants including Arnulf, Hawise, the girls Beda and Gunhedris (who preferred to be called Hedda), and some fifteen villeins. There would be more on the morrow, Guy had promised, but this night, Cat could not but think that Rivaux had not one-tenth of the men of the Condes.

Freshly scrubbed, her hair neatly braided in a single plait down her back, she wore her best gown in hopes of gaining his attention, and was sorely disappointed when he declined to eat. "Nay," he told her, "there's too much to do ere I sleep." Stung that he could have dismissed her so lightly when she'd gone to such pains for him, and in front of those she would rule in his name, she nonetheless held her peace. She would tell him of it when he came to bed, she decided. If he had any care for her, if he would love her at all, then surely he must hear her out then.

As the small supper consisted of spitted rabbits and boiled fish from the river, accompanied by stale bread, it was not a lengthy affair. And no sooner had the bones been cleared than the sun began to set, sending most of the people to seek pallets laid out at the base of the tower. The more fortunate, the men of some standing, claimed the common chamber of the tower itself, while Hawise and Catherine climbed the stairs to the solar.

Cat looked around the room with some pride. Her hands might be blistered and her knees raw, but the place was clean and almost inviting. Already two rush mats lay on either side of the curtained bed, and more would be made on the morrow. Seeing her own bed and her own hangings reminded her how very tired she was. Down below, men argued as they drew lots for sentry. Cat walked to the narrow arrow slit that served for her window and looked out across the small valley. The lowering sun cast rich, warm color over the winding river and formed a beautiful background for wispy gray clouds on the horizon. She drank in the beauty of it and forgot the ugliness of Rivaux.

Coming back to sit on the bench, she began unbraiding her hair. It was still damp from its earlier washing, but as her fingers combed through it, it fell in rippling waves down her back and over her shoulders. Hawise looked up from where she folded down the covers behind the curtains.

" 'Twas but braided," she protested.

"Aye, but my lord likes it down," Cat told her. "I'd have you brush it for me." Then, seeing the fatigue in the older woman's face, she relented. "Nay, sit you down and I will do it myself."

Cat finished her hair and argued within herself whether it was preferable to wait for him fully clothed or in bed. But then she was tired enough that she feared to be asleep when he came up, so she decided to sit up and plot what she would say. When it came right down to speaking with him about how he'd changed, she knew not how to phrase it without angering him. But he *had* changed, she reminded herself stoutly, and if ever she was to have peace with him, she had to do it. She'd delayed too long already in keeping her promise to her father.

The evening wore on with no sign of Guy. Hawise, after urging her mistress to go on to bed, sighed and sought her own pallet belowstairs. Cat pulled out the shirt she'd worked and studied it to keep her resolve, and still he did not come. Lit only by one large tallow candle on a spike, the room darkened and tall shadows loomed eerily against the rough stone walls. She moved restlessly to the arrow slit to look out at the night sky, and she heard the muffled voices of sentries posted by the broken wall. The moon was almost full, shining through streaks of deep gray clouds, and the air was clean from the earlier rain. She breathed deeply and made up her mind: if he would not come to her, she would seek him out.

The old tower was square, with stairs that wound between the three floors cut into the thick outer wall. And while the top floor housed the lord and his family, the middle billeted the servants and men-at-arms who comprised Rivaux's household, and the bottom held what passed for a hall as well as screened-off space where the officers of the household worked. Holding her candle before her, Cat picked her way carefully down the steps, pausing to listen but briefly to the exhausted snores of Guy's men, and then going on down.

The main hall was deserted, but Cat could see a light and hear voices from behind a screen drawn across the end. Edging closer, she was certain that Guy spoke with William, for she heard him say, "I'd not have brought her here if I'd known 'twas like this.

Jesu! She is Roger de Brione's daughter! ' 'Tis but burned sticks and broken stones!' she said!''

"My lord—''

"Nay, I'd not listen,'' Guy decided wearily. Sinking back onto his bench, he reached for a cup of wine. "One thing I swear to you, William: if it takes me half a lifetime, I mean to build for her a grander keep than the Condes. Aye, even if it beggars me.'' His hazel eyes were bleak, his strange irises more green than gold. "I am Guy of Rivaux, count of this land, lord of Belvois, Celesin, Ancennes—Henry also gives me back Vientot—and I cannot bring her to better than this? By the rood of God, I swear I will kill Robert of Belesme for what he has done to my lands and my people!''

"My lord . . .'' Catherine hesitated momentarily and then moved forward as he turned to face her. "I would speak with you.''

"How long have you been here?''

"It matters not—I have come to speak with you,'' she repeated.

"And by your leave I'd retire, my lord.'' William spoke hastily, rising from his bench. "Every old bone in this body complains this night.'' He covered his yawn with his hand and waited for dismissal.

"Aye, seek your bed.'' Leaning back with his cup in his hand, Guy studied Catherine warily. Even in the flickering yellow light that illuminated her face, he could tell she was paler than usual, and her expression was tentative, as though she feared to speak her mind. To stall for time while he stilled racing pulses, he sipped from the cup and watched her over the rim. She was so beautiful that it made his heart ache almost to look on her. Her unbound hair shimmered, its dark waves taking red from the pitch torch that hung on the wall above her, falling from the neat part in the middle to cascade forward over her shoulders and down past her breasts. The metal threads in her purple gown glittered different colors, making it seem that she was cloaked in radiance rather than cloth. His mouth was so dry that he closed his eyes to her and swallowed deeply of his wine. He could hear the stiff silk rustle as she moved, and when he opened his eyes, she stood over him.

"You bathed," she observed lamely, noting his still-wet hair.

"Aye, I soaped and Arnulf poured buckets of water over me, if you would call that a bath." To avoid her, he reached toward the tally sticks as though to study them again.

"My . . . Guy, I know not where to begin, but—"

"Then do not say it, Catherine. I fear I'd not like to hear it."

"I have to say it." She moved even closer to peer into his face. "Are you drunk?"

"Nay—aye—I do not know." He looked up defensively. "A drunk man is the last to know if he is or he is not," he muttered. He raised his hand and then dropped it. "In truth, I think I am but bone-weary."

"You do not look drunk," she decided. "When Brian has too much wine, everyone knows of it. He—"

"I'd not hear of Brian FitzHenry!" he snapped angrily, lurching to his feet. "God's bones, Catherine, can you think of naught else? Can you speak of naught else to me? You've not changed in five years, have you? You still cling to foolish dreams of Henry's bastard! Well, I take leave to tell you that you'd best put him from your heart and your mind, Catherine of the Condes! 'Tis I who have you and I who mean to keep you!" Pushing past her, he would have left her standing there.

"He isn't there, Guy."

She spoke quietly, but her words cut through the air like an arrow thudding into a tree. He stood stock-still, unable to decide if he'd heard her aright, afraid to ask her to repeat what she'd said. Exhaling slowly until his lungs were almost drained of air, he could hear every beat of his own heart. "He isn't where?" he managed to ask finally.

"He is not in my heart—at least he's not there as you think he is." She waited for him to turn back, but he stood motionless. With a deep sigh, she realized he was not going to ease her confession for her. Staring at his back, willing him to face her, she kept her voice calm despite the pounding in her chest. "If I love Brian FitzHenry, 'tis as brother and naught else, Guy. And if I think of him and speak of him, 'tis because I know him well as brother and friend. I was prepared before Tinchebrai to be wife to you and none other."

He closed his eyes and swayed, whether from the effect of her words or the wine, he was uncertain. Part of him wanted to turn to her, to open his arms and cling to her, but part of him held back. She was alone and at his mercy in Rivaux—did she but seek to ease her lot now? Not a week before, she'd stood on the practice field at the Condes and accused him of killing Brian FitzHenry. He desperately wanted to believe her, he desperately wanted her to love him, but wanting something like that had never made it happen for him— not with his grandfather, nor with his father, not even with the monks. Nay, there was none but William to love him. What passed between him and Catherine was but the fire of lust, he supposed. But some perverse corner of his heart had to know.

"And now?" It was more croak than question.

She wanted to face him, she wanted to touch him, but the thought that he might rebuff her held her back. Moving closer, she spoke to his shoulders. "I would still be wife to you and none other. Even if I cannot have what my parents have, I'd be your wife. I'd lie with you, I'd bear your heirs for you, I'd hold your lands for you when you are absent from them, I'd—"

"Stop it! 'Tis what you think I would hear!" Using anger for his shield, he spun around to face her. "Do you think I am such a fool that I can be swayed with words? Nay, Catherine—not when these eyes have seen you with *him!* Not when these ears hear *his* name on your lips almost daily! Think you I did not see you in his arms after Tinchebrai?" He took in her stunned

expression and nodded. "Aye, I was with the prisoners that day, Catherine."

"Because I knew him! 'Twas of you I asked! I feared
you were dead! Belesme came for me, urging me to
flee with him—he said the day was lost!" Tears spilled
onto her cheeks and ran unchecked down them.
"Sweet Mary, but you wrong me!" She moved closer,
clenching her hands at her sides, and stared upward
into his flushed face. "Did you never think how 'twas
for me? Belesme said he knew not if you had fallen,
Guy. And after I escaped him by rolling beneath a
wagon, Curthose's camp was overrun by common soldiers bent on ravishment. I hid until I saw a knight in
Maine's colors, and then I ran to him, not knowing if
he would save me or take me. 'I am Catherine of the
Condes,' I told him, and he brought me to the king. I
did not see you there, but I saw Brian, a boy I had
known all my life, Guy. Aye, I threw myself in his
arms—I admit it, but 'twas because I was frightened
for you." Taking an angry swipe at her tears with the
back of her hand, she drew up to her full height and
lowered her voice to a husky whisper. "But I swear to
you that I never did anything to dishonor you or me,
Guy of Rivaux—with God for witness, I swear it."

He knew she spoke the truth in that at least, but it
was not enough. He closed his eyes against the re-
morse he felt.

"Nay, look at me! I am not done, Guy. Would you
hear more of that day? Would you know that I went to
King Henry to beg for mercy on you when I knew you
lived? Would you know that he refused to listen, telling
me that I would be given to Robert of Caen anyway,
whether I willed it or not? And would you know that I
begged a silver mark that Brian could ill afford to lose,
and I used it to bribe your guard that I might have one
last meeting with you ere you left Normandy?"

"Stop it. There is no need—"

"No need? Nay, there is every need! Have you forgotten that 'twas *you* who refused to see me? *'He said*

that King Henry forbids it,' '' she mimicked the guard. ''Aye—and I knew 'twas you who turned me away, for I'd already bribed the fellow. I knew then that you did not want me, that Curthose had forced you to take me against your will, and I expected you to recant the marriage. But you did not. For five years—*five years, Guy*—I was neither wife nor maid in my parents' house, and I did naught to dishonor you!'' Despite her best efforts, the tears flowed freely now. Her voice dropped again as she continued, ''And then you came back, and—''

''I saw you on the wall with Brian FitzHenry the day I rode in, Catherine.''

''Aye, and would you know why? Because we had quarreled over what we would be to each other. Despite the fact that my husband did not want me, I could not bring myself to give my body to anyone else—not even to Brian.'' She paused for some response and was disappointed. '' 'Tis most strange you should speak of that, Guy, for 'twas then that I knew I did not bear him the love of a woman for a man, that he was brother to me and nothing more,'' she continued finally.''Aye, and he knew it also.''

''I believe that not,'' he muttered. ''For how can you explain that he set himself against me from the time I rode in until the day I left, Catherine? How is it that he gibed and goaded until I accepted his challenge on the quintains? And how is it that you ran onto the field to aid him when he fell?''

''Jesu! I cannot believe that you are so thick-witted, Guy of Rivaux! If Brian FitzHenry chose to challenge you, 'twas for my father rather than for me. Aye, you may stare if you choose, but 'tis true. In all of his years at the Condes, Brian has ever striven to achieve my father's skills as a knight, but he has not the body or the temperament for it. In truth, I can see now that 'twas my father's son he wanted to be rather than my husband. He came back to the Condes because he had no place, and 'tis the only home he has ever known.

Neither his mother nor his father values him, Guy, but my father does.'' She stopped again, looking up through watery lashes to see if he listened.

''That has naught to do with me.''

''Oh . . . aye, it does,'' she countered. ''Look through Brian's eyes, if you will, and see how it is when an admired knight rides in to your house, sits higher than you at your lord's table, beds the girl you once thought to wed, and gains favor with the man you love as a father. Brian envies you, Guy, but not for the reasons you think. You have everything in his eyes, and he has nothing. You should pity rather than hate him.''

It was as though he'd turned to stone. She scanned his face for some sign that he believed her, that he cared for her. His flecked eyes betrayed turmoil in that they were neither green nor gold, but his face was oddly arrested. Yet, whatever thoughts troubled him, they were his alone. She reached out across the abyss that seemed to separate them and then dropped her hand without touching him. She'd done her best to keep her promise to her father—she'd laid her heart almost naked before him—and there was naught else that she could think to do. If he cared not enough to listen, she had lost. Defeated, she turned to leave, hoping that he would say something to stop her, but there was only silence.

It took all of his self-control to let her go. She'd told him nearly everything he'd ever wanted to hear of her, and yet somehow it was not enough. Wearily he walked back to pick up his cup and refill it. The table was littered with the tax tallies of what Rivaux had paid Henry in his absence, and Guy reluctantly sat down to count them again. He'd boasted to William that he would build Catherine a keep greater than the Condes, and yet 'twas far from certain that he could even meet his obligation to Normandy. But Henry knew Rivaux had been raided. Perhaps if Guy applied to have his taxes postponed . . . His thoughts trailed off, turning yet again to her. He could not think of aught else, it seemed.

Leaning forward to brace his head with his hands, he tried again to concentrate on the slender notched sticks of wood, but found the task too difficult in his state of mind. He was just too tired to make sense of them, he decided. He ought to go to bed. Reluctantly he pushed back and straightened up, reaching for the wine. His hand stopped in mid-reach—nay, he'd had enough to drink already.

He isn't there, Guy. He isn't there, Guy. He isn't there, Guy. Her words echoed like a pulse in his ears, beating over and over again until he squeezed his eyes to distract his thoughts from it. Rising, he stretched and looked at the cluttered writs and tally sticks on the table, only half-seeing them. *I was prepared before Tinchebrai to be wife to you and none other.* Jesu, but she left him no peace. Try as he would, he could not keep the image of her in Brian FitzHenry's arms from his mind. He'd been tired and sick at heart over the loss of the battle, and then to see Cat in Brian's embrace . . . Nay, he'd not think on it—it was too painful still. Did she think to fool him with her words here this night?

I would still be wife to you and none other. Even if I cannot have what my parents have, I'd be your wife— I'd lie with you—I'd bear your heirs for you. . . . Catherine of the Condes had cost him everything once—his lands, his wealth, almost his life. He saw her again as she once was, a girl of thirteen bent on escape from him. His fingers reached to touch the scar on his cheek—aye, she'd marked him then. She'd marked him then. She'd fought him with her claws and her wit until she'd been forced to wed him, and then, seeing the battle against her marriage lost, she'd accepted him with good grace. *I was prepared before Tinchebrai to be wife to you and none other.* And suddenly he had to admit that she meant it. Five years of bitterness dissolved as those words echoed again in his mind. Catherine of the

Condes—the beautiful Cat—was his in name and fact. He fingered the scar on his face, and for the first time in days, he could smile. Just as surely as she was his, she'd marked him for hers also.

Despite his aching muscles and his awful fatigue, he felt suddenly elated. Catherine of the Condes wanted to be wife to him. She who had had everything was willing to take him with nearly nothing. *Even if I cannot have what my parents have* . . . Few people ever had what was between Roger de Brione and Eleanor of Nantes, and he could never be like her father, nor was Catherine like her mother, but there was a fire between them as great as any man had a right to dream of. He reached to lift one of the torches from its holder in the wall.

The climb was steep and dark, but he was scarcely aware of it. In the solar, the single candle stand dripped melting tallow as the candle wick flickered and smoked in a sea of liquid. His eyes searched the square room for her until they reached the bed. Holding the torch away from the hangings, he looked down where she lay, curled with her back toward him.

"Cat . . ." Although she did not stir, he suspected she was still awake. He turned and tossed the flaming torch across to the empty brazier, where it popped and sputtered against the last floor sweepings that had been dumped there. Still clothed, he eased his body down behind hers and reached for her. "I would be husband to you and none other, Cat, I swear to you." With one hand he smoothed her hair against the pillow, and with the other he clasped her closer. Choking back a sob, she turned against him, and he began kissing her wet face, tasting the salt of her tears.

❧ 27 ❧

Dawn came through the arrow slit like a shaft that widened as it crossed the floor, laying a wedge of light in the otherwise dim room. Catherine stirred slightly beneath the weight of his arm and then came awake. He still slept, his deep even breathing breaking the silence of the solar. And 'twas small wonder that he did, she decided as she remembered how they'd passed the night.

Easing her hair from beneath his arm, she propped herself up to study him. In sleep, his face was relaxed, his expression softer, gentler, reminding her of the way he'd looked before Tinchebrai had changed his life, before he'd become embittered over the loss of his lands. His black hair, where it lay against her own dark locks, was blacker than any she'd ever seen. Impulsively she reached to smooth the tangled fringe back from his forehead, and his breathing broke cadence, hesitating briefly before again evening out. His divided eyebrow gave him a faintly quizzical look in sleep, as though it disbelieved his dreams, and the scar she'd given him was white where it had healed into a fine, thin line. She regretted marking him now, for it was the only blemish on the handsomest face she'd ever seen. And as she watched him, she thought she detected a faint quiver at the corners of his mouth.

Taking the end of a thick strand of her hair, she leaned

closer and tickled his nose with it. She was rewarded with a twitch that told her he was far more awake than he wanted her to think. Bending her head to brush his lips with her own, she was unprepared for the quickness of his response. His flecked eyes flew open and his arms came up to imprison her against the hardness of his chest as he wholeheartedly answered her kiss, tasting, possessing, plundering her mouth with his tongue. It happened so suddenly that she collapsed over him, a prisoner to his awakening desire. His arms tightened and his hands explored her body hungrily, sliding over the bare shoulders, back, and hips to elicit an answering passion.

Afraid that Hawise would come to awaken them, Cat tried to push herself up. "Nay—not now," she managed to whisper even as she felt him stir beneath her. It was a mistake, for she'd given him access to more of her body. He half-lifted her higher, raising her breasts above him and teasing a nipple with his tongue until it hardened. "Hawise . . ." she protested feebly as she felt again the intense desire that radiated from his touch.

"Shhhh—the door is barred," he murmured against her breast before he began to suck.

Her back arched as her hands supported her body over his and her legs straddled him, giving her a false sense of power, of control over the strong, virile man beneath her. She would savor what he was doing, she would enjoy giving him leisurely access to her, and she would prolong the exquisite feel of him as long as possible. But even as she felt him rise against her, her own body betrayed her with its need. Already she wanted more of him, wanted to urge him to touch her there, and she felt the wetness that gave her away. She would have rolled over on her back and spread her legs eagerly, but his hands held her hips.

"Nay—I'd look at you, Cat."

His voice was soft and intimate, sending new shivers of excitement through her. Her eyes, which had been closed to concentrate on the feel of what he would do to her, opened slowly to look down on him. His black head was visible only from the top as his mouth teased and tormented her breasts, tasting first one and then the other. His hands positioned her hips over his as his mouth moved upward to murmur against the hollow of her throat, "Would you learn to ride, Cat?"

Now she could see the gold flecks in his eyes. One hand moved beneath her to test the wetness there, and when she moaned in ecstasy, he waited no longer, easing her upward only enough for his body to enter hers. She reared back, gasping, and then settled over him, feeling the exquisite, indescribable pleasure of having him inside. When she dared look down again, his eyes were gold with his own pleasure. "Ride me, Cat—ride me," he urged her as his hands stroked her hair, her back, and her hips with restless eagerness

For answer, she began rocking back and forth, her brow furrowed in concentration at the sensations that tautened her belly and made her eager for more. Her hair fell forward like a silken curtain between them, and still he watched her, enjoying what she would do to him. "Move, Cat—move," he whispered as he began to rock in rhythm with her. "Move." Biting her lip, she leaned forward to tease him with her breasts while moving ceaselessly as the tension built between them. Her brown eyes were almost black with passion, and her breath came in rapid rushes as she labored to bring herself release, driving against him now, pitching and rolling her hips until he could be passive no longer. He grasped her hips with both hands and thrust upward in mindless need until he heard her cry out again and again and again before she fell to lie on him, quivering to receive the flood of his seed. He held her close, her knees still locked at his side, and he tried to catch his breath.

"Sweet Mary," she whispered between parched lips as her head rested against his shoulder. "You must think me wanton."

"Nay—I think you the joy of my heart, Cat."

She rolled off him and he let her go, half-turning to watch her. Lying with her eyes closed, she was silent for a time as her breasts heaved beneath her tangled hair. Finally she spoke, this time quietly. "What am I to you?"

"You are my wife."

"I'd be more than that, Guy."

He could see her swallowing still to calm her ragged breathing, and he knew what she wanted of him. His fingers combed the straggling hair back from her face with unaccustomed gentleness. He hesitated, still afraid to say the words that would give her power over him, until she opened her eyes and met his gaze soberly. "Aye—I love you, Cat," he murmured softly, knowing he meant it, knowing that words were words and, spoken or unspoken, they did not change the fact she already held him in thrall to her.

"I feared to disgust you, that you would think . . ."

"Cat . . . Cat . . ." He reached to pull her closer. "Disgust me? 'Tis I who should disgust you! The more I have of you, the more I want—nay, 'tis delight I feel. 'Tisn't every man who gets a woman like you." A slow, almost foolish smile spread over his face. "Aye, I love all of you—your face, your hair, your eyes, your skin . . . even your claws. And 'tis not an easy thing for me to say it, Catherine of the Condes, for I know not what you think of me."

"I think I have loved you since before Tinchebrai. I was disappointed that you thought me too young," she admitted. "I did but fool myself with Brian, for I did not want him this way."

For once, Brian FitzHenry's name meant nothing to him. Cat—his Cat—had just confessed to loving him, and nothing else mattered. He settled back into the luxury of the feather mattress and cradled her against him with his arm. Rivaux would be rebuilt, his lands would again make him wealthy, and his sons would be powerful. With Catherine of the Condes beside him, all things would be possible.

When Hawise came up the stairs to call them, Cat started to rise, but he held her fast. "Nay—I'd hold you longer, love."

The hall was swept bare, the trestle tables and benches taken outside to be scrubbed thoroughly, and the walls whitewashed even to the arched supports. Cat surveyed the results with pleasure, thinking she'd show Guy that she was as competent a chatelaine as her mother. Directing boys sent over from Guy's castle at Belvois, she set them to work removing caked grease and refuse from the floor with knives. Outside, the din of workmen was almost deafening, as some labored to pull up the charred remnants of the old wall while others hewed timber for the new one.

Drawn to the courtyard for a sight of him, she stood watching as bare-chested men worked in the early-summer heat to rise and set heavy posts. Her husband was among them, working side by side with his villeins, carrying, pushing, steadying, and bracing timbers. The muscles that had been used for swinging heavy broadsword, mace, and battleax now rippled in common labor. From time to time he stopped to wipe his dripping hair back from his face with his forearm, but then he returned to his task with more enthusiasm than any of his peasants. Inside the new stockade wall, others worked to pull down the rest of the once unfinished stone shell, loading the rough-quarried rocks onto carts and then drawing those carts beyond the wood-staked outer perimeter.

A shout rose from the yard as a shaggy band of men, goaded by William de Comminges and another of Rivaux's knights on horseback, walked over the horizon. Guy paused to lean on the heavy mallet he had just used to drive supports into the ground and waited for William.

"I saw smoke in the woods," William explained

from his saddle as he rode up. "Aye—they belong to Rivaux." Nodding to a stout fellow in rags, he added, "When Belesme burned their huts and Henry did not come to their aid, they took to the forest, he says." His grizzled face took on a much-tried expression. "I would have you tell him, my lord, that you do not mean to take his hands for poaching."

Even as he spoke, the man fell to his knees before Guy, begging, "Have mercy, my lord, but I had to eat! Have mercy!"

"Where are the others?"

"None are left save us, my lord."

His divided eyebrow rising skeptically as he did so, Guy counted but eight men and no women. "Belesme killed everyone else?" he asked.

"You'll start him sniveling again, my lord," William cut in. "As he told it to me, there were but few who survived the slaughter when Belesme and his men fell on them. This man claims to have lost his wife, his two daughters, and his son—says Belesme himself spitted the babe."

"Where are the rest of the women?"

"He says there are none—that none made it to the forest with them."

Guy, angered that Belesme had managed to murder most of his people, started to strike out at those who'd survived, to ask why they had not fought for the women, and then mastered his temper. They were, after all, unarmed save for picks and staffs, and no match for mounted raiders. Nay, the man he'd punish would be Robert of Belesme. Aloud he addressed William: "Feed them and give them axes—they can cut wood. I'd have this wall finished before I begin to build in stone." To the man still groveling at his feet, he shook his head. "You had to eat—I'd not begrudge you that." When he perceived the fellow meant to grasp his leg and kiss his foot, he nearly kicked him away. "Get up," he ordered curtly. "No man serves me from there."

"I'd delouse them first," William muttered. "Lady Catherine would not be pleased to have the place overrun with vermin."

"See if there is enough lard, then." Guy picked up the heavy mallet again and turned toward the square tower. Seeing Catherine in the arched doorway, he beckoned her out. The fatigue lines that etched his brow softened as he watched her walk toward him.

She shielded her eyes against the bright sun and looked where William herded his find. "Sweet Mary, but how can they have lived this year and more without anything?"

"The forests protected them and gave them food." Dropping the mallet, he slipped an arm about her shoulders and walked her toward the end of the partial wall. "But there are no women to help you, Cat."

"As long as I have Hawise, I can manage. Besides, there are Beda and Hedda."

" 'Tis too much for you—I should have sent you to Belvois until this was done." He reached to lift one of her hands and examined it. "You were not meant for this."

"Neither were you, but we are doing it. Nay, I'd not leave you now."

"Still, I'd not have you do it. Your father would have my head on a pike if he knew." His flecked eyes stared distantly for a moment as he seemed to see something else. "But it will not always be like this, Cat, I swear to you. You are countess in name now, and one day you will be countess to lands and wealth so vast 'twill take an army of scribes to count what you have." Collecting himself, he squeezed her shoulders and propelled her toward a large, spreading tree. "Sit you down where 'tis cool and rest." Taking his undertunic from where he'd tied it at his waist, he spread it out on the ground for her. As soon as she sat on it, he dropped down beside her and picked up a stick. "Let me show you how Rivaux will be," he told her as he began to draw in the dirt.

Leaning to rest her arm on his sweaty back, she watched as he made two wide concentric ovals broken by four small circles. Then, at one end of the inner one, he made a small square, and in the open space he set a large rectangle. Along the outside of it all, he drew the river and showed the ditch coming off it.

"Here is our outer wall—'twill be stone, and as thick as two men lying across it. The towers are round, as they are harder to bring down with siege machines." He pointed to the inner circle with the stick. "And here lies the wall of the inner bailey, Cat. I mean to keep the tower we have, but 'twill be inside the wall. And here"—he went back to where he'd drawn the river—"here you see how I mean to fill the ditch."

"But what is this?" she asked, indicating the large rectangle in the inside.

"That?" His face was almost boyish as he turned to her, and the flecks in his eyes were pure gold. "That is your house, Cat. I mean to build a palace for you."

❧ 28 ❧

The sun beat down mercilessly through the months of July and August, and still the work did not stop. No sooner had the wooden inner wall been completed than every man Guy could conscript from not only Belvois but also his more distant possessions of Celesin, Ancennes, and Vientot came to till his fields, build wattle-and-daub hutches between the river and his partly constructed stone outer wall, and to work on that wall itself. Now some thirty feet of it stood, an unfinished sentry over Rivaux's land.

And inside the wooden stockade, Catherine presided over immense changes. Where she'd found little more than a chicken yard, she'd made a neat herb garden, and already the plants grew enough to show promise of seasonings and medicines for the winter. From the tangled roses that climbed the old tower, she and Hawise and the two girls brewed rosewater and made sweet sachets for clothing chests. Not content with these housewifely endeavors, she managed to beg enough labor of William, who now shared the duties of seneschal and captain of the keep, to build a large kitchen, a smokehouse, an alehouse, and a bakery at the base of three sides of the old tower. And while he had grumbled that he courted rebellion from the overweary men, he nonetheless managed to see she had what she needed. He even obtained a woman skilled

300

in ale-making from Ancennes, as well as cooks and bakers from Vientot.

Even the lowest of the peasantry, those who'd come in from the forest, including perhaps another ten or twelve who made their way after William's original discovery, threw themselves into their lord's service. It began to look as though the late planting would still yield enough harvest to feed everyone even if it would not also meet Guy's taxes. By August, every little hut boasted at least a couple of chickens, and most also had either a cow or a pig provided from Belvois stock.

Despite the exhausting dawn-to-dusk labor, Guy considered this the best summer of his life. No matter how tired he was, no matter how impossible his schemes seemed, he had Catherine waiting for him at end of day. At night, they explored each other, discovering more of each other, sharing dreams, and planning a glorious future for the House of Rivaux, one where their sons and daughters would be envied and admired for their power and beauty. For the first time in his twenty-four years, Guy of Rivaux was content.

Laboring to lift a stone into a cart, he strained until his flat belly felt concave as he hoisted it and carried it. The sun beat down, burning his already deeply tanned face and shoulders. Sweat poured, to drip from his chin and run in rivulets to commingle with that on his chest. The curling mat there was almost straight from the steam that rose from his body.

"My lord—riders!" William shouted from the partial wall.

Guy grunted as he eased the stone onto the cart with an effort. Hostile riders were the nightmare that kept him going when his body ached beyond endurance. Wiping his dripping face with his arm, he reached for the broadsword he kept never further than a few paces. His palms were so wet that Doomslayer threatened to slip within his grip.

"How many?" he yelled back.

"Mayhap twenty!" William shaded his eyes to

count, and turned around to tell his master, "Aye, and they carry Normandy's banner!"

Guy leaned thankfully on his hilt, bracing his bone-weary body with the blade tip in the ground. With so much turmoil and so many petty wars in the wake of the Angevin's claim to Maine, he feared to be drawn into the conflict ere Rivaux was ready. But he had no quarrel with Henry—not anymore. Aye, in his eager-ness to buy Guy's loyalty, Henry had forgiven Rivaux's taxes for the first year.

He watched curiously, waiting for the riders to get close enough that they could be seen beyond the glint of the sun on their helms, and then he recognized the leader. For an instant his stomach knotted and then relaxed.

Brian FitzHenry rode into their midst and lifted his helmet from his thoroughly soaked head. He looked around until his eyes settled on Guy in disbelief. "Jesu! God's blood, my lord—I'd scarce know you!" Then, taking in the famed broadsword, he felt the need to amend. "That is, I'd not expected to see you—"

"Building my own wall?" Guy asked, grinning. "Aye—I bid you welcome to Rivaux. Come down and I'll give you the kiss of peace while we each stink too much to notice the other."

Brian hesitated, surprised at Rivaux's easy greeting. After that day on the Condes' practice field, he'd not expected ever to be able to make his peace with the man. Nodding finally, he slid from his saddle to face one he'd long considered an enemy.

Guy wiped his hands on his braichs and walked to grasp Brian by both shoulders, kissing him lightly on his wet face. Stepping back, he gestured to the men around him. "See to the setting of those stones and then rest for water." Draping a sweaty arm around Brian, he guided him toward the keep itself. "That you are not a greedy neighbor come to pull down my house makes you most welcome," he told the younger man. "Aye—and Cat will be happy to see you. How left you the Condes?"

"I left it the day you did." Brian looked down to where Normandy's leopard was embroidered on a badge on his shoulder. "But Aislinn tells me that Earl Roger means to return to Normandy ere the snow falls."

"You saw Aislinn?"

"Aye, I stopped at Mayenne on my way here." Brian's brow furrowed for a moment and then cleared. "She's not well, but I'd not tell Cat."

"That surprises me. I'd expected him to be ill rather than her."

"He is. He can scarce stand unaided now, and the old man cares not, since Linn is with child. It is as though Geoffrey has no value left to him, and the babe is everything." He stopped walking abruptly and looked up at Guy. "I fear for her—I do. The babe does not sit well with her in the heat, and Count Hugh will blame her if she loses it. I tried to persuade him to let me take her back to her mother until the babe comes, but he would not hear of it."

"Brian!"

"You will have to hold your nose, Cat," Brian warned her as he opened his arms to her. "Jesu, but are prettier than ever—I swear it," he murmured as she hugged him. "Linn bids me give you her love."

"You've seen Linn?"

"Aye."

"Sweet Mary—how does she fare?"

Brian's eyes met Guy's over Catherine's shoulder briefly in warning. "Linn is always Linn, Cat—she is well."

"And Geoffrey?"

"He'll be dead within the year."

"Aye," she sighed, stepping back. "She feared as much." Her eyes traveled over him, taking in the badge he wore. "You serve your father now—I am glad for you."

"I went to Rouen and told him I would do whatever he willed except fight Belesme for him." Lifting a small stone in the yard with the toe of his boot, he looked away. "He crossed through the Vexin a fortnight ago and threatens Evreux—my father thinks he means to fight his way to Belesme itself. 'Tis why I am here—I am come to warn you. The last time, he came this way and burned Rivaux."

Catherine and Guy exchanged glances of consternation, each thinking of the still-unfinished wall. "I have not the men to spare to send you to the Condes, Cat," Guy decided. "You will have to go to Nantes."

"Nantes! Nay, I will not! My place is here, with you!"

He shook his head. "Nay, I'd dare not fight with you here."

"You'd dare not fight with less than half a wall either! I'll not go!"

"Ah, Cat, 'tis to be expected of you, is it not?" His flecked eyes warmed as they studied her and his mouth twisted into a wry smile. "Full half the time you tell me where you will not go."

"Guy, listen to me! I'd not go to Gilbert! You think me safe there? Nay, but I'd not be—my grandsire is coward born—I'd be safer tethered outside these walls like a goat than at Nantes!"

"Nantes has high walls, Cat," Brian cut in. " 'Tis not likely that Belesme would take the time to lay siege there."

"You stay out of this!" She whirled on him fiercely, demanding, "What can you know of it? If Belesme so much as came to his walls, my grandsire would throw open his gates in fear!"

"Cat . . . Cat . . ." Guy caught her and held her trembling against him. "If he is such a coward, opening his gates is the last thing he'd do."

"I'd not be sent away!"

"Shhhh—'tis late summer already," he reasoned, "and Robert does not raid after the snow falls. 'Twill not be for long, Cat, and I'd have you safe."

"But Rivaux—"

"I'll stay here—I've got twenty mounted knights," Brian offered. "And 'tis not likely that Belesme will stop anywhere where he can expect a fight. He is not what he once was—he has no lands left in Normandy to succor him."

"If he is not what he once was, then why did you not wish to fight against him for your father?" she sniffed, trying to hold back tears.

"I would not deliberately stand in his way, Cat," he said. "I still fear him, but mayhap Rivaux need not. Robert of Belesme would not spend a thought as to whether to face me, but I'd think he'd not want to try Guy if he could avoid doing so."

"Sweet Mary, but I think you both mad!"

"You can rage, you can hiss and spit, Cat, but you'll not change my mind," Guy told her. If Belesme is at Evreux and is repulsed there, the Devil may turn on me. Nay, you'll go to Nantes this day."

"This day! This day? Nay—I will not!"

"Aye—you will. I'll send for you when the wall is finished or the snow falls, whichever should come about first," he promised.

Turning to Brian, she appealed for support. "Brian . . ."

"Nay, Cat, I'd not stand between you and your husband." His brown eyes were serious, but his voice held a hint of self-deprecation. "I told you I would stay here, did I not? And when have you ever known me to risk my bones foolishly? If I stay, you must surely know that I do not think Belesme will come this way again. Besides, for all he knows, he took all there was to be had the last time."

"Jesu! Why was I woman born?" she demanded in exasperation. "If I were a man, you'd not sent me away."

"You were woman born for me, Cat, and I'd keep you safe," Guy answered. "Come, let us find Hawise."

"Wait!" Her mind racing, she licked dry lips and stalled for the time to change his mind. " 'Tis midday already . . . and I'd take clothes with me . . .

please . . .'' She sucked in her breath and made her appeal. ''Please—I'd go on the morrow.''

He couldn't send her without at least some of her things, and he would have to see an escort armed and readied. ''Aye,'' he decided, glad for one more night with her. ''Aye, you'll go on the morrow.''

''Brian, where is Guy?'' Catherine demanded as she met him in the main hall.

''Bathing.'' His brown eyes took in her purple gown appreciatively and he nodded. ''I see you are wearing your best finery in hopes of changing his mind.''

Ignoring the latter remark, she focused on the first. ''Bathing? But he's not upstairs.''

''Nay.'' He grinned. ''To keep you from washing me, he took me to what passes for the bathhouse here, Cat, and I finished first. Not that I was inclined to linger— having coarse fellows pour buckets of cold water over me whilst I soap my body is not what I call a bath.''

''Why did you not offer to take me to the Condes?'' she asked suddenly.

'' 'Tis too far.''

''Or Nantes even?''

''I value my skin.''

''Then why did you offer to stay here?''

''Because I saw how little of the outer wall is done.'' Noting the skeptical lift of her dark eyebrow, he sighed. ''Aye, and I'd redeem myself for what happened at the Condes.''

''Why?''

''God's blood, Cat!'' he exploded finally. ''Can you do naught but question me? If the truth be known, I suppose 'tis because I would be like him. I made a fool of myself over the quintains, and I'd not have you or Aislinn or him think me unwilling to make amends. Is that meet in your eyes? I am not much the warrior, Cat, but I can set my men to helping finish your wall.''

''You think Belesme will come here, do you not? You can tell me, Brian.''

"I would if I knew, but Count Robert does not tell me what he plans," he snapped with asperity. "Leave me be. If you would know what I know not, ask your husband. I'll warrant he does not know either, but at least he has the means to silence you."

"Jesu, but you were not used to be so sharp-tempered, Brian."

"That was when I had wine in my cup and a woman in my bed. But you and Linn would have me different, and now you like not what you see. In truth, I know not what either of you would have of me."

"Your pardon, then." She paced away from him anxiously. "But if you will not speak of Belesme, then tell me of Linn."

"There's naught to tell," he responded evasively. "I saw her at Mayenne, and that is all."

"All? Brian FitzHenry, I have known you most of my life, but I have never before known you to be so sparing of words. If Geoffrey is dying, how is Linn?"

"She grieves for him, as you would expect."

"She is well-treated?"

"Aye," he lied.

"Sweet Mary, but must I pull every word from your mouth? I'd have you tell me of my sister—I'd know if she looks the same, if she sent any word to me—anything!"

"She loves us all well, Cat. She spoke of you and Pippa and Bella, saying she wished she had been kinder to you all, for she'd not realized how she would miss you. And she is homesick for the Condes—she'd see her mother and father again."

"When Geoffrey dies, she'll go back."

"If Count Hugh does not try to keep her so he will not have to return her dowry," he acknowledged in an unguarded moment.

"Nay—he would not dare."

"She carries Mayenne's heir. I would to God she did not." His brown eyes were distant for a moment and then his attention returned to her.

"She carries Mayenne's heir? Holy Mary, but then . . ."

"Aye. But I will tell you this, Cat: babe or no babe, I mean to go to my father if Mayenne will not return her to her parents. I'd not see her rot in Mayenne forever."

"My father would not let that happen."

"If he knows of it."

"He would know."

"He is in Harlowe much of the time now, Cat," he reminded her. "Nay, but 'tis possible he would not. But I would not speak of this either." He leaned against one of the central pillars that supported the ceiling of the hall. "Let us speak of you instead—'tis my turn for questions."

"There is naught to tell."

"Are you happy here?"

She met his eyes squarely and nodded. "Aye, I am."

"Your lord pleases you?"

"Aye."

A gleam of amusement lit his brown eyes. "And now you see how it is, Cat. If you ask someone about something that scarce concerns him, you will get more words than you would listen to, but if you pry into his inner thoughts, you get very little."

"Are you telling me not to meddle in your concerns, Brian—is that what you would say to me? After all we have been for each other?"

He grinned broadly. " 'Tis what I always liked about you, Cat—you have a quick understanding."

"Brian—"

"And so do I. Nay, I'd not speak to him of Nantes."

"I'd not quarrel with you tonight of all nights, Cat," Guy told her as he barred the door to their chamber.

"And I'd not quarrel with you either, but—"

"Nay." He turned around and put a finger to her lips. "Listen to me again but once—I'd not say it twice. I am sending you to Nantes to keep you safe, whether there is need or not. I'd not lose you, Cat."

"But I could go to Belvois!" she burst out, drawing back. " 'Tis closer and—"

"Nay. Most of the Belvois men are here, and I cannot spare enough to truly garrison the keep. My hope is that its walls will discourage Belesme if he comes, but I'd not take that chance with you inside. You go to Nantes. Coward or no, Gilbert is safe within those walls."

"Please, Guy, I'd not leave you."

Her eyes filled with tears that tore at his resolve. "And I'd not have you go, but I'd not have you fall into Belesme's hands if he should come this way." His hands reached to clasp her shoulders, and his flecked eyes were intent on hers. "Do not tear me apart, Cat."

"Nay, but . . ." She bit her lip and looked away, unable to meet the pain in his gaze. "Guy, I cannot bear it that you stay here."

"Aye, you can." He stepped closer and his hands slid from her shoulder down her back, pulling her into his embrace. "If I can stand it, you can also, Cat, for you are dearer than life to me." He felt the stiffness leave her body as she leaned into his. "But I'd remember you for aught besides tears this night," he added softly, his voice dropping almost to a caress. "Aye, I'd undress you and love you while there is still the time." One of his hands felt for the end of a plait and his fingers began to unwind the golden strip that fastened it. "Aye, and I'd lie beneath the rose scent of your hair." Her arms slid around his waist and held him tight as a sob escaped her. He stopped unworking her braid to smooth his hand soothingly over her crown and cradle her head. "But I'd be content to just lie holding you, if it be your will," he murmured above her. He could hear her sniff back more tears, and his other arm tightened protectively around her. He wanted to send her even less than she wanted to go, but the thought of what a man like Belesme could do to her was frightening and real. "Nay, Cat," he sighed finally, "but you cannot change my mind about

Nantes. The Robert of Belesme that raids now is far more terrible than the one you knew in Rouen." Resolutely he set her back so that he could see her face. "He has fallen into such evil that had I not Rivaux to rebuild, I would offer my levies to Henry and go after him in hopes of ridding Normandy of him forever."

Nodding, she tried for a semblance of a smile, but her mouth merely twisted. "Then I am glad Rivaux is not rebuilt. I'd not have you face him—not now . . . not ever."

"Look at us—we are expecting the worst, when we do not even know if he will come this way," he said to lighten her mood. "I'll warrant that in a month's time 'twill all be past and I'll be coming for you at Nantes."

A month. It sounded like both forever and not too far away. "You think 'twill be over in a month?"

"Aye, no more than six weeks for certain. Did you not hear Brian? Belesme never raids past the first snowfall—he withdraws into France for the winter, where he waits for the spring." Lifting her chin with his knuckle, he managed a smile that warmed the gold flecks in his eyes. "Come—cry peace with me and give me a kiss. We'll go to bed, and I will hold you."

"Nay."

"Nay?"

"I'd not spend my last night with you being held, Guy." A reluctant smile played at her mouth and then broadened. "But neither will I do all the work either— you can smell my hair when we are done." To hide the flush that rose in her face, she bent her head and reached for the ties of his chausses.

❧ 29 ❧

"Would you favor chess or tables perhaps?"

"Nay."

Gilbert of Nantes eyed his granddaughter with a touch of exasperation. In the three weeks she'd been with him, she'd been quiet and withdrawn, and now she appeared to be getting sick. The unusually warm September did not set well with her, leaving her pasty and queasy much of the time. "Mayhap we could walk in the garden and I can show you where your mother once—"

"Nay."

"God's teeth, but what ails you, girl? Three daughters I had, and not one of them as puling as you! I'd not have young Rivaux complain to me that I let you sicken whilst you were here!" He spoke with feeling, as though berating would somehow make her well, and then sighed, for Catherine was the comeliest of his granddaughters and he truly liked her. Unlike her mother, she appeared to have a docile nature. To cheer her, he rose and stood over her. "Aye, but I suppose you cannot help it, can you? The spice merchant comes from Spain this week, I am told—mayhap I can get you some oranges to tempt your appetite."

Catherine's gorge rose and her stomach revolted at the thought of food. "If I am unwell, Grandpapa, 'tis but because of the child I carry. 'Twill pass."

311

"Child! Eh . . . what's this, you say? A babe?" He came alive at the thought, rubbing his hands together almost gleefully. "Well, now, if you would not make an old man glad! Your grandmother and your mother never could get sons for Nantes, Catherine, but young Rivaux has good blood in him. Aye, a son for Nantes mayhap!" he chortled enthusiastically.

"I just pray I have a son for Rivaux," she managed miserably.

"What you need is air and rest and some of those oranges. Aye, and I'll see if the fellow has anything for a weak stomach also," he promised.

Gilbert surprised her. She'd been prepared to dislike and despise him, but it appeared that in his old age he had mellowed. Certainly he had been gruffly kind to her, offering to amuse her a dozen ways, ordering rich fabrics from the cloth vendors and setting Nantes's seamstresses to making pretty gowns for her, and regaling her with tales of how things had been in the Old Conqueror's time. In turn, she listened silently to his boasting, gaining his affection.

"A son for Nantes," he mused half to himself. "Aye, but I think you'll be the one to bear a son for Nantes. My Mary could not do it, nor could Eleanor or Margaret, and Adelicia does not matter, for her son cannot inherit, anyway—aye, 'tis you who will have the next Count of Nantes, Catherine," he decided definitely.

For a moment she could almost smile despite her sickness, for if it should prove to be a son, the babe would have enough titles one day to make even King Henry envious. Aye, her son would be lord of the Condes, Count of Nantes and Rivaux, and Earl of Harlowe if he lived long enough.

"Aye, but we would celebrate this, Catherine. I'll call for my best wine."

"Nay."

"Oh . . . aye." He nodded, remembering her sickness. "Well, there's naught to say that I should not celebrate, is there?"

"I'd go home—I'd return to Rivaux."

"I promised the one who brought you—William, was it?—that I'd keep you here until your lord sent for you, Catherine." His black eyes were like coals beneath his white brows as they watched her. "Aye, and it pleases me to have you, anyway. 'Tis lonely for an old man with naught but ungrateful daughters."

"Mayhap you should pass Christmas in the Condes. Maman—"

"I doubt she would welcome me," he cut in testily. "Nay, your mother was naught but a trial to me, and well she knows it. But I'd not speak of such things when you are ill—I'd not harm the babe by oversetting you." Satisfied that he'd mollified her, he turned to reach for a flacon of wine and poured himself a cup. "To an heir for Nantes," he told her as he raised it to his lips. "Aye, mayhap Rivaux will name him Gilbert for Nantes." When he looked back, her eyes were closed and beads of perspiration were visible on her forehead. Her face had that ashen hue of one about to be heartily sick. "Oh, God's teeth," he muttered as he sought to catch her. "To your lady! Hawise! To your lady—to Rivaux!"

"Nay, I am all right—'tis but the sickness. 'Twill pass."

"My lord . . ."

Gilbert turned on the hapless servant who stood tentatively within the door. "Not now," he snapped. "Can you not see she is unwell? Hawise! Hawise! Where *is* the woman?"

For answer, Hawise pushed past the young man in the doorway to reach her mistress. Putting her arm around Catherine, she murmured soothing words as she had done ever since the girl had been a small child. "This does not last long, sweeting," she soothed, "and then all will be well. Let your poor Hawise take you to your bed."

"Nay, I will be better—'twill pass."

"My lord—"

"Jesu! Can it not wait? God's blood, but the girl is sick!" Gilbert shouted at the fellow who still waited. "Nay, get out of here."

"Just let me sit," Catherine begged.

Nodding, Hawise motioned to the count to help his granddaughter, and between them they eased her onto a bench. Cat leaned forward, her head in her hands, and tried to control the rising nausea. The room spun around her, and the voices seemed far away and unreal.

"My lord, there is a man—"

"Are you still here? Have you no ears? I am surrounded by fools! All right, out with it, and be gone!"

"He comes from Belvois, my lord," Gilbert's man tried to explain. "He says 'tis of utmost import that he speak with you."

"Belvois? Send him to the kitchens—I'd come down later."

"Nay." Cat swallowed hard and raised her head. "Send him here. Belvois is one of my husband's keeps."

"Take her to her bed," Gilbert ordered.

"Nay, I'd hear him." Cat shook her head determinedly and held on to the bench beneath her. "Please, I pray you."

For the first time since she'd been at Nantes, Gilbert eyed his granddaughter with disfavor. "Art as stubborn as your mother, I fear, Catherine," he muttered. A weak-willed man given to retreat, he turned back to the servant with a sigh. "Aye, I will see him."

"Let your grandsire tend the matter," Hawise urged. "This will pass sooner in bed, and well you know it."

"I'd hear whoever comes from Belvois first," Cat defied her through clenched teeth.

The wait seemed interminable, with Catherine determined to defeat the waves of nausea and her grandsire pacing impatiently, cursing and muttering about how she would harm her babe. Holding her peace, Hawise dipped a cloth in a ewer of water and wrung it out before wiping her mistress's face with it.

"Belvois is no concern of yours or mine," Gilbert muttered. "A woman should stay out of a man's affairs, and I'd not see the fellow."

"I'd know how 'tis he comes here rather than Rivaux."

"Aye, but he'd have no reason—" He stopped short as a boy was brought in to kneel before him. "Get up and speak your piece," he growled.

" 'Tis Belesme, my lord! He lays siege to Belvois!"

"Holy Mary!" Cat gasped involuntarily as she leaned into Hawise's stomach and felt the older woman's arms go around her. Belvois was but ten leagues from Rivaux itself, and it had but a small garrison. If Guy tried to relieve it, or if Belesme should turn southward to Rivaux itself . . . Catherine dared not let herself think further.

"Why come to me?" Gilbert demanded irritably. "I am not suzerain to Belvois. Go to Rivaux."

"I pray you, my lord—I have been in my saddle night and day . . ." The boy paused and looked toward Cat. "My captain bade me escape and come to you—said you shared a bond of blood with Rivaux through the Lady Catherine, and—"

"And he cannot go to Rivaux," Cat interrupted, her heart thudding painfully with fear. "Rivaux has naught but one wooden wall to breach, and no men to spare, Grandsire." White-faced, she looked at Gilbert and her dark eyes pleaded. "I ask your aid for my husband—I pray you do not wait until Belesme reaches Rivaux itself." Denying the awful dread that threatened to betray her, she tried to keep calm. Gilbert was weak-willed, everyone said, and it was up to her to have the greater will now.

"Rivaux will have gone to relieve his own keep ere I can get there," he temporized, stalling whilst he found the means to avoid her appeal. "Aye—'twould take me a fortnight to raise my levies."

"Count Robert has fewer than one hundred men," the boy offered.

Casting him a look of pure malevolence, Gilbert cleared his throat, his own mind racing. One hundred men was not many, but he had no wish to meet Robert of Belesme across a field. Not now, not ever. Speaking finally, he allowed, "I could perhaps send fifty mounted men-at-arms—but no more than that—and 'twill take two days ere they can be ready."

" 'Tis not enough!" Cat disputed. "Aye, and you can spare twice that without calling your levies, can you not? And I'd not have you send your captain, Grandsire—I'd have you go with me."

He was too stunned by the change in her for the full import to sink into his consciousness. He fingered the stubble of his beard for a moment, trying to decide how long he could delay. "Aye—but 'twill take four days to arm and provision them."

"Four days?" She fairly howled in indignation. "Nay, I'd not thought it of you! Did I not know you better, I'd think you meant to wait until Rivaux itself is taken! But as you are Count of Nantes, I know it cannot be so!" She pulled away from Hawise and rose to face him. "Aye, despite what is said of you, I know my grandsire is no coward!"

His face reddened dangerously as he exploded, "Who dares call me coward? If 'tis that bastard father of yours—"

"My father is no bastard!" she shot back. "And nay, 'tis not he who says so!" She cast about wildly for the means to goad him. " 'Tis Belesme! Aye—he warned Curthose you would run!"

"He ran also!"

"But they all said it: de Mortain, Curthose himself, and—"

"And all are gone now," he scoffed, "but yet I

live.'' His eyes narrowed suspiciously. ''And what said Rivaux of the matter? Did he call me coward also?''

''Nay, he disputed it,'' she lied. ''And do you think he would have sent me to you if he thought you craven? Nay, but he would not! He values me well, Grandsire! He sent me here because he knew you would keep me safe!''

''And so I shall, girl! But I cannot take an army to Rivaux if he asks me not—nay, he should send to Henry!''

''Why? Henry did not protect it the last time, did he? And lest you forget it, Guy fought against him at Tinchebrai—nay, he'd not aid us!''

'' 'Tis not my affair. Rivaux has no oath of mine.''

''But he has a bond of blood! I carry your heir and his in this body! One day Rivaux and Nantes will be ruled by my son—does that mean naught to you?'' she cried. When she saw he was unconvinced, she lowered her voice and managed in a calmer tone, ''All right, send de Searcy with me, then. I'd not have you risk yourself for my husband, Gilbert of Nantes.''

''I did not say I would not go,'' he protested. ''But I think it a fool's ride, for Belesme does not stay long anywhere in Normandy. He does but burn and kill and leave.''

''Which is why we must leave on the morrow if we are to be of aid to Guy. Please, Grandsire, for the sake of my heir and yours, help me hold his patrimony.''

Her eyes met his and held until he had to look down for fear she could see the cowardice in his heart. Aye, he'd go, but he'd make certain he arrived too late to cross paths with Robert of Belesme. ''All right, Catherine—for the son you give Nantes, I will do it.''

''I am going also.''

''Nay, you are not—I'd not take a girl with an army. You will stay here and take care that you do not lose the babe you would have me fight for.'' He shook his head, muttering, ''Aye, and I pray 'tis a son you carry.

I'd not have you cheat me as your mother and grandmother have done.''

'' 'Twill be a son,'' she promised. ''Save my husband, and I will bear a son to rule Nantes and Rivaux.''

❧ 30 ❧

Bone-weary from three fruitless days in the saddle, Guy set a plodding pace for the return to Rivaux. When word had come that Belesme laid siege to Belvois, he had gathered Brian and every man he could spare to go to his people's aid, but even as Guy and his men crossed the river that wound between the two estates, Belesme had inexplicably pulled back and faded into the woods, taking his ragged army into deep underbrush that made pursuit dangerous and difficult. Once again, the dispossessed Belesme had struck in the heart of Normandy with impunity.

" 'Tis strange that Count Robert would draw back from a smaller force," Brian mused aloud, putting into words the thought that had perplexed Guy since Belvois.

"Aye."

"Mayhap he grows overcautious with age," the younger man went on.

"Belesme? Nay—never. But I own he surprised me. If you do not count the occupants of the house he burned, he left no dead." Almost by rote, Guy said a silent prayer for the three people who'd burned in their thatched wattle-and-daub hut, and then crossed himself. Jesu, peasant or no, 'twas not a way he'd choose to depart this world.

"Aye," Brian murmured agreement. "I'd expected

319

him to burn the fields and all the villeins' huts if he could not take the place. Mayhap we surprised him early.''

"How long does it take to set torches to drying grass?'' Guy responded rhetorically. "Nay, if he burned them not, 'twas because he had no wish to do it.''

"Well, I cannot make sense of it, but then, I know not the man.''

"I knew him once, and I cannot make sense of it either. Given what was between us before Tinchebrai, I'd expected him to face me at Belvois.''

"Mayhap he knew not how many men we brought.''

"He knew. If there is naught else that Belesme knows, 'tis how to count those against him—how else can he choose where he raids so well? He does but strike heavy blows and run. Still, I'd thought he would have tried to ruin me though my lands at the least.''

Curiosity got the better of Brian. He half-turned in his saddle to ask, "But what can be between the two of you? He cannot blame you for his losses—nay, 'tis my father he hates.''

"He wanted Cat for revenge on Roger de Brione, I think. He asked Curthose to send her to Mabille, but Curthose gave her to me instead.''

"I should hope he did—e'en my uncle Curthose was not such a fool as that. Jesu, Cat to Belesme? And when he was wed at that? Nay, there'd have been none to stand for it.''

Guy leaned forward in his saddle and tried to ease the aching in his back. Unlike Brian FitzHenry, who seemed able to sleep astride a horse, he'd had no sleep in three days, and his mind was beginning to reflect it. It seemed he could not even carry the same thought long, and the puzzle over Belesme's strange maneuver defied understanding to the point where he'd not think on it any longer. He wanted to be at Rivaux, he wanted his bed, and he wanted Catherine—aye, above all, he wanted Cat.

"Art too tired to sit your horse," Brian muttered. "Were I you, I'd stop here for the night and lay my pallet on the ground."

" 'Tis still daylight. Nay, but I'd sleep in a bed this night."

"Mayhap you are right. I could use a comely wench to warm my bones after this ride."

"Not in my keep. There are but Hedda and the kitchen girls, and Cat would not like it if you were to lay one of them."

"Do you never think of it?"

Despite his overwhelming weariness, Guy looked over at Brian suspiciously, wondering why he would ask. But in the month since Brian had offered his service to protect Rivaux, Guy had discovered much to like in his former rival. Besides, he had nothing to hide.

"I'd not tell Cat," Brian prompted.

" 'Twould make no difference if you did." For a moment, Catherine's face seemed to float before him as it often did as he drifted into sleep, and Guy's longing intensified until he could scarce bear it. "Nay," he answered finally, "I'd do nothing to destroy what is between us." He caught Brian's skeptical look and nodded. "If I burn, I burn alone until she is come back from Nantes."

"Art besotted then."

"For a man reported to lay every willing wench who breathes, I've not seen you try it at Rivaux."

"Nay," Brian sighed. "I gave up all my vices at one time, but 'tis a hard task trying to be worthy for someone." A rueful grin spread across his round face, and despite his own fatigue, a twinkle sprang to his brown eyes. "Aye, I did not say I meant to. I suppose if you can be true, then so can I."

"Do I know the lady?" Guy felt compelled to ask.

" 'Tis of no import—she'd not have me, anyway."

"Cat?"

"Nay."

They fell to silence, each lost in his own thoughts. Guy's turned again to Catherine as he wondered how she fared at Nantes. On his return to Rivaux, William had reported that she already had Gilbert enthralled with her beauty and docility. Guy could not help smiling at the report—his Cat docile? Aye, and the old man was plying her with gifts to ease her homesickness, offering in a letter to keep her for the winter, saying, "She is the delight of my life, the joy of my old age." His dotage, more like, Guy snorted to himself. Nay, he'd not have Cat stay away from Rivaux one day longer than necessary. Even now he prayed that the harassment of Belvois was but Belesme's halfhearted last attempt to wreak havoc ere he withdrew again into France. Word placed his summer's death count high, with scores of villages burned and razed, hundreds of peasants burned or hacked to pieces to satisfy his blood lust, and dozens of knights captured and tortured to slow deaths. Nay, mayhap he was but on his way back to France and would not take the time to outwait Belvois.

Guy's horse picked up its pace on its own, a sign that they were nearing Rivaux itself. Jogged from his reverie, Guy realized he'd not even noted that they'd reached the wide shallows of the river that ran between his lands. God's bones, but it would be good to eat hot food and sleep in a feather bed again. And he hoped William had been able to keep every man working in his absence, for he liked not feeling vulnerable in his own keep.

The water was swift over the rocky bed, swirling around his horse's knees as he urged the animal across. The cold wetness seeped through his boots and soaked the bottom of his braichs where they were tucked in, chilling him, but he did not care—he was nearly home and the feather bed beckoned. Beside him, he heard Brian cursing that he was ruining his boots and had not a pair to spare.

Reining in on the opposite bank, they waited for the

forty men who rode with them to finish the crossing. Guy looked to Rivaux, to the outer wall and the piles of quarried stone. Aye, there'd been a few more feet of it done, as near as he could tell. But it was still daylight and work had stopped—William must be getting softer than he'd suspected, if he did not glean every minute's work from his men. Using his pommel for leverage, Guy rose in his saddle to look more closely. There was no sound of carpenters at work inside, nor was there any sign of activity at all, he had to admit as he listened.

The short hairs at the back of his neck prickled in warning and he raised his hand for silence as the others joined him. Craning his neck toward the fields, he could see they were undisturbed. Haystacks raked from the harvests dotted the land like silent sentries among neatly defined patches of gold thatch and green grass. Uneasy, he looked for the wisps of smoke from the cooking fires in the huts, and was reassured to see some. He was overtired, he guessed, and his mind would deceive him into fear. Sniffing deeply, he smelled bread from his own ovens and dismissed his fears. Aye, a weary body made him foolish.

As if by silent signal, the draw that spanned his ditch creaked downward, opening the stockade itself. Guy spurred on almost eagerly now, not waiting for Brian or any of the others. The men behind him, sensing the nearness of their own ease, whipped their own tired mounts in a near-race for the gate. The wooden platform bounced beneath the pounding hooves and the iron supports banged noisily as they poured three abreast across the bridge and into the inner bailey. Silent ostlers moved to grasp reins from the riders while the bridge raised behind them, securing Rivaux from the world they'd left.

Guy had removed his helmet and was in the process of dismounting when he noted the stranger who held his horse. And out of the corner of his eye he could see the crossbowmen who stepped from behind Catherine's new kitchen and bakery. Turning around, he saw more of them posted above him on the stockade wall itself, crouched from outside view. His whole body felt numb as he slowly turned back to his own square tower. There in the wide, arched doorway stood Robert of Belesme.

"Nay, do not think to fight, Guy of Rivaux," Belesme told him even as Guy's hand crept to the hilt of Doomslayer. "You would be cut down ere you could clear the scabbard."

"Where are my people?" Guy demanded, his heart racing as he contemplated his chances. But the bridge behind him was closing, making escape impossible. They were doomed, every Rivaux man in the keep, and he'd led them blindly to their deaths. Impotent rage, directed at himself for being a fool and at Belesme for what he would do to them, made Guy reckless. Still partially shielded by his horse, he grasped his sword and prayed he could reach Belesme before he was cut down. Lunging forward, he gave the shout, "For Rivaux and St. Stephen! For Rivaux and St. Stephen!" They had not a chance, but he'd invoke the name of the martyr and die fighting rather than be skinned or boiled in his own keep.

Half a dozen green-shirted men tried to grasp him from behind, while the bowmen held their fire, but he shook them off, nearly carrying one fellow with him. He almost reached Belesme, thinking irrationally that he was as big as, if not bigger than, the older count now. Robert made no move to evade him, but stood watching him with those strange green eyes of his, until Guy raised Doomslayer to strike. The last words he heard were, "Take him, Piers," as he fell to the ground.

"Would you have me place him with the others?" Piers de Sols asked his lord as he knelt beside Guy's inert body.

Robert of Belesme stepped forward to move Guy with the toe of his boot, and then, satisfied that he was indeed unconscious, he dropped to his knees to examine where Piers had hit him with the rock. Expertly he lifted the young man's eyelids to study his pupils, and then he rolled him over to feel the lump that was already forming beneath the thick black hair. Having seen every nuance of a man's progress toward death, he considered himself an authority on whether someone would live or not. Apparently satisfied, he rose and wiped his bloody hands on his green tunic.

"Nay, I'd have him brought to me when he wakens. Disarm him and tend the cut on his head.

Guy came to consciousness slowly, aware first of the woman who hummed softly at his bedside while she changed the cool rags on his brow, and then of the awful ache that threatened to split the back of his head. Stirring gingerly, he could tell he was in his own feather bed, and as his cognitive powers returned, he began to wonder if he'd been dreaming, if his head pained from some other injury. His hand crept to the back of his head and he felt the lump there. The place was tender beneath blood-matted hair. Ever so slowly, he opened his eyes to stare at the woman who hovered over him. Her eyes were as green as Belesme's.

"Nay, do not move too quickly," she cautioned him. Then, seeing his confusion, she leaned closer to explain, "I am Mabille."

Mabille. The witch of Belesme, the woman who had borne Count Robert in what some said was a pact with the devil. The woman said to be so vile she lay with her own son after she poisoned his father for him. She appeared to float above him like a faery creature slow to age, with smooth white skin and red hair that mingled with silver. He stared blankly and tried to understand how it was that she tended him. His eyes traveled warily around the room, taking in the details of his own chamber. Aye, he was in his own bed.

"Drink this—'twill ease the pain." The bed ropes

creaked as she sat beside him and reached to lift his head. "And, nay, 'tis not poison."

"Still, I'd not drink it."

Her laugh was almost musical as she lifted the cup to his lips. "Do you truly think I'd waste the time to stitch your head beneath that black thatch you call hair if I mean to poison you?"

"I'd think you meant to save me for Robert's knife," he answered candidly. He tried to rise and push her hand away, but fell back from the intense pain in his head.

"I am not unskilled in simples. Drink it." This time, she slid her arm behind him. "Piers, hold him," she ordered a man who sat nearby on a stool. "Now, we'd have you mended enough to see my son, Lord Guy," she almost crooned as she held the cup again to his lips and coaxed, "I swear to you 'twill not harm you."

The man Piers came closer and braced Guy with his arm, asking, "Do you want me to force it down him?"

"Nay," she answered, "he will drink."

Despite all he had ever heard of her, Guy saw none of her reputed evil in the green eyes that met his. But then, she would be full of guile, he supposed wearily. Aye, and a swift poisoning would be preferable to the death he knew Robert of Belesme would inflict on him, for even in his befuddled state he could remember the tales of how Fuld Nevers had been skinned alive. He nodded and took a deep sip of the bitter liquid.

"Aaarggh," he managed with a shudder. "What is it?"

" 'Tis for pain. Lay him back, Piers." She leaned to set the cup on the bedside bench and then sat back to watch him. "I'd not harm you, Guy of Rivaux," she murmured softly.

Telling himself he was in the midst of an awful dream, Guy closed his eyes and leaned back. The bitter mixture she'd given him pitched and rolled in his stomach for a time and then he felt strangely calm. His eyes were heavy and his mind floated as though it were separate from his body. He tried to open his eyes and focus on her, but her streaked red hair hung like a veil over him, blotting out her features save for the green eyes that watched him.

"You have poisoned me," he muttered thickly with a tongue that barely worked. The last thing he remembered at all was the feel of her cold hands smoothing his rumpled hair back from his face.

Mabille of Belesme rose finally and collected the assortment of medicinal herbs and little pots she'd brought with her. "He will not wake before the morrow, but I'd not leave him unguarded."

"How fares he?"

Mabille turned around at the sound of her son's voice and found him standing at the unbarred door. "You surprise me, Robert. I'd thought you to be below with the prisoners."

"I mean to spare them." He shrugged at her expression of disbelief and added, "But I have told the men they can have any they find beyond these walls."

"He took a hard blow with the rock—his head must be like steel."

"Would you have expected it to be otherwise?"

"Nay, but it surprised me that he tried to fight."

"I knew he would not do otherwise," Robert told her proudly. Moving to the side of the bed, he looked down where Guy lay curled like a giant child. "I asked how he fared."

"Well enough. He woke and I gave him some of the bark you stole from that Eastern trader outside Gisors. It aids the pain."

He lifted a black eyebrow and looked up. "And he drank it?"

"Aye—'twas better in his eyes to be poisoned than what he believes you would do to him."

Curious, he studied the younger man's face for a time before he reached his scarred hands to touch hair as black as his own. His fingers traced the fine, straight profile and the high, defined cheekbones, and a slight smile formed at the disfigured side of his face. ''Nay, I'd not harm him.''

He was a prisoner in his own keep, attended by Belesme's men rather than his own, and yet Guy found himself treated as befitted his rank. Mabille herself tended his head and brewed the potions that eased his pain once he woke the second time, but she steadfastly refused to answer any of his questions about the men and women who lived at Rivaux. "Nay, but Robert will tell you in his time, Lord Guy," was all she would say.

"But I would at least know how the old one—how William de Comminges fares," he persisted. "And the man called Brian also."

"What are they to you?" she asked finally.

"William has been with me since my birth."

"And the other one?"

Well aware of Robert of Belesme's bitter hatred for Brian's father, Guy deemed it best to avoid that relationship. "Brian comes from Wales to serve me. I'd not have him harmed either."

"Wales. Aye, Robert had lands there once, but those lands were taken," she remembered bitterly. "Shrewsbury he was, and King Henry disinherited him, saying he was traitor to the crown, that he made Wales a fief of his own."

"I fought at Shrewsbury and throughout the marches, but the Welsh rebel there still."

''And they always will if Henry thinks to rule them from Rouen—or even London.'' A smile curved what had once been a generous mouth. ''Aye, we have heard of your deeds in France.''

''My lord of Belesme would have him brought down,'' someone called to Piers de Sols through the door, sending a shiver of apprehension through Guy's body.

If even one-tenth of the stories about Belesme's legendary cruelty were true, it would not be unlike him to have made certain his prisoner was well enough to endure hours or days of torture. Aye, Guy had seen evidence of his blood lust himself and had listened as Rivaux's survivors from the earlier raid had told of the slow deaths of those who'd been taken. Belesme did but play with him, drawing out the manner of Guy's dying, letting him think he would be allowed to live, Guy was certain, and yet somehow that did not explain Mabille's gentleness.

''Well, my lord,'' Mabille murmured, turning to him, '' 'twould seem you may ask of your people yourself.'' Over her shoulder, she told Piers, ''Dress him.''

''I would dress myself.''

Piers rummaged through the chests that lined one end of the solar and found Guy's best tunic, the one he'd worn to see Henry in Rouen. Guy, who faced probable death, stilled his fears by studying Robert's man. There was little about Piers de Sols that fit Belesme's reputation, for the man seemed neither cruel nor unpleasant. When he came back with Guy's tunics, chausses, and shoes, Guy asked him, ''How is it that you serve Count Robert?''

''I am his squire these nineteen years, my lord. I have served him in every battle save Tinchebrai, and would have served him then but for broken bones.''

''Jesu, but how can you?''

Piers cast a covert look at Mabille and shrugged. ''He has been good enough to me.''

''Then may God punish you for his blood sports,''

Guy muttered as he slipped on the linen undertunic and then reached for his chausses.

"Nay, he does not ask me for that. I've killed no man other than in battle, my lord."

His hands steady, Guy pulled on his hose and tied them beneath the undertunic. For the briefest moment he considered overpowering Piers and taking Mabille hostage in hopes of treating with Belesme, but then realized that none of them were armed. And 'twas said that the love between Robert and his mother was a strange one—that more than once he'd nearly killed her himself. But if he could use one of them for shield—nay, he sighed inwardly, he could not—Belesme would not treat for them. If anything, he'd bring out Guy's men and begin executing them before his eyes.

Piers held out the overtunic and waited for Guy to pull it on. The black hawk of Rivaux spread its wings as he smoothed it, and Guy felt a fool for the way he'd been taken. He would have minded dying less if he'd struck a few blows first, but to have been caught by a ruse filled him with shame. He should have known that Belesme would not have stayed at Belvois, that he had not the men to sustain a siege into the winter, and yet Guy had ridden out and left Rivaux with far too small a garrison. How had Robert gotten William to surrender? he wondered, and new fear clutched at his heart. Had he killed William already?

"Art ready, my lord?"

"Ah . . . aye." There was little use postponing the inevitable. Guy squared his shoulders and hoped he would not die a coward. "Aye."

He followed Piers down the steep steps, passing the room where Rivaux's men usually slept. The chamber had been swept bare save for a few rough benches and boxes and the rolled pallets that lined one wall. Did any of their owners yet live—and if so, then where?

Piers's heels clicked on the flagged floor as they crossed the main hall to the room where Guy kept the

records of his estate. The thought came to him as he
reached the screen that he was glad he'd made his
peace with Catherine before he'd sent her away. A stab
of near-physical pain cut through his breast as he
thought of her—she'd mourn him deeply, he knew.
Aye, but he'd had what few men had had—for a time,
he'd had Catherine of the Condes to love him.

Belesme warmed his hands at a small fire in the
brazier. Guy stared at his back for a moment, noting
for the first time that the older man's tunic was faded
and worn.

Piers paused at the edge of the wooden screen and
cleared his throat. "I have brought the Count of Rivaux, my lord."

"Leave us, then."

Robert of Belesme turned around slowly, his green
eyes traveling over Guy with a strange light in them.
He appeared to stop when he reached the black hawk
on Guy's chest, and there was a flicker of something—
disdain perhaps—that crossed his face. The dent in his
cheekbone was even more pronounced than Guy remembered it, and the smile that twisted his mouth was
made crooked by his disfigurement. Now that he was
sure he was going to die, Guy felt like every moment
dragged, making every observation unbelievably acute.
They were of a like height, he and Belesme, but he
thought perhaps he was outweighed by as much as a
stone, maybe more. Noting the jeweled dagger that
hung from Belesme's belt, Guy considered his chances
for overpowering and taking him, knowing full well
he faced the man everyone had acknowledged the most
dangerous in Normandy for twenty-five years and
more.

"You might do it," Belesme told him almost pleas-
antly, "But then again, I might carve your lights out
and roast every man in Rivaux if you err in the trying." Abruptly he changed the subject, gesturing almost wearily to where the constant drizzle wet the

frame of the unshuttered window. "It grows chill for September—I'd hoped to avoid the rains."

When Guy was silent, the older man leaned to pick up a steaming cup from a low table and held it out. "I mulled some wine for you—you will need it ere we are done."

"Is this like the hyssop the Romans gave Christ?"

"Nay, 'twill but warm you." He moved closer with the cup and his green eyes searched Guy's face as though they looked for something. "Here."

The metal cup was hot when he took it, but Guy raised it to his mouth to sip.

"Have a care—you'll burn your tongue out," Belesme murmured, still watching him.

" 'Twill save you the trouble later, then."

A faint smile again twisted one side of his mouth. "Nay, if you think I mean to kill you, you mistake the matter." Robert lifted his cup and drank deeply before wiping his mouth on the sleeve of his tunic. Illogically, Guy remembered there had been a time when he would have been too fastidious to soil his clothes with food or drink. "Nay, I'd not harm you, Guy," Belesme repeated softly. He stared harder, as though he would see something beyond mere appearance, and when he spoke again there was something akin to the old pride in his voice. "Though I think you no more afraid of me than I would have been." He moved even closer, until Guy could see the age lines on what must have once been a handsome face. "Aye, but you have not the look of her," he decided softly.

Taken aback by the sudden change in Belesme's tone, Guy felt as though he were part of something unreal, some faery dream mayhap. "The look of whom?" he managed to ask.

"Alys."

"I never favored her, I am told."

" 'Tis as well you did not—she was a foolish creature." Robert waited for him to rise to the bait, but he did not.

"I never knew her, as she died birthing me," Guy admitted, wondering where Belesme led him.

"Nay, but there is more of your father in you than you will care to admit."

"I scarce knew him either, so if you hope to gain a fight with me over either of them, you'll not do it," Guy retorted, betraying his bitterness. "All I ever had of my father was Rivaux, and it was granted grudgingly to me when there was no other heir to name."

"Not quite."

There was something so compelling in those two words that Guy felt the warning hairs on his neck rise and his flesh chill. He had the sense that Robert enjoyed the slow telling of this as much as he enjoyed a slow killing. He took another drink of the hot wine to stave off the unease he felt.

"Aye, Alys was a foolish, silly maid wed to an old man who could not even do the deed," Belesme continued conversationally. "She hated him—aye, you may stare, but she did. And she was a comely thing if one did not consider her foolishness, I suppose. I spent part of the winter here when she was but newly wed."

Guy's stomach knotted and his palms grew wet at the impossible thought that came to mind. "You have no reason to tell me this now that they are both dead, my lord."

"Aye, I have every reason, Guy." Robert of Belesme moved to look out into the courtyard at the gray, drizzling rain that fell there. "I was but twenty-one and newly knighted—Old William delayed that as long as he could, out of dislike for me, but that's naught to the tale—and Alys thought to use me to rid herself of a cold and useless husband. My handsomeness excused my own coldness then, but there were not many as wanted to lie with me at that. Except Alys. She was restive, wanting what Count Eudo could not give her, and she turned to me."

"Nay!"

Belesme spun around at the vehemence in his denial

and nodded. "Aye, but she did." His green eyes grew distant, as though seeing again what had passed, and he continued, "She had dark hair, not so dark as Eleanor's as I remember, and eyes that were more gold than brown. I used to close mine when we were together and tell myself she was Eleanor of Nantes. 'Twas not Alys I wanted—'twas Eleanor."

"I do not believe you—'tis lies you tell!" Guy disputed hotly, despite the chill in his heart.

Ignoring the outburst, Robert went on, "Old Eudo was blind. Because I never lay with the castle wenches, he thought me safe enough—'twas even rumored that I shared William Rufus' strange taste for men rather than women. It wasn't until Alys conceived you that he discovered he'd been cuckolded. First she begged me to kill him, and when I would not because the Old Conqueror valued him too much, then she begged to go with me, saying she would tell him of it. I told her not to be a fool—to bed the old man any way she could—but she was too stupid to listen. She still thought to rid herself of him through me." A harsh laugh escaped him as he remembered. "Aye, she told him she carried my babe, Guy, thinking he'd challenge me and I would kill him anyway. As I was as big as I am now and was already noted for my skill at arms, I knew he would not force a quarrel. I told him I would leave and say nothing of what had happened here." His eyes met Guy's now and held. "As well you know, 'twas my offer he took. He'd no wish for any to know of his shame, so he kept her—he beat her until 'twas difficult to recognize her, but he kept her."

The knot tightened in his stomach and his gorge rose, threatening to make him vomit, for Guy knew deep within himself that Robert of Belesme spoke the truth. It explained so many things now—why he had been despised by both his mother's family and by the man he called his father, why he had been sent away to the loneliness of a monastery when most boys went to foster, why he had to fight his terrible temper—dear

God, but he was the son of Robert of Belesme! He bore the terrible Talvas taint—the blood that flowed in his veins was the Devil of Belesme's. The witch Mabille was his grandmother. His very soul was damned to hell for the blood and madness he carried within him.

"Aye, Guy of Rivaux—art my son."

"Why could you not have just killed me—why did you tell me this?" Guy asked numbly.

"Dead you serve no purpose, but living you fulfill what I promised to Eleanor of Nantes." Belesme reached to take the empty cup from Guy's nerveless fingers, and turned away to set it on the table. "Did you never wonder how 'twas you were given Catherine of the Condes?"

"Curthose needed men."

"I gave her to you—I pushed him into turning to you."

"You demanded she be sent to Mabille, as I remember it," Guy contradicted as he fought hard within himself against the horror and self-loathing he felt.

"And you think he did not know how it would be for her? Nay, my demands forced him to do something to protect her from me. He needed men and money, aye, and I gave him the means to get them—and I gave the girl to you."

"Nay, 'twould make no sense. You wanted her for revenge on de Brione—"

"And bring all Normandy down on my head then? I never wanted but Eleanor of Nantes in my bed since first I saw her—something your foolish mother and my countess would not believe. I knew Catherine of the Condes was not for me. She bears his blood as much as Eleanor's." Belesme walked the few paces back to face Guy. "But the day I went to the abbey to tell Eleanor she came to me, I vowed to her that my son would rule Nantes."

"I think you are mad."

"Aye. But my son *will* rule Nantes, Guy. My blood

will triumph over them all—all who thought to thwart me in this: Curthose, Henry, Roger, Gilbert, even Eleanor. You defeat them for me—you defeat them all.''

"Sweet Jesu. And you tricked me at Belvois—you came here to tell me this?''

"I can tell none other." Belesme's eyes met Guy's squarely. "Aye, you hate me, but I hold your fate in my hands," he murmured with chilling softness. " 'Tis fitting that the son most like me should fulfill what I once promised, is it not?''

"Nay, you lie to me—'tis all lies, Robert!" Guy denied suddenly, unable to bear the burden of what Belesme had told him. "If I were your son as you say, you'd not have burned Rivaux!''

" 'Twas not yours when I burned it—Henry held it. I did but take revenge for you, Guy."

"I'd defeat you. I have but to go to Henry and tell him of this, my lord. I'd tell him I do not want Nantes.''

"Nay, but you are not the fool your mother was—you'd know the cost. Henry hates me as much as I hate him. Think you he would let you live when he vows to rid all Normandy and England of the family of Belesme? And what of your wife's family? Think you that they would welcome my son as they have Guy of Rivaux? Or Catherine? Would she want my bastard for husband?'' He leaned so close that Guy could feel his breath. "Nay, you'll hold your peace and know what you do for me.''

"I know you are mad.''

"Madness is in our blood, Guy.''

"I'd not have this blood! Nay, I have it not! 'Tis lies, lies—all of it! You seek to destroy de Brione through me—and I'll not do it!'' Guy's voice rose in horror as he stared at Robert of Belesme.

"Lies? Look at me,'' Robert commanded harshly. "We are of a height not common to most men, are we not? And your hair is as black as mine, your face much as mine once was before this.'' His fingers touched his caved-in cheek. "Aye, and even your eyes betray what I have given you."

"You are the only one to see it," Guy spat out, and then he stopped, arrested by the memory of how Eleanor of Nantes had looked at him.

"Men have short memories, Guy. Too often they see what is now rather than what once was. But Mabille noted the resemblance as soon as she saw you." He stepped back and his eyes raked Guy from head to foot. "And I would not have you think I take no pride in you, for you have gained lands as I have lost them, you have the battle skills I once had, and you have Eleanor's daughter to wive. Aye, look at yourself with that black hawk of Rivaux blazoned there—'tis as much vanity as ever I had. There is that of me in you. And look at me . . ." He gestured to his own faded, spotted green tunic. "As you rise, I fall to this. Aye, my day is nearly done, and yours has just begun. You will carry the blood of Belesme to sons who will rule vast lands, and as you know it, I will know it also."

"May God in his mercy give me no sons, then."

"My family always has sons." Abruptly Belesme turned and strode to the window. "When the rain ceases, we will leave. I take but provisions for my men from you. I have no gold to pay for the food, but I leave your people as I have found them. I did but come to tell you what you do for me."

"I will hunt you down if you raid again in Normandy."

"Nay, the monks had you too long. I saw that when we were together at Curthose's court." Belesme shook his head, his face still toward the open shutter as he braced himself against the sill. "To kill your father is forbidden you."

❧ 32 ❧

Gilbert scanned the horizon anxiously, his eyes darting along the lines of trees that dotted it, fearing to find some sign of Robert of Belesme. Ever since they'd reached Belvois and been told that Belesme had withdrawn, he'd wanted to return to Nantes, but Catherine would not hear of it. They would go to Rivaux first, she told him. And the more he tried to delay the sharper her tongue got, until he wondered how he could have ever thought her sweeter-tempered than her mother.

But just when his sense of ill-usage threatened to explode into anger, he'd look over at her and see how sick she was. He'd tried to leave her at Nantes—had done so, in fact—but she'd followed them, and he'd let her come finally, thinking she would slow him down and lessen his chances of meeting Belesme. But she had not—she'd lost her breakfast and her supper almost every day and still managed to sit her horse and keep the pace. As much as he hated to admit it, he felt a grudging sense of pride in her. Aye, she'd bear a strong son for Nantes. With her spirit and Rivaux's strength, that son would hold Nantes against all enemies.

"What say you to a rest, Catherine?" he asked, noting the now familiar ashen color of her face. "Art overtired, child."

" 'Tis not much further."

Ahead of them, Gilbert's outriders reined in and signaled a halt. One of them wheeled and rode back to warn his lord, "There are riders crossing into the forest beyond the river. Eustace cannot be sure from here, but he believes 'tis Belesme from their green shirts."

"Belesme?" Cat's eyes widened in dismay. "Where?"

" 'Twould appear they come from Rivaux."

She reeled from the news as though from impact, and Gilbert hastily leaned to hold her in her saddle. "Nay, it cannot be," he soothed. "There is no smoke."

"I'd have you pursue them," she managed as she clutched at her pommel for strength. "I'd not have them escape again." Her stomach weighed like a rock within her at the thought of what Belesme would have done to Guy. "Sweet Mary, but I'd not have him go unpunished if he has harmed my husband."

"You look like death itself," Gilbert muttered, his arm still bracing her. "Nay, but we stop here."

"My husband is at Rivaux! Guy is at Rivaux! Nay!" She broke away from him and dug her spurs into her horse's flanks. The animal, unused to such treatment, leapt forward and ran straight toward the river.

"By the Blessed Virgin, you've got to stop her!" Gilbert called out to the outriders. "Catch her ere she harms herself! Or the babe!" Alarmed by her sudden action, he spurred after her. "Catherine! Catherine! There's naught you can do! Oh, Holy Mary, stop her ere Belesme sees her," he prayed aloud as he rode.

Gilbert's men, unused to seeing him ride toward trouble rather than away from it, rallied and followed with their weapons drawn. To a man, there was not one of them who did not feel for Catherine and who did not want revenge. If Belesme indeed came from Rivaux, there'd be little chance her husband survived.

" 'Tis Belesme, you fools!" Gilbert shouted as

some of them passed him to pursue the green-shirted men. "Catherine! Catherine! Hold up, I say!"

But she cleared the hill ahead of him and headed into the river. Her horse floundered a moment, giving Gilbert the fright of his life, and then found its footing. The thought that Roger de Brione would have his head if anything happened to her made him brave enough to follow her. But she'd chosen a deeper place to cross and he dared not chance it in full mail. Still shouting at her to stop, he rode down the bank to the shallows and splashed across. By the time he reached the opposite bank, she'd turned toward Rivaux.

"Nay! Catherine, you cannot! 'Twill mark your babe! God's teeth! Are you deaf and daft, girl?"

Ahead lay the timbered wall with its partial stone surround. Despite her fears, she looked to the gate, fearing to see Guy's head there, bearing that gaping grimace of death so common to those who died under torture. But the pikes above the gate were empty and the bridge was drawn. Above her, she heard someone shout, " 'Tis the Lady Catherine!" and almost immediately the iron-and-timber draw began its creaking descent.

Behind her, her grandsire still pursued, splashing out of the water and yelling for her to halt. Afraid that he would stop her, she kicked her horse again and made for the lowering bridge, jumping the small gap even before it clanged into place against the iron moorings, and crossing into Rivaux itself.

"Lady Catherine! What the . . . ?"

"William, where's Guy—where is he?" she shouted hysterically. "I saw Belesme and . . ." She choked, unable to go on, as the old man reached for her. Weak from illness and emotionally exhausted from her fears, she clutched at his shoulders and buried her head in his woolen overtunic as he set her down. "Eh now, lady, there is no—"

"Cat! Sweet Jesu! How came you here?" Guy had been on the stockade wall on the other side when he'd heard them lower his bridge, and he'd come running across the courtyard and bailey. She stared blankly at him for a moment, and then, disentangling herself from William de Comminges' clumsy embrace, she threw herself into his arms, babbling that she'd never thought to see him again. He closed his arms around her and clung to her as much as she clung to him, rubbing his cheek against the top of her head and murmuring, " 'Tis all right, Cat . . . 'tis all right, love," over and over while she cried.

"Lord Guy!" Gilbert reined in at the sight of him and stared, feeling very much the fool. Nonplussed, he looked around him at the men who'd stopped working to watch the strange sight of their lord and lady embracing in broad daylight. His gaze lit on William and he demanded testily, "You—fellow! I'd have the tale from someone—what in God's name goes here?"

William looked over at Cat and Guy before turning his attention to Gilbert. "Naught's amiss—not now."

Guy stepped back shakily for a closer look at Catherine, unable to believe he held her in the flesh. "God's bones, Cat, but I thought to never see you again. Let me look on you." Then, seeing her pallor and perceiving that she was thinner than when she'd left Rivaux, his face creased in concern. "You have been unwell."

" 'Tis nothing."

"Nothing!" Gilbert exploded behind her. "Nothing, you say! God's blood, my lord, but do not listen to her! For two weeks and more, she's not been able to keep food in her stomach, but she would not rest until I rode to Belvois—and when I left her at Nantes, she came after like a damned wolfhound tracking its prey!" he told Guy with feeling. "And then we saw Belesme, and she thought the worst. 'Twas Christ's own miracle that she did not die crossing the river, I tell you! Look at her—she is more than half-drowned! Aye, if the babe is unmarked after this, 'tis but that he bears the blood of Rivaux!"

Guy's hands tightened on Cat's elbows, and for a moment she could not tell whether he supported her or she him. But when she looked up, she thought it was pain rather than joy she saw. Looking away quickly, she managed to murmur, "Aye, I'd thought to tell you when we were alone."

Not to be put off, Gilbert of Nantes dismounted and pushed his way to Guy. " 'Twas thought we saw Belesme, my lord."

"Aye."

Seeing no signs of a siege and no burning buildings, Gilbert was confused, but with his usual inborn resiliency once danger passed, he reached the conclusion he liked best. Beaming at his granddaughter's husband, he nodded. "Then 'tis well she insisted we come, my lord, for he dared not tarry when he saw the men of Nantes. Aye, he's on his way back to the safety of France, I'll warrant."

"With more food and mail than we could spare," William snorted, "but, aye, he is gone at least."

"And you are unharmed?" Cat asked Guy anxiously, almost unable to believe it could be so.

"He had not the time to spare roasting us—he thought he was pursued," William lied hastily.

"And he was. Had I not had Catherine in my care, I'd have tried to take him," Gilbert boasted, not realizing that every man in Rivaux knew him for the coward he was. Looking up at Guy, he gestured to Cat. "She's been sicker than her granddam ever was, my lord—I pray it passes soon—but I'll admit right now that there's not many, man or woman, who'd make the ride she just made when she thought you dead." Laying a hand on her shoulder, he leaned closer. "Aye, she ought to have been a son herself."

"You are so weak you tremble, Cat," Guy murmured as he braced her with his arm. "You belong in bed." Without waiting for her protest, he lifted her and headed for the main portal of his hall. "Get the door," he called out, and a dozen men vied to do his bidding. Over his shoulder, he told William, "See Gilbert and his men fed and his horses tended."

"Aye, my lord." William eyed the Count of Nantes with a hint of humor and nodded. "Aye, you come tell me how 'twas that you routed Belesme."

Despite the steepness of the stairs, Catherine was light in Guy's arms, worrying him, for he'd never seen her ill or helpless before. At the top of the steps he leaned to wrench open the door, kicking it wide with the toe of his boot. "Your gown is soaked," he muttered as he set her down beside the bed.

" 'Twas the river."

"Aye, you risked too much to come here, Catherine." He bent her forward over his arm and pulled at the lacings under her arms clumsily. "God's bones, but I am a poor tiring woman after Hawise."

"I can undress myself."

"Nay. Look at you—you are sick unto death and chilled to the marrow of your bones. Here . . ." Lifting the back of her overgown, he pulled it up over her head and tossed it in a heap at her feet. He could hear her teeth chatter as he worked almost feverishly to undress her. Discarding her damp chainse, he thrust her between the covers of the bed and looked about for the means to warm her quickly. The brazier hearth was cold and the logs still damp from when they'd been brought in earlier. He sat on the bench beside the bed to remove his boots and then eased his body in next to hers, rolling to the center of the feather mattress and enveloping her naked body in his clothed one. "Got to warm you ere your lungs congest," he murmured, settling against her.

He was big, he was warm, he was safe. She shivered and burrowed beneath him to draw strength and heat from him. Too exhausted and weak to think even, she closed her eyes and clung to him until she went to sleep.

Guy lay quietly, his wild, tumbling thoughts in contrast to the stillness of his body, until he felt her relax and heard her breathing even out. For a day and a night he'd tried to tell himself that Belesme had lied to him, but in his heart he knew differently. And then he'd tried to tell himself that it made no difference what blood he carried, and again he knew it was not so—the name of Belesme was hated and feared throughout Normandy and England, and the blood was tainted with madness. The blood he would pass on to the babe Catherine carried within her—the blood of Belesme. A sense of aching loneliness washed over him, a loneliness he'd never thought to have again since he'd known for certain that Catherine of the Condes loved him, a loneliness made more terrible by the knowledge that he dared not tell her the terrible legacy he'd give their child. And there was fear also, fear that there was within him that which could somehow make him like Belesme—fear that Catherine's love would turn to hate if she found him out. Aye, 'twas a bitter, dangerous secret he bore, one that would cost him his wife, his lands, and his life even. And he could not ease the guilt he felt, for there was none to tell of it, none who would not turn away from him in horror. 'Twas little wonder that he'd been so unsuited to monastic life—he was Satan's spawn.

Catherine moved trustingly against him, nestling in the hollow he'd made of his chest and belly and thighs. The arm he'd wrapped around her was beginning to tingle from its cramped position, so he eased it from beneath her and brushed over her hips and legs. In other times, touching her would have brought forth such desire in him that he would have been consumed by it, but now he felt that to touch her like that would be to defile her. Her skin was warmer beneath his hands now. Denying his own loneliness, he rolled away and rose from the bed.

Padding to a large chest, he drew out his warm fur-lined cloak and carried it back to spread over her. In a little while he'd have one of the kitchen boys bring up coals and start a fire in the brazier, but not just yet.

Voices from the common room below floated up as Gilbert of Nantes expounded on how Belesme had seen him and run. Unwilling to face the fool, Guy gathered up another cloak, wrapped himself in it, and sat on a bench against the wall, leaning back to indulge in yet another bout of self-loathing.

❧ 33 ❧

At first, Catherine thought she but imagined the change in him. There was so much to do ere winter set in: the continuing work on the outer wall, the restocking of Rivaux's depleted larders, the counting of crops and men on all of Guy's lands for Henry's taxes—the list was overwhelming. But as she began to adjust to the babe within her womb and to take over again the running of the household, she began to worry over her husband.

He made too many excuses to be gone to Belvois and his other castles when she thought William could have acted in his name. And while he was always kind, courteous, and gentle with her, it seemed he used the babe as an excuse not to bed her, telling her she was not well enough. His temper was uneven to his men and to his servants, so much so that many preferred to go through her to him, and yet when she taxed him with it, his temper got worse rather than better. Even Brian, whose stay provided them with needed men, was not proof against Guy's ill humor.

She sat on a cushion beneath the window, plying her still-indifferent needle and pondering her unhappiness, unaware that he stood just within the door. From time to time she looked out to the trees behind the walls and saw the few bright-colored leaves that now clung to otherwise empty, barren limbs, and tried to tell herself that it was but that she did not like winter, or that it was some malaise brought on by the changes in her body.

He watched hungrily as the graying light illuminated her dark braids and profiled her lovely face. She was becoming an obsession with him, an obsession in which his waking hours were spent torn between fear and desire and his dreams were haunted by her and Belesme. At night he lay beside her and struggled with a body that ached for her until he could not bear it. But it frightened him to get too close to her. Ever since Belesme had left Rivaux, Guy had thought of little other than how she would feel if she ever discovered the truth, and every time she looked at him now, he feared she would see something in his face or his eyes and know.

Finally, when he could stand watching her no longer, he jammed on his helmet and crossed into the room itself. Startled, she looked up, and the smile on her face froze at the sight of his mail.

"I am come to bid you Godspeed, Catherine."

"Again?" Her voice betrayed her dismay. "But you have but been here less than a week, my lord."

"Aye, but I go to Vientot—there is grumbling there over the taxes I levy for Henry."

"Cannot William go?"

"Nay, he is needed here."

She wanted to cry out, to scream at him that he was needed at Rivaux even more than William de Comminges, that *she* needed him. She bit her lower lip to still the trembling, and nodded, afraid to speak for fear of releasing a flood of tears. Vientot was the furthest of his possessions—it would be weeks before she saw him again.

"William will see to your needs, Catherine." He stared helplessly, knowing he disappointed her. Finally he turned away. "God keep you safe while I am gone."

"Wait!" The word escaped her involuntarily, but it

turned him around. "Can you not . . . would you not come closer that I may kiss you farewell, my lord?"

"Aye." He tried to keep his voice light, but he could not still the almost painful thudding of his heart. He moved closer to stand over her.

He was magnificent and forbidding in full mail save for his gloves, which were probably fastened to his saddle, since he did not like the feel of them in general. His new surcoat, the one Hawise had worked for him at Nantes, was even more impressive than the one he'd worn to court, for jewels winked from both the hawk's eyes and its talons. But even shadowed by his helmet, his eyes betrayed a sunken, haunted look—another sign of what she already knew. He'd scarce slept since she'd returned to Rivaux.

"I'd see your face," she managed as she rose.

"Oh . . . aye." He dislodged the helmet and lifted it off his head to tuck it under one arm.

Before he had a chance to guard himself, she stood on tiptoe and circled his neck with her arms, pressing her body against his, and moving parted lips over his in invitation, kindling desire between them. His free arm caught her to him, molding her breasts and hips against the hardness of the cold steel mesh as their lips met and his tongue took possession of her mouth. To her, it was proof that at least she still had the power to move him.

"Sweet Jesu!" he muttered, thrusting her from him suddenly. "I'd not meant to do that." Conscious of the need to escape or be lost, he stepped backward quickly and jammed his helmet on his head, twisted the nasal over his nose, and started for the doorway, leaving her feeling spurned.

" 'Tis the babe, isn't it?" she blurted out through tears. "You do not want the babe!"

He stopped, not daring to turn back. "What makes you say such a thing?" he asked finally.

"Because everything is different between us! And naught's changed with me but the babe, Guy," she choked, trying to stop crying. "And you have no right to treat me thus, for 'tis you who gave it to me—'tis your son I bear!"

"Naught's different, Cat." He closed his eyes for a moment to gain control of himself. " 'Tis but that you are overset because of the babe, and your mind tricks you. All is well between us."

"Nay, you'll not blame me, Guy of Rivaux—not when you *have* changed! I . . . I . . ." She burst into tears, unable to continue.

"Aye, then 'tis me, and I am sorry for it," he sighed. "But my men wait, and we will have to speak of it later. Godspeed, Cat."

"You cannot keep leaving me! You have to tell me what is wrong!"

He had nearly reached the safety of the doorway.

"You love me no longer! You have another woman!" she flung at him.

He turned around slowly and shook his head. "Nay, 'tis not so, Cat. If anything, 'tis that I love you too well." He faced her across the wide expanse of the room. "But I must go to Vientot. You will be all right—I leave Brian and William with you."

Cat's eyes were still red when she emerged from her solar several hours later. She crossed the courtyard purposefully and walked the length of the new wall until she found Brian FitzHenry in an argument with one of the men from Belvois about the depth of an arrow slit.

"You have not the room for a crossbowman to kneel," he told the fellow. "Nay, you misread the plans."

"Brian."

"Jesu, what ails you Cat? You should not be out here without a cloak—you'll harm your babe."

"You and my grandsire are the only ones who seem to care about it anyway," she told him bitterly. "For all Guy thinks of it or me, I should have drowned in the river.''

"Make it a foot deeper," he told the workman before turning back to her. "Now, Cat, what nonsense is this? Never say you have quarreled with Rivaux again?''

"Aye." She met his eyes and nodded. Sighing heavily, she announced tonelessly, "I'd go home, Brian—I'd have you take me home to the Condes.''

"What?"

"Do not screech at me, Brian, please. I cannot bear it.''

"Have you taken leave of your senses, Cat?" he demanded. Then, lowering his voice, he took her by the arm and propelled her away from the workmen to tell her, "Nay, but I could not—'tis against the laws of God and man to interfere with what is between a man and his wife.''

"Those are strange words from you—how many husbands have you cuckolded?''

" 'Tis different, and well you know it. I am not fool enough to cuckold Guy of Rivaux, if that is what you are offering.''

"I am not—I'd not be so base. What I ask of you is that you take me home.''

"To the Condes? God's blood, but 'tis too far.''

"To the Condes . . . to Nantes . . . to Harlowe. I'd not stay here.''

"Ask de Comminges, then, Cat. I dare not attempt it.''

"I'd expected more of you, Brian, for you are like a brother to me," she reminded him. "To ask William is like asking Guy if I may leave him.''

"Your husband would kill me, Cat. And if he did not, your father would.'' His brown eyes considered her soberly. "What has happened to overset you so?''

"My husband loves me not.''

"Jesu," he sighed in disgust. "It is not true, but even if it were, 'tis no reason to leave his house. He makes you a countess, you are chatelaine here, he does not beat you even as you deserve—nay, but you know not when to count your blessings and thank God for what you have been given.''

"I thought you of all people would understand.''

"I understand too well—you would leave your lord over a quarrel with him and bring his wrath down on me. Nay, he mistrusts me enough already.''

"Then why do you stay here? Why did you ask your father for leave to defend Rivaux's walls with his men? If you fear him, why stay?''

"Because 'tis close to Mayenne.''

She sucked in her breath and stared, her own misery forgotten for a moment. "Sweet Mary,'' she breathed in shock.

"Aye, 'tis strange, is it not?'' He nodded. "All those years I thought I loved you, but 'twas not so. So I wait here for Geoffrey of Mayenne to die, that I may take her home ere the old man makes her his prisoner for her dowry.''

"Does she know?''

"About Count Hugh's plans?''

"About you.''

"Nay.''

"I'd not thought you knew she lived, Brian—never once in all those years do I remember a word of love between you.''

"There were none, but I think I was blinded by you, Cat. You are the one every man looks on and admires, whilst Linn is but Linn. Away from you, there are many who would think her a beauty, but in your presence, she fades. I did not note how truly beautiful she was until she kicked me awake and told me to leave you be and make my own way.''

"She must have kicked your head,'' Catherine muttered dryly, "for I have never heard such a thing. You and Linn? She'd never allow your whores, Brian.''

"I can accept that. Have you heard of my lying with any of the women here?''

"You are serious, aren't you?"

"Never more serious or sober in my life, Cat. If Aislinn of the Condes chooses me freely, I'd not ask God for more."

"And if she does not?"

"Then I will go to Wales and fight for my mother's husband, I suppose." He turned to stare unseeing at the workmen on the wall. " 'Tis no easy thing to wait for a man to die, Cat."

"We could bring her here. Aye, 'tis not far, and mayhap Count Hugh would let her visit me."

Perplexed by the sudden change in her, he looked back. "I thought you wanted to leave Rivaux."

"Aye, I did, but mayhap with Linn here I'd not miss Guy so. I'd go with you to get her, and Count Hugh would never suspect your interest." Her troubled eyes met his again. "In truth, Brian, I know not what I wish to do, but I'd not live like this. I need Linn or Maman."

"Linn is with child also—I doubt Mayenne will let her come."

"Geoffrey yet lives, and she is his wife rather than Count Hugh's. Nay, the choice is Geoffrey's whether she stays or goes. I'd ask him, Brian."

"You will have to tell de Comminges of it."

Hawise put her hands on her hips and drew her mouth into a thin line of disapproval. Despite her status as tiring woman to Catherine, she spoke with the audacity of one long in service. " 'Tis folly, Cat, and well you know it. Nay, but your lord would be displeased to even think you rode that far with his babe in your belly."

" 'Tis your place to pack rather than censure," Cat retorted.

Unabashed, the plump woman shook her head. "I've known you since you were birthed, and I can tell you that your mother and your father would tell you not to go—not without your lord's permission."

"My lord is not here to ask, and I've not seen my sister since I left the Condes, Hawise. Besides, 'tis not that far. I'd take my purple gown, and the red one also, and the golden net for my hair, I think. Aye, and I give you leave to pack another gown also. We will not be staying overlong, as 'tis my intent to ask that Linn come here."

"And leave a sick husband?"

"Aye, else she will be at Count Hugh's mercy when Geoffrey dies."

"That is between Earl Roger and the count," Hawise reminded her. "You'd embroil your lord in a quarrel not of his making, and him with an unfinished wall."

" 'Tis not your place to scold me, I said. Leave me be and pack my things—Brian says I cannot take above three boxes."

"And that is another matter, Cat. 'Tis not likely your husband will welcome the news that you've ridden out of Rivaux with Brian FitzHenry, no matter where you go."

"He will not," Cat conceded, "but 'tis none of your concern. If you cannot keep your tongue civil, I'll have Beda in your stead."

"Mayhap he will beat you."

"Nay, he'd have to come home first."

34

He saw the pack animals in the outer bailey and the mounted escort waiting in the courtyard when he rode in. And then he saw her, dressed and ready to ride, crossing the open yard ahead of him as he came over the lowered bridge. In that moment he knew a fear greater than that which had been plaguing him: Cat thought to leave him.

The escort scattered before him as he rode into its midst, and she turned to gape, speechless, as he tossed his helmet to a startled ostler and dismounted. A host of emotions paraded across her face as she backed away from his determined advance—shock, hope, dismay, were mirrored in turn in dark eyes made enormous by his wrathful gaze. William took a step forward to stay him and then dropped his hand, while Brian sat uneasily in his saddle above them. The clatter and bustle of preparation froze into silence as all watched their lord face his lady.

But when he spoke, it was with a calm that belied his anger and his fear. "I'd speak with you alone, Catherine," was all he said to her, disappointing those who thought to watch.

The gold flecks in his eyes receded, chilled by the green. For a moment her chin came up in defiance, and then she exhaled sharply and nodded, looking away. "Aye."

355

She turned back toward the tower to hide the sudden fear she felt, but his hand caught her wrist painfully as he leaned over her to mutter for her ears alone, "You can walk or be carried, but afore God, I'd not stand here and quarrel in front of mine own men." Without waiting for a decision, he pulled her none too gently toward the doors.

"God's blood, but I think he means to beat her," Alan breathed to break the silence.

"He'd best not." Brian spoke grimly, dismounting.

"You'd not dare to interfere."

"Of a surety I would."

Guy pushed Catherine up the narrow stairs and through the solar door before turning to kick it shut with his heavy boot. Releasing her wrist suddenly, he unbuckled his sword belt and stood Doomslayer in the corner by the door. His hands worked the fastenings of his mail coif at his neck while he walked to face her.

"Tell me how it is that you thought to leave me."

"I was not leaving you! As I recall the matter, 'twas you who left me," she added defensively.

The thin white scar on his cheek tightened as he tried to control his conflicting emotions. "Then where did you think to go?"

" 'Twas Mayenne, Guy."

"Mayenne?" He stared blankly at her for a moment. *"Why?"*

"I'd see how Linn fares. I am told her lot is even unhappier than mine own." Her heart beating heavily in her breast, she raised her eyes to his. "And now that I have answered you, will you tell me how it is that you are come back but one day since you left?"

"I could not leave the quarrel between us," he admitted simply. " 'Tis wrong of me to punish you for mine own dark moods."

"Then . . . then you are not angry with me?" she asked.

"Only when I saw you ready to leave with the

FitzHenry. My first thought then was that I'd kill him and beat you.''

"You have naught to fear of Brian. He did not truly wish to take me without your permission.''

"I feared to lose you.''

He towered over her, seeming bigger than ever in his mail, and his face still bore the imprint where his nasal had lain against his cheek, but his rumpled black hair and those flecked eyes of his were the most endearing of any she'd ever seen. He opened his arms to her and folded her against him as she leaned her head into his shoulder.

"Sweet Mary, but I feared to lose you, Cat.''

Fierce pride in this big man who loved her flooded over her. She clasped him tightly, rubbing her cheek against the roughness of the mail beneath his surcoat. "Nay, you fear nothing—art as fearless as Belesme, Guy.''

The muscles in the arms that held her tensed and his body went rigid for an instant, and then he mastered himself. "As long as I have you, Catherine of the Condes, I fear nothing,'' he said.

"What do you mean to do about Vientot?'' she asked suddenly, remembering why it was that he'd left her.

"Send William to collect the rents and taxes for me. I'd spend my winter here with you.''

"Guy . . .'' Her hands released his waist and came up between them to press his chest as she leaned back. "I . . . that is . . . well, the babe sickens me no longer, and . . .'' She reddened at the amused gleam in his eyes. "Well . . . I would!''

"Would what?'' he asked, grinning. "Come, there's naught you cannot say to me.''

"I . . . I'd lie with you again, Guy.''

The gold flecks became more prominent, warming his eyes. "Whenever you wish it—I am prepared to do my duty by you whenever, wherever, and however you

want, Cat.'' His grin softened to a crooked smile.
"But I'd as lief get out of my mail first.''

A sobering thought occurred to her. "But I will become big-bellied and you will think me too ugly.''

"Nay, I will not. I promise we will find a way.''

"Cat! Cat! Are you all right?''

Catherine turned in Guy's arms at the sound of
Brian's voice on the stairs. "Aye,'' she called back.
"All is well, but would you ask Hawise to see to the
ordering of a bath for my lord?''

There was a pause before he answered. "Aye, but
since we are already saddled and ready to ride, I mean
to go on to Mayenne.''

Her passion spent, Catherine lay with her head cradled against his shoulder. It had been as good between
them as it had ever been, and now he was silent as he
caught his breath. Her fingers crept to play with the
dark, curling hairs on his chest as she mused aloud,
"What think you we should name the babe? If 'tis a
daughter, I would call her Aislinn or Eleanor, unless
you would name her for your mother. What was your
mother's name?''

After a brief hesitation he answered simply, "Alys.''

" 'Tis a pretty name. Would you wish to name her
that—or we could save the name for a later daughter—
what say you?''

"I'd not name any of them Alys. Eleanor or Aislinn
is fine.''

"If 'tis a son, I'd expect you to name him,'' she
continued in the same vein. "What was your father's
name?''

This time, there was a sharp intake of breath beneath her head. "Eudo—there have been four counts
of Rivaux so named.''

"Eudo?'' She wrinkled her nose in distaste and
sighed. "Well, he could have more than one given
name, I suppose.''

"You needn't worry—I'd name no son of mine

Eudo. For one reason, I hate the name, and for the other, I hated the last to bear it.''

Her fingers ceased playing on his chest and she rolled to prop herself up on an elbow to look at him. ''Then what would you name him?''

''I had not thought of it.''

''We could name him Roger for my father,'' she ventured.

''Nay, there is but one Roger de Brione. A Roger of Rivaux would be unable to equal him.''

''What about Guy?''

''And be like the Alans of Brittany? Once 'twas impossible to remember whether 'twas Alan I or Alan II when people talked, and now 'tis Alan III and Alan IV. Nay, I never favored the name Guy, anyway, and I'd not give Rivaux a Guy II.'' The image of Robert of Belesme went through his mind, sobering him. ''Truth to tell, I think I would rather have a daughter.''

''And I would rather have a son like his father.''

He was unprepared for the chill that such innocent words gave him. He'd thought that in those hours on the road to Vientot he'd come to an understanding with himself—that he'd come back to Catherine and hide the terrible guilt, the terrible secret he bore from her— that he loved her so desperately that she could save him from himself. But he feared what she would do if she ever knew that the babe within her carried the blood of Belesme.

''Guy, are you all right?'' she asked suddenly.

''Oh . . . aye.'' He rolled on his side to face her and reached to stroke the smoothness of her hip. ''I was but gaining strength.''

''Strength?''

Easing closer, he bent his head to tease the nipple of her already swollen breast with his tongue, and was rewarded with a moan that ignited again the fire between them. ''Aye, I'd taste of you again,'' he whispered as her hands twined in his hair and her body responded to his words.

* * *

"We cannot stay abed through supper," she decided. "But I'd not go down and face the men when I'll warrant every one of them knows what we have done."

"What difference does it make? We are wed."

"Aye, but to spend half a day and more like this . . ." She colored and rose hastily from the bed. "Well, 'tis sinful . . . and . . ."

His eyes traveled over her still-naked body, taking in every curve of her with pride. "If this be sin, I'd go to hell gladly, Cat."

"I would you be serious. I cannot face them tonight—I'd have you tell them that I am ill."

"And let them think I have come up here and beat you until you had to seek your bed? What a reputation you would give me, wife."

"Still, I'd not go down this night."

"We can say you bathed me—everyone will know that for the truth."

"For hours and hours?"

"Well, maybe you deloused me also—it can take hours to pick the nits, I am told."

"Ugh!"

"But as I have not been seen suitably scratching, we might have difficulty with that story," he told her, grinning.

"Stop it! Being a man, I suppose you would not understand, because I am told that men take pride in such things, but I'd not have it thought that I have spent my day behaving like the castle whore."

"Jesu, but you mean it, do you not?" Rising from the bed, he came up behind her and clasped her to him, nuzzling her bare shoulder. "I know not what castle whores you have met, Cat, but I can tell you with authority in the matter that they do not linger at the task." Releasing her, he padded barefoot to one of the chests to draw out his clothes. "But since it troubles you, I'll sup tonight without you and send Hawise up with food."

"I'd not face her either—not tonight."

"You have to eat, Cat," he told her reasonably. "All right, I will bring you food myself, but I take leave to warn you that I am a poor tiring maid." He eyed her tangled hair and shook his head. "You'll get naught but one clumsy braid from me."

"What are you going to tell them?"

"Nothing. They can guess, for all I care about it. I'll warrant there will be those who think we have comported ourselves with wanton abandon this day, and then there will be those who think I've beaten you until you cannot stand. Let them think what they will."

"I'd rather you said I was sick with the babe again."

"I try not to tell falsehoods."

After tying his chausses, he pulled on a plain linen shirt that hung to his knees. Straightening, he came to face her, and his eyes searched her face. "Are you ashamed of loving me, Cat?"

Taken aback, she blinked and stared. "Ashamed? How could I be ashamed of loving Guy of Rivaux? Art good, kind, handsome, and a warrior in the bargain, Guy—nay, I am proud to call you husband." Impulsively she threw her arms around his neck and tiptoed to hug him. "Aside from your temper, there's naught I'd change about you."

His arms returned her embrace, but looking over her head, his face was bleak.

With a worried eye, William watched Guy drink more than was his custom, and he was more than half-certain that he knew what ailed his master. More than twenty-four years had passed since Guy's birth, and William had begun to relax his vigilance, thinking there was none left alive to know the tale, none but Belesme and himself. And now he believed Guy knew it also. But it went against William's nature to think on it, much less speak of it, unless he knew for sure.

He leaned back on his narrow bench and braced his back against the wall, openly watching the man he'd reared from a small boy. Aye, Guy knew, he decided finally, for there was naught else to account for the change in him since Belesme had come to Rivaux.

Guy reached to pour himself another cup of the rich red wine, but William leaned forward suddenly to stay his arm. "Nay, but I would speak with you whilst you can still stand, my lord. And the Lady Catherine would not like it were I to help a drunken fellow into her bed."

" 'Tis not your place . . ." Guy retorted, and then thought better of it. "Aye, you are right—I drink too much," he sighed. "And I am overtired."

William glanced around them, noting the thinness of the company since Brian FitzHenry and his escort had left, and leaned closer, lowering his voice. "I have been with you since Lady Alys bade me keep you safe, my lord. If there's aught you would know of it, we can walk the walls alone and speak. Or if not, I'd hold my tongue."

Guy looked up and his divided eyebrow lifted in surprise. In all the years William had served him, Guy had never been able to glean more than the barest of facts about the Lady Alys or Count Eudo, and now he offered what Guy had once thought he wanted to know. Hope that Belesme had lied flared briefly, and he nodded. "Aye, I'd walk the wall."

The night air was cold enough that Guy could see his breath in the moonlight as he climbed a deserted portion of his new stone wall and stood to look out over the huddled huts below. This was his land, his patrimony—this was Rivaux. His heart swelled with pride in what he'd built—his wall, the foundation for a new church, new huts for his people—aye, he was lord of everything as far as he could see. He breathed deeply to clear his head as William came up behind him.

"There was a time I never thought to see it again,"

Guy murmured. "Between Curthose's beggaring me and Henry's sending me into exile, I thought I dared not think of having it again. I thought I'd lost everything at Tinchebrai."

"I knew Henry would call you back, my lord. You were destined for greatness from your birth."

"My birth," Guy snorted bitterly, "Aye, and how long do you think I would have this if my birth were known?" He swung around to face William in the pale moonlight. "You knew," he accused. "You knew, and you told me not."

"I knew—aye."

"Would you ever have told me?"

"Nay. 'Twould have served no purpose save to harm you."

"I have heard Count Robert tell the tale, William, and I'd hear my mother's side of it now."

"All of it? I'd not know where to begin, Guy."

"Did my mother lie with Robert of Belesme?" he demanded.

"Aye."

"Then I'd hear all of it. If I am truly his son, there's naught to spare me now."

William pulled the wide sleeves of his overtunic over his hands and then folded them together for warmth in the chill breeze. "Your mother was the Lady Alys, daughter to the Vicomte of Varanville, wed to Count Eudo at thirteen." William cleared his throat and prepared to go on. His eyes took on that faraway look of one seeing the past relived. "Count Eudo was more than fifty—I know not how old for certain—and he'd buried two wives before he took Alys. Three living sons he'd had of them, Roland, Ralph, and Walter by name, and there was a daughter, Mathilda—full half of the girls in Normandy were Mathilda in honor of the Conqueror's duchess then. Anyway, all of his issue were older than Alys when she came to Rivaux."

"What did she look like?"

William appeared to consider, and sighed. "She was

a little like your own lady, but she had not the spirit. She had dark hair and brown eyes so light that sometimes 'twas said they were pure gold, and she was slender—more so than Catherine, I think—and she had a laugh that was most pleasant before she came to Rivaux. I came with her as master of her household on her marriage, so I remember her best for what she was at Varanville.''

"Go on."

"Count Eudo was too old for a young wife, Guy. It was whispered in the stables that he could not so much as lay the serving wenches anymore, but Alys had a dowry that he coveted—she brought him Belvois on her marriage. There was no blood in her marriage bed, but none blamed her for that.''

"Did he love her?''

"Eudo?'' William's voice raised incredulously at the thought. "Nay—he thought of her not at all, save to tell her to be modest and mind her prayers.''

Guy could almost be sorry for the young girl sent to an indifferent and self-centered old lord. "Go on,'' he prompted again.

"When the fall came, the Old Conqueror passed through on his way to Mantes, bringing his court with him. Among them was a man he'd once fostered himself, Robert of Belesme. Even then, 'twas difficult to find any to like Belesme, for neither his arrogance nor his cruelty knew any bounds. Old William—the Conqueror—did not like him overmuch, either, but he said that on the battlefield there was none to compare with Robert of Belesme even then. They quarreled—Belesme and the Conqueror—over some blood sport where Robert had dragged a peasant from his cottage at Domfort and had killed him slowly with his knife, castrating him in front of his wife and daughters for some insult the fellow was said to have offered him. The castellan of the keep appealed to William as overlord for justice, but when William would have heard the case, no witness could be found. Anyway, William did not take Belesme with him to Mantes.''

''And Belesme met my mother.''

''Aye. 'Tis difficult to tell it now, but Count Robert was as comely a man as there was to see then, but cold—aye, those green eyes frightened better men than me. But to Alys, a lonely girl shut up here, he was someone to entice. Evil is like a flame, Guy—it draws good people sometimes much as fire draws moths in summer.'' William stopped and spat over the side of the wall. ''But he never seemed to notice any of the women, and as there were two stories credited about him—one that he lay with his mother and no other, and the other that he lay with men—well, there was no reason to think he knew the Lady Alys even lived.''

Guy hugged his clothes tightly to his body and tried to keep warm. ''Belesme said she wanted him to kill my . . .'' He stopped, aware that he still tried to think of Count Eudo as his father. '' . . . to kill her husband,'' he finished lamely.

''I know not why she lay with him, but she did, and I'll not understand it to this day.''

''Belesme told me the rest—there is no need to finish the tale. You do but confirm what he said. If I would know anything more, 'tis why you have cared for me.''

''Lady Alys died in childbed when she was but fourteen, Guy. Had the old man not beaten her daily, I think she might have survived, but by the time she had her lying-in, she was wearied of it. The birth was hard, for you lay wrong and did not turn. When she began to bleed heavily, she asked to see me, and she told me she thought she would die. She would not hear otherwise, and I suspected she knew. She said that if the babe was a son, Eudo would not let him live, and she asked that if you were born alive I would take you to her family.''

''And he let you?''

"Nay. Her women told him it was not over whilst I wrapped you under my shirt and rode for Varanville as though devils were after me. At first, I thought your grandsire there would kill you himself, for you were a reminder of Alys' wantonness, but the old priest would not let him. He finally wrote to Eudo that you lived and promised to rear you to hide his daughter's shame," William remembered.

"We lived in a peasant's hut beneath the castle walls with a kitchen wench to give you suck, until the old vicomte decided it was not meet that I who was son of a knight should live thus. Then he let me bring you to his table, but even though he acknowledged you as his grandson, he treated you worse than the lowest bastard in the keep until he ate spoiled lampreys and thought to die. The old priest said 'twas a sin what he did to you—I think you were mayhap two or three then—and he reminded your grandsire that Holy Church considered you had been born in wedlock despite what Count Eudo said. When he recovered, your grandsire met Eudo on the matter, and 'twas agreed that to keep the world from knowing he had been cuckolded, Eudo would recognize you, as he had other sons to inherit. And so that neither of them had to look on you, you would be sent to be taught by the monks. They took you away from me then."

"Aye, I remember."

"But your brothers died. One by one, they died, Guy—but you have heard of that. And when Robert Curthose would not stand with Count Eudo against de Mortain, the old count never forgot it. Rather than let Rivaux become Curthose's on his death, he recognized you as heir. By then, you were overold to foster, and I was asked to train you, as I knew the whole, and it pleased me to do it. I knew if you were Belesme's son, I could make you mayhap into the finest, fiercest fighter in all of Normandy."

Despite the faint light, Guy could see the sparkle of tears in the old man's eyes and was deeply moved. All

of his life, he'd been able to turn to William de Comminges, and now that he knew why, it humbled
him.

"William—"

But the old man was not quite finished. Nearly
breaking with emotion, William's voice dropped almost to a whisper. "And, afore God and his saints,
Guy of Rivaux, I think I have done it. You've naught
to be ashamed of—art the best knight I know."

" 'Twas you who taught me all I have become,"
Guy responded quietly.

"You are Robert of Belesme's son in nothing but
blood, my lord—there's naught else of him in you."

" 'Tis the blood that haunts me—'tis the blood of
madness—'tis the blood of Satan that flows in Belesme's veins."

"If Belesme is mad, 'tis because of Mabille."

"And who is to blame for her madness, then?"

"Her father."

"And his?"

"Jesu! You will have to put these thoughts from your
mind, Guy, else you will go mad. You are what you
make yourself—not what blood you bear." William
spoke earnestly. "Had I not believed that, I'd have left
you for Count Eudo to kill."

Guy stared silently over the edge of the wall to the
broken rocks far below them. "Think you I do not
argue it with myself? Aye, I have thought of little else
since Belesme spoke to me."

"My lord . . ." William reached to comfort for the
first time since Guy had been a small boy.

"You do not understand—I fear to lose Catherine."
It was as though the words were wrenched from him,
pulled from deep within, as Guy gave voice to his
greatest fear. "And I do not think I could bear it if
she turned away from me."

"Tell her—'twill make no difference."

"Nay. But I live in dread that one day she will see

Robert of Belesme in me and know the child she bears carries Devil's blood.''

Sensing that argument was futile, William shook his head sadly and dropped his hand. '' 'Tis a secret that can give you no peace, my lord.''

❧ 35 ❧

"The FitzHenry returns, my lord, and 'twould appear that there are more riders in pursuit."

"Brian?" Cat turned around from where she had been showing Guy the fabric she'd bargained from the cloth merchant. "Art certain?"

"Who follows him?" Guy demanded tersely.

" 'Tis too far to tell, in truth, but would you have the draw lowered?"

"Aye, and I'd have the bowmen in position should there be trouble. Tell William to secure the inner wall—nay, I will tell him myself," Guy muttered, already halfway to the stairs. "Jesu, but I am not ready for this—he should have tried for Belvois."

"Mayhap he had not the time."

Catherine followed them down to where William already armed the bowmen and gave them their positions. Alerted by the sentries' shouts, peasants from the huts below pressed outside Rivaux's gate, while laborers within brought out pitch vats. Seeing that Guy meant to order his defenses, Cat turned and climbed the back steps of the timber wall to watch.

Aye, it was Brian all right, riding as though hell pursued, splashing across the river, while several of his escort broke away and turned to delay those who followed them. As they drew closer, she could see that Count Hugh himself came after him.

"Aislinn!" she shouted, recognizing the rider beside Brian. Running back down the wooden steps, she nearly collided with her lord. "Guy, he brings Linn! Merciful Mary—'tis Linn who comes!"

"Aye, and 'tis Mayenne that follows," he told her grimly. "Stand back when they come in—I'd not have you trampled. By the looks of it, there could be a fight."

The entire household was in earnest preparation now as men-at-arms struggled hastily to pull on coats of mail, while boys ran from slit to slit with supplies of arrows for the crossbows. In a matter of minutes the nearly finished wall bristled with shafts deftly fitted against tautened bowstrings. The drawbridge went down so quickly that the sound of its hitting the mooring reverberated through both baileys, only to be drowned in the din of riders crossing over it, followed by villeins armed with cudgels and pitchforks tramping on its wooden floor.

"God's blood, but I'd thought we'd not make it," Brian breathed as a cheer went up from the men on the wall. Behind him, the last fellow had barely climbed over the rising bridge when the men of Mayenne emerged over from the river shallows.

"Brian, what . . . ?"

Before she could even ask him what had happened, he'd turned to Guy. Cat looked up at Aislinn, who still tried to catch her breath. Her face and hands were ruddy from the cold, and she had the sniffles, but otherwise she appeared to be all right.

"Geoffrey's dead, Cat."

For an instant Catherine thought Brian had caused the death, and she stared upward in disbelief. "Geoffrey's dead?" she repeated.

"Aye, Count Hugh would have him ride out two days ago when he could scarce sit in the saddle. He fell from his horse and broke his neck."

"Sweet Mary," Catherine murmured, saying a

quick silent prayer for his soul. "But that does not explain—"

" 'Twas a hunt, Cat, and Geoffrey would not have gone but for Count Hugh. When he fell, they all gathered round to discover him dead, and Brian grasped my bridle and told me to say I was going back inside the castle. While they made a litter for his body, we ran, gathering Brian's escort as we fled."

"Oh, Linn, I am so sorry . . ."

"Nay, I am glad to be out of there, and 'tis better that my husband is dead. He had so little pleasure in living."

Geoffrey of Mayenne was dead, and his widow had fled to Rivaux ere he was buried. Apparently her shock was evident, for Aislinn sought to explain. "I was a good wife to him while he lived, but I came to hate his father. I knew that if I did not leave then, I'd never see the Condes again—Count Hugh intended to wed me to one of his men to keep my dowry."

Behind her, Catherine could hear Brian arguing with Guy over what he had done, saying that Aislinn had been little more than a prisoner at Mayenne. "But you cannot expect him not to fight over her," Guy retorted, "Not when she carries the heir. And I'd not fight with an unfinished wall."

"You would not have left her, either."

"I would have taken her to Belvois."

"That way was cut off by Mayenne's men. Besides, he'll treat—he'll not want to make an enemy of you."

"Your faith in my power overwhelms me," Guy muttered dryly. "And what am I supposed to do with her—send her to the Condes when her father is gone to England?"

"I'd have you keep her here until I can speak with Earl Roger and my father."

The acrid smell of melting pitch floated over them, a grim reminder of what they faced. "Alan, I'd be armed," Guy told his squire. Meeting Cat's worried eyes, he nodded. "Aye, I mean to treat with May-enne."

"You'll not give her up?"

"I know not what I'll say to him, but nay, I'll not give her up. But . . ." He turned to Brian and sighed heavily. "But I would have been warned that I was gaining an enemy."

"Would you have me speak with him?" Brian asked.

" 'Tis not your keep he would threaten. Catherine, take your sister inside and see she is made warm."

Unclad, Aislinn was thinner than Catherine remembered, despite her swollen abdomen. She shivered as Hawise rubbed her limbs to warm them, and Cat heated honeyed wine. Beda held a blanket close to the brazier, where a roaring fire had been set, and when it was almost hot to touch, Hawise pushed Aislinn into Cat's bed and covered her with it.

"You are nigh frozen," Catherine muttered as she brought the wine to her sister.

"It was a long ride—I'd not thought to make it." The younger girl took the cup and sipped from it, then leaned back, sighing. "I know Lord Guy is angered with Brian, Cat, but I could not stay there. You know not how it was."

Catherine signaled to the tiring women to leave and sat beside the bed. "Guy will stand for you, Linn, but I doubt you can keep the babe from Count Hugh."

"Aye—the babe," Aislinn remembered, and her voice grew bitter. " 'Twas why I was married, was it not? Poor Geoffrey wanted to die in peace, but there had to be a babe." She closed her eyes for a moment and pulled the covers closer, as though to shield herself. "I suppose I should count myself fortunate that I conceived while Geoffrey could still do the deed, for I heard Count Hugh say that before he'd let Anjou have Mayenne, he'd get me with child himself."

"Jesu!"

"Aye, ever was I afraid of him, Cat. When Geoffrey

grew worse, his father sought my company, taking me from my husband's bedside, saying that I should enjoy a whole man's company. I think if I had not the babe within me, he would have ravished me.''

''Did Geoffrey know of this?''

''Aye, I think he did, for when Brian came to see us, Geoffrey told him to take me away while he could.'' Aislinn's eyes filled with tears and her lower lip trembled. ''He wanted to die, Cat—there were no pleasures left for him. And his father would not understand—'twas as though he thought Geoffrey became ill to thwart him. When Brian wished to hunt, Count Hugh made him—*made* him—ride with us, knowing full well that he could not sit his horse. He killed his own son, Cat.''

''Shhhhh—do not think on it, Linn. You are safe here, I promise you. Drink your wine, and I will hold your hand as we did when we were small, until you sleep.''

Aislinn obediently took another sip, but shook her head. ''Nay, take it away. I am too tired to drink.''

Cat took the cup and set it aside before leaning over to tuck the covers closer about her sister. ''You will stay here until the babe is born, and Guy and Papa will decide what is to be done.''

''I wish Papa were here.''

''So do I, but we have Guy, after all, and I doubt Mayenne will wish to force a quarrel on him.''

''You would have been proud of Brian, Cat—he did not hesitate in the least. He risked his life for me.''

''He loves you.''

''We are the only sisters he knows.''

Catherine opened her mouth to set Aislinn straight, and then thought better of it. Brian FitzHenry could do his own wooing. Instead, she reached for her sister's cold hand and held it. ''Try to rest, Linn.''

''Aye.''

Aislinn closed her eyes and lay quietly while the wine and the bedcovers warmed her. After a time, she was so still that Cat thought she'd gone to sleep. Gently disengaging her fingers from Linn's, she rose and tiptoed toward the door.

"I pray 'tis a girl, Cat," Aislinn murmured suddenly. "Then he will not want the babe."

After much shouting back and forth between William on the wall and Count Hugh before the gate, it was agreed that Guy would go out to discuss the matter under flag of truce. But for reasons of safety, Guy chose to do so in full mail. More than one fool had been felled by arrows while he spoke, he told Alan as he adjusted his helm over his face.

"I'd go with you."

Guy looked down at Brian from the height of his horse. "Nay, you'd but anger him further."

"I'd hear what lies he would tell you. You cannot know how he has treated Linn, my lord. Had I known of it before we left Mayenne, I'd have tried to kill him first. But she did not tell me until we were nearly here. If you'd not believe me, ask one of them." He gestured to where the men who'd ridden with him huddled over the fire that heated the pitch. "Aye, there's not a man among them as would not wish him dead."

"I believe you, but I'd go alone." His eyes were heavily flecked, giving no insight into his thoughts as they stared from behind the polished helmet. "If 'tis just Guy of Rivaux he faces, he either goes home or makes his quarrel with me. If it is both of us, there is already a quarrel."

Nudging his horse forward with his knee, Guy indicated to the gateman he was ready. As a precaution against a ruse or a rush for the bridge, Rivaux's bowmen fitted their notched arrows in the crossbows again and waited. Villeins soaked rag-covered torches in hot pitch and handed them up to the defenders on the outer wall.

Guy rode out slowly, leisurely even, always conscious of the dramatic effect of his presence. While still in range of his archers, he stopped and leaned forward to rest arms on the pommel of his saddle.

"I am come to see how it is that you invade my lands, Hugh of Mayenne," he called out clearly.

"I come in peace, my lord," Count Hugh answered loudly. " 'Tis curious that I am given this welcome when I but seek my son's wife. Send her out to me, and we will leave Rivaux." He edged his own horse closer, being careful to stay just beyond arrows' reach. "She carries the heir to Mayenne."

"She has requested shelter, and I'd not turn my wife's sister away." Guy clicked his reins and moved to meet the older man on open ground. "If you would seek her return, you'd best discuss it with her father, for I am told her husband is dead."

Hugh of Mayenne watched Guy uncomfortably. There was a studied arrogance about the Count of Rivaux that almost frightened him. He sat there too easily, his free hand resting on the hilt of Doomslayer, his flecked eyes cold in an impassive face. A shiver traveled up the older man's spine, making him shudder. It was as though the younger man would as soon cleave him in half as speak to him. Hugh licked his lips nervously, but managed to protest, "Nay, but there is no quarrel with you—I'd but take the girl and go. As you see, I have few men and treat with you unarmed."

"She wishes to return to her father."

"This is not her father's house, my lord."

"Aye, but Earl Roger is gone to England. She turns to me as husband to his heiress."

"She comes to you as Henry's bastard's leman," Hugh spat out, unable to believe that Guy would care what happened to Aislinn of the Condes.

" 'Tis my kinswoman you insult, Hugh."

"The bastard fled with her ere my son was cold—what else am I to think?"

"If you accuse her, I will be compelled to defend her honor," Guy told him coldly.

"Jesu! She's naught to you!" Recovering, Count Hugh tried a different tactic. "You cannot wish to be burdened, my lord. Send her back with me, and when the babe is born, I will send her to her family. You have other concerns, do you not? He looked upward at the bristling wall. "Aye, your wall is unfinished yet—you've not the time to fight over a woman."

Hugh of Mayenne's words were meant as a veiled threat, but Guy ignored them. " 'Tis nearly done."

"I'd ransom her from you."

"I'd stand her champion. Accuse her if you will, but stand ready to defend any accusation on the field of honor, my lord. I said I'd not turn her away, and I'll not."

" 'Tis your final word?"

"Aye."

"Then I pray you do not regret this, my lord of Rivaux, for the next time I come for her, 'twill be with an army!" Wheeling, Hugh spurred his horse and rode back to his men, muttering aloud, "God's teeth, but he is an arrogant whelp!"

Guy sat there until Mayenne reached his escort and turned back to him. Lifting his hand in a mocking salute, Guy then eased his horse slowly back into his keep.

"Jesu!" Brian exhaled as he met him. "Does he mean to fight?"

"Not this time."

❦ 36 ❧

Despite Mayenne's threat, the harsh winter passed quickly and almost without incident. After Guy wrote to Roger informing him of Aislinn's presence at Rivaux, her father sent permission for her to stay, and she provided good company for Catherine as both awaited their babes. Work on Rivaux's stone outer shell continued as weather permitted, and was finished about the same time as the last spring thaw. And Henry, as Normandy's duke rather than England's king, unbent enough toward Guy to keep the feast of St. Catherine with them in November. During that time, he was persuaded to send his writ to Mayenne stating that the Lady Aislinn "hath of her own free will and conscience departed her late husband's house in favor of her sister's, and doth have all permission to do so, provided Mayenne's heir be returned to his patrimony once weaned."

Christmas came and went with new robes throughout the household, owing to Henry's abatement of Rivaux's annual taxes for that year only. Indeed, Guy had prospered sufficiently that when Catherine's women had their Christmas chairing, the custom whereby they held the lord of the castle in his chair until he paid them gifts, they were rewarded with new cloaks apiece. Only the news that Eleanor of Nantes had taken her two youngest girls and gone to Harlowe to be with her lord marred Catherine's enjoyment of the feast. But then, Earl Roger and all of them were expected back in the Condes by Easter feast, and plans were made for Aislinn to return to her family home as soon as her babe was born.

The spring thaws of March brought rumors of renewed raiding by Robert of Belesme, first in the Norman Vexin and then closer to Rivaux, but such was the fear of him that if rumors could be believed, he had the power to be at opposite ends of the duchy on the same day. There was a collective sigh of relief when the last stones were fitted in Rivaux's high outer wall. Not content with this measure of security, Guy at once set about the construction of round towers to be built in four places inside the wall. And, true to his promise to her, he ordered the breaking of ground for the magnificent house he intended to build for Catherine.

On 2 April, 1112, Aislinn was delivered of a daughter born too early, and on 4 April they buried the babe beneath Rivaux's chapel floor. For Catherine, now heavy with her own child, Aislinn's tiny daughter was yet another reminder that the descendants of Gilbert of Nantes seemed to be all girls. Nonetheless, she clung steadfastly to the belief that she carried a son for Guy.

When Aislinn did not mend quickly, Catherine took it upon herself to write to Brian, who had returned to Rouen with his father. Drawing close to the fire in her solar, she dipped her quill in ink and carefully began:

Brian FitzHenry,

I heartily recommend me to you this 7th day of April, and trust my message finds you well. Cecilia of Mayenne came into this world on 2 April and departed it shortly, may God in His mercy take her small soul. My lord husband wrote to Count Hugh of it this day, and dispatched the message forthwith.

She paused to look over what she'd written and sighed. She wanted to tell him to come back to Rivaux, but there seemed no politic way to put it, for Aislinn would not wish her to meddle in her affairs. But Cat knew Brian loved her sister, so she dipped her pen again to continue:

Aislinn does not mend well for disappointment in the babe, and I fear for her health. My lord father wishes her home again and promises to accept her will in whether she weds or not. I am told there have been several inquiries as to her person and her dowry, but Count Hugh delays in returning what my father granted on her marriage to Geoffrey. God willing, Linn will return to the Condes, leaving here 22 April with William for escort.

I am unhandsome but well and hope to be delivered of my son next month. It would please me greatly were you to stand godfather to him. I thought to ask William, who has served my lord so well, but he declines, saying he is too old for the task.

Reading it again, she was satisfied that he could not help but know what she wanted him to do. She added her closing and sanded the whole, shaking the white sand back into the small leather pouch she kept for her writing things. Aye, he'd know it was time to come for Linn—and she'd given him twelve days to do so. Otherwise, he would have to go to the Condes and attempt to persuade Eleanor that he had changed. And he had changed, for he drank no more to excess, nor did he fill his pallet with serving wenches and whores. Rolling the letter carefully, she inserted it in a cylindrical case and affixed Guy's seal at one end.

"Give this to Sir William for dispatch," she ordered her new page, a small redheaded child sent by a neighboring lord to be trained in her household.

"Aye, my lady."

She could hear the boy run on the stairs and sighed at the boundless energy of children. Her own babe stirred within her, shifting from one side to the other. It had to be a son, for no girl could possibly make her ribs so sore.

"Did you not think to tell him not to run on the steps?"

She shifted on her seat and turned at the sound of Guy's voice. Grinning, he came across the room to clasp her shoulders from behind and hold her against him. "Aye, I cannot think de Searcy would thank us if the boy killed himself ere he even got to where he played with swords."

She leaned back against his woolen tunic, savoring the rough, hard feel of him. His hands slid down over her swollen breasts to tweak a nipple through her gown, and she felt a surge of desire and then disappointment as he drew back.

"Nay, 'tis too close to your time," he murmured above her, smoothing her hair against her crown instead.

"I will be glad when I am not so ugly."

"Ugly? Naught's ugly about you, Cat. Big belly and all, you are still the loveliest lady in Christendom, I swear."

"Art blind then." She ducked away from him and rose awkwardly, clutching her gown to her swollen abdomen as though to hide it. "Sweet Jesu, but I will be glad when it comes."

His expression sobered. "Do you fear it?"

"I think that must be why God gives us so long, Guy," she decided. "When 'tis time, we feel 'tis overlong and are ready to part with the burden. If I fear anything, 'tis that 'twill be a daughter, or even worse, that 'twill die like Aislinn's."

"I'd be glad of a daughter."

For a fleeting moment she glimpsed the haunted look

in his eyes, but mistook the reason. "You are afraid also."

"Aye."

"Because of what happened to your lady mother?"

"Aye."

"I am full grown and healthy, my lord, and the babe sits well within me. If my mother, who is far smaller than I, can be delivered ten times, then so can I."

"I hope 'tis not ten times, Cat—I'd not put you through this so often." He moved closer to wrap her in his arms and nuzzle the part of her hair with his chin. "Art dearer than life to me, love."

To accommodate the babe between them, she had to lean forward to slide her arms around him. "I'd have a dozen sons for you rather than give up lying with you," she murmured against his shoulder.

"What would you think of having the babe at the Condes with your mother to attend you?"

She stood very still within his arms, uncertain and afraid of his meaning. "Why do you ask?"

"Henry summons me to Rouen. I'd not go, Cat, but I dare not refuse him—he is overlord to all I hold."

"But *why?*" she gasped in dismay. "Why is it that he needs you now? Can you not tell him . . . can you not write . . . ? Nay, I suppose you cannot," she sighed. " 'Tis but that I would have you here for my lying-in."

"I'd be here—you know I would—but I cannot depend on how long Henry means to keep me. I know not even why I am called," he admitted frankly. "But Linn goes to the Condes, and I'd have you go with her. You will have William for escort, and he will see to the fitting of a cart so that you do not have to ride on horseback. If you leave this week, you should be there with weeks to spare." Releasing her, he lifted her chin with his knuckle. "Aye, 'tis not how I would have it either, but at least I will know you are as safe as may be."

"Why cannot I stay here?"

"If I cannot be here, I'd have you with your lady mother, your sisters, and women with skills in childbed."

"Sweet Mary, but I'd not have you go," she whispered, nearly choking on her disappointment.

The last place he wanted to be was Rouen, miles apart from her, not when the last few months had been the best of his life. It was no abuse of the truth when he said she was dearer than life to him, and he was afraid to leave her. Despite her brave words, women did die in birthing, and she would be torn apart bearing a child, he feared. Even as the babe moved between them, it frightened him to think he had passed on the blood of Belesme. What if she looked on the child and saw Belesme in it? That thought had haunted him from the time he learned she carried the babe. Now it had reached such proportion that he had to will himself not to dwell on it, a near-impossible task given that she expected him to share her pleasure in his child.

"I will plead your illness," he decided finally. "Mayhap Henry . . ."

That he would do it was proof enough for her. "Nay," she decided, sighing again, "I'd not cost you his goodwill, Guy. 'Twas wrong of me to tear at you for what cannot be helped. 'Twill be good to see Maman again." Her hands clutched at the woolen tunic as though to hold him as long as she could. "When do you ride?"

"I am bidden to be there Monday."

" 'Tis but four days!"

"Aye, I will have to leave on the morrow, but you and Linn will have William to tend to your needs," he tried to reassure her.

The whole household was subdued as news of Guy's departure spread. The isolation of winter had lulled everyone into a sense of self-sufficiency, and now those who had looked forward to the birth of their lord's heir as being the final link in the chain of normalcy for

Rivaux were to be denied. It was a sudden and all-too-grim reminder of their feudal state, where raiding and rebellion could again tear apart their peaceful world. Even William de Comminges, whose fifty-five years of life had been regularly punctuated with war, uprisings, suppression, and the interminable preparation for those things, was reluctant to see the peace of the winter past come to an end.

"God's bones, my lord, but we have only finished the wall, and now we have not the security of staying behind it," he grumbled to Guy.

" 'Twill not be for long, I hope. Henry summons Normandy's council, most probably to levy more taxes—I have heard that his daughter's wedding last year still beggars him."

"Art not such a fool, my lord," William scoffed. "You leave me with women whilst Henry rails at the baronage for aid against Belesme, and well you know it."

It was always difficult to fool William. "All right—aye, I think he means to ask for aid, but I give you the greater task. I'd have Catherine safe at the Condes before Belesme raids again. Robert is mad enough that I cannot trust he will not come here, and I'll not be home."

" 'Tis a long journey for one near her time."

"Hawise judges she has another month before the babe comes."

"Humph! I've seen them count wrong before, but aye—I'll do it."

"If anything should happen . . ." Guy hesitated, afraid to put his worst thoughts into words. "If Catherine . . ."

"I'll send to you at Rouen with orders that the messenger is to follow you until he finds you. But she is well, my lord, and there is naught to suspect otherwise."

"Aye, but the babe . . . Oh, Jesu, William, but I'd not have her bear it," he finished finally, looking away.

"You speak as though you think its feet will be cloven, Guy. 'Twill not be so. 'Twill be but an ugly, shriveled creature as you were once, and then 'twill grow as you have.'' William raised his hand to touch his young lord and then dropped it. "Nay, but there's no speaking to you, is there? You have haunted yourself with what you fear, and naught I can say will convince you that the evil of Belesme is in his mind and not his blood."

"Then you cannot explain Mabille or William Talvas, can you?"

"I know not what made them as they were, my lord, but I'd ask you this: do you see madness in yourself?"

"There is a violence in me, William."

"God's blood!" the old man exploded. "Art a fighting knight and a man! Aye, you kill in battle, but is there a pleasure in the killing?"

"Nay."

"I saw you cleave eight men outside Ludlow, my lord, and then I saw you empty your guts when 'twas over. Think you Belesme has ever done the same?" With the authority of a king's prosecutor, William shook his head. "Nay, you have not, and therein lies the difference between you. If every man who had a temper thought himself insane, Normandy would be naught but madmen!" Then, sensing that he had overstepped the bounds between a knight and his lord, he exhaled heavily, muttering, "Your pardon, my lord, but 'tis wrong of me to tax you. If I offend you, 'tis but for the love I bear you."

"William." Guy moved to clasp his man awkwardly, holding him briefly and planting a solemn kiss on his cheek. "You are the only father I have ever known. I pray you never fear to speak your mind to me."

Embarrassed by a flood of emotion that threatened his composure, William patted Guy clumsily on the shoulder. "Here, now—'tis unseemly," he responded gruffly. " 'Tis proud I am to serve you."

"I pray for your safety as well as Catherine's." Noting the reddening of the older man's eyes, Guy eased his arm about William's shoulders. "Come, let us walk the wall together this night, that we may see what we have made."

❦ 37 ❧

When he rode into Rouen, Guy was surprised to find no signs of an impending council, and it worried him to have been summoned alone. After sending Alan to apprise the ducal household of his arrival, he took lodgings in the city and awaited Henry's pleasure. It did not take long. Within hours, a messenger brought word that Guy was to present himself for audience forthwith. Again he chose to go as a warrior lord rather than a courtier.

"God's blood, Rivaux! Art fearsome this day!"

Guy swung around before he reached the doorway to the audience chamber. "Brian! Jesu, but I'd thought you'd be on your way to the Condes by now." His face broke into a crooked smile that lifted the scar on his cheek. "Linn goes there next week."

"Aye, I had that of Cat's letter."

"She wrote to you of it?"

"With your seal affixed. Do you not know what your lady wife does?" Brian demanded, grinning.

"Cat keeps me meek—these are but the trappings of my rank." Guy laughed. Sobering abruptly, he returned to the matter at hand. "Then you know about Aislinn's babe? We fought to save it, but it was too small. We ate mutton for a week after, because 'twas thought the skins of freshly slaughtered lambs might

386

give it warmth. In the end, I think it was just too small to suck.''

'' 'Tis probably God's blessing she died, then, for Mayenne would have used the babe to keep Linn's dowry,'' Brian pointed out. ''But I am sorry for Aislinn—'tis hard for a woman to lose her babe.''

''I doubt he will give it back anyway.''

''Aye, he will—now that Earl Roger has returned to Normandy.''

''De Brione is back? I'd begun to think he'd moved to England, and his return was but a rumor. I know that Cat does not know of it, but she will be glad enough to find him at home.''

''He is here—my father summons him also.''

''Then there *is* a council.''

''Nay, but ere he is done, you may wish he had called one. Come on—I am on my way in also, but for a different reason: I mean to beg to go.''

Puzzled, Guy stood back to let him pass, and then followed. The room was almost empty except for the ever-present clerks in their plain priest's robes, who sat scratching their pens constantly in the execution of Henry's writs. It was said in Normandy that learning was a dangerous thing. In the less than six years since Tinchebrai, the Conqueror's youngest son had managed to issue more writs than his illustrious father and his ineffectual brother had in all their years put together. And that did not count what Henry issued in his English kingdom.

The duke was standing, overshadowed by the taller Roger de Brione, and both men turned to greet Guy. Henry's eyes traveled over him, pausing briefly on Doomslayer, and a faint smile curved his mouth.

''What say you—did your daughter not get herself a fine husband?'' he demanded of Roger.

''Aye, though I did not think it at the time,'' de Brione answered. Turning to Guy, he could not resist asking, ''She is well?''

''She is well but for the babe. I am sending her with

her sister to the Condes to be with Lady Eleanor for her lying-in.''

"And if she is delivered of a son, he will be too spoiled for anything ere you get him home," Henry interrupted. "But it sorrowed me to hear of the Lady Aislinn—may God grant her infant peace." Looking back at Roger, he added, "Count Hugh disputes it and accuses Rivaux of hiding his heir from him."

'' 'Tis a lie, and well he knows it. I could have sent the babe's body back to Mayenne, but I was not certain he would even give her Christian burial," Guy retorted.

"He does not want to give back Linn's dowry, no doubt," Roger muttered dryly. "But if he thinks I will not sue for it, he is mistaken."

"Aye, but there is time to settle that later. For now I am more concerned with putting an end to Robert of Belesme's continuing encroachments on my duchy." Henry glanced to where the clerks sat, and added significantly, "Writs avail me not where he is concerned."

Guy and Roger exchanged surprised glances at the duke's open admission that he could not control Belesme. And Guy experienced a sense of unease as it occurred to him why Henry had summoned them: he expected them to make war on Belesme. Each time Henry had come to power, first in England and now in Normandy, he'd attempted to destroy his old enemy, and despite his successes in expelling him from his lands, Henry simply could not rid himself of Belesme forever. And the hatred between the violent and vicious count and the man who'd sought to rule him had reached such a state that Belesme now considered any town, any castle, and any loyal vassal a target for merciless revenge. It was still a source of comment and distrust that he had merely stripped Rivaux of food and supplies the fall before, when scarce a baron in all of the duchy had not lost men and crops to him.

Waiting until he was certain of their full attention,

Henry proceeded, "Aye, there can be no peace in Normandy whilst he is free to strike at will. I dare not be gone from this duchy for fear of the anarchy that arises from his raids. The time has come, my lords, for him to face my justice," he finished dramatically.

"You wish our levies—so be it."

"Nay, Roger, 'twill not serve. He knows he cannot face an army, and he will flee to fight elsewhere rather than chance a pitched battle." Henry paused for effect and then continued, "What I am asking is that between you who have the skill to do it, you seek the means to take him prisoner and return him to Rouen." Henry's brown eyes were calculating the effect of his request as they shifted from Roger to Guy. "Aye, there's not many to ask for such a task, and well I know it. But you have both fought the Welsh and know how to counter raids. And aside from you, there are few in Normandy willing or able enough to go after him and fight as he does."

"Or foolish enough," Guy muttered. "Jesu, but he is like quicksilver, floating about, aiming a blow, and fading to fight again another day."

"And he inspires others to anarchy!" Henry snapped. "Any petty landholder with ten mounted men thinks to rape and steal, knowing full well that if he burns the place and kills everyone, 'twill be blamed on Belesme. But I am not fool enough to believe that even Robert can be all over the duchy at the same time, and 'tis what some would have me think. Aye—last week, he was reported in the Vexin and the Contentin on the same day. Now there are village priests who preach that he is the Devil made flesh, and that there is no way to defend against him!" Henry snorted derisively. " 'Tis a good way to fill the parish coffers, but prayers are foolish when 'tis only steel he respects."

" 'Tis impossible, Your Grace—he would have to be cut off from retreat and followed across lands belonging to other barons. And with no base in Normandy, he will be hard to find.''

Looking at Guy, Henry's eyes and voice suddenly grew cold. ''I know Earl Roger has the stomach for it, but I am not so certain about you. Lest you forget it, my lord of Rivaux, you came back to Normandy a pauper and were given your patrimony—aye, and your other possessions also—in return for your loyalty. Am I to think you too craven for the task I give you?''

''The Welsh Marcher lords would refute that,'' Roger cut in abruptly. ''Nay, he is but concerned to be away from his wife before her lying-in.''

Surprised by his father-in-law's defense of him, Guy met Henry's gaze with equal coldness. ''There is no man living who has ever called me craven, Your Grace,'' he told him evenly.

There was something in those strange flecked eyes that made Henry's blood chill. Not even the Conqueror's son was proof against the controlled anger he saw there. Even as he watched, the gold warmth faded to green spikes that spread from the pupil. It was the color, he told himself later—the green reminded him of Belesme. ''I did not accuse you, my lord—I asked,'' he told the man before him, backing down.

''An army is useless,'' Roger mused, barely aware of the confrontation before him. ''It gives too much notice and is too unwieldy to fight as Robert now fights.''

''Aye, but if he is cornered, he *will* fight. And I know not how old he is, but I'd not like to meet him in single combat.''

''He is forty-six, Brian,'' Roger answered. ''And still he has skills like none other. He can punish a man with any weapon chosen until 'tis a blessing to die.''

''Yet you bested him once, my lord, and could do so again,'' Guy ventured.

''Aye, but I've not spent every year since in constant warfare as he has done,'' Roger admitted. ''And had I not fought for Lea, I do not think I could have done it then." He fell silent, mulling in his mind the prospect of taking to his saddle for weeks and months against his life's enemy. Then he slowly summed up his liege's expectations. "What you would ask of us is that we bring him in alive by any means we choose, is it not?"

"Aye. I give you my writ authorizing his arrest."

Grimly weighing his chances, Roger nodded. "Then so be it."

Henry watched him, his brown eyes intent. Realizing that he could not in good faith refuse his liege lord without raising suspicion, Guy let out a heavy sigh. "Aye, so be it."

"I'd go with you."

Almost in unison, they turned to stare incredulously at Brian, and he reddened but did not answer. "You have to take men-at-arms, Roger—I'd ask that you take me." The air was heavy with things unsaid as Roger and Henry shook their heads. "I know what you would say to me—that I am untried and indifferent in arms, and you both love me too well to see me fall." Brian stopped and turned to appeal to Guy. "Tell them . . . tell them, my lord, that I am not the same man who left the Condes last year."

Knowing full well that Brian desperately wanted the approval of both men, Guy felt a sudden kinship for him. "Aye. Aye . . . you can ride with me."

"You'll not be sorry for it, I swear to you."

Once it was agreed on, there was not much left to say. Henry promised to subsidize them through remission of rents and taxes not to exceed the cost of men and arms, directed the issuance of writs allowing them pursuit throughout Normandy, and bade them collect whatever they needed to be in their saddles within the week. Then he dismissed them, admonishing them to practice care against Belesme's cunning and treachery. Having been a victim already of his cunning, Guy considered it an unworthy reminder.

Withdrawing into a deserted alcove to ponder what

they'd promised, the three men debated the best approach. Guy spoke first, asking his father-in-law, "How many men are in your escort?"

"I brought but twenty men-at-arms and five bowmen. And in yours?"

"Thirty-one. I have enough enemies that I rarely travel with fewer. And of those, all but my body servant and four archers are knights and squires. Brian?"

"The men I brought to Rivaux belonged to my father," Brian admitted. "There is but myself and my squire, and I have money enough for mayhap a pair of mercenaries."

"Less than sixty then," Guy calculated. "And I doubt Belesme can have many more than that now—mayhap a hundred at the most. Nay, I'd not have mercenaries unless Earl Roger wishes it. I prefer to stand with mine own men."

"Then we are agreed," Roger murmured appreciatively as Guy considered their forces.

"Most of mine have been with me since Tinchebrai, and followed me into Wales, so there's naught to fear that they will break and run if we meet Belesme." Guy stopped for a moment. "God's bones, but I'd thought to be planting crops at Rivaux now, but instead it appears I will be living in my saddle."

"The telling of the tale will be in whether we can not only find Robert but also take him," Roger observed to both of them. "We must make certain that we lay a better trap for him than he does for us. I wish I had killed him the one time I could, for God's justice has been slower than I'd expected."

But Guy stared unseeing for a moment, hearing Belesme again as he'd heard him at Rivaux, saying, *"To kill your father is forbidden you,"* and wondered if he could commit the sin of patricide when the need arose. They'd been ordered to bring him in for Normandy's justice, but Guy knew Belesme would choose to die rather than be taken. "Aye, I wish you had killed him also," he admitted somberly.

Roger, who had been absent from the Condes for nearly a year, left them to write to Eleanor of the quest for Belesme. Brian watched him go with an almost bitter twist to his smile. "He does not expect much from me, does he? 'Tis as though only you and he go, but then, he fostered me and thinks he knows my skill. I suppose 'twill be years before he can think of me as aught but a whoremaster and a sot."

"Nay. You mistake the matter—he loves you well."

"But 'tis not the same as respect, is it?" Brian reminded him. "When I would have had Catherine for wife, he refused me, saying we were of the wrong tempers for each other, when in truth he did not want me for his son. Now I fear he will say the same of Linn."

"Cat tells me he gives her the choosing this time, so full half your battle is won there."

"Aye, but I'd earn her," Brian sought to explain. " 'Tis difficult to understand, I suppose, but I'd have him think me worthy of her." His eyes met Guy's, revealing inner pain. "But I'd not expect you to know how 'tis for me—you are much admired for everything. There's none to doubt you."

"You mistake the matter then, Brian FitzHenry, if you think that. I have spent my whole life striving to win the love of others. You at least have had that."

"Aye, they love me but find me wanting."

"God's bones, but what a sorry pair of fellows we are, if we've got naught to do but dispute how we are loved." Guy draped an affectionate arm around him. "Come, we'll see to our equipment and share a skin of wine in my lodgings. You know," he added almost cheerfully, "now that I know 'tis not Cat you want, I find I like you."

❧ 38 ❧

"There is that about this place that I cannot like,"
William muttered as he raised his hand to halt them.

Ahead the road narrowed where it entered forest,
and behind them was the ford they'd crossed over a
swollen stream. With the cart carrying Catherine and
her sister, 'twould be impossible to effect an orderly
retreat if the need arose. He detached two riders, ordering them to go ahead and return.

Catherine, already made miserable by the rough jostling of the cart, followed his gaze anxiously. Somewhere in the thicket a horse whinnied, sending a shiver
of apprehension through her. Despite her lord's stric-
tures, she wished she had ridden a horse.

"You expect trouble, Sir William?" she asked with
a calm she did not feel.

"My bones warn me that we are watched. Garay,"
he ordered his squire, "take the cart back until . . .
Oh, Holy Mary!" He wheeled his horse, shouting,
"Draw the column to cover retreat! Archers! Cover
your lady!"

Rivaux's two riders emerged from the forest with
green-shirted men in pursuit. " 'Tis Belesme," someone yelled. " 'Tis Belesme!"

The cart bounced over rocks and broken limbs,
swaying so wildly that Catherine clung tightly to the
side while trying to hold Aislinn. "And 'twas said

riding horseback would harm the babe," she muttered.

But Aislinn, white-faced with fright, sat rigidly, praying under her breath, "Mary, Mother of God, intercede for us . . . Merciful Father, deliver us."

William kept his retreat as orderly as possible, given that Guy had the more seasoned men with him. As the first of the pursuers reached him, he swung his mace expertly and caught the man squarely at the side of his helmet. Reeling from the blow, the fellow lost his seat and fell, to be dragged by his horse, bouncing along the ground before being trampled by the ensuing melee.

The skirmish was engaged as the Rivaux men sought to block their attackers from reaching Catherine's cart. "For Rivaux and St. Stephen! For Rivaux and St. Stephen!" someone shouted to rally them. William feinted with the mace and then swung wide to catch another, who slumped in his saddle and clung to his pommel, stunned. "God aids us!" he yelled above the din. " 'Tis not Belesme—'tis Mayenne! 'Tis Mayenne!"

" 'Tis Mayenne—'tis Mayenne! Sweet Jesu, 'tis Mayenne!" The cry went up and grew. "For Rivaux and St. Stephen! Let us take Mayenne!"

The cart hit the rocky ford with a bounce, snagged its wheel, and tottered crazily before turning over. Aislinn was flung clear and scrambled up frantically to find her sister. "Cat! Cat!" The last thing Catherine thought before she hit the water was that she would lose the babe.

William saw the wagon axle break, but could not draw off for the men that surrounded him. His heart sinking, he swung furiously to clear the way, sending two more of Mayenne's men to the ground. When one sought to disembowel William's horse, he was knocked from behind by a Rivaux man and sent sprawling on his own sword.

"Draw off! Draw off! 'Tis Belesme!'

Incredibly, the green-shirted men who attacked them were now scattering, breaking off contact to flee. William spurred his horse toward the ford as riders splashed across and thundered past him in pursuit. When he reached the overturned cart, two had already reined in, and one had slid down to lift Aislinn from the water.

"I am all right . . . I am all right. 'Tis my sister . . . 'tis Catherine of the Condes!" she cried frantically, trying to break away and get to the cart. "She's in there!"

Before William could dismount, the taller one was off his horse and pulling at the wrecked cart. Incredulous, he heard him order, "Get the other side, Piers," and realized it was Robert of Belesme. Heedless of his own safety, William swung down and joined them in trying to right the wreckage. As they heaved, silk pillows fell out, floated in the water until they were soaked, and then sank. A box broke open, spilling Cat's purple gown onto the wet rocks.

Several times they slipped on the lichen before they gained sufficient footing for leverage. Belesme pulled off his heavy gloves for better grasp, gripped the side of the cart from beneath, and heaved, righting it. The unreal thought that Belesme's strength came from the hard training of his trade went through William's mind as the cart, or rather what was left of it, sat at a steep tilt over one wheel. The one called Piers leaned over Catherine's limp body to feel along her jawline.

"She lives, my lord," he told Belesme.

"Hold the wagon that it does not fall again," Count Robert ordered William brusquely, and then, when William braced his back against the lower side, he lifted her free of the wreckage. She was unconscious but breathing, and her gown was soaked. Even as he carried her from the broken cart, Aislinn saw the spreading stain on the back of her dress.

"She has burst her waters," she blurted out. The three men looked at her blankly for a moment, until she explained the significance to them. "The babe will come."

"My lord . . ." One of Belesme's men rode back. "Mayenne escapes. Would you have him pursued?"

"Nay. Take what prisoners you can and hold them." To Piers he instructed, "Get Mabille's box from my saddle."

Catherine awoke on the hard ground, conscious of waves of searing pain that clutched at her insides, wrenched them, and subsided, only to come again. Opening her eyes, she saw Robert of Belesme standing over her, and for a moment she thought she'd gone to hell. Another pain tore at her, sending an involuntary cry from her.

" 'Tis your babe, Cat—'twill pass."

Cat stared wildly until she focused on Aislinn. "Sweet Mary, Linn," she whispered, "Where am I?"

"There was a wreck, but you are safe," Aislinn sought to reassure her. "But the babe comes."

The terrible pain eased, and Catherine tried to turn her head. She was surrounded by a dozen or so mail-clad men. William leaned over her anxiously. "Lady Catherine, you are all right, but you will have to be moved to a warmer place. Can you aid yourself?"

"Aye . . . nay!" She bit her lip, tasting the blood, as another gut-wrenching contraction seized her. She was going to bear her child on wet ground in full view of a band of men.

"Lift your arms, Catherine," Belesme commanded harshly. He knelt awkwardly beside her and scooped her from the muddy stream bank, rising precariously and carrying her to where Piers lay folded blankets. "Cover her with your cloak."

It took a moment for William to realize he was being addressed. Nodding, he unclasped his cloak and laid it over her. When he straightened up, Robert of Belesme was emptying the contents of a leather pouch into a cup of wine. Stirring it with his finger, Belesme knelt again by Catherine.

" 'Tis bitter, but will ease you," he told her, lifting her head.

"Nay, you would poison her!" Aislinn protested. "Sir William—"

"If I wanted her dead, I'd have left her in the water." To Catherine, who was in the throes of another pain, he urged, "Drink it."

She tried to drink, choked, and fell back, breathless. But he was not to be denied. He forced her head up again and ordered her to try again. It was bitter, and for a brief space she thought it would come up. " 'Tis gall," she managed, swallowing to keep it down.

" 'Tis an herb my mother uses for pain, Catherine."

To make matters worse, Aislinn pushed on Cat's stomach as Hawise had done on hers weeks before, forcing downward with both palms until Cat thought she could not stand it. "Have you a knife?" she heard Linn ask those around her. "I have heard it cuts the pain."

"The only thing a knife cuts in a birthing is the cord," Belesme answered her.

The pains never subsided, Mabille's bitters not withstanding, and Cat was certain she was going to die unshriven somewhere on the road to the Condes. She labored as Hawise had shown Aislinn, pushing, straining to relieve herself of her aching burden until her back felt as though it would break, humiliated at first by her audience, and then not caring. Robert of Belesme mixed for her more of the bitter bark and forced her to drink it, and throughout her ordeal, it seemed that every time she opened her eyes, she saw the chill green of Belesme's over her.

After a time, the others drifted away to deal with their prisoners, and she was vaguely aware of those who begged for their lives. She knew not how long she labored, only that she tired, and still the pains came, closer, harder, until she screamed. Aislinn moved to her knees to catch the babe and William held her flailing arms, and still Robert of Belesme hovered over her, his green eyes watching as though he were Satan come to take her babe from her. Catherine felt the sharp tear as she pushed the child from her body, and she fell back, wet and exhausted.

"You are nearly done," Belesme told her as he stirred still more of the bark into wine and gave her a third drink of it.

The others turned away when the final pain delivered the afterbirth, but Belesme knelt beside her head to tell her, "You have given Nantes a son, Catherine."

"He does not breathe," she heard Aislinn whisper, and she tried to crane her neck to look downward. She saw Robert of Belesme take her babe in his hands and put his mouth to its face. She tried to scream out, but no words came, and then she heard the faint, plaintive cry. In the fancies of her mind, she'd thought he meant to suck the soul from her child, but in truth, he'd breathed life instead.

"You'll live to be a fighting man like your father and his father before him," he murmured to the infant as he drew his sword and cut the cord himself. The babe's wail intensified until its whole body shook before he thrust it at Aislinn and rose. Standing over Cat, he looked down. "Art as strong as your mother, Catherine." She saw his bloody hands before he turned away, and irrationally wondered whether the blood belonged to her, the babe, or someone else.

But she had a son—she'd borne Guy of Rivaux a son. Freed at last from the pain, her body was strangely light and her mind floated, echoing the glorious news that she had a son. Aislinn wrapped the babe in someone's hastily given undertunic and laid it in Cat's arms, where it cried for a time and then lay blinking, its slate-blue eyes unfocused beneath its thatch of black hair.

* * *

"My lady."

William shook her awake, prying her from her deep, drug-induced sleep, and Catherine's first thought was that she'd dreamed she had a son. She was warm now and snug within blankets on a narrow bed. Opening her eyes, she saw the whitewashed walls and the crucifix affixed over the narrow door.

"Jesu, where am I?"

"The Abbey of St. Martin."

Her hand crept to her abdomen and found it flaccid and empty. "My babe? I dreamed I had a son, William."

"Nay, 'twas no dream, my lady." His weathered face broke into a broad smile and his eyes twinkled beneath his bushy silver brows. " 'Tis a fine son you have for Rivaux."

"I told Guy 'twould be a son." Twisting her head to look around her, she returned to William. "Why are we here?"

"We were beset by Hugh of Mayenne not far from here, and lost full half of our escort. While you fled, your cart overturned, and—"

"Aye, I remember that. And Belesme came."

"He routed Mayenne. 'Tis believed Count Hugh thought to overrun us and take the Lady Aislinn back to Mayenne, while blaming the raid on Count Robert. But Belesme had passed him undetected several miles before and sought to find out why 'twas he came under the colors of Belesme."

"Aye, he was there when the babe came," she recalled. "I had thought him Satan come to take my son's soul." Her muscles ached as she stretched them. "But he mistook the matter—he said I had a son for Nantes. In his madness, do you think he thought me Maman?"

"There's none to know what he thinks."

"He breathed life into my babe, William—I saw him do it."

"Aye."

"The men from Mayenne," she remembered suddenly. "What did he do with them?"

"He killed them."

"All?"

"Aye."

"So now you are awake. We had thought Robert of Belesme had cast a spell from which you would not wake, Cat." Aislinn walked in, carrying a wriggling bundle in her arms. "As yet, we have not found a wet nurse, so you will have to try it. He is little, but he has an appetite." Coming closer, she laid the babe on Cat's chest. "And as we are in a convent, none of the sisters has milk, so we have fed him sugar in a wet cloth."

At the thought that Catherine would have to expose her breasts, bachelor William rose, inclining his grizzled head. "I'd thought to stay here until you are able to travel," he told her, "and then we will press on to the Condes. I have sent to Celesin, which is closer to us, requesting more men for escort."

Aislinn watched him go before settling comfortably on the side of the cot. " 'Tis fortunate we are, Cat, that we live," she murmured as she lifted the blanket from the babe. "First I thought you dead in the cart, and then when I saw 'twas Belesme who came, I thought he would kill us all." She picked up the infant and watched him screw up his face to cry. "Here—I am told you put him on a nipple and tickle his cheek until he sucks." She waited while Catherine obediently bared a breast and then laid him against it, tickling him. His mouth opened like a rosebud to receive the nipple, and he took a tentative pull, drawing milk. Instinctively he began noisily sucking. Satisfied, Aislinn sat back. "You know, Cat, I think he did it because of Maman. I do not think he could bring himself to kill Eleanor of Nantes's daughters."

"He gave my babe breath, Linn."

"Aye. Now *that* I do not understand. But when one

is mad, as he must surely be, then 'tis impossible to know how it is that he kills one and spares another.''

"William said he killed Mayenne's men."

"He took them with him when he left us, and I could hear them begging him for the means of their dying, Cat, but he killed none while he was with us. Aye," she sighed, "we all knew he would later. William said he wished he could save them, but he dared not try it."

Unable to dwell on such things, they fell silent, each watching the tiny infant at Catherine's breast. Cat reached to ruffle the black hair and study the small face. Aye, she'd given Guy his heir, this son born of their love. "God grant that you are half the man your father is," she whispered softly to him. Looking up for Aislinn's approval, she was struck by the intense longing in her sister's eyes, and she felt almost guilty for being so happy.

"Nay, Linn, but your time will come also," she told her gently.

Aislinn shook her head. "Men would rather have me for sister than wife. Even Geoffrey did not feel passion for me."

"Geoffrey probably was too ill to feel much of anything, Linn, but I know your time will come—I know it."

❧ 39 ❧

He had a son born of the blood of Belesme. The fear
that he would pass on to another generation the vi-
ciousness and violence of Belesme had been realized.
And Catherine, in the absence of her lord's will in the
matter, had chosen to name him Richard for her father's father, Richard of Harlowe. And although the
babe had come early, he thrived, she'd written. Aye,
but he had the blood of fighters, and could not be
expected to do otherwise.

Guy replaced her letter in the case and returned it
to his saddle pouch. It did no good to read it for the
hundredth time—it was in truth fact and could not be
changed. But she was safe at least. As the horse beneath him pounded his backside, he allowed himself
to think of her, wondering if the babe had somehow
changed her.

"God's bones, but what I would not give for a bed,"
Brian grumbled good-naturedly beside him. "By day,
my bones are jarred from dawn to dusk, and by night
they are cramped from lying on the ground. You know,
by the time I ever see the Condes again, I'll not be
able to walk like a man."

"At least 'tis not so hot this week as last," Guy
responded.

"Aye—I stewed then." Brian lifted his helm from

his head and set it before him on his saddle. "Jesu, but does your neck not ache?"

"Only when I am awake."

Wincing as he did so, Brian turned his head to look back down the column to where Roger rode with the archers. They'd gotten half a dozen more from the Bishop of Sees in hopes that they might lay a trap for Belesme, and Roger wished to discuss how they were to be deployed. "How long since we left Rouen?" he muttered as he turned back to Guy. "Seven weeks? Or is it eight?"

" 'Tis nine."

"Aye, and we have heard that he goes to de Mortain's old keep in Avranches, but there's naught to show of it except a few words from a dying man."

Guy understood his frustration all too well. For over two months they'd sought to engage Belesme, only to find themselves outdistanced or outwitted, arriving always after he had struck. Aye, they never so much as saw him, but they'd buried burned and maimed corpses the breadth of Normandy. The last time had sickened him the most, for many of them were children found huddled in a charred heap where they'd sought refuge together. As his men had attempted to pry apart the seared flesh to give them separate burial, more than one had sickened at the stench and the sight. And with each new sighting of Belesme's mad vengeance, Guy would look on the dead and know 'twas his own father that had done it.

"Art silent," Brian chided him.

"Aye."

"You tire of the task also."

"I would that it were over, but who would not? I'd be at Rivaux with Catherine and William, enjoying the safety of my new wall and building Catherine's house."

"You forget Richard—you've not seen your son."

"Nay, but 'tis Catherine I would see above all others."

"Aye, I suppose it is." Brian was thoughtful for a moment, and then twisted in his saddle for a better look at Guy. "What do you think Aislinn will say to my suit?" he asked suddenly.

"I think she'd be a fool not to take you."

"But will she?"

"I know not what is in her heart, Brian, but Aislinn of the Condes is no fool," Guy answered.

"And Roger? Do you think he'd let her come to me? I am but Henry's bastard, after all."

"He would have given Cat to Robert of Caen once."

"Aye, but my father favors Robert—he is made Earl of Gloucester now."

Guy appeared to consider the matter, for he knew how much Aislinn meant to Brian. "I think," he decided slowly, "that if you are part of bringing Robert of Belesme to Henry's justice, that he cannot deny you reward this time."

"I pray you are right."

But suddenly Guy was not attending him, as he leaned forward and raised himself against his pommel, his whole being intent on what he smelled. Brian stopped also and sniffed the air, and his face betrayed his dread. It was faint from distance, but the odor of smoke mingled with that peculiarly distinct smell of burning flesh.

"I think we cannot be far behind him this time," Guy muttered grimly.

Guy removed his helmet and tied a cloth over his face before he walked among the dead. The lord of the small keep above them trailed him and Roger and Brian, explaining how it was that he could not open his gates to give his people refuge, until Guy could stand it no longer.

"These were your people! As lord, you were sworn to protect them!"

"But 'twas Belesme, my lord—'twas Belesme," the knight pleaded, as though that were excuse enough.

"And there was not time. Had I lowered the bridge, 'twould have been myself he murdered!''

"How many were there?'' Roger asked.

"Not many—some twenty villeins and serfs, I think. Those that serve the household were inside. And there—''

" 'Twas how many Belesme had with him that I meant to ask,'' Roger cut in curtly.

"When Satan comes, he needs not many. I—''

"Just tell him how many men rode with Count Robert!'' Guy snapped, already sickened by the sight of a woman lying faceup in the road, her eyes staring sightlessly, her bloody legs splayed, her babe ripped from her belly and lying beside her.

"There was not the time to count them, but—''

"You watched from the wall,'' Roger reminded him coldly. "You must have noted enough.''

"Bertrand said there were at least seventy—maybe more.''

Despite the revulsion Guy felt, he walked to where the woman lay and stared down at her. She was younger than Catherine, and the babe had neared its term, for it looked almost perfectly formed, with small hands and feet and face. But Belesme's men wanted to leave no living, for they'd even bludgeoned the back of its tiny skull. Guy remembered the feel of his own babe kicking against his back when Catherine had placed her swollen belly there at night. For a moment he doubted God's justice in allowing Belesme's blood to go on while letting the innocent be slaughtered.

He felt a hand grasp his shoulder and squeeze it, and he turned to face Roger. " 'Tis no fault of yours, Guy,'' Roger told him as his blue eyes mirrored sympathy. "You must not think it.''

"Sweet Jesu, but they ravished her also,'' Brian muttered beside them as he also stared downward. As Guy watched him, Brian knelt close to her eyes and murmur, "Almighty Father, to thee we commend these souls, asking thy mercy on them.'' After making the sign of the Cross above each of them, he rose and turned away to bring up the hard biscuits he'd eaten earlier.

"There are enough left within the walls to bury them, my lord," Guy told Roger. "If he was here but hours ago, I'd go after him."

They ate and slept without a fire, their pallets unrolled on the forest floor among trees so dense that there would be no way mounted riders could come through. Seeking the solace of solitude, Guy had laid his bedding some distance apart from the others and he sat on his blanket and ate salted fish and dried biscuits in the darkness and tried not to think of what he'd seen.

He lived a nightmare, it seemed, an endless dream whereby his body was punished and his mind tortured in his pursuit of Robert of Belesme. As he sat there, he pondered the end to it. If they did manage by some stroke of fortune to corner him, what then? Could even one born of Belesme take him?

He heard the crunch of boots behind him and turned to stare upward in the moonless night as someone stood over him. And somehow he knew that it was de Brione, not by anything he could see and not by spoken word. It was more a sense of presence.

"You give yourself too hard a task, Guy."

When Guy did not answer, Roger dropped down beside him to sit cross-legged on his pallet. For a time both were silent, and then Guy could stand it no longer. "That I would bring in Belesme?" he asked warily.

"Nay—the other. You cannot carry a burden of what you fear to be."

Guy stared hard into the pitch-darkness and tried to see the other man's face, but even with eyes that were adjusted to the lack of light, he could make out nothing but the faint glitter of de Brione's eyes. His stomach knotted in fear of what Roger must be thinking.

"I have watched you, and I have ached for you, knowing how it must be for you."

"Nay. No one knows how it is for me, my lord. Nothing I would have ever came to me without my fighting for it: my life, my lands, Catherine—nothing. And yet each time, I fought hard and won, but this time I cannot. I do not think I can take him."

"You could—despite what is said of him, he is neither Satan nor Satan's spawn, Guy. I have fought him since I was but fifteen, and I can tell you that he is a man like any other, save that he is more clever and more skilled than most. But . . ." Roger's eyes caught whatever light there was as they met Guy's soberly. "But I'd not have you fight him if it can be helped. I'd not have you kill someone of your own blood."

"Jesu!" Guy exhaled sharply, his whole body arrested as time stood still. "You must hate me for it," he managed finally in a hollow voice.

"Nay. 'Tis you who would hate yourself. You cannot be faulted for whose blood you bear—only for what you become, Guy, and you need have no shame for what you are."

"How did you know?" Guy's heart thudded as he wondered if Belesme could be seen in him.

"Eleanor. She knew him better than any, and she thought there was a resemblance in ways she could not explain to me. At first, I thought it but her woman's fancy, and scoffed at her for it."

"But later?"

"But later, as I have lived with you these nine weeks past, I came to see what she saw." Considering the matter, Roger sat very still for a time, and only the sounds of insects at night broke the silence. "I think," he said after a time, "that you look much as he once did, but everyone forgets all but how he appears now, so 'tis unlikely that Henry will note it. If anything, 'tis that you and Robert both could draw people with your handsomeness, but would turn them away, Belesme from arrogance, and you from caution. You fear love and he disdains it.''

"Aye, I fear it,''Guy admitted. "But I accepted that Catherine was everything to me before he came to Rivaux. I'd not tell her—I'd not have her turn from me.''

"My daughter is proud and willful, but she is fair. I think you fear for naught.''

"I'd not have her know that I gave her a son of his blood.''

Roger sighed and rose with an effort. "We all must struggle with the demons within us, and you mayhap more than most. But I see no madness or evil in you, and I expect none. Nay, but I am proud to claim you for my son, Guy of Rivaux—you are what you have made yourself, and I like what you have become.''

"You think Cat will forgive me, that she will not care?'' Guy asked incredulously.

"She had naught to forgive. But I suppose I have to leave you to discover that for yourself.''

"Wait . . .'' Guy pulled himself up with a low branch and dusted his hands. "I'd not tell her, still.''

"That is your right to decide. I did but come to tell you that if we manage to make Robert fight, I will try to take him myself. God knows, but there can be no stain on my soul for it.'' Roger reached to clasp Guy's shoulder quickly and then dropped his hand. "Your secret is safe with me, Guy. I'd not betray you.''

As Roger's footsteps faded in the forest, Guy lay back down, turned on his side, and pulled his blanket over his shoulder. The ground was hard, but he was so tired that it was difficult to care. Roger knew and professed not to care. Roger knew Robert was his father. The thought whirled through his mind, repeating itself over and over. It was impossible that he could not care—impossible. But Roger was the most honorable man Guy knew. *"Your secret is safe with me. I'd not betray you,"* echoed again in his mind. Roger knew and would protect him.

Yet when he finally did drift into the netherworld

between consciousness and sleep, it was neither Roger nor Belesme who came to him there. He pulled his blanket closer and could smell the roses in Catherine of the Condes' hair, could feel the warmth of her skin beneath his, and could hear her whisper love words to him alone. The tension eased somewhat as his mind gave her presence beside him, but in the last instant before he dreamed, he was afraid.

❧ 40 ❧

Peasants who had fled into the forests came out cautiously to tell them that Belesme had passed but an hour or so before. The story was the same—villeins ridden down in the fields where they worked, their wives and children either burned in their huts or dragged forth to be slaughtered. Guy thought that a man ought to become inured to the suffering and destruction after a time, but it had not yet happened. His gorge rose, sticking in his throat as he looked around at the pitifully broken bodies. He'd seen men cleaved nearly twain, their guts spilling onto the ground, their brains spattered on other men's shields, but at least those men had fought sword against sword with a chance for survival. Now he was faced almost daily with the destruction of the innocent and unprotected.

Brian had disappeared behind a still-smoldering hut, and Guy thought he'd gone to be sick. Following him to comfort him, he saw the younger man bending over a woman impaled by a pitchfork, her agonized moans more moving than screams. As he watched, Brian spoke to her, made the sign of the Cross over her, and drew his sword to end her death throes. When Brian turned back, Guy could see tears streaming down his face.

"Brian—"

"He *is* the Devil, Guy—he *is!* Once I did not care,

411

but now I can see 'tis God's will that we find him and kill him even as he has killed! I care not what my father has said—he has to die for this!'' He bent to wipe his bloody sword on blackened grass. ''I pray 'tis I who strike the blow—I do.''

''We have to catch him first,'' Guy reminded him soberly. He looked at the blood that spilled from where Brian had sliced across the woman's neck, and his eyes turned a bleak, cold green. In single combat, Brian was no match for Robert of Belesme. And his new-found love for Roger de Brione was too precious to lose. Nay, if anyone took Count Robert, it would have to be himself. ''Come on, we are not far behind.''

''Are you ready to ride?''

Roger came around the hut and stopped, his blue eyes taking in the woman's body and Brian's drawn sword, before traveling to his foster son's face. Word-lessly he moved to drape a comforting arm about Brian's shoulders, and together they walked back to their standing horses. Guy reached for the pitchfork, removed it with an effort, and tossed it aside. God in his mercy would have to forgive him, but he was going to put an end to Robert of Belesme's evil if he had to kill him.

''How many do you see?''

Guy stretched in his saddle to look below, where Belesme and his men openly took their ease on the bank of a small spring. Belesme himself had dis-mounted to wash his hands in the water. ''Mayhap seventy, mayhap more,'' he answered Roger.

''We'll lose too many of our own,'' Roger muttered.

''I say we ride him down now,'' Brian urged. ''He is on foot and can be taken.''

''Nay. He'll see us ere we can reach him. 'Twould give him time to mount. And there's too great a risk that he will escape again.'' Roger shook his head and continued to stare at the scene below. ''I do not think he knows he is followed yet, and I'd surprise him.''

"They build a fire—mayhap they mean to stay here," Guy observed. And then, even as he watched, he saw several men unpack tents.

"God's blood, but he's bold. He must think there are none to dare."

"Or else he means to draw us out, Brian." Guy turned to Roger to add, "I heard in Wales that it was a favored ruse used to bring the Welsh into the open. I'd pull back eight or ten furlongs and wait for nightfall."

"Aye."

"Nay—he has prisoners," Brian protested. "They have brought women for sport."

"Holy Mary." Guy looked again, and even from the distance he could see girls pushed from where they had been hidden by the horses into the open area. "So he has."

Roger's eyes were troubled as he considered the discovery of prisoners. "Aye, you may be right that he means to draw us out—'twould be like him to have his blood sport and wait for us at the same time. Or it may be he truly does not know we are here. And I know not how to tell which it is."

" 'Tis evening. I'd wait and fall on them—I'd give them no more chance than they give," Guy decided.

"But they will kill the women," Brian reminded him.

"Aye, I know it."

"And you'd let them?" he asked Guy incredulously.

"I doubt he will kill them forthwith, for he has been known to keep the comely ones for days," Guy answered brutally. "I'd not see them dead, but neither would I lose my men and not get him. I cast my lot for waiting until night falls." His eyes were heavily flecked with green as they met Brian's. "I'd listen to screams for a few hours rather than scatter Belesme and his men now and risk that he gets away to raid again."

"I'd not expected you to be so harsh, my lord."

Guy was torn by the plight of those below him, but held his ground. "Nay, but I'd not lived had I been soft, Brian."

Roger looked from one to the other. Like Guy, he realized the need to wait, but he sympathized with Brian's horror. "Aye, we move back until night falls," he decided finally.

"So you cannot hear them?" Brian gibed.

" 'Tis not likely they will survive the melee anyway," Roger answered him.

Saddle girths were tightened, blade edges were honed, and pitch was melted over a small fire as the men milled around, tensely awaiting darkness. The archers, who would be useless at night, busied themselves helping wrap the horses' hooves to damp the sound of them. And in his own way, each man there prayed it would soon be over. This was what they'd waited for, suffered for, and striven for in the nine week since they'd left Rouen. They'd live or die trying to take Robert of Belesme. And there was scarce a man among them unafraid.

Alan spat past the fire and cleared his throat diffidently. Though knighted at Rouen, he still was in awe of Roger. "My lord, do we do as Normandy asks—do we take him alive?"

"If 'tis possible—aye."

Alan's face creased thoughtfully. " 'Twill be difficult to note which is Belesme in the dark, and he will be hard to take, I think."

"Roger . . ." Guy waited for his father-in-law to turn around. " 'Tis twilight. By the time we reach them, 'twill be blackness." His eyes searched the darkening horizon. "Aye, there is no moon tonight."

"Then we ride."

At the signal, everyone mounted quietly while a few prayed silently. Guy's squire and one of the men-at-arms handed up the unlit pitch-wrapped torches as the others filed past. Once they began to ride, there would be no speaking, no sounds other than the metallic chinking of mail and the plodding sound of the wrapped horses's hooves on the hard ground. Even the spurs of knighthood that most of them wore were either packed in saddle pouches or the rowels were deadened with thongs to keep them silent.

Sixty-three men rode double file slowly along the narrow rutted road until they were less than three furlongs from Belesme's camp, and Roger reined in. With precision, the line widened, stretching across the crest of the hill above the spring.

Below, sentries paced near where the animals were tethered, their hazy figures dimly outlined by the small fires that warded off insects. Guy studied the seeming peacefulness of the scene beneath them and thought of how many times his father must have fallen on his victims in similar circumstances. The night sounds chirruped in his ears as Roger finally shouted, "For Normandy, men!"

They came down over the hill like a small horde of metal-clad men, riding breakneck for the center of the camp. The startled sentries gave up cries of alarm as they fell, either cut down by swinging maces or trampled beneath the wrapped hooves. Brian swung his sword to cut the ropes that penned Belesme's horses, loosing them and running them ahead to confuse those who hastily rolled from pallets or emerged from the tents. With his eye on the largest tent, Guy leaned to light his torch from one of the fires. The pitch caught and flared even as he flung it. Behind him, Alan did the same, as did others, and soon the silk was engulfed in flames. A woman screamed hysterically from within.

Half-clad men fought desperately, blocking Guy from Belesme's fiery tent. He raised Doomslayer, swinging the heavy blade in arc after arc, hearing the sickening sound each time it bit through flesh and bone. Blood spattered from severed arteries, spraying his surcoat and his leg, as he fought his way to Belesme, waiting for him to emerge from the flames. Kicking away the last man in his way, Guy heard Brian curse and cut him down, and he dismounted. Inside the tent he could hear a man coughing, and he suddenly realized that if it were indeed Robert, he'd chosen to die rather than be taken.

'Tis forbidden you to kill your father echoed in his ears almost like the voice of God. "For the love of God, spare me!" the woman screamed as she staggered from the tent with her hair on fire. Guy grabbed her and threw her on the ground to smother her hair, and then he thrust himself through the fiery flap. Belesme was outlined in flames, lit from behind in red and orange light that made him look like a picture of Satan in hell. As Guy moved closer, the count doubled over, no longer able to breathe from the smoke. Guy dropped to the ground and crept to reach him as the wind caught the burning remnants of the tent and lifted them, sending showers of popping sparks all around him. His hands reached Belesme's and he inched backward on his stomach, pulling his father after him through the burning grass. His head pounded and his lungs felt ready to burst before he himself was pulled feet first from what was left of Belesme's tent. Brian grasped Guy's singed head and rolled his body over Guy's to smother his burning surcoat.

"You fool—you would save him!" he shouted at him.

"The woman—is she all right?" Guy gasped.

"She's bald, but she lives," Brian muttered as he sat up on Guy's chest. "Sweet Jesu, but you gave me a fright." Looking over at where Belesme lay choking from the smoke, he demanded, "Why? Why did you not let him burn?" He leaned to grasp the sword he'd discarded when he'd rolled onto Guy, but Guy stayed his hand.

"Nay, give him to Henry's justice—he is unarmed."

Brian stared in disbelief, but he released the hilt.

"Are you all right?" Roger dropped to kneel beside

Guy, his blue eyes strangely reddened. " 'Tis over, Guy. We have won—they are all dead or taken."

"Our losses?" Guy asked, afraid to hear.

"But three dead and eleven wounded. I thought to lose four when I saw you go in there, but Brian covered you, fighting like a madman and pulling you out."

Brian rose, still angered that they had not killed Belesme, and stalked away. "Aye, I disappointed him," Guy managed through the ache in his throat and chest. "I am sorry for it."

Roger glanced to where his men already sought to secure Robert of Belesme's hands. "If you think he will endanger you or Richard, I'll do it still," he offered in a low voice meant for Guy's ears alone. "I am not above loosing him and letting him fight."

"Nay. To tell would be to defeat his purpose—I've naught to fear of him anymore."

"You are certain?"

"Aye."

"Henry's justice will be grim," Roger promised him. "If he is fortunate, he will be executed, but 'tis more like he will face what faced your enemy de Mortain, and he will be blinded and imprisoned for life. For Robert, that will be hell."

His breath coming easier now, Guy sat up and partook of the fresh air. "Then 'tis meet that it happens this way, for he has no fear of dying. He would have stood in there and burned rather than be taken."

"He has enough enemies that 'twill be difficult to get him to Rouen."

"Roger . . . ?"

"Aye?"

"Did any of his prisoners survive?"

"About half of them." Roger pulled up a handful of grass to clean Avenger's blade. "It was a difficult decision not to fight earlier, but it was right. Armed, Robert would have fought and many more would have died."

"Brian did not think so."

"Brian has but lately thought himself a soldier. 'Twill take time for him to learn that we cannot right all wrongs, I think. But he will learn it." Roger's eyes followed with pride the man he'd fostered. "Aye, he will. When he had no purpose, I despaired of him."

"I think you have Aislinn to thank for what he has become. He'd have her, you know."

"He has but to ask."

"I'd tell him."

"Nay. You and I will leave him be, Guy. 'Twas my mistake from the first—because Henry did not love him, I sought to ease his life. But life is hard and harsh and cruel, and it served him ill to protect him."

Once they had Belesme trussed like a pig for roasting, Guy's and Roger's men raised him to stand on hobbled feet. He stared past them at Guy and Roger, and for the briefest of moments his eyes warmed and the harsh lines of his face softened before it became cold again.

"You should have killed me," he told Guy as they dragged him past.

Guy watched him go and felt relief. It was over and the Devil of Belesme had been taken. Roger knew and did not care. In a few days' time, after they saw Henry again at Rouen, they would go to the Condes. He still had to face Catherine, and he was still more than a little afraid of what she might think of him, but he would do it.

"I wanted to kill him, but I could not," he said aloud.

"You are what he could have been, Guy."

Once the camp was secured, Guy sat brooding beside a small fire, his thoughts on Robert of Belesme. He'd both fought with and against the man, he'd been used by and had triumphed over him, and now it was nearly over. He had but to take the man almost none knew for his father back to Rouen for Henry's justice and reap the rewards of what he'd done. He now could see Robert for what he was: a tortured, violent man determined to destroy himself and everything in his path. Even the lurking fear that Robert was Satan incarnate had faded when 'twas a man he dragged from the burning tent.

It would be a long and bitter trip back to Rouen, with all of Normandy demanding Robert of Belesme's head for his crimes, and Guy had no doubt that they would have to fight to keep possession of their prisoner every furlong of the way. And Henry would be waiting to mete out his justice with as little mercy as his father, the Old Conqueror, had done. Aye, he'd spare Count Robert's life, consigning him to years of imprisonment as a blinded, castrated, empty husk of a man. Guy picked up a stick and broke it before casting it into the fire, where it caught and was quickly consumed by the flames.

Guy rose from his solitary fire and stretched his tall frame, his face red from the illumination of the campfire in the dark. Kicking dirt over it, he snuffed it out and turned to the tent where Belesme was held. Even now, the man drew him as much as he repelled.

"I'd speak with him alone," he told the two guards within the tent.

Seemingly asleep, Robert of Belesme lay on a straw-filled pallet with his eyes closed, but after the others left, he struggled to sit and face Guy. The light from the lone candle was so faint that his green eyes appeared black.

"You risked your life thinking you saved me from hell." He spoke low.

" 'Twas you who once reminded me, 'tis forbidden me to kill you. I'd not have your soul weigh on mine." Guy moved closer to stand over his father. His heart thudded and he wondered why he'd come.

"You'd be forgiven. Hell holds no terrors for me, Guy, for I have lived in it already."

"You know not what is on the other side."

"I have glimpsed it often enough—I have seen it

written in that last moment on a thousand faces." Belesme managed a bitter, twisted smile as his eyes met Guy's. "But 'tis strange to hear that from your lips. Mayhap the monks did less than I thought."

"Why did you come to Rivaux?" Guy asked suddenly.

"You are my son—I wanted to share what was common between us before 'twas over. It was a boasting, I suppose, for I took pride in what you had become," Belesme admitted. "And I wanted someone to know that whether I lived or died, I had won."

"Won?"

"Aye, I kept my promise to Eleanor. My blood—my son—will rule Nantes."

"You cannot know that."

"I have seen the babe, Guy. 'Tis a direct line of blood, mine and hers, that will rule Gilbert's lands."

" 'Twas madness, my lord. A hundred things could have changed that ere it ever happened."

"Aye, but it did not."

There was that arrogance, that overweening pride that Guy remembered about him from those days when they'd both served Robert Curthose against Henry. And, in a different way, he shared that pride and arrogance.

As if he could look into Guy's mind, Belesme nodded. "Aye, we fought together once. I suppose I should even think it fitting that 'twas you who brought me down at last."

"Like the young wolves with the old?"

"Aye." Robert's eyes pierced like shards of glass once more. "I was wrong at Rivaux—the greater sin is letting me live, Guy."

"Do you fear Henry's justice?"

"Nay, 'tis hell for me either way. But you think yourself damned now for the blood I have given you. Kill me and atone for it."

"I'd not have your blood on my hands."

"Then put it on mine."

Guy looked down to where thongs bound Robert's seared wrists and then to the chains that hobbled his feet. Across the small tent were what was left of his scorched clothes. Guy moved away to lift Belesme's belt from the bench and remove the dagger. Returning, he dropped it blade-first into the ground beside his father and then silently lifted the tent flap and left.

The Condes looked much as it had almost exactly six
year before, but to Guy of Rivaux it was no longer the
awe-inspiring fortress he'd once found it. As they
reined in and waited for the bridge to be lowered over
the river-fed ditch, he scanned the walls for Catherine.
At the windows of Eleanor of Nantes's solar, Aislinn,
Philippa, Isabella, and their mother waved brightly
colored silk scarves that caught the summer sun, but
there was no sign of Cat.

Beside him, Brian FitzHenry removed his helmet
and waved wildly to them and to the garrison that lined
the top of the outer wall. A loud cheer of welcome
rose as the bridge banged against its moorings to open
the inner, more peaceful world within. Roger took the
bridge first amid shouts of "Harlowe! Harlowe! Harlowe!" As Guy's horse crossed beneath them, the
chant changed to "Rivaux! Rivaux! Rivaux!" and Guy
suddenly felt an overwhelming sense of belonging.

The intense exhilaration of being there blotted out
the earlier fatigue of their deciding to ride night and
day from Rouen. The entire outer bailey was filled
with shouting, cheering people as they rode in, and
ostlers were pushed aside by the press of those who
vied to touch the bridles, the horses, the tunics, and
the mail of the men who'd caught Robert of Belesme.
Brian slid from his saddle, only to be engulfed by the

throng, lifted, and carried into the main courtyard. Guy, eager to see Catherine, edged his horse through the enthusiastic crowd before he dared to dismount. Ahead, he could see Aislinn running from the main hall portal. Brian struggled free of his admirers and stood uncertainly for a moment before opening his arms to receive her. And Aislinn, sweet and supposedly gentle Aislinn, astounded all who chanced to be looking by twining her arms around his neck and kissing him eagerly through her tears.

"Sweet Jesu, but I love you!" Brian shouted at her to be heard above the din.

Still looking for Catherine, Guy turned in his saddle and searched the crowd with his eyes. She stood across the courtyard, her babe in her arms, watching him with a misty smile on her face. Behind him, someone pulled Roger from his horse also, and Guy, fearful of being lost in the excited, milling people, chose to ride to her. Just before he reached her, she thrust the babe at a startled William de Comminges, and when Guy slid from his saddle, she reached up on tiptoe to dislodge his helmet and take it off.

"I never wanted to kiss cold steel," she told him as she tossed it onto the ground and stepped into his waiting arms. "Sweet Mary, but I have missed you," she murmured into his shoulder as she rubbed her cheek against his surcoat and slid her arms around his waist.

"I was afraid you were not coming to meet me," he teased into the top of her shining braids.

"I wanted you to see Richard, and I'd not have him crushed by the crowd."

"Richard? Oh . . . aye."

She jabbed at his back through layers of surcoat, mail, and gambeson. "Your son, Guy," she muttered indignantly.

"I did but think to tease you, Cat—'tis good to know you've still got your claws." His arms closed around her, savoring again the rosewater fragrance in her hair, enjoying the feeling of her body against his once more.

"Art the love of my life, Catherine of the Condes," he spoke low above her ear.

She hugged him more tightly and then pushed away. "Well, whether you would see him or not, Guy, you have to look at him. I went to too much trouble to give you this son for you to ignore him."

Guy's eyes met William's over her shoulder, and he read the pride in the old man's face. "Aye, I'd see him. Come with me, both of you, and we'll look at young Richard of Rivaux."

"Nay, I . . ." William held back diffidently as the infant squirmed in his arms. "You belong with your lady."

"Nay, William, but he'd not have either of us without your aid," Cat protested. "Come on . . ." Her nose wrinkled as she sniffed at Guy, and she grinned. "If naught else, I'd have you help me get him out of all this steel and into a tub of bathwater. Sweet Jesu, Guy, but you stink," she complained happily, threading her arm through her husband's.

William adjusted the babe on his shoulder, craning his neck to look lovingly on the black hair that covered its head. Smoothing his roughened hand over it, he held the babe's back gently and followed them with the pride of a grandfather ready to display his greatest treasure.

" 'Twould be thought you walked on eggshells, Sir William," Hawise harassed him good-naturedly. "Would you that I carried him?"

"Nay."

Catherine turned to take her babe from him when they reached her tower chamber and held it out to Guy. "Behold Richard of Rivaux, my lord—'tis time you looked on him."

Guy knew a pang of fear as he took his son and stared down on the small face. The eyes that blinked solemnly and stared back were almost blue-black rather than the feared green. He relaxed slightly, allowing himself to exhale before he carried him to the bed. His heart beat faster as he unwrapped the swaddling bands to examine his babe. Richard kicked, exercising his legs and his lungs at the same time.

"He has ten toes, Guy," William observed dryly behind him. "Aye, and he looks much as you once did, so there's hope he'll be a handsome-enough fellow."

"He is a handsome fellow already," Cat said, "and you've got him crying."

Guy lifted him gingerly to hold him to the window. "Aye, he is that. Hey, Richard, is this any way to greet your sire?" Jostling him gently, he watched his son give half a hiccup and stop. "Is he big enough?" he asked curiously.

"They grow. Here, I'd take him before you drop him or curdle the milk in his stomach," Catherine told him as she reached for the babe. " 'Tis time he slept anyway, and you need your bath if you are to eat at Maman's table tonight."

The Condes welcomed back its lord with a feast rivaling that of Easter or Christmas, and Guy was caught up in the gaiety that surrounded him. Eleanor, grateful to have Roger home at last, watched him with the air of a young girl and listened to him tell of how Robert of Belesme was finally taken. Brian paid little attention to anything but Aislinn, and finally Catherine leaned to whisper to Guy, " 'Tis all but settled between Papa and King Henry—they will wed at Christmas."

"Roger and King Henry?" he asked with a lift of his divided brow.

"Linn and Brian, dolt!" She laughed, then sobered. " 'Tis good to have you back, Guy, and even better to see you tease me again."

His flecked eyes warmed with gold as they traveled over her. "Teasing is but one of the things I like to do with you, Cat." He was rewarded with the slow flush that crept into her cheeks. Leaning closer, he whispered into her ear, his breath sending a visible shiver through her, "For ten weeks and more I've sat in my saddle, so tonight 'tis your turn to ride."

She had to close her eyes to hide the flood of desire that washed over her. It seemed that everything about him made her want him: his handsomeness, his strength, the incredible warmth of his body, those beautiful eyes when they met hers—everything. When she dared look sideways at him again, he was watching her appreciatively as though he knew her thoughts. A slow smile spread over his face, lifting the faint scar on his cheek. "Art more beautiful than mortal man has a right to expect, Cat."

Her hand reached to touch the fine line where it cut downward, and she felt the warmth of his skin and the faint trace of his freshly shaven beard. "I've always been sorry for it, Guy," she admitted.

"Nay, I've never minded it—it marked me for yours."

The rest of supper seemed interminable, but in truth it had lasted but two hours when Roger rose and stretched, saying he was tired and would seek his bed, but that anyone else was welcome to eat or drink his fill. Eleanor lingered behind but long enough to bend over Guy and murmur for his ears alone, "There's none I'd rather have for Cat, my lord." He looked up startled, thinking perhaps it was the wine, but she met his gaze soberly and nodded. "Aye, we share a pride in you, Guy of Rivaux."

"Nay, 'tis I who am proud to be kinsman to you," he murmured to cover the intense relief he felt. If Eleanor of Nantes, who had suffered so much at Robert of Belesme's hands, could find it in herself to accept him, Guy knew everything was all right.

"I'd go up also," Catherine whispered as soon as her parents had left. Her hand covered his, stroking it, tracing fire beneath her fingertips, telling him she desired him as much as he wanted her. He drained his cup and nodded.

"Aye."

Furtive giggles and knowing looks followed them as they left, but Catherine didn't care. Every fiber of her being, every bit of her body was alive with the thought of what it would feel like to be loved by him again. Already her thoughts had aroused her body until she knew it would be a fiery, intense coupling, quickly over, but followed by a more leisurely exploration of each other.

The wet nurse held Richard, now asleep at her breast. When she saw Catherine and Guy, she covered herself and rose to lay the sleeping babe in his cradle. "He is as full as a tick at day's end, my lady." She smiled as she dropped a hasty obeisance. Looking upward to Guy, who towered over her, she added, "I sleep in the cutout chamber below. If you'd have me take him with me . . ."

"Nay. If he wakes, we will summon you." He moved to stare down at the sleeping form of his son, who lay on his stomach, his face turned to the side, his mouth moving as though he sucked in his sleep. The overwhelming innocence of the babe comforted him and brought forth a fierce, protective love.

"Guy . . ." Catherine came up to stand behind him, placing her hand on his shoulder, and he turned into her embrace. "You think him beautiful, do you not?" she asked anxiously.

"Beautiful?" He appeared to consider the babe a moment, and an unholy gleam warmed his eyes. "Aye," he decided as his arms tightened around her, "and I'd like to make more like him, if you'd have the truth of it."

She leaned her head against him, knowing that once he kissed her there'd be no more words. "I'd have him be like you."

"Cat . . ." He'd meant to lie with her first, to seek the easing of his need for her, but he felt compelled to tell her. "I'd have him be like your father, Cat. There is that about me that you do not know. I—"

"If you are going to tell me about your tainted blood, I'd not listen to it," she told him softly.

"You know?"

"Aye, but it does not matter."

"Your mother?"

"Nay—'twas Belesme himself. He was there when Richard was born—he cut the cord himself. I meant to write to you of it, but there seemed no way to tell of it. But I knew, Guy. I knew when he let us live. I saw him look at my babe, and at that moment I thought I saw you there."

"Jesu! And you can live with that? You can—"

"Shhhhhh." She stopped his words with her fingers on his mouth. "Aye. I love you, Guy."

It was as though the final fear fell away, leaving his soul cleansed of its stain. She loved him and she did not care about Belesme. He looked deep within those dark eyes of hers and saw the mirror of his own love for her. His hand moved to cradle her head as he bent to taste of her mouth, taking what she freely gave. He had no more devils, within or without, left to fight.

Author's Notes

The principal characters in *Fire and Steel* are products of my imagination, although I like to think that Catherine of the Condes and Guy of Rivaux and their supporting cast could have lived a life such as I have depicted.

The character of Robert of Belesme is based loosely on a real historical person, Robert de Belleme, whose reputation and exploits have long fascinated me. Although little in-depth detail is known about his life other than when he lived, what lands he held, whom he married, and whom he supported in the struggles that ensued after William the Conqueror's death, I could not pass up an opportunity to use him in *Lady of Fire* and *Fire and Steel*. The chroniclers of the day mentioned him often enough in passing that I came to wonder about a man whose extraordinary military abilities, political power, and great wealth were matters of record and yet were insufficient to prevent his downfall. His excesses of extreme cruelty in a violent and cruel time were such that his comings and goings between Normandy and England were reported in the *Anglo-Saxon Chronicles* in the same light as famines, pestilence, and other natural disasters. He was hated and feared by king, baron, and commoner alike, to the extent that I once had a history professor say that there were those who believed that the English expression "the bogeyman will get you" came from Robert de Belleme and his raids.

I admit openly to literary license in the use of this character, although I believe him capable of acting as I have portrayed him. The real Robert de Belleme was captured after years of vicious raiding in Normandy and spent his final years blinded and castrated, incarcerated in Henry's dungeons. In my story, I leave it to the reader to decide how my Robert of Belesme ended.

The character of the Conqueror's youngest son,

Henry, is portrayed as realistically as I could make him. He is found variously in this book as King Henry and Duke Henry, used interchangeably after the Battle of Tinchebrai, because many Normans holding lands in both England and Normandy would owe him allegiance in both capacities. To avoid further confusion, he is the only Henry in the book.

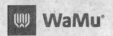 **WaMu**®

Anything else we can do for you?

- Checking & Savings
- Retirement
- Home Loans
- Home Equity Loans & Lines
- Credit Cards
- Small Business Accounts & Services

Just let us know — in person, at wamu.com or by phone at 800.788.7000.

```
     DATE           TIME        MACHINE
  07/30/08        09:36 AM      S2R06172

*************6011
1111 LOUISIANNA SUITE 100
HOUSTON          TX

TRANS NUMBER      7399
WITHDRAWAL                        $20.00
FROM SAVINGS

CURRENT BALANCE                   $10.00
AVAILABLE BALANCE                 $10.00

     Sit, bank and relax!

  Bank here or there with
  a WaMu Free Checking(tm)
 account & online banking.

    It's free and easy!
```

About the Author

Anita Mills lives in Kansas City, Missouri, with her husband, four children, sister, and seven cats in a restored turn of the century house. A former English and history teacher, she has turned a lifelong passion for both into a writing career.